THE REST JUST FOLLOWS

Glenn Patterson is the author of eight previous novels, the most recent of which, *The Mill for Grinding Old People Young,* was the 2012 One City One Book choice for Belfast. He is the co-writer of *Good Vibrations* (BBC Films/The Works), an award-winning movie based on the life of Belfast punk impresario Terri Hooley. He lives in Belfast.

Further praise for *The Rest Just Follows*:

'Delicately drawn and acutely observed . . . an extraordinary novel about the lives of ordinary people.' Tony Clayton-Lea, *Sunday Times Irish Edition*

'*The Rest Just Follows* feels very real – almost painfully so at times – and never pat or cliched. These characters ring true, their situations are believable; the writing is unadorned, the tone honest and a little wistful . . . A warm-hearted, well-crafted and engaging book.' Darragh McManus, *Irish Independent*

'The language in the book, particularly at the start, is in the vernacular of Belfast children, and there is a marvel in it being both authentic and intelligible . . . The book works as a reassu͟ ͟ ͟ ͟ ͟ er you to sanity a͟ ͟ ͟ ͟ ͟ ͟ *nes*

'Tender, humane and quietly devastating . . . A subtle and compassionate look at the people and places that shape us, and the moments that can alter the course of a life, or lives, forever.' Lucy Caldwell, author of *All the Beggars Riding*

Also by Glenn Patterson

Fiction
Burning Your Own
Fat Lad
Black Night at Big Thunder Mountain
The International
Number 5
That Which Was
The Third Party
The Mill for Grinding Old People Young

Non-fiction
Lapsed Protestant
Once Upon a Hill: Love in Troubled Times

The Rest Just Follows

or Up Here

GLENN PATTERSON

FABER & FABER

First published in 2014 by
Faber and Faber Ltd
Bloomsbury House
74–77 Great Russell Street
London WC1B 3DA

This paperback edition first published in 2015

Typeset by Faber and Faber Ltd.
Printed and bound by CPI Group (UK) Ltd, Croydon CRO 4YY

Extract from *Bedsit Disco Queen* reproduced with the kind permission of Tracey Thorn

The right of Glenn Patterson to be identified as author of this work has been
asserted in accordance with Section 77 of the Copyright, Designs and Patents Act
1988

A CIP record for this book
is available from the British Library

ISBN 978–0–571–30523–0

2 4 6 8 10 9 7 5 3 1

'When you're young and moving in some-what limited circles, it's not as though you have a world of choice. The people you meet are just the people you happen to meet and the rest all follows.'

Tracey Thorn, *Bedsit Disco Queen*

Starting

I

From ever he could remember Craig had had the feeling that his life was somehow being watched and weighed. Nothing happened by chance. That woman who sat down across the aisle from you on the bus and started talking to your mum about the holidays and were you getting away anywhere nice yourself was not a random stranger but a spy. The conductor too: 'How old is the wee lad? Over five? That's a half then.'

When people he did not know turned up at the door – and there being no phone in the house in those years people had a habit of just turning up: second cousins once removed, old neighbours of his parents, returned from Canada or Australia, or so they said – Craig would hide in his room, sometimes under his bed.

'He's a wee bit shy,' his mum said and he was happy to let her think it.

There was a programme on the TV, the Christmas after he turned seven, bigger boys and girls talking about school and pocket money and what they wanted to be when they were older, all stuff like that. It showed them too when they were the same age as him and it was strange that some of the things they said back then seemed to know the teenagers they would turn out to be, almost like the second bit had come before the first.

It was hard to explain.

Craig's mum tutted. His dad put down the paper. 'What?'

'Listen to those voices.'

'What's wrong with them?'

'What's wrong with them?' That was the way his mum and dad talked: one said something and the other said it back and added something of their own. 'They're all English.'

'So?'

'So you'd think sometimes we didn't exist. No one ever comes near us.'

'Do they not?' His dad said it like he knew the answer and it wasn't one his mum thought.

His mum tutted. Craig wondered. About women on buses and second cousins once removed and whether one day it would be him sitting there in the box in the corner of the living room, bigger and uglier as his granddad would say, plucking at his trousers, trying to account for himself.

'Quiet boy,' his teacher wrote on his end-of-year report. 'You would hardly know he was there.'

*

Maxine Neill's teachers vied with one another year on year to sing her praises. 'A joy to teach . . . sets the standard for others to aspire to.'

Mr Jackson who had her in P5 and who had taught Victor and Tommy before her told her, between him her and the gatepost, that it was easy to see who had got the brains in the family.

The headmaster had had to cane Tommy one time in

front of the whole school for writing a bad word on the door of a cubicle in the boys' toilets. Tommy said it wasn't him, swear on the Holy Bible, but nobody believed him. Nobody ever believed Tommy. He had one of those faces.

Maxine was only in P1 then. She wasn't able to see because of the heads in front of her, but she heard the *swish* of the cane – one, two, three, four, five, *six* times.

Tommy came into the box room that night after she had had her tuck-in and told her she wasn't to listen to what anybody said, he didn't cry. All right?

He didn't cry.

Maxine looked out from under the covers into that face of his. Said nothing.

*

As soon as he had worked out the catches on the side of his cot St John's brother Paddy would turn up in St John's room at night. The first few times it happened St John took him back along the landing to his own room, gave him Teddy Arbuthnot, put up the side of the cot, secured the catch, and ten minutes later there was Paddy once more, standing by the bed, two inches from St John's face, smiling. Paddy was still in night nappies. St John didn't want him honking up the bed. The ninth or tenth time it happened he bundled together spare blankets from the box on the landing and laid them on the floor between the bed and the wall. A nest, he said. Paddy clambered in, cooing his delight. St John fell at last into a deep sleep. Deep, deep, deep . . .

St John's mother woke him and Paddy at 4 a.m. to tell them that their father would not be coming back.

'Is he *dead*?' asked Paddy from the nest, thinking not unreasonably (Paddy was six now) of Rory, the red setter who had not come back from a trip to the vet the summer before last.

'No, he's not dead.' St John's mother made it sound as though a gesture that a poor dumb animal was capable of would be beyond that man. Moonlight leaked in around the bedroom curtains tipping her hair silver. She wound a strand around her fingers, trailed it across her lips. It must have tickled. She laughed. 'He just won't be coming back,' she said and went to break the news to Sibyl and Bea.

'Brandy,' whispered St John, sniffing the air she left in her wake.

They found her when they came down for breakfast stretched out on the kitchen floor. The wall-phone dangled off the hook, straining out the time at ten-second intervals: at the third stroke it will be eight-twelve and twenty seconds . . . at the third stroke it will be eight-twelve and thirty . . . eight-twelve and forty . . . fifty . . .

'Mo!' said St John. Mo was what Sibyl had called her when she was little, whether from falling short of 'Mummy' or from hearing other people call her Mrs Nimmo no one knew, and, it being Sibyl, no one corrected. 'Mo, wake up! We've got to be in school in half an hour.'

'At the third stroke it will be eight-thirteen precisely.'

'I think she's dead,' Paddy said.

*

Craig knew that the late arrival in the outsize blazer was headed for him even before the form teacher had found his name in the register.

'Nimmo, Nimmo, Nimmo, Nimmo . . . Saint John?'

'Sinjin,' the boy said, and thirty pupils burst out laughing, relieved to have found a focus for some of their own feelings of strangeness and discomfort.

'I beg your pardon, *Sinjin*,' the form teacher said and was rewarded with another thirty laughs, all the louder for being licensed. 'You may sit there for now.' The form teacher indicated the desk beside Craig who alone of the class had remained silent, though not out of any fellow feeling. Quite the reverse. It was a ridiculous name and he was dumbly furious that the boy should bring it any-where near him. Having successfully negotiated the first half hour of his first day of First Year he was now to be lumped with the freak.

He faced the front as the big blazer fitted itself into its allocated space, every movement accompanied by an effort from somewhere in the room to keep the laughter going.

When the bell rang for the start of the next period he squeezed through the gap between the desks before St John Nimmo had a chance to stand.

7

Bad luck stuck if you let it.

He was fucked if he was going to.

*

Five miles away right-handed Maxine Neill was writing her name on the cover of her homework diary left-handed, an arsy-versy declaration that the school needn't think for a minute it was getting the real her. She wrote her form, 1K, for Kilroy (Mrs), and on the first page the date, 1 September 1974. She calculated – in her head, note – the days to her release date, 30 June 1979: one thousand seven hundred and sixty-four, including the leap year.

She would count each and every one of them.

Anybody with half a brain could see that she should not have been here, that her Eleven Plus result had been an aberration. She had had eighties and nineties, for God sake, in the past papers they had practised on. In the final one before the tests themselves she had got *all but three* answers right.

Her parents said sure not to worry, she had done her best, that was all anyone could ask for. And the secondary school hadn't done Victor or Tommy or any of her cousins a bit of harm. It hadn't done them a whole lot of good either that Maxine could see, and she saw plenty. There was hardly a sweetie shop or a chippy in the neighbourhood that didn't have someone belonging to her ringing up the cigarettes and strawberry bonbons or spreading the sheets of newspaper ready for the teatime rush.

Never mind the days, she was going to count the hours.

(Forty-two thousand three hundred and thirty-six.)

The last thing St John needed at the end of that day was to come round the bend of the driveway and see Mo about to launch herself off a stepladder in front of the drawing room's big bay window.

He tore up the front steps and in the door.

The bedroom curtains were in a heap at the foot of the stairs, sun-spotted velvets, dusty damasks, racing cars, for those nights when Paddy could be persuaded to keep to his own room.

The word that flashed through St John's mind was round-up. The urgency left him. He stood in the drawing-room doorway. The stepladder was as old as the house itself, one of the rope stays had been replaced with twine. Not so much a ladder as a prop from a public information film: *Stop! Before you set foot on that . . .*

Mo, on tiptoes on the very last tread, was wielding a poker, trying to dislodge the curtain pole from its fittings.

'What's happening?'

'From now on,' she said without turning her head, 'we will observe natural rhythms, sleep when it is dark and rise when it is light.'

Bea shouted from the first-floor bathroom. 'You might have left us a blind in here.'

The lower pane of the bathroom sash had been broken by a tennis ball two summers ago and replaced 'temporarily' with plain glass.

'Oh, Bea, grow up,' Mo shouted back. 'Who on earth is going to see you?'

Sibyl appeared at the banister in knickers and over-the-knee socks. 'Let me think . . . Dr Lennox?'

'He's at least fifty yards away, over a hedge. And he's a *doctor*.'

'He's a dirty old fucker,' Sibyl said under her breath and disappeared again.

Mo grunted. One end of the pole thumped against the floorboards and the curtains slid off it with a rattle of rings.

'Is anybody going to help me here?' she asked. 'Don't all rush!'

It was light next morning at twenty past six.

Sibyl, St John, Bea and Paddy gathered bleary-eyed in the kitchen. The milk had been left out on the sideboard overnight and had gone off. The breadbin was empty. They waited the best part of an hour then Sibyl said, right, that's it: she was going to go and wake her.

She was back within the minute.

'She's not there,' she said at the same moment as Mo let herself in at the back door wearing their father's sheepskin coat, a tie-dyed scarf round her head.

She set a basket on the table. 'Eggs.'

'Eggs?' said St John. There wasn't a shop in Belfast open at that hour.

'That's right.' (Paddy and Bea were lifting them out, small and large, brown and white.) 'Hens lay them.'

There was not either, that St John knew, a farm within five miles. Mo was putting on an apron over the sheepskin coat. She set a cast-iron pan on the stovetop and put a thick slice of lard into it.

'How many do you think you could eat?'

'All of them!' Bea and Paddy shouted together and Sibyl yanked open the cutlery drawer.

St John was late for school again: late, but beautifully replete.

*

The freak fell asleep in the middle of the second period, Geography, face down on the atlas that had only a minute before been set in front of him. Uprichard, the beardy geography teacher, came and hunkered down by the desk. He cocked his ear, letting on to be entranced by the snores. They were a right cast of comedians the teachers in this school . . . *n't*. Then he took hold of the corners of the atlas and pulled. The freak's forehead bounced off the desk. He scrabbled for his pen in the groove beside the inkwell and blinked at the blackboard, which was as blank at that moment as his own expression.

'Welcome back from the Land of Nod,' Uprichard said, making his pitch for *Opportunity Knocks*. 'For tomorrow you can bring me four sides of foolscap expanding on your explorations: flora, fauna, average annual rainfall' – each item on the list emphasised by a tap on the bap with the atlas and greeted with a thirty-throated guffaw – 'highest mountain, longest river, cash crops and staples, et cetera, et cetera.'

Craig, at the rear of the room, shook his head. You stupid, stupid bastard, you deserve all you get and more.

He made an extra special effort of avoidance in the corridor afterwards. Despite being forced to sit beside him for roll call in the form room indeed he gave the freak a wide berth almost the whole of that first term. Went in, did his work, went home, as straight as he was let, worked more. He doubted that more than a handful of people in the class could remember his name, unlike St John Nimmo's, but that was all right. Craig was bedding down, taking the long view.

*

Wednesday was games day – the choice for girls was netball or netball – and between the messing around on the court and the messing around in the changing rooms afterwards Maxine was generally a half hour later getting out, which meant she would often be passing the country-bound bus-stop when the one boy in her primary school to have got the Eleven Plus was arriving home from town. (She would like to know what *he* got in his practice papers. She couldn't even remember seeing him, much less hearing about him.) Unfortunately for him the boys from her new school would often be passing too on the way back from their games. (Football or football.) Sometimes if his bus was running a little late they would wait for him, passing the time decorating the shelter with their nicknames and their anatomically exaggerated artwork. Her brother Tommy would be there, even though Tommy had left school at the first available opportunity the Easter before. He was helping out the bread server a couple of days a week, but he was usually finished up well before lunchtime, which suited him right down to the ground that he never stood straight on if there was a wall to slouch against.

Maxine tried hard not to take pleasure in the chasings that inevitably resulted from the coincidence of the boy on the bus and the boys loitering at the stop. (There was a word for taking pleasure that way. Maxine had read it but never heard it spoken.) It was part of the contract. As soon as he opened the letter saying congratulations you have passed he became a fruit and a snob, in the same way that, Maxine feared, the letter she had got saying bad luck you didn't carried an unwritten 'milly' tag.

Anyway she was pretty sure that if Tommy and the others had wanted to do him real harm they could have caught him easy enough. She would follow in their wake and always before she had reached the turn-off to the estate Tommy and the rest of the pack would come sauntering back towards her, Tommy every now and then breaking into a limp-wristed, knock-kneed run, the others falling about laughing at the impression.

It was right there in the letter: a fruit and a snob.

One afternoon, taking a shortcut across the waste ground that had used to be the Spar, she found an empty pencil case with a key ring on the zip showing the grammar-school crest – she recognised it from his blazer – and the initials CR printed on the inside in purple felt pen. Something Robinson she thought it was you called him.

Felt-tips in other colours lay scattered about, pencils, biros, a perspex protractor, splintered. It put her in mind of the days immediately after the Spar was bombed, the packets of Penguins and Club biscuits they scavenged but were afraid to eat in case there was glass in them.

She gathered up what she could fit back in and still get

the zip to close – the universal law of pencil cases: once emptied they never could hold half of what was in there to begin with. For a couple of weeks she carried it around in her bag, rehearsing her lines for when she came to hand it back – 'I don't suppose this belongs to you . . . I don't suppose *you* belong to *this* . . .' – but the only time she saw him was after games on a Wednesday and even when the boys from her school were distracted by fighting with one another or putting the finishing inverted-teardrop touches to another enormous dick, he always hit the footpath at such a run that she hadn't a hope in hell of catching him.

*

Craig needed a compass. His own – straightened into a dart that had narrowly missed his ear – he had last seen embedded in a lino tile at the end of what had until eighteen months ago been the Spar's household and cleaning aisle. He had stooped to pluck it out as he ran past, but nearly cowped right over, and the boy who had chucked it – a boy he remembered from his P1 year, getting the cane in front of the whole school – was closing on him fast, so he left the thing there, a mark of just how far their antipathy extended, along with all the other pens and pencils and bits of plastic that together with the compass had made up his Helix Oxford Set of Mathematical Instruments.

He hadn't said a word to his parents, not about that chasing, nor any of the chasings that had gone before it. The less he let on to anyone about what was happening the sooner it was all likely to stop. He would have to replace what he had lost out of his pocket money – they called it pay at home, all 75p of it – item by item, week by week. With any luck, and taking into account other necessary expenditure, he would have the entire pencil case's worth, if not the pencil case itself, for the start of the new term.

In the meantime he was on the final question of a snap maths test, which required him to draw a circle with a radius of 2.5 cm.

Peter Long, who normally sat next to him in Maths, had been sent home at break with gastroenteritis. Craig glanced over his shoulder. The two Jills were leaning forward as they worked, faces obscured by curtains of hair, auburn to the left of him, dirty fair to the right. No way in.

'Three more minutes, class,' Mrs Gascoigne shouted from her perch on the radiator in the corner by the window; she was sucking a confiscated brandy ball, which she moved now with an indiscreet clack off her teeth, from the right side of her mouth to the left, 'then pass your exercise books to the front for collection.'

Craig faced about. Across the aisle at a diagonal the outsize blazer was as rigid as a scaffold. He reached out his hand and touched the shoulder. In the chess club, which he had started to attend (spectator only) in the lunch break, Tuesdays and Thursdays, they would have dismissed the move as a cheap pawn that left him vulnerable to counterattack. But that was chess and this was Maths and all around him exercise books were already being closed, ballpoint pens clicked and retracted.

'Lend us your compass there, will you?' he whispered.

St John Nimmo turned, tortoise-slow. His skin was as

smooth as waxed wood. He looked down at Craig's palm, open and waiting, then just as Craig was about to tell him to forget it, felt behind him on the desk and handed the compass over. The spike was bent inwards and possibly backwards.

'That's just flipping great,' Craig said.

St John Nimmo performed a complicated manoeuvre with his mouth that Craig finally recognised as a smile. (There was something in there that he was trying to hide, or maybe something not in there that ought to have been.) 'You just have to knock the other leg a half a centimetre to the side each time. Trust me.'

Which was the start of the counter-attack.

3

'What I want to know,' St John said, 'is what happened to seven, eight and nine.'

The Break-time Tobacco Appreciation Society was today considering the merits of Player's No. 10. The Society tended, given the brevity of the break and the constraints of its members' finances, to stick to the shorter and therefore cheaper brands: Sterling, Sovereign, Gold Bond, Embassy Regal, Embassy Red, Three Fives, Craven 'A', Player's No. 6.

'Can't help you with eight, but seven was transferred to Piccadilly and I think Black Cat got number nine.'

The Break-time Tobacco Appreciation Society was in its third term and had grown out of the Crafty Fag Club, which itself had begun meeting on an ad-hoc basis in the spring of the second year. Crafty fags and tobacco appreciation had from the outset been a potential weak point in Craig's strategy of anonymity, but having got the taste at the age of ten when he found a packet of his granddad's Rothmans down the back of the sofa, he had been resigned to trying to adapt his habit to his grammar-school life. If anything, that life had ingrained the habit. What better way to settle the nerves after a three-hundred-yard dash from the bus-stop pursued by shouts of 'bum-boy'?

St John, who had had his first puff shortly after his twelfth birthday (didn't like it), his first complete cigarette just before his thirteenth (nearly puked), was in comparison a novice.

The Society's regular meeting place was between two industrial-size waste bins at the back of the refectory, which, caught as they were at that quarter hour of the day between having been emptied and being refilled, did not smell too overpowering, although high enough to neutralise even a Capstan Full Strength. As for actual smoke, it was, ahead of the uneaten custard and imperfectly mashed potato, the refectory's principal by-product. The Society could have swollen to ten times the size and its exhalations would have gone undetected by even the most suspicious eye. As it was it had a core membership of two.

'That' – St John crushed the cigarette against the wall, rubbed the black smudge with his thumb, his thumb against his trouser seam – 'was not one of my favourites. I would go so far as to say it was high on my list of cigarettes not to smoke again as long as I live.'

'Like scrapings from the Devil's hooves,' Craig said and dropped his cigarette down a drain: *pssht*. 'What have you after this?'

'Two Physics then French. What's yours, History?'

'Correct-o.' This coinciding and perhaps inflected by the production from his inside pocket of a packet of Polo, its first two-thirds now a twist of foil as dull as ash. 'History, Maths, Maths.'

Their paths had diverged at the end of the first year when St John jumped at the opportunity to drop Latin, taking him into the single-language stream. Craig had kept Latin on, in fact had opted to add Spanish. St John would have jumped at Spanish too, but the rule was no second language no third. (In the language peculiar to the school both the rule and the hypothetical question that gave rise to it made perfect sense.) All of which disguised the fact that they would in all likelihood have been separated anyway. Craig had by sheer hard work kept up with – or at least kept sight of – the year's high fliers. St John had by sheer coincidence scored one per cent either side of the class average in all but two of his summer exams. (Divinity thirty-six per cent, Latin – inevitably – twenty-one per cent, thirty-three below the average, nineteen below the second worst score.) The occasional bomb scare aside, when the streams re-converged into one broad third-year river tumbling towards the all-weather tennis courts in the shadow of the Biology block, the Tobacco Appreciation Society was the only chance they had to meet between ten to nine and twenty to four; actually given the journey Craig had to get there in the morning, the speed with which he left in the afternoon, often their only chance to meet at all.

St John took a Polo, inserted the tip of his tongue into the hole, at the same time craning his neck to see around the bins. 'All clear,' he said, or as it came out, 'Aw clia.'

The bell for the end of break was ringing as they emerged. A teacher traversing the open space between the Maths block and Modern Languages caught sight of them and frowned, but there were so many pupils on the move, one very small one – 'You boy!' – finding himself perhaps at the opposite end of the school from where he needed to be – at something a little above a fast walk – 'No running!' – that the danger passed.

'Any thoughts yet about tomorrow?' Craig asked.

'My sister has some Gitanes.'

'Sibyl?' Craig had yet to meet either of them, but already St John's sisters loomed large in his imagination.

'Bea,' said St John. Bea was thirteen to their fourteen, Sibyl was two years older again: almost off the scale. 'I found the packet when I was looking for my *Zeppelin IV*, shoved away down behind her pillow.'

Whatever St John had thought *Zeppelin IV* would be doing down there. (Craig was an only child, the ways of siblings and sisters in particular were beyond him.)

'Will she not miss them?'

'Probably, but who is she going to tell?'

'Point,' said Craig, and peeled off left, taking with him the same faint whiff of low-grade tobacco and yesterday's steak-and-kidney pie overlaid with peppermint that St John carried straight on, across the quad, to the temporary Physics labs.

*

St John walked home for lunch most days. No: walked home most days with his lunch – an unvarying meat paste (Mo's great 'discovery') on sliced pan – in his blazer pocket. He would eat it sometimes as he walked. Sometimes he threw it over a wall into the grounds of an old people's home. Not infrequently he would have a wank the moment the front door was closed, although that was not the main attraction over staying in school. (For there were places there too, of course there were.) He liked having the house to himself, the absolute stillness of it, even for the bare dozen minutes that the walk left him (ten minutes walk and wank) before he had to set out on the return leg. He couldn't have told you where he drifted to in those minutes, or how he knew without having to set an alarm or even check his watch that it was time to come back to the here and now.

Today he had the added incentive of Gitanes. Strike while the iron was hot and Bea was out. There was a lot of house, but Bea when she was in it these days was disinclined to quit the one hundred and twenty square feet of it that contained her unruly bed with its shifting coverlet of *Just Seventeen*s and *Jackie*s: 'Tampax comics', in Sibyl's withering judgement, never mind that until as late as last summer her own room had been virtually carpeted with them.

He pulled up from under his shirt the string necklace with the key on the end of it. They all wore them, even Paddy, for those occasions when it slipped Mo's mind that she was to collect him. St John was never entirely sure how to characterise what it was that Mo did that kept her out of the house all day. When forms were to be filled in at school, under 'occupation of parent/guardian', he wrote 'projects'. Typically a project involved a big house somewhere down the country, whose owner, a friend of a friend, was at his or her wit's end with this or that room. For weeks at a time there would be talk, and thought, of little else. Swatches of fabric took over the kitchen table. Drawings annotated with Mo's eccentric spelling wafted to the floor every time a door was opened. The phone never stopped.

And then suddenly it did.

'There's no point trying with some people,' was as much as would be said, although not before Paddy had been obliged to make his own way home from school a couple more times and drag the key up from under his shirt.

Paddy of course was not in the least put out. He stood on an upturned flowerpot to reach the lock and once inside helped himself to bowl after bowl of Rice Krispies, with or without milk (the supply was still unreliable), until the others arrived, an appetite for Rice Krispies, St John supposed, being what eight-year-olds had instead of hormones.

St John's own hormones were at a low ebb this particular lunchtime. Two periods of Physics followed by French subjunctives would, he reassured himself, stem the sap of any man or boy. His zip remained determinedly up as he closed the door and crossed the hall to the stairs.

The curtains had come back, after a mostly muslin fashion: large, unhemmed bolts stitched together and fastened to the window frame with drawing pins. Light diffusion was the new idea. It had gone together with unobstructed air circulation until an opportunistic burglar threw his leg over the sill of the open drawing-room window, while Mo, St John, his sisters and brother were who knows where in the house, and helped himself to the TV. The downstairs windows were now nailed shut.

Upstairs, where the sashes still worked, windows faced one another at either end of the long east–west-aligned first landing and the least sunlight, early or late, turned the air between them a hazy amber.

Halfway along the left-hand wall, as the stairs returned you to face the front of the house again, stood an old blanket box to which at some point a rectangular cushion had been glued. It was the sort of thing that Mo might do, although the depleted stuffing, the sheen that the cretonne cover had acquired (do not dream of calling it chintz in her hearing), bore out her claim that it had been like that when she had picked it up at auction with the Pair of Persian Rugs.

Emphasis on 'she': the past since that morning Mo had woken them with the news that their father would not be coming back had undergone a singular revision. For all that he was mentioned now he might never have been a part of it at all.

The blanket box was St John's favourite place in the house to sit and it was to the blanket box – as enticing in that amber light as a fresh-baked loaf – that his feet now unconsciously tended, so that he was side-on to Bea's room rather than on the point of entering it when a door opened at the far end of the landing and Mo herself appeared, wrapped in her Japanese-print dressing gown.

'Oh,' said St John.

'What are you doing home from school?'

Her face was flushed, her hair untidy.

'It's lunchtime.' He patted the blazer pocket where his sandwich wasn't. 'I just thought . . . for a bit of a change.'

She nodded. She had not moved from in front of the bedroom door. For a moment he thought of charging straight at her, catching her off guard, to find out what, or who, she was protecting. But only for a moment.

'Well, I'd better get back,' he said.

'Yes.'

He faced about, his footsteps as he walked away from her

heavy, as though he was walking through true amber, which would harden before he reached the stairs, preserving the awkwardness of the moment for all eternity. He turned with his hand on the banister. She was still watching him.

'Is everything all right?'

'Of course.'

A large rhododendron grew to one side of the driveway, just short of where it met the street, and hard up against the wooden fence, or what remained of it, between their garden and the house next door's. This was where St John without a further backward glance proceeded to hide, perched on the stump of another shrub that had succumbed like the major part of the fence to rhododendron sprawl.

He was not the only recent visitor. Two Gitanes butts were conspicuous among the brittle brown leaves that made up Planet Rhododendron's floor. There were sweet wrappers too, a Tudor Crisps packet shrivelled by careful application of a match or a lighter to a miniature simulacrum of itself.

He could not see the upper part of the house at all, but without disturbing the branches too much – he might have been a bird foraging, encouraged by the unexpected bounty of the old-people's-home shrubbery – he was able to work himself a pretty good angle on the steps leading up to the front porch. He watched them for an hour or more – for the remainder that is of lunch and most of the seventh period – reckoning that whoever was in there would leave well before Paddy's finishing time at three.

Mo had never made a secret of her boyfriends. The only mystery to St John was where in a city as closed up as Belfast she found them. One guy, Jan, a very blond and according to Sibyl much too young Dutchman, had even come to live with them for a few weeks last summer. There had, it's true, been an element of subterfuge there, Paddy who was particularly fond of him asked that Jan be given the room next to his. (It would have been a maid's room once upon a time.) Jan walked into it every evening when Paddy was going to bed and walked out of it again the following morning, having managed in the meantime not to crease a sheet or dent a pillow.

Perhaps it was just being caught out in the middle of the day that had embarrassed her, the unexpectedness of St John's appearing on the landing like that . . . God forbid she would think he was sneaking up on her . . . *spying*. He pressed down a branch. Nothing was stirring. He rested his head a moment on the back of his hand.

A bang. He opened his eyes. He was in a wooden cage . . . No, a bush: the rhododendron, and the bang just now was the front door closing.

Footsteps, in a hurry, crunched on the gravel. A man passed less than a yard from the verge, visible only from the waist down. St John slipped sideways off the stump on to the leaves, his landing drowned by the footsteps as they carried on down the driveway and on to the street. He scrabbled to get clear of the rhododendron's branches, no care now for the noise he made, coming out head and hands first on to the gravel. He looked left down the street towards the junction with the main road. No one. He looked right. A moment later and he would have missed Dr Lennox turning into the mews that joined St John's street to his.

4

Maxine did not carry on with her counting beyond Valentine's Day 1975. The five-barred tally gates on the back of her first-year homework diary terminated in an ornate 'Woody' in another hand, the girls in her class having decided that year to send each other cards from their favourite Bay City Roller. Maxine didn't care for any of them particularly – you could find boys decked out in the same gear on any street corner round her way (there were no Marc Bolans, no David Bowies, more's the pity) – but after turning up her nose at Alan, Derek, Eric and Les, in alphabetical order, the choice was made for her.

'I *knew* she was a Woody girl . . .'

The verses on the Valentines were still quite tame – 'I love you, I love you, I love you almighty, I wish my pyjamas were next to your nightie. Don't be mistaken, don't be misled, I mean on the clothes line not on the bed.' The girls were none of them over the age of twelve, only a handful had yet been inducted into the Dr White's Club, a name that had done nothing to prepare Maxine, the newest member, for the associated mess and emotional mayhem. It almost went without saying that her mum had done nothing to prepare her either, aside from supplying the aforementioned sanitary towels and reminding her where the Disprin were to be found, although Maxine would probably have died of embarrassment – for her mum as much as herself – had she tried to say anything more. Both Maxine's parents subscribed to the view that life was a series of challenges to be overcome with the least amount of upset. Their rare meals out together as a family were rounded off with a sigh of relief and the expression that that had 'seemed to go off all right'. Granted, in recent years hotels, restaurants, cafés and all such places of public resort had become bomb magnets, but Maxine had memories from before that whole carry-on even began of her dad gunning the car home at the end of a day at the seaside, of the speed with which her mum rinsed out the flasks and the Tupperware before they threw themselves into their chairs either side of the TV: 'There!'

Woody and Dr White's lore had their limitations, but at least with her school friends there could be laughter as well as bewilderment and dread at the changes they were experiencing. The fact was that Maxine had made friends with ease. The teachers' expectations were in general not high and by aiming just a little higher she was able to shine and still keep plenty in reserve. She was the class's plaiter-in-chief, the fabricator of complex folded-paper fortune-tellers.

She coasted through that year and the next. She might have coasted through the three remaining years and out the other side had the police not turned up at the house early one morning and battered down the front door. Maxine was too afraid even to leave her bedroom. She heard them, though – six of them, she thought – charge up the stairs and into the boys' room next door. She heard the shouts and curses, the upsetting of lamps and photographs, the sound, unmistakable even on this the first time of hearing, of hard boots connecting with soft body parts.

It could only be Tommy. Victor had got a job on the rigs just a few weeks before, but even if he had been at home it could still only be Tommy.

They kicked him all the way down the stairs and out the gate to the Land Rover. Maxine, bending a slat of the venetian blind with her forefinger saw, bright against the turgid morning light, his yellow Adidas shorts, which were all that he slept in, his skinny white legs striped red by the boots and batons as the policemen pinioning his arms shoved him – a crack on the knuckles of the hand that tried in desperation to cling to the frame – through the rear doors.

Afterwards the thing that struck her was that she had not once in the three or four minutes between the police arriving and roaring off again heard a peep from either of her parents. She found them in the front room, in nightdress and pyjamas, staring out of habit towards the corner where the TV sat, although they had pulled the plug themselves when they were going to bed the night before. There was glass on the carpet tramped in from the hall, a Hummel chimney sweep lying broken on the hearth, dislodged from the mantelpiece by the thundering of the feet on the stairs. But otherwise, she half expected one or other of them to say, it had seemed to go off all right.

Maxine sat on the sofa separating their armchairs.

'What did he do?' she asked.

'We have no idea,' her dad said at last. A tear ran down her mum's cheek and dripped on to the ruff of her housecoat; a moment later a tear ran down the other cheek. She had cried the same way at the end of *Love Story*. 'No idea at all.'

'Here, is it true your brother was lifted for making guns?' This before Maxine was through the school gate. She had fondly hoped that no one else had witnessed that morning's events. There had been no open doors, no lights even, at the windows (another place there might have been whistles and bin lids), but there had obviously been fingers, like hers, pressing down on the slats of the blinds, other fingers in phone dials, tongues working overtime.

Boys crowded round her in the corridor wanting to know did Tommy really split one of the peelers' eyes open. The girls from her class linked her arms and dragged her down to the toilets – 'Can yous not see she's upset? She doesn't want to talk' – then bombarded her with a whole load of questions of their own. Did her brother have a kind of uniform that he wore, a balaclava? Which one of them was it he was in, the UVF, the UDA? She didn't have to answer if she didn't want to, but, like, had he any mates they hadn't met . . . ?

Even the teachers had got wind of it. Her head of year called her in and asked if she wanted to sit out PE, maybe go home early. Maxine said yes to the first (who wouldn't?), but could think of nothing worse than the second. If instead he had handed her an hour's detention she would have thanked him: thanked him doubly for two hours'. When the last bell rang she hung back for as long as she possibly could – until the caretaker chased her – then dawdled out the gate to find her friends still waiting for her. With Maxine at their centre they forged again a chain of schoolgirl solidarity that sprawled across the footpath, breaking for no woman or man, and definitely not for a simp in a grammar-school blazer getting off his bus.

Maxine hadn't seen him in she didn't know how long. Perhaps he had eventually worked out that he could save himself a lot of grief by catching a later bus on her school's games days, although it was part of the contract that the contract itself was finite, the chasings and name-calling terminating eventually with a collective shrug. *Ach, let him alone.*

Today, though, was different. Karen Thompson on the end of the chain nearest the bus-stop asked him where the fuck he thought he was going.

'Home,' he said. He looked like he had grown about a foot and a half since the days when Tommy had hunted him for sport.

'Not on our footpath you're not,' Karen said. 'Go and find your own.'

He thought about it for a moment.

Heather Nixon – Knickers – two girls to Maxine's left stamped her foot, 'Boo!'

He actually jumped. Of course they wet themselves.

Maxine was about to say she didn't care what footpath he walked on, but before she could get a single word of it out he had stepped down on to the road, and the girls cheered.

They walked her to the front door, which had not only been replaced since she left for school but had had a first coat of paint applied, then carried on down the road singing to the world about being Belfast girls who wore their hair in curls and wore the skinners to their knees.

The chimney sweep had been glued and set back on the mantelpiece. If Maxine had not seen it herself this morning lying on the hearth she could almost have been persuaded it had never been broken at all.

It was when the police released Tommy without charge the evening of the following day that the problems started, for Maxine as well as her brother.

There were only two ways you walked away from an arrest like that without at least going through the courts. One was to refuse to speak no matter what was said or done to you – and no one, least of all Maxine, would have credited Tommy with such fortitude; the other was to give the cops all they asked of you and more.

Maxine saw the graffiti on the gable end of a house directly facing her own when she left for school on the morning after his release. 'Tommy the Tout.' A couple of mornings later it was joined by a crudely drawn fist, face-on, and a black circle above it representing the barrel of the gun he was now staring down: 'Bye-bye Tommy.'

Tommy himself lay low, literally – stretched out on the sofa from the day's beginning to its end. He wouldn't get up to answer the door; he was afraid even to pick up the telephone. Somebody, though, must have phoned Victor, because he arrived home from the rigs at the end of that week, a fortnight earlier than expected. He said he would have a word with a few boys he knew, see if he could work something out. It took him the best part of two days going from one drinking club to another. Maxine was not invited into the front room to hear the news he brought back. She listened at the top of the stairs with her ear to the wall. (Four long hairs, roots and all, were caught on the head of a screw in the banister.) Victor's voice was pitched too low, but she heard Tommy echoing his brother's words, turning his statements into questions.

'I go or the whole family goes? Forty-eight hours?' And then a statement and a question of his own: 'I never told them nothing. Why doesn't anyone believe me?'

When the police returned for him a second time before the forty-eight hours was up it was by arrangement, for his own protection.

Maxine's mum and dad waited for a call or a letter – even just a line that let them know how he was, where he was – but no call or letter came, no line.

As for Maxine, she spent the first few weeks of her brother's exile in Coventry. Not a single person in her class would speak to her. The teachers too seemed to think it politic to ignore her. Only the summer holidays came to her rescue: sixty-two days that could not have passed slowly enough.

*

It was the summer of the Silver Jubilee. The red helicopter carrying the Queen and Prince Philip from the Royal Yacht to Hillsborough Castle passed right over St John's house from whose attic window Mo played the Sex Pistols at full volume, 'God save the Queen, the fascist regime . . .': 'a horrible noise, but a sweet sentiment.'

She had migrated to the attic at some point during the night, having been drinking since early evening, a dinner party to which somebody significant had been invited and at which he proved himself to be not so very significant or even very interested in her at all.

Sibyl had climbed the attic stairs around lunchtime to try to talk her down and had wound up drinking with her. Sibyl it was who provided the record and ran the extension lead for the record player up from the landing. Of the three remaining Nimmos Paddy was nominated to answer the door to the neighbours who came to complain, or rather, since they didn't like to think of themselves as complaining types, to reason. 'Look, a lot of people find this whole Jubilee business a bit crass,' Paddy reported their words verbatim and apparently without irony, 'but – a lovely summer's day – if you could just, you know, keep it a little bit quieter . . .'

'I don't see what she's got against the woman anyway,' said Bea, who tended to like or dislike things in inverse proportion to other people's liking or disliking them, a stance that often left her in a minority in her own house and a majority in the world at large. 'It's not like she asked to be born a princess.'

'Any more than you asked to be born a pain in the hole,' St John said. St John was in bad form. Craig had been meant to come over – the first time since he was about six that St John had invited anybody to the house – but an hour after he was due to arrive he had phoned to say he was giving up and going back home: the buses were all up the left with the extra security. (The phone boxes were permanently up the left, which was why it had taken him an hour to ring.) The part of St John that was relieved his friend hadn't after all witnessed the madness in the attic had been wrestling with the part that wanted to know why he hadn't been able to find some way around the irregular timetables and the road-blocks.

It was this latter part, when they were arranging where to

rendezvous a few days afterwards to compare Jubilee-visit notes (St John was already editing his), that decided to withhold the offer of the house the second time.

They met instead in the Wimpy on Wellington Place. Craig was all antsy, fiddling with napkins, flicking the big red plastic tomato with his fingernail, tapping his feet, tapping his feet, tapping his feet . . .

'You'll never guess what happened to me after I phoned you the other day?' he said.

'Give up.'

'I met a girl.'

'You're not serious.'

'I think I might be.'

*

Maxine had been in the house by herself a little after half past ten that morning of the royal visit when there was a knock at the door. From force of habit she put her eye to the tiny spyglass that Victor had insisted her parents had fitted in the new front door. Its fisheye ballooned the head of the person doing the knocking, made a tuber of the nose.

'Knickers,' she said under her breath. She wiped toast crumbs off her pyjamas, which were otherwise clean and presentable and turned the lock. 'Hiya.'

'Hiya,' said Heather Nixon. 'It's a wick summer, isn't it?'

Maxine had been mourning the passing of each and every day, but, yeah, she said, I know what you mean. Heather looked up and down the street. No one there. Maxine suspected that this was not so much the opportunity as the motivation: all her other friends had gone away.

'Fancy coming in?' she said.

They spent what was left of the morning painting their nails – finger and toe – and listening to the radio. (Heather guessed the 'Golden Hour' year was 1973 after the first four notes of 'Whiskey in the Jar'.) They were distantly aware of the sound of a helicopter, tonally different from the helicopters that provided the soundtrack to the city's days and nights, traversing the sky from north to south. Each tilted her head a little towards the window, left a word momentarily hanging between them . . . 'What was that you were saying?' 'No, you go.' 'I forget.'

Only once did Maxine ask herself was this wise, when Heather, passing the boys' room on the way into Maxine's, paused for a second to read their names, which Tommy had stencilled there donkey's years before. 'You're lucky there's just you now,' was all she said, though, then launched into this whole thing about her wee sister and a missing necklace, which Heather knew rightly had been sitting on her side of the chest of drawers when she went out the day before.

At a certain point Heather suggested that they walk down to the Spar. (It had reopened the year before, half the size of the old one and everything in it twice the price.) She didn't budge from the edge of the bed when Maxine said she had better get dressed, but neither did she let up in her chat. You would have to be some kind of perv yourself, she seemed to be saying, to let me sitting here bother you.

Before they opened the front door Heather pulled out a little tube and applied a slick of lip gloss to both their mouths.

'The fellas don't stand a chance,' she said.

Across the street the gun-barrel farewell to Tommy had been painted over with news of some more recent offence: SP + DK = House breakers NO MORE WARNINGS.

A neighbour's little girl played two-ball against it, spinning round after every third throw, lifting one leg to let the balls bounce under it before she caught them and threw again. A bit further on two boys lay on the footpath pushing stones down a drain with lollipop sticks.

They saw no one over the age of eight until they rounded the last corner before the Spar. 'Oh, God, look who it is,' Heather said then.

Maxine didn't recognise him straight off without the uniform.

'Here, give us one of your fags,' Heather shouted before Maxine could stop her. Heather had asthma. She didn't even smoke. He hesitated on the kerb opposite, as though still mindful of past injunctions about where he could and could not walk; but only for a moment. Heather squeezed Maxine's arm. 'Oh, frig, he's coming over.'

He produced a ten-deck of some obscure brand from his jean-jacket pocket and shook a filtered-tip out towards Heather. 'Nah, you're all right,' she said, as blatant as you like. 'I just put one out.'

'Me too,' said Maxine, since he didn't ask. His eyes, which were three different shades of green, barely took her in at all, but flicked like a down-and-up switch between the top of Heather's blouse and the glossed lips of her fast-moving mouth.

*

'Heather Nixon,' said Craig in response to St John's asking him what this girl was called. The next question – 'What's she like?' – was harder to come at. 'She's funny' – he nearly said *loud* – 'and she has' – he and St John had very rarely talked about girls; he shied away from the first thing that came into his head – 'a nice mouth.'

'I'll recognise her when I see her then,' St John said, and paused. 'When will I get to see her then?'

Craig shrugged. 'I don't know, some time, maybe, soon. I'll bring her down here.'

But Heather did not like going into town: too dangerous. Even the bus was dodgy, taking you past areas where you knew you were not welcome. (Bricks, admittedly, were sometimes thrown to reinforce this point, bottles, bags of dog shit.) Craig, in truth, soon ceased to care. She had a pretty one-tracked mind, had Heather. If they never quite went all the way that summer they went pretty far pretty often pretty much anywhere they could lean or lie unseen for five or ten minutes. Some days, they went round to Heather's friend Maxine's, since there was never anyone there but her during the day. Always at some stage Heather would remind Maxine of a message she was supposed to have said she had to do – 'Oh, yeah, right' – and off Maxine would go for half an hour and leave them at it on the living-room sofa. (It was on that living-room sofa in fact that they got as close to all the way as they were ever to get, as close as any two people could get without going there.) A couple of times Craig asked Heather if she thought her friend minded. 'Of course she doesn't. I would do the same for her if it was my house that was empty. Mind you, she'd have to find a fella willing to have her first.' She bit her lip. 'I'm a bad bitch sometimes, amn't I?'

'You are,' Craig said and she squirmed with the pleasure of hearing it confirmed. 'You really, really are.'

They were all sitting in Maxine's back garden one afternoon, Maxine in one deckchair, Craig in another, Heather sideways across his lap, when Heather sprang to her feet. 'I need to run round to the house and set the timer on the oven,' she said. 'Our Alison's too dense to remember.'

Craig, taking this as some novel reversal of their normal routine, went to get up. 'No, I mean it,' she said. 'Wait here. I'm only going to be a minute.' But ten minutes passed then fifteen and still she didn't come back. Craig and Maxine barely exchanged a word. Craig was annoyed that Heather hadn't taken him with her. Maxine, he felt sure, was annoyed that Heather had left him behind for – God – *twenty* minutes now.

She stood up suddenly and strode down the back garden to the door.

'Sorry,' she said. She had her hand to her mouth. He thought she might have been laughing. He looked down at his shirt. The second and third buttons were open where Heather had had her hand. He did them up again and glanced up at the house in time to see Maxine turn away from the back-bedroom window.

She came out a couple of minutes later with two plastic tumblers pinched together between the thumb and forefinger of her right hand.

'Here,' she said and he took one of the tumblers from her. He looked inside. Ribena.

'Thanks.'

She had something in her other hand that she tucked under her arm as she walked to the free chair. He lost her for a moment in the sun's glare. He sat up shielding his eyes.

'I don't think it was fair,' he said. 'Heather going off like that and leaving you stuck with me.'

Her eyebrows, over the rim of the plastic tumbler, shrugged.

'Actually I don't think it's fair us always coming round here to . . .'

'To?' asked Maxine half into her Ribena.

'Get in your way,' he said feebly.

They sipped their drinks.

'Are you going to show me,' he said at length.

'Show you what?'

'That other thing that you brought out with you there now.'

Her hand reached down to the blind side of the deck-chair. 'How do you know I brought it out to show you?'

'The way you were hiding it.'

They both laughed at the illogicality of what he had just said and because they were glad to have banished the silence laughed more, flopped back against the canvas. Which is how Heather found them when she came up the alley, giving out about her sister . . . She stopped.

'What's so funny?' She threw herself into Craig's lap. There was no weight in her, but her momentum tested the frame to its limits. His bum practically touched the ground. 'Did you miss me?' she said and at that precise moment it would have been very hard indeed for him to say no.

Maxine launched the last of her Ribena towards the flowerbed.

The Monday after that they went back to their schools.

*

'What, dumped you just like that?' St John asked.

'Her exact words were, "I can't really be arsed with this any more,"' Craig said.

They were back behind the refectory. New shirts, new ties, St John in the blazer he had finally grown into in the middle of last year and had ever since been growing out of, a pack of Chesterfields they had clubbed together for to get the new term off to a good start.

'She sounds like a bit of a mad woman.'

The bell rang for the end of break. Craig took a last drag. 'I'm not fussed to tell you the truth. O levels coming up.'

'In about eighteen months' time.'

'Yeah, but you've got to get the head down early.'

5

St John's problem was not to do with getting his head down, but keeping his head up. Irrespective of which regime was in place at home he never seemed to be able to fit all the sleep he needed into the out-of-school hours and while there had been no repeat of the first week's Land of Nod fiasco scarcely a month passed without a detention for inattention, scarcely a week without a piece of chalk bouncing off his desk, or the wall he was leaning against, his name exploding from the lips of the chalk-chucker. *Nimmo!*

His grades slipped and slipped. Then they slid.

Twice Mrs Daniels, the head of year, sent him home with a letter for Mo. Both times Sibyl forged replies: thank you for your concern . . . quite capable of dealing with the matter myself . . .

The third letter went by post requesting that Mo attend a meeting in the headmaster's study at two o'clock on the following Tuesday afternoon.

She had started volunteering a few weeks before in the War on Want shop on the Lisburn Road, having apparently exhausted the supply of people in large houses with whom there was no point trying. Half the clothes that were donated she bought before they even got to the racks. She arrived at the meeting two minutes late in a fake snow-leopard wrap and a red sweater dress St John had never seen before either, the clothes she left the house in that morning carried in a large plastic bag containing besides a die-cast manual juice extractor (it looked like something out of that *Star Wars* film), lying on its back, chrome lever raised in stiff-armed salute. St John sniffed discreetly and was relieved not to smell drink.

The headmaster greeted her across the vastness of his desk with a smile of calculated width and duration. From behind him his six predecessors looked on, their gowns, thick with varnish, almost indistinguishable from the mahogany panelling on which they were mounted, their smiles, if anything, more meagre still than his.

St John knew from the set of his mother's shoulders that she was not going to be cowed by the occasion, unlike Mrs Daniels who looked suddenly as though she wished she had never been elevated to head of fourth year.

'Thank you for coming, Mrs Nimmo,' the headmaster said. 'I do not make a habit of arranging meetings in the middle of the day, which is as inconvenient for me as I am sure it is for you, but this is unfortunately a problem that will only get more serious unless addressed at once.'

He turned his head towards St John. 'Have you anything you want to say?'

Mo touched her son's hand. 'You don't have to say anything.'

'Mrs Nimmo, this is not a trial.'

'Isn't it?'

The headmaster sighed. 'Mrs Daniels?'

'Well, it's very simple, at least on the page it's very simple.' She had an actual page in her hand. It trembled. 'St John's performance in the first two terms of this year is far below GCE standard in every one of his subjects.'

Mo held out her hand for the page, which Mrs Daniels in trying to hand over dropped and had to bend to retrieve from under her seat. Her face when she sat up again was flushed.

Mo studied the text, frowning, turned the page over to make sure there was nothing she was missing. Her plumped-out lip said not. She passed it back, without so much as a glance, to Mrs Daniels.

'St John came up through your own Prep School,' she said to the headmaster. 'Seven years of fees in return for which I was guaranteed that a place would be found for him here, no matter what the outcome of the qualifying exam.'

'Which I passed,' St John wanted to remind them all, but held back sensing it would not help the case his mother was constructing.

'Since then you have accepted another four years of fees . . . Frankly if you had not called a meeting soon I would have been on the phone to you looking for an explanation for the shocking performance of your teaching staff.'

St John thought for a moment he might choke on the laugh he swallowed.

Mrs Daniels sat forward. 'I can assure Mrs Nimmo, Headmaster, that St John's teachers have been doing their utmost to ensure that he keeps pace with the rest of the class, but they each have twenty-five other pupils to attend to.'

'Oh.' Mo looked directly at her, shaping the exclamation rather than speaking it, although even that, and the raised eyebrow accompanying it, was too much for Mrs Daniels whose flush became a full-blown blush.

The headmaster cleared his throat. 'There is also the small matter of these.'

He passed across the table Sibyl's forged letters. Mo barely glanced at those either. 'I'm sorry,' she said. 'My handwriting can be a little hard to read at times.'

'I don't know what you take us for, Mrs Nimmo,' the headmaster started to say but was interrupted by an enormous explosion, which set the past headmasters shivering on the walls. The headmaster (extant), Mrs Daniels, Mo and St John, without being aware of it, rose two or three inches from their seats. Almost immediately there came the sound of sirens, which carried on – away from the school, thankfully (they sank back on to their seats) – for several minutes, and which had the effect of drawing their thoughts off the matter in hand and towards whatever might lie at the sirens' journey's end. The car-tax office, as it turned out. No one killed or badly hurt, such sometimes is the whimsical way of large explosive devices in confined urban spaces whose occupants have only been given two minutes to get the fuck out.

The headmaster looked at Sibyl's letters, balled in his fists, as though unable to account for their presence. 'Well, perhaps we should leave it there for now,' he managed at length. 'And let us hope we do not have cause to meet like this again.'

Mo was already on her feet. She tightened the wrap, picked up the bag with the clothes and the juicer.

'If you and your staff do your duty I guarantee you that St John and I will each do ours.'

She reached across the desk to shake his hand. She turned

and shook Mrs Daniels', startling her up off her seat again.

St John returned to his class, bemused.

Later, passing the drawing room, he overheard Mo talking to Sibyl. 'I recognised the woman as soon as I walked in, from the WoW shop. I sold her the *Story of O*.'

St John stepped in from the hallway. 'What's the *Story of O*?'

'Twaddle,' Mo said.

'I didn't know you sold that sort of thing,' said Sibyl, confirming for St John the nature of its twaddle.

'Special stock. I had a lovely lady come in with her son-in-law carrying a big box full of stuff belonging to her late husband. I don't know whether it was her or him had put the *Arden Shakespeare*s on top, but *O* was one of the milder offerings buried underneath.'

She told St John and Sibyl she had been considering withholding their allowance for a fortnight ('We get an allowance?' asked Sibyl), but had decided instead to let them donate it.

She was starting a Juice Fund.

For the whole of that week and the week after that and the week after that again the house was coming down with oranges and lemons and grapefruits. On one occasion Mo brought home a lime, in the city at that time rarer even than young blond Dutchmen. There were jugs of every conceivable blend in the fridge, all of them with the same faint taste of chrome, cubes of coloured ice in the freezer, husks spilling out every time you took the lid off the bin. Then, inevitably given its age and sudden overuse, the spring went in the arm and though several replacement springs were tried the mechanism was never the same again. Still the juice extractor retained its place on the countertop along with the broken egg timer, the electric can opener (fused) and the never-used fondue set. Every so often in passing, in the years ahead, St John would flip the arm up into its fascist salute then watch it sink slowly back to its side.

He got the five GCEs he needed to be accepted back in to do A levels, Maths and any four others. (French, Biology, Art and – a miracle almost worthy of study in the subject itself – Divinity.) He stood in the covered walkway beside the office where the envelopes were being given out, checking and rechecking the long strip of perforated paper.

'So?'

Craig.

'I'm in.'

'Brilliant.'

'You?'

'Yep, in too.'

'Let's see.'

Craig produced an envelope of his own, a similar strip of paper inside. St John read down it. 'A, A, A, A, B, A, B, A . . . I'll say you're in all right.'

They had wandered without thinking up the back of the refectory, although two minutes in the opposite direction would have taken them out the school gate and into the anonymity of the August-morning streets. They sat with their backs to the wall, their shoulders almost touching. The bins on either side of them were padlocked for the summer, the flues above them entirely smoke-free.

'Have you any on you?' St John asked.

'I've sort of been stopping,' said Craig.

'*You?*'

'Sort of. Trying to.' He pulled out a slightly creased No. 6. 'I've got this.'

St John deliberated a moment then pulled a Twiglet of a roll-up from his pocket. 'I've got this.'

'Is that what I think it is?'

'I don't know, are you thinking tea leaves?'

'Tea leaves?'

'I heard Sibyl talking about it on the phone to someone. I tried it the other night.'

'What's it like?'

'Makes you feel a bit light-headed.'

'So do No. 6 sometimes.'

'A different sort of light-headed . . . drifty.'

'I don't know.'

St John folded back a match from a half-used book with the name on the front of a Dublin hotel. 'Give it a go.'

He struck the match. They looked at each other over the flame. 'All right,' Craig said.

He dipped his head to light the No. 6 and passed it straight away to St John, who in turn passed him the Twiglet.

It never reached his mouth. They registered the footsteps a moment before they heard the woman's voice.

'Is someone there?'

'Shit.' St John crushed the No. 6 against the wall. Craig, panicking, tried to flick the Twiglet on to the roof of the refectory. It bounced off the fascia board to land in the middle of the passageway.

The footsteps faltered. 'Come out at once, whoever you are.'

Craig's face drained of colour. 'We're fucked,' he said as the voice called out again: 'School rules apply in the summer too!'

'Well we can't just hide up here,' said St John and before Craig could stop him stepped out to find himself face to face with Mrs Daniels, the Twiglet smouldering on the ground between them. When Craig emerged, a heartbeat behind him, St John was already laughing.

'Quiet, for God sake,' Craig said out the corner of his mouth, but 'Oh,' was all that Mrs Daniels said. 'Oh.'

*

Maxine had gone to collect her CSE results the Thursday before. A top grade there – 1 – was the equivalent of a GCE C. She pulled out the slip . . . she'd got three of them. She closed her eyes. She had been expecting more. Teachers – everyone in her class – had been expecting more.

She opened her eyes, glanced around, and of course there was no one there to see her shame. Most of her friends weren't even bothering to turn up for their results. They had walked out the gates on their last day of school and straight on to the broo. Maxine had walked out with them, like, and signed on too, but always with the intention of signing off again in September when she went back to school. No, not 'back', 'on', to another school, the school she should have been at all along.

Now when she walked out the gate she turned right, to-wards town. She wanted to blame somebody, but she didn't know who . . . Her parents, her teachers, the whole rotten system of grammar and secondary schools, but she kept coming back to fucking Tommy getting himself arrested – how many hundreds of days ago? – as the moment when she was thrown off course. On and on she walked, pounding the pavement, past all those places Heather Nixon was too chickenshit to pass even on the bus (nobody said boo to her), through the wasteland of roadworks and slum clearance that used to be Sailortown, through the Royal Avenue security gates, barely breaking stride to be frisked, until she arrived footsore in the city centre.

She wandered for a time the entries off High Street, looking for an out-of-the-way bar where an underage girl could slip in without remark, but between the wire cages and the cameras, the clusters of men in the doorways comparing football coupons and betting slips, her courage finally failed her.

She bought a can of Fanta out of Woolies and sat with it on a bollard at the edge of Corn Market. A load of punks were crowded round the fountain (*sink*, more like) in the middle of the square, 'Outcasts' stencilled across the shoulders of one leather jacket, across another 'CRASS' and that odd symbol with the cross that so confused Maxine every time she saw it.

They didn't even attempt to hide the carrier bags they passed around, heavy with glue. Maxine had tried lighter fuel a couple of times, but it was a scary kind of rush and she hated the head it left you with in the morning. Right now, though, she would have sniffed anything that you waved under her nose. She threw back the remains of her Fanta for the cheap brain-fizz that provided and when she was able again to stop blinking her eyes there was a fella, seventeen, eighteen tops, standing in front of the bollard, looking at her.

His hair was cut short and dyed plum. He wore a T-shirt ripped at the shoulders (his arms looked to have been knotted together from the discarded material) and a pair of red-and-black-striped jeans so tight you could see the shape of him like something on the butchery counter, shrink-wrapped.

'Sorry, was I staring at you and your mates?'

He glanced behind him at the fountain. 'Oh, I'm not with them.' And as he said this she thought that there was perhaps something a little too *precise* in his look. He pointed at a second-floor window. 'I work up there.'

A sign jutted out, black and white and red from the Victorian brickwork: Berlin.

'I was looking out and I saw you sitting and I thought, fuck it, I'll ask her.'

'Ask me what?'

'To model.'

Maxine laughed. 'I don't think I'm model material.'

'Your hair, I mean.' He reached out a hand and touched it. Cascade of bangles tinkling in her ear. She shivered. 'I have to do two cut and dyes by next Tuesday, one guy, one girl.'

His hand was round the back of her neck now, flicking the hair clear of the collar. 'It would be pretty full-on, like, but it wouldn't cost you a penny.'

Whether it was the Fanta or the fact that she hadn't eaten since the night before (even the thought of breakfast this

51

morning had turned her stomach) her head was light. She stood up and stumbled against . . .

'What did you say your name was?' she asked.

'I didn't. It's Max.'

'No!'

'I know.' He grimaced. 'My parents had delusions of grandeur.'

'No, no, it's just' – she put a hand to her chest – 'I'm Max*ine*.'

'Well, there you go, it was obviously meant to be,' he said and took her by the arm and led her across Corn Market to the door that led to Berlin.

It was amazing. Stepping through that door really was like stepping into another city, not Berlin – not yet – but a version of Belfast past: the tiled hallway, the light cast from the stained-glass fanlights, the mailboxes with their brass handles and nameplates . . .

The staircase was three feet wide easily, its banister anchored to a huge mahogany newel post decorated with pineapples and pomegranates and bunches of grapes. Doors with frosted glass opened off the first landing – Maxine read 'shipping broker' in passing and something that looked very like 'furrier'. From behind another door she thought she heard the sound of sewing machines. For a mad panicky moment as Max steered her still up she wondered if she had seen the red, white and black sign outside at all, if she hadn't actually been dragged down a wormhole to a previous century, and then they were at the top of the second flight of stairs and Max was opening the door and there she was, there it was, Berlin, as 1979 as Belfast got.

She could not work out at first who among the people

sitting and walking about were the clients and who were the stylists – they all appeared to be smoking – and who were the strays wandered in off the street to listen to the jukebox, which stood off in one corner and when she entered was playing a song she had never till that moment heard but would ever afterwards associate with that day, that whole period of her life.

'That's incredible.'

'"Shot by Both Sides",' Max said over the top of it. 'Magazine. Here, give me your jacket there.'

And only then did she remember that she had on underneath this awful blouse with frills and bows that her mum had bought her for Christmas and that she had been too lazy, and guilt-ridden, to take back.

'I'm a wee bit cold,' she said.

'It never warms up in here, even with the driers going all day.' Max gave his stringy arms a rub. She caught a glimpse of a single brown nipple. For all that was holding the T-shirt together he might as well have been topless. 'Wait here till I see if there's a chair free.'

A girl wandered over from the general direction of the till, preceded by a long breath of smoke. 'Is Max doing you?' she asked and Maxine said yes, he was. 'Don't let him talk you into anything you don't want.'

'I wasn't thinking of it.'

'No one ever is with Max,' said the girl and smiled a smile that was not meant for Maxine but for Max himself who was returning at that moment with a cape for her shoulders.

'Found a chair,' he said. 'Right by the window.'

'What does the jukebox take?' Maxine asked as he

53

installed her in front of the mirror.

'Ten pee, or three for twenty.'

She slipped off her jacket under the cape. 'Well if I gave you twenty would you go and put that "Shot by Both Sides" song on again for me three times?'

He was an hour over the cutting alone, an hour in which Maxine, who had resolved not to meet her own gaze for the duration, had nothing to look at but his chest and neck, Adam's apple in perpetual motion, the underside of his chin. She was aware of people – stylists, clients, strays – wandering over to see what he was at, aware of their muttered approval. At moments he seemed to her to be cutting freehand, leaning back, as though the scissors were directing him and not he them, at other moments he moved in so close, tracking down a single hair, that her nose was practically inside his T-shirt. It smelled surprisingly clean.

Once, towards the end of the hour, he had to ask her to sit still. 'This is the really important bit.' She wanted to tell him it wasn't him, it was the envelope with her CSE results in it, folded over in her back pocket, apparently swollen to ten times its original size and digging into the left cheek of her bum. But she didn't say anything. And she didn't move again until he said it was OK.

When it was time for the dye he took her into a tiny side room – alcove, really: a sink, a chair, no window. The stuff he prepared was the colour and consistency of blackcurrant yoghurt. He pasted it on with a brush (already she was conscious of how little hair she had left) and pulled a plastic hood down as far as her eyebrows, the tips of her ears. 'If this starts to burn,' he said, 'shout.'

Having not even now the option of her own face to look at, she watched him in the further hour he left her sitting there come and go across the alcove's doorway. She watched him at the window, perched on the sill, as he must have been when he looked down into Corn Market and saw her. She watched him bum cigarettes, smoking with his elbow resting in the palm of his hand, watched him get too close too often to the other girls who came his way, as plenty did. She was pretty sure he knew she was watching as well. Something about the scale of his gestures, like the actors she had seen on the class trip to the Arts Theatre (about which the less said the better), making sure they could be understood right up in the back row.

He came in every so often to check under the hood, poking at the roots with the pointed end of a plastic comb. 'Another wee while yet.'

You're enjoying all this, you so-and-so.

It was a sweet relief when he finally leaned her head back over the sink and switched on the taps. The jets from the showerhead were a hundred separate needles driving into her scalp. Then – 'Bear with me' – he applied another dye, low down on her nape, and abandoned her again. The place was already starting to empty. Juniors with brushes as wide as the stairs she had climbed to get here pushed hair promiscuously across the floor. (It thrilled her to think of her own hair tumbled in with all the rest.) The jukebox fell silent. She didn't know where Max had got to. He wasn't on the windowsill, or flitting around the other stylists' chairs. She was beginning to think he had actually forgotten her when he appeared, asking her to lean back over the sink again, just a moment or two – was that water OK? – there, that would do it.

He led her out of the alcove by the hand and sat her down in the chair beside the window again. The blow-drier came out, two more pairs of scissors, the electric trimmer, a brush with bristles right the way round. Ten minutes more. She looked at her hands in her lap.

'All right.'

He stepped back and finally she raised her eyes.

'Oh, fuck,' she said and started to cry. A white, white shell, cut in a perfect semicircle around her forehead, descending to a point, a right-angle practically, midway down her ear, shading into scarlet at the nape . . . She was beautiful. Even the awful blouse was rescued by association. It looked daring, deviant somehow.

The girl who had spoken to her earlier took photographs with an instant camera – front, back, left side, right side, three-quarter view, head down, chin raised. The Polaroids were passed from hand to hand as one after the other they bloomed into colour: *that one – no, that one – oh, wow, yeah . . .*

When they had all had their say and she was getting her jacket on, Max asked her if she was in a hurry home. Suddenly she was not.

'I've a bit more clearing up to do,' he said. 'I'll meet you at the fountain.'

The punks who had been there earlier were gone. The office workers were gone, the shop workers and shoppers were gone. Soon the security gates would be shut and then the only way out would be the pedestrian turnstiles. After ten or fifteen minutes she saw Max leave with an older guy she took to be the owner. They stood chatting briefly before the owner raised his hand for Max to slap, turned towards High Street, and Max with a single glance behind him came over to the fountain. 'I have a key,' was the first thing he said.

So up the stairs they went again, past the shipping broker and the might-be furrier, the now-silent sewing machines. She was under no illusions, not then, not a few minutes later when he was lying her back on the towels that he had tossed about the floor for a blanket, unbuttoning her blouse with one hand, his shrink-wrap jeans with the other.

'Quick,' she said (she didn't want to give him the satisfaction of telling him he was fucking gorgeous), 'I'm getting cold.'

It was after nine when she got home. Her parents had been up the walls. Turns out there had been a bomb down the town. The car-tax office again. Maxine hadn't even heard it. Their panic, though, turned to open-mouthed confusion when they saw her standing in the living-room doorway. There was no point in asking her what she had done, so all that was left them was to ask her why she had done it, over and over and over again. Why, Maxine, *why*?

Maxine started work in Berlin at the beginning of September, answering the phone and working the till and sometimes, if it was really hectic, sweeping the floor. It was Saturdays only, cash in hand: seven pounds fifty, along with her share of whatever the stylists decided to donate to the juniors from their tips. Between the shops at lunchtime and what she put into the jukebox she barely had enough left some weeks to pay for the bus home.

So, Max reasoned, don't get the bus home.

So a lot of nights she didn't.

She told her mum and dad she was staying with one of the other girls and once or twice she really was. Mostly though she went to Max's brother Ben's place on the Ormeau Road. Ben was twenty-three and married and didn't give a fuck. Audrey, Ben's wife (she was twenty-one), had done up the spare room in peach and cream with lace trims around the valance, the lampshades, the quilted stool before the dressing table, the handmade cover for the box that sat on top, from which came the peach-and-cream tissues Maxine used to mop herself with two or three times a night.

She was wrong about the owner. The salon was run by two brothers, Dermot and Pete, neither of whom was the guy that Maxine had seen Max leave with that first day. That was Andy who had used to work at Sassoon's in London and had done Rod Stewart's tints. (Rod had tipped him in coke and threw the rolled-up twenty in with it.) And then there was Stevo and Gerard, who was sweet, everybody said so, and Paula and Áine and Cathy K – the other Cathy, Cathy Q, had left more than a year before but the K stuck – and the ever-changing cast of juniors with whom, tips apart, Maxine, with no ambitions beyond answering the phone on Saturday, was never lumped. And Max, of course, the rogue.

There was a girl came in every second Saturday, incredible-looking, elfin-cut jet-black hair, red PVC raincoat, whatever the weather, collar up, belted tight. The Billy Girl everyone called her. She was one of Pete's, hardly spoke to anyone apart from him and – at a stretch – Dermot the whole time she was in, but stood looking into the jukebox until it was her turn. (Her haircuts consisted of two dozen very precise snips, which took Pete about half an hour to line up and which Maxine, sitting at the till, was instructed to take no payment for.) Only once did Maxine see her put her hand in her pocket to put a record on. 'The Laughing Policeman'. The song had been a staple of all their childhoods. There wasn't a month went by but it got an airing on *Junior Choice*. At the opening bars everyone in the salon turned, smiling, to see the Billy Girl still frowning into the jukebox. Dermot mouthed *Oops* and as one they returned in silence to their occupations until the final *ha-ha-ha-ha-ha* freed them to talk again. Maxine, who was close enough that she could have reached out and put a hand on the shoulder of her PVC raincoat, had found herself close to tears.

Andy claimed that the reason she kept her raincoat belted all the time was that she had nothing on underneath but a corset and suspenders. No, said Áine, you *wish* she had nothing on but a corset and suspenders. Max told them if they needed someone to find out, one way or the other, they knew who to ask, this with a wink to Maxine to say he was only kidding around.

'Yeah, right,' she said.

She knew he was seeing other girls behind her back. It wasn't like he wanted for room. She left him six whole days – and nights – in which to do it. Her relationship with him, like her relationship with Berlin, was strictly Saturday only. Which is not to say she was in any way lukewarm towards him, God, no. She would race up the two flights of stairs some Saturday mornings barely able to breathe with

6

Craig sometimes likened the sixth form to the final phase of the Great War. Many had fallen in the preceding years and those who remained had grown in ways that would have been unimaginable to their fresh-faced, newly enlisted selves. (That he was, at coming seventeen, the same age as some of the fallen of France and Flanders was not lost on him.) There were half a dozen in his Latin class, half that again in Ancient History. Even History, with a cohort of eighteen, was forty per cent down on the numbers before the Big Push of the O levels.

The course plotted from first year had brought them closer and closer to home. Only now that they were reduced to the seriously committed were they allowed to dwell for any length of time on their own country's past, although no more recent than the years following the Great War itself, the events leading up to Partition, which, he learned, had to be considered in the same historical sweep as the assassination of Archduke Franz Ferdinand and the attrition of the trenches.

It felt strange – transgressive almost – to be sitting in class discussing the same sets of initials as were heard with dreadful regularity on news bulletins today – IRA, UVF – shorn of all the passion, and the opprobrium, that normally attached to them.

That, said his teacher, was the meaning of the 'vantage-point of history', a place above the fray.

His teacher, Mr Harrison – Hammy – had only been at the school a few years himself. He had asked Craig in passing one day, a couple of weeks into the term, what primary school he had gone to. Craig said the name. Hammy nodded: thought so. 'I know it well,' he said. 'Played football against you a couple of times.' From some of the other things he said it was clear that he felt a distance between himself and the older teachers, a distance not entirely dictated by age. 'Most of these people have never had to fight to get anything. It all came to them on a plate.'

Craig had History last two periods on a Thursday. It was not unusual for the class to carry on after the bell had rung. 'That's the end of what the school is using your parents' fees to pay me for,' Hammy would say, 'but if any of you want to sit on a while and chat . . .' The kettle would come out from the deep drawer in the base of his desk, an assortment of cups, uniformly brown inside, a small jar of Maxwell House, a large one of Coffee-Mate. Treatises had been written, he said one day, on the role of coffee in the advancement of Free Thought. Though clearly not by any of the coffee pickers, Tanya Morgan said. See, said Hammy, stirring a cup, you prove my point and theirs!

Craig was nearly always the last to go. He would offer to rinse the cups then he and Hammy would walk together, still talking, through the empty corridors to the staffroom. As the weeks went by Hammy would tell Craig to hang on while he nipped in and got his coat and carry on talking until Craig's bus came along. Their conversations ranged here and there over the subject that bound them. History, Hammy said, taught you that there was no more redundant word in English than 'unprecedented'. The protests, for instance, that were cranking up again in the Northern Irish prisons? The government thought it was showing its strength by refusing to concede the demands for free association, for freedom from prison work and prison uniform, but all it was doing was pushing the prisoners towards ever more extreme forms of self-abnegation: first the no-wash protest, now this business with the excrement smeared all over the cell walls. Finally there would be a hunger strike – just as there had been in 1920, you could set your watch by it – prisoners would in all likelihood die, bringing down who knows what on all our heads. You only had to look at how the marches were being orchestrated on the outside. The political wing was starting to assert itself.

'So, what, should they just give in?'

'They should allow them the illusion of the smaller victory to deny them the certainty of the larger,' Hammy said then added quickly with a smile, 'History tells us what is likely to happen, unfortunately governments tend to be composed of lawyers and economists and wealthy businessmen, not history teachers.'

Hammy helped out Scottie Campbell, one of the PE teachers, who coached the boys' First XI hockey team, and sometimes drove the minibus for him to away matches. (Craig intuited that this was not so much a pro-hockey stance as an anti-rugby one.) Word quickly filtered through the sixth form that on trips back from matches up the country Hammy would pull the bus in at a pub along the way

– it didn't matter where they had been playing, he always knew a suitable pub – where team and teachers alike could slip in a pint or two under the guise of refuelling on sausage and chips. Before long he was turning up with Scottie on the edge of the company on nights when the hockey crowd were out under their own steam in town. It was on one of those nights early in the summer term that Craig met him in the Washington Bar.

The 'Wash' had two distinct advantages for the schoolboy, and -girl, drinker: snugs where the obviously underage could not be readily seen and a back door giving access to the ill-lit street behind in the admittedly unlikely event of a police raid. Craig had gone along hoping to meet a fifth-form girl who had been smiling at him in the corridors for the last few weeks and whose brother, he had learned from a girl in her class, was the First XI goalie. Apparently – this from another girl – she was always hanging out with the hockey ones. Apparently – Craig by now suspected that the smiling girl was using her friends as go-betweens – they were all going to the Wash that Saturday night.

So he went too and they were there all right, *she* was there, hanging off the arm of one of her brother's teammates. She ignored Craig completely – her two friends, hanging off the arms of two other hockey players, ignored him. No, not ignored: made a point of ignoring. He had only himself to blame. He would have turned around and walked out if he hadn't thought that he would be drawing more attention to himself. Besides it was fifty minutes till the next available bus. He called a pint and stood with it at the bar. He had barely drunk a third when Hammy came in with Scottie Campbell, still in their own school uniforms of sports jackets and knitted ties. Craig had heard enough about the two of them by this stage not to feel the need to hightail it out the back door. He nodded when Scottie nudged Hammy, standing with him at the far end of the counter. They raised their glasses to one another and for a quarter of an hour or so that was that. The two teachers angled their bodies in such a way as to suggest to anyone happening in that they had no knowledge of any of the other clientele. Craig meantime kept one eye on the clock, the other on his pint, which was emptying faster than the hands were turning. About ten minutes before he had to leave for his bus, Scottie passed him on his way out to the toilets. Hammy picked up his glass and wandered over.

'All right there?'

'Yeah, not bad.'

'Funny, I wouldn't have connected you with this lot.' He jerked his head towards the snug in which nine-elevenths of the school's best hockey players were ensconced with a significant proportion of the fifth form's most attractive girls.

'Pure chance,' Craig said.

Scottie came back from the toilets and stopped at the snug's open door. Craig looked at the clock.

'Bus?' Hammy asked. 'I can give you a lift.'

'Ah, no.' Craig had exposed himself by coming here tonight. He had no wish to compound the fault. 'It'd be taking you way out of your way.'

'Nonsense.' Said like a teacher. 'Where are you exactly?'

Craig named the estate then the street.

'Sure, that's no problem,' Hammy said. He threw back

the last of his pint. 'Time I was heading anyway.'

'But what about . . . ?'

Hammy spared him the embarrassment of having to say the name. 'Him?' He gestured to Scottie that he was leaving. Scottie showed him in reply the new pint that had appeared in his fist. 'There'll be no getting him out of here now until closing time.'

The car – Craig was useless on makes; it looked like it might be red, though . . . the red car, so – was in a temporary car park on a bomb site at the corner of Sandy Row. A handwritten notice – felt pen on cardboard – behind the window of the attendant's hut read 'All Day Parking £1.00p'.

'That's one thing we can thank the Provos for,' said Hammy. 'Cheap parking.'

The word – Provos – sounded strange coming from him, as though he was saying it to pass himself. Craig wanted to tell him it was all right, 'IRA' was as acceptable to him out of the classroom as in.

Hammy tried to open the door the first time with the key for the boot. 'Sorry, it's just new. Well, new to me.'

Craig had seen him drink at least two pints in the Wash and there was no knowing where he and Scottie had been between school's end and them fetching up there. Fellas Craig knew, though, regularly drove with four or five in them and the way Hammy reversed out of the parking spot, looking over his shoulder, one arm flung across the back of the passenger seat, dispelled any doubts he had. Hammy was well in control.

He put his foot on the brake suddenly, back end still in

the car park, front end sticking out into the road.

'It's Alec, by the way.' His right hand was reaching across the steering wheel. Craig shook it. He only just stopped himself from saying 'Craig'. 'I don't know where Hammy came from,' said Ha— . . . Alec. 'I mean, Harro, OK, don't like it, but OK. But *Hammy*? It's like something out of *Tales of the Riverbank*.'

He took his foot off the brake, worked his way up the gears to third. They drove in silence until they were clear of the city centre. Groups of guys ran across the road from shadow into shadow, squinting to see in the window of every car that passed, expecting the worst. The drivers, for their part, routinely ignored red lights, preferring the blared horns of cars approaching from the left or right to the prospect of having to sit for even half a minute on a street they didn't know. Harrison (Craig just couldn't cope with the Alec) shook his head. 'When I think of what this town used to be like,' he said.

'You that old you can remember?'

The words just sort of slipped out. Harrison made a face.

'Stories my dad used to tell me about running around when he was our age.' *Our*. He shook his head again. 'There's a difference between living and just not dying.'

Craig instantly salted the line away for future use. It might mean provoking an argument with one or other of his parents, but these days that was not so very difficult.

An army patrol passed at speed, headed for the town. Harrison watched them in the rear-view mirror.

'Left here,' Craig said.

'Left?' Harrison looked forward again. 'I would normally

go . . . all right . . .' He flicked down the indicator. 'Left.'

Another silence. Craig was trying to think of something to fill it when Harrison suddenly said, 'So where are you headed next?'

Craig had enough wit to recognise that this was not a request for more directions. 'After A levels, you mean? I'm not sure.'

'Don't tell me you haven't thought about university?'

'I have, but . . .'

'First one in the family, et cetera, et cetera, don't want to presume too much?'

'There's a wee bit of that, yeah.'

Ahead of them a traffic light turned from green to amber. Harrison slowed to a halt before it had climbed to red. There wasn't another car in sight. The engine turned over. Craig looked out the passenger window, but he could tell without turning that Harrison was watching him. The old anxiety – stirred earlier by the snub in the bar – flared. He narrowed his eyes at the red light. Change, for fuck sake. Change.

'We need good young historians coming through,' Harrison said to the back of his head as finally red became red-amber, became green. The car lurched forward. 'If you can get over the cultural cringe that is.'

To protest would have been to give in to the very cringe he was being told to get over. So he blushed instead, grateful for the cover of darkness and for the sight up ahead of the entrance to his estate.

'Anywhere around here will be fine,' Craig said and almost instantly wished that he hadn't. A crowd, about a dozen strong, was gathered in the lee of the Spar. Harrison must have read into that one nervous glance the entire story of Craig's post-primary years.

'I might as well drop you to your door.'

They compromised – a final check by Harrison in the rear-view mirror – on the top of his parents' street.

'Think about what I said,' Harrison said as Craig got out.

He hit the horn a long beep with his fist as he drove off. He was all right to drive, but he did still have a few drinks in him.

Craig knew it would be the first question his parents asked when he walked in the door. 'That wasn't you getting out of that car?' He was a good quarter of an hour earlier than he would have been if he had gone for the bus, an hour and a quarter earlier, at least, than if the goalkeeper's sister had not so pointedly turned her back. He lit a cigarette and stood on the corner smoking, between the lights of his parents' living room and the lights, growing fainter, of his history teacher's car.

'There's a difference between living and just not dying,' he said aloud. 'And I don't want to just not die.'

He and St John had given up on the bins behind the refectory as beneath the dignity of sixth years and, of course – despite Mrs Daniels' inexplicable failure to report them – permanently compromised. There were free periods now most days and several cafés within walking distance happy to have the custom. To one of these – the Four Eyes – they wended their way in the hour before lunch on the following Monday. Craig had been itching to tell someone since he stubbed out his cigarette on Saturday night and went in to find that his parents had already gone to bed. ('There was nothing on only

Parkinson.') St John, though, was distracted, nodding along to the preamble, about your woman, remember, was smiling at me in the corridor the other week, without really seeming to take it in.

Craig interrupted himself to ask if everything was all right.

'Fine,' St John said. 'Just a lot of homework I didn't get done over the weekend.'

'Were you out?'

'Out? No.'

'I wound up in the Wash,' Craig said, hoping to get the story back on track.

St John stood up. 'I need the bog.'

He was gone fifteen minutes.

'Are you sure everything's all right?' Craig asked when he got back.

'I dozed off.' St John smiled, but his eyes told a different, more troubled story. 'I sat down to, you know, and the next thing I'm waking up with my head on the edge of the sink.'

He pushed up his hair to reveal a red groove running diagonally from his right eyebrow to the left side of his scalp. Craig stared at it a few moments then burst out laughing. St John joined in a second or two behind, throwing himself back in his seat and rubbing his forehead.

'What am I like?' he said.

*

It was three when he got to sleep the night before. The night before that, Saturday, he hadn't slept at all.

It had all started the night before that again with Paddy

wetting the bed. He was, as Mo kept reminding him, walking round the room, yanking off blankets and sheets, Almost Eleven Years of Age. Paddy sat on the floor, wrapped in an old quilted bedspread that St John had trailed in from the room next door, crying into his knees. It was Bea, sitting down beside her kid brother and stroking his hair, who asked the question.

'Is someone giving you a hard time in school?'

'No,' he said then hiccupped. 'Not in school.'

Mo had stopped in the act of skinning a pillow.

'Where then?' Bea asked.

Another hiccup. 'Cubs.'

Mo tore the pillowcase away, tossed it on to the pile on the floor.

'I knew it,' she said. 'I should never have let you go near that church.'

Paddy had petitioned all through the previous school year to be allowed to join the troop attached to the nearby Church of Ireland. Mo had pointed out the problem of the 'attached to' condition. The Nimmos were not now and never would be attached to any church. Sibyl broke the deadlock. She offered to go with Paddy to the required number of church services per year. It wouldn't make her any more of a hypocrite than the lechy oul' lads she saw traipsing through the church gates with their pastel-hatted wives, not mentioning any names . . . she faked a cough and forced one out under cover of it, 'Dr Lennox'. (St John glanced at Mo: not a flicker.) So Paddy went to Cubs every Tuesday night and church with Sibyl one week in every four. (It was even better than she had hoped: the faces on them when they saw her . . .

71

priceless.) Almost all of his spare time was spent on activities for badges – three months for his Collector's badge alone, although St John had tried to tell him that winter might not be the best time to be scouring the streets for lollipop sticks. He had even gone away to a weekend camp in Tullymore Forest. The others had practically to restrain Mo on the Saturday night from driving down and bringing him home. And sometimes for badness they would ask him to recite his Cub Scout Promise when she was within earshot.

> I promise that I will do my best
> To do my duty to God and to the Queen
> To help other people
> And to keep the Cub Scout Law.

And now here he was sitting on his bedroom floor, wrapped in a bedspread, sobbing his heart out.

'What have they been saying to you?' Sibyl asked, for she had joined them too by now, sitting down on the other side of Paddy from Bea.

'Let's talk about it in the morning,' Mo said.

'No, we're all here, let's talk about it now.'

'In the morning,' said Mo and before Sibyl could object again swept up the pile of bedclothes from the floor and left.

When they went down to breakfast in the morning – Paddy had ended up nesting in St John's room – Sibyl and Bea were waiting, a plate on the table between them piled high with toast.

'She's gone out,' Sibyl said.

'Where to?' asked St John.

Sibyl shrugged. 'Who knows? There was a note.' That

was more than there usually was. Bea pushed it across the table to Paddy who leaned over to read it. 'Back soon.'

Bea gave him a slice of the toast.

'It was about her, wasn't it?' she said as he bit: 'the teasing.'

Paddy shook his head. He chewed slowly, swallowed at last. 'It was about my daddy.'

'Soon' turned out to be half past six. Mo rapped the door with her forehead, prevented from opening it herself by the bundle in her arms. St John would have put money on her not coming home empty-handed. He had been half hoping for fish suppers. The bundle wriggled and something – St John for a split second couldn't have said what – sprang out of her arms on to the tabletop.

'A rabbit?' said Paddy. It was a light golden colour, the ears apart, no bigger than a guinea pig.

'I got him for you,' Mo told him. The rabbit shuffled to the edge of the table and looked down at the tiles below but clearly didn't fancy its chances. It shrank into itself. Mo set down a cabbage leaf that she appeared to have been keeping, literally, up her sleeve.

Sibyl and Bea wandered in.

'I got a rabbit,' Paddy said. He picked it up in his arms, cabbage leaf hanging out of its mouth.

Sibyl scratched the animal's ear, scratched her brother's. 'We need to talk,' she told Mo.

'We'll just get the rabbit organised,' Mo said and turned to the cupboards beneath the sink, opening doors, as though there might be a hutch lurking behind one of them, ready-made.

'No,' said Sibyl. 'We need to talk right now.'

7

'You have to understand, I was only thinking of all of you. There didn't seem to be anything to be gained at the time by going into all the gory details and then you were so young . . .'

'I was nearly thirteen,' said Sibyl.

Or twenty-one: St John had a memory from way, way back, of his father saying that Sibyl had been born eight.

'But the others,' Mo said, without conviction. 'Paddy . . .'

They were in the drawing room, progeny distributed about the two great velvet chesterfields that comprised the whole of the room's soft furnishings, parent by the fireplace, occasionally picking up a poker and moving around the ashes that had lain there undisturbed since the previous Christmas, or perhaps the Christmas before that. Between times she sipped from the glass of rosé at her right hand (Sibyl had moved the bottle over beside the settee on which she sat) and, after her fashion, opened up.

'I had been sitting one night waiting on him coming home. There were a lot of people then being picked up off the streets and shot.' There was a man picked up and shot about a week ago, but even in St John's memory of these things he knew it was not the common occurrence it once was. 'And then of course *your father*' – she seemed for a moment baffled anew by the connection – 'your father never

ever learned to drive. He preferred there to be someone always on hand for him, i.e. Muggins here, most of the time.' She shook away the unwelcome memory. 'Anyway, about half past one the phone rang – I nearly pulled it off the wall trying to grab it before it woke any of you – and the voice asked me was I who I am and then said he was the police, although I knew that even before he told me. Well of course I was panicking, but there was a bit of me too was thinking, hold on, they wouldn't just *phone*, and then I could hear the smugness in his voice. He told me your father had been arrested earlier in the evening under the Special Powers, Northern Ireland, Act, and that he could be held under the provisions of the Act, paragraph . . . I forget which – twenty-three – under paragraph twenty-three he could be held indefinitely.'

'You mean he was *interned*?' Bea said.

'He wasn't the first person we knew who was,' Mo said quickly. 'The police in the early days weren't that particular when it came to "subversives". There were pacifists and all sorts lifted.'

'Why did you throw him out then?' Sibyl up to that point had been quiet. 'Stand by your man and all that.'

Mo filled her glass again. Sibyl reached for the bottle as she went to set it back on the hearth and took a swig, fortifying herself, sensing perhaps that they were approaching the nub of the Cub Scout taunts. The rabbit's nose and whiskers appeared from under one of the sofas.

'Oh, believe me, I would have walked to the ends of the earth for him at one time. If you had asked me five minutes before the phone rang I would still have been saying I'd march to the door of No. 10 Downing Street if something like that ever happened.'

'But,' said Bea.

'But then the policeman told me where he had been arrested, a flat off University Avenue.' She interrupted herself. 'Paddy?'

'I'm all right,' he said, past the thumb hooked slackly in his left cheek.

'So . . .' She sighed. 'I could hear he was waiting for me to ask it, but I had to ask it anyway: what was my husband doing in a flat on University Avenue? And the policeman said, do you mean at the precise moment the officers went in? Well I didn't know which of them I hated more just then, the policeman for the enjoyment he was getting out of it or your father for his . . . his . . .'

'Bastardness?' Sibyl suggested.

'What was he doing?' Paddy asked. Bea leaned across the sofa and whispered it to him.

'They arrested her too. I knew the name at once. She was one of his Ph.D. students. He had had her and a couple of the others round for drinks.'

St John dimly recalled a night in this very room, Sibyl and him doing the rounds with plates of cheese and pickle and little things in puff pastry. Girls in long skirts, stiff as statues, boys in ties that clashed with their shirts, the laughter intermittent and much too bright.

'You told us he had gone on a research trip,' said Bea.

'No, that was another time, and he had, or at least he told me he had. Anyway, they kept him for a fortnight in the Crumlin Road. I went to see him one day when you were all at school. I had made up my mind I wasn't taking him back, but walking into that place, well you'd need to have a heart of stone not to feel a flicker of doubt, and then there he was in front of me, bold as brass, telling me he was changing his name to the Irish. I asked him was this all to do with her, for he had as much Irish in him as' – she looked around for something; found it under the sofa – 'that rabbit, and he stood up and launched into this whole attack on me, on marriage. There was a war on in our country and I was reducing it to silly bourgeois values, I was only play-acting at being bohemian.' She made it sound, as he must have made it, the worst accusation you could level at anyone. 'He actually asked the guards to take him back to his cell. The IRSP ones had accepted him on to their wing.'

'Brilliant. Our father's an Irp.'

For on the street, even on the Nimmos' street, *Irps* was what the Irish Republican Socialist Party had become. Divis Flats, their power base, had been rechristened their Planet.

'So where is he now?' St John asked.

'Derry. He teaches in a college over the border. They have children him and her.'

'You mean we have half-brothers and sisters?'

'Brothers, two of them, but he has made it very clear he wants no contact at all between you. I think he's worried about bourgeois contamination.'

'I hate him,' Bea said.

'Me too,' said Paddy.

Sibyl got up.

'Where are you going?' Mo asked.

'Out.'

'But it's . . .'

'I'm not a child,' Sibyl said and Mo meekly brought the wine glass to her lips.

Paddy fell asleep soon after. Mo tucked him up on the sofa then lay down on the other sofa and before long she too was sleeping.

St John and Bea turned out the lights and went into the kitchen. There was too much to try to take in to think about bed. Sibyl came back about two, coughing her lungs up.

'Are you on the ciggies now too?' St John asked.

'Wise up,' she said, 'and get me some honey.'

'Please.'

'I'll get it myself.'

On the Sunday they all mucked in to build a hutch for the rabbit, which after a great deal of discussion they had agreed to christen Ethelred, for his gait, which was unsteady.

It was amazing the materials that could be salvaged from the outbuildings and the ramshackle garage: hardboard sheets, two by fours, corrugated perspex of varying degrees of transparency, a whole bale of chicken wire gone to rust, save for a coil, three feet long, at the very core. Mo sat with her back against the wall, on a little canvas stool that they had also unearthed, smiling, keeping her own counsel. Two days later she went away and didn't come home for six weeks.

*

Max told Maxine that the Billy Girl was having a party. Apparently she had this amazing house somewhere around Sans Souci, there were going to be hundreds at it.

'What do you think?' he asked. He was propped up on one elbow in the single bed they had made their own in Ben and Audrey's spare room. They had just been wakened by the protracted mewling that signalled the onset of Audrey's orgasm, or -asms, it was hard to tell once the real hollering started whether it was one thing they were listening to or many. Maxine refused to let Max touch her while it was going on – that would just be disgusting, she said, though in truth it was not so much revulsion she felt as inadequacy. What did Audrey have, or know, that Maxine did not? Or more to the point what did Ben have, or know, that Max did not? She had not had cause to complain otherwise. Max was as fun and exciting and as considerate a first lover as she could have hoped for. But still, those sounds . . .

Best try to talk, take your mind off them.

'I think,' Maxine said, 'the form with parties is you wait until the person having it asks you.'

'Max-*ine*.' Max threw himself back, as extravagantly as the narrow bed allowed, on to the pillow. 'It's not fucking *Anne of Green Gables*. She told Pete and Pete told Dermot and Dermot told Andy, which he wouldn't have if Pete hadn't said it was all right to, and then Andy told the rest of us.' He rolled over to face the wall taking her share of the bedclothes with him. 'Well, you can suit yourself, I'm going anyway.'

Maxine didn't want to tell him she was a bit afraid of the Billy Girl. She had turned up one Saturday with a bottle of vodka in her bag and half a dozen what looked like communion glasses (though it was hard to imagine her ever setting foot in a church), which she filled and lined up on the counter beside the till, rims touching. Then one after the other she picked them up and drank them off, before replacing glasses and bottle in her bag. At least she had laughed after that. She had laughed that much Pete had to take her out for a walk around the block before he could sit her down for her twenty-four snips.

She tugged the corner of the sheet that was just peeping over Max's shoulder. He held on to it. She tugged harder and he span round like a top, facing her, poking right into her.

Audrey was beginning to get into her stride – 'more' and 'harder' and 'oh-oh-oh'. Max's penis pulsed, depositing a single sticky droplet in Maxine's navel.

'Sorry.'

He made to draw back. Maxine reached under the covers and reeled him in again. 'Will you do one thing for me?' she said. 'When you feel me start to come will you give me your hand to bite on?'

*

Craig had bumped into Harrison a few more times around town, Scottie invariably in tow. On the final Thursday of term, though, as they walked back towards the staffroom, Harrison said they should try to meet up over the holidays, 'keep the conversation going'. Craig was flattered – who wouldn't be? – that the teacher seemed to be as stimulated by his pupil's company as the pupil was by his. They settled on the upstairs bar of Robinson's, the second Thursday of the Twelfth fortnight. To be honest, Craig half expected him to have forgotten, but as he came round the top of the stairs that Thursday night in July there Harrison was sitting. They both raised their hands: How!

'Are you all right for a drink?' Craig asked.

'I've one just coming,' Harrison said and Craig looked over his shoulder to see a girl step away from the bar, arms outstretched, a pint in one hand, a short in the other, a mixer between the two girdled by her fingertips. The weight of the drinks seemed to drag her forward, causing her to accelerate the closer she got, but when Craig took a step forward to help she shook her head firmly.

'Don't!' She touched the base of the mixer down first, the glasses following with the precision of a lunar-module landing. 'There.'

'Ros, this is Craig,' Harrison said, 'Craig this is Ros.'

She nodded. 'You want anything?'

'I'm OK.'

'Go on ahead,' said Harrison. 'Our round.'

Plural. 'All right, then. A pint. Tennent's or Harp, whichever they have.'

'One's as bad as the other,' said Ros, and turned and went back to the bar.

'Do you recognise her?' Harrison asked.

Craig looked at her again. Medium height, medium build, medium-length mousey hair. Not a single thing about her that stood out more on close inspection than on first glance.

'I'm not surprised.' Harrison interpreted his hesitancy benignly. 'She would have been going into the sixth year when you were in first. Way before my time, of course. You have to tell people that or they start getting ideas.'

Craig thought of Tanya Morgan and the other girls in his class, the ideas some of them had, and the dim view they would take of him wasting himself on someone so unremarkable.

Ros was back. 'Tennent's.'

'We met at UU, didn't we?' Harrison said to her, then to Craig. 'I was doing my MA. Ros is still there.'

'What do you do?' Craig asked.

'Research.'

'Into what?'

'Not into, on.'

'Ros is a historian too. Russian Civil War.' Harrison took her hand. She smiled, grimly. She wasn't amused by something. Craig feared it was him.

They worked their way through a couple of drinks – and it did feel like work – with only Harrison seeming totally at his ease. When, after half an hour, he got up to go to the toilet Ros and Craig were left to fend for themselves.

'I'm sorry if I gatecrashed your night out.'

She shrugged. 'It's Alec, isn't it? It's what he does.'

'Is it?'

'He takes people up, eggs them on.'

'People like me, you mean?'

'They become his projects. He throws out lines to them, ideas.' *There is a difference between living and just not dying.* 'I keep telling him to write that stuff down, publish it, make that his project.'

He came back, still rubbing between the fingers of one hand with the fingers of the other, making doubly sure they were dry. 'Anybody ready for another one?'

'Do you know what, I'm fine thanks,' Craig said. 'I should probably be going.'

'We must do this again before the end of the holidays,' Harrison said.

'We must,' said Craig, while over Harrison's shoulder Ros twisted her mouth into an expression of disapproval.

A date was floated, a Saturday night, a few weeks hence. 'Actually, I have something on that night,' Craig said. He wasn't making it up: it was one of the few nights of which he could genuinely claim it, but however it came out, Harrison clearly smelt a rat. He glanced behind him at Ros who was inspecting her fingernails, glanced back at Craig, who was in that moment again a seventeen-year-old schoolboy, and in the silent moment after that.

'Maybe when we get back from holiday,' Ros said unexpectedly.

'Sure.'

Harrison smiled.

*

Right up until the day of the party Maxine was in two minds about whether to tell Max she wasn't going after all. She hadn't even – as a disincentive to herself – brought with her to work the clean pair of knickers she had got into the habit of stuffing into her bag before running out the door on Saturday mornings.

At lunchtime, though, she had gone to Boots with Áine and bought a new lipstick. When they got back to the salon she asked Max if he would touch up the red at the back of her hair. She had kept it in the style he had first cut it for getting on for a year now and there was still not another person in Belfast with hair like it, which was something else she had to be grateful to him for: he had saved the best for her.

Berlin after closing time on a Saturday. An anteroom. An impromptu bar. Tonight no one was going home. Friends had started to gather from shortly after four. Carry-outs congregated on the alcove's countertop. Andy took charge of the punch – three parts vodka, one part orange juice . . . fuck a load of Mundie's wine on top – in a basin that half an hour before had been used for mixing the last of the day's peroxide. Gerard had scalded it three times before pouring in the drink, although Stevo said the Mundie's on its own would have done the sterilising trick.

Dermot and Pete themselves were nipping back for a swift one between cuts. Maxine started on rum and coke while Max was painting on the dye. He was telling a story about a girl he had known at school who had given some fella a blowjob, like not just a quick suck, a proper with-issue blowjob, and her friends the next day were all dying to know what it had been like, you know, the *taste*, and she had wrinkled her nose and said, well, it was all right, I suppose, I mean, don't get me wrong now, you wouldn't eat a pie of it . . .

And of course everyone erupted at that: you wouldn't eat a *pie*. Maxine held Max's hand resting on her shoulder. How could she not go with him to the party?

All this time she had been going three days a week to the Tech on College Square, to study for her resits, which had come now, which had gone. She had not banished totally the hope that a grammar school would accept her on the strength of these new results to study for her A levels. The way her birthday fell she would still be only a few months over seventeen when they took her, eighteen still when she was sitting the exams. With each week that passed, though, the idea of wearing a uniform again, even one that permitted black tights for sixth-formers, was less and less appealing. And for every month she felt she aged between a Monday and a Friday the next Saturday would age her double.

By the time they left Berlin they were already half trashed, sixteen of them, primped to within an inch of their lives and proud of it, toting the remains of the carry-outs between them and extra rations of Dax, and Elnett Hairspray. They had to line up to squeeze through the turnstile at the bottom of Arthur Street, sending one person after another into hysterics with cracks about too many pies. Even the group of skinheads on the benches outside the City Hall failed to faze them. (There were anyway, Maxine knew, good skins and bad skins – Spidermen – just like there were Mods and 'black' Mods, for whom the main attraction seemed to be the flaunting of the Union Jack.) They all piled on to a bus just leaving from Donegall Square then had to get off again when the driver, who had shouted down the aisle at them a couple of times already about their drinking and their dirty talk, threatened to drive them to the nearest cop shop, but at least by then they had a quarter of a mile less to walk, and, besides, half of them had managed to sneak on without paying while their friends were crowded round the ticket machine.

The juniors pooled their money and stopped for more drink at the off-licence next to the Club Bar. Maxine decided to go in with them on it, even though she and Max normally split their carry-outs between them. 'Anyway, it might be no bad thing to have your own tonight,' he said. 'If this place is half as big as they're all saying I could end up losing you in it.'

'As long as you don't lose me for too long,' she said close to his ear and taking hold of his wrist shoved his hand right down her pants and out again before anyone else had seen, before Max's fingers had a chance to flex, though flex they did now in the night air, a thin line glistening from the centre of his palm to the heel of his hand.

The house was massive.

Another couple of rooms, Andy said, it would probably have qualified for its own MP.

'Is that an actual turret?' Cathy K asked.

The sixteen of them suddenly looked rather small on the driveway. The sixteen of them could probably have had a party comfortably in the rhododendron that had colonised almost the entire flowerbed nearest the street. Even Pete looked a little circumspect as he approached the big front door and – a last glance over his shoulder at the troops: the *uninvited* troops – raised the knocker.

The door swung back almost immediately – as though it had been a lever he had raised instead of a knocker, or as though someone had been watching their approach. A girl stood there, not as striking, but quite obviously the Billy Girl's younger sister. She was barefoot, holding a book folded open on itself.

'I'm Pete,' said Pete. 'And this is Dermot, from Berlin.'

'I think you mean *with* Berlin,' she said. 'There are enough of you.'

She stood aside to let them through. Maxine, bringing up the rear, was half expecting to be handed a ticket. The girl did not follow behind, but lit a cigarette and climbed with it, and the book, on to a low cupboard built into the side of the porch between the outer door and the inner one, through which Maxine now passed into the hallway where the Berlin squad, confronted with a bewildering choice of rooms, all of them laying claim – at least in terms of noise – to being where the party was really at, had once again been becalmed.

'Kitchen,' Max said determinedly and off he marched, with nothing but logic to direct him, towards the back of the house. Maxine had not taken more than two steps after him when the Billy Girl herself appeared on the stairs. Maxine had to try *not* to see up her dress, though what she thought she did inadvertently catch sight of bore out Andy's surmise about her red raincoat.

She looked over the banister as she came down, singled Maxine out for a 'hi'. She actually smiled. At the bottom, she draped her arms around Pete's neck and kissed him full on. He looked as surprised as anyone.

'The only room out of bounds is at the top of the house. My baby brother is up there pretending to be asleep. Other than that . . .' she spread her arms wide, 'do what you like.'

'You might be sorry you told this lot that,' Dermot said.

The Billy Girl shook her head. 'I don't see how.'

Maxine had never been, or seen, anywhere quite like it. There was as much furniture in her parents' front room as there was in the entire downstairs, which was five, maybe six times the size. The only floor coverings were enormous rugs (Maxine wanted to say Persian, but didn't know how you told for sure), worn through in places to the backing. The curtains were basically rolls of raw linen.

A lot of smoke was being generated in the room immediately to the right of the hallway. Two sofas (granted each on its own would have equalled in area the three pieces of her parents' suite) had been pulled into a V shape with the opening facing the fireplace. A serious-looking bong was being passed among some serious-looking bong-smokers. Too serious. Maxine backed out, leaving a couple of Berliners behind her.

Within about five minutes of the Billy Girl giving them the licence to roam, indeed, the group of sixteen had been reduced to three, Maxine, Áine and Gerard, who being sweet said he would stick by the two of them. Maxine remembered that she had been on her way to the kitchen before the Billy Girl appeared on the stairs and threw her, but by the time she reoriented herself and found her way there, along a passageway, past more doors to the left and to the right, Max was nowhere to be seen. The back door was open on to a broad cobbled yard in which candles, a couple of feet high some of them, had been lit. Beyond that an arch opened on to total black. A gabble of voices came from out there. She strained to but could not break it down into its constituent parts.

'Let's try upstairs,' Áine said, but there seemed to have been a new influx of guests into the hallway and somehow in trying to thread their way through them, Áine too got lost.

'Just us now,' Gerard said. 'Hold on to me tight.'

He opened his arms for a hug and from two feet missed her entirely. He wasn't sweet, Maxine realised, he was paralytic. 'Do you need some air?'

'Um . . .' His shoulders lurched – once, twice – in the unmistakable prelude to boaking. Maxine, acting faster than conscious thought, pulled the neck of his T-shirt out and bent his head forward a split-second before the third, productive heave.

'Oh, shit,' he said, when he had come up again for air. The stain ran past his waistband down the front of his trousers. Maxine led him back down the hallway and through the kitchen. Outhouses opened off the yard. The first contained a toilet with no chain, cardboard boxes stacked on the seat, almost as high as the wall-mounted cistern. The second was the coal bunker, or had been. The door grated on slack when she tried it. The third had no door at all. It smelled faintly of weed-killer. She pushed Gerard inside.

'Here, let's get you out of that.' She dragged his jacket off then worked his arms inside his T-shirt. She gripped it by the shoulders. 'All right?' He nodded. She pulled, shuffling her feet apart to avoid the splash.

She wiped his chest with a dry corner of sleeve. The bones on him. He made Max look like Charlie Atlas. Whether he stumbled then or made another attempt to hug her, his head came forward to rest on her shoulder. She used the T-shirt to push him upright. 'Take that out there somewhere,' she said, pointing to the archway. He went obediently, and God forgive her she decided she wouldn't hang around for him coming back.

There was a short passage to the right of the kitchen as she came out leading to a room she had previously missed. She wondered if this was where Áine had disappeared. She went in. A red light-bulb, a curly-haired guy playing she didn't know what on guitar to four swaying girls, none of them Áine, or anyone else Maxine recognised for that matter. This was stupid. She should just go home now, treat herself to a taxi for once.

'*Maxine*?'

She turned.

'Jesus, it is.'

For a moment in the red light she didn't recognise him either.

'Do you not remember me, a couple of summers back, I used to come round to your house with Heather?'

'Craig,' she told herself.

'I like the hair,' he said. 'Mad.'

'Are you one of the hairdressers?' the boy beside him asked. He had hardly registered with her until that moment, but as soon as she looked at him she saw the family likeness.

'This is . . .' *Singeing*, it sounded like. 'It's his sister's party.'

One of the girls swaying along to the guitarist told them to shush.

'It's his sister's party,' Craig said again.

'Come on we'll go somewhere else,' Singeing said.

'Actually,' said Maxine, 'I was about to head.'

'Really?' Craig said.

'Really?' she asked herself. She smiled. 'Nah.'

The Billy Girl was Sibyl to her brother, whose own name, he explained after Maxine had twice baulked before it ('Don't worry, everybody does it,' he said), was properly Saint John. 'Like Worcester,' said Craig, not very helpfully.

They had parked themselves on a large chest on the landing. A cushion was coming unstuck from the lid at three of the four corners. Partygoers wandered past in front of them, in and out of rooms.

'Do you not mind?' Maxine asked.

'There's nothing to take,' St John said. 'Whatever there was went up to my kid brother's room.'

'I know, but, the bedrooms . . .'

He shrugged. 'It's a party.'

Maxine, through all the business with Gerard, had managed to hang on to her quarter share of the juniors' carry-out. That quarter she now split three ways, which worked out at two-thirds of a tin of Tuborg Gold each. They passed the tins between them with the same instinctive grasp of protocol and mathematics as Craig and St John displayed in supplying the cigarettes they smoked (Benson & Hedges, both of them). Maxine, who was sat between them, took the occasional puff to be sociable, now from the left side of her, now from the right.

She and Craig talked about Heather. Maxine resisted the temptation to tell him about the 'Knickers' name. She was in England now. *Heather*? I know, the girl that wouldn't get on a bus to go into town getting on a boat across the water. She was working as a receptionist in a dentist's surgery in Nottingham. God, Craig remembered her once nearly having hysterics at the thought of going for a check-up . . . Was she sure? *Dentist's* surgery?

'So this is where you are?'

Maxine looked up to see Max coming along the landing towards them. She sat forward. 'Max, this is St John, he's' – a hesitation – '*Sibyl's* brother, and this is Craig, he used to go out with a friend of mine.'

Max barely acknowledged them. It wasn't jealousy, she thought – Max would not have considered either of them a match for him – so whatever was irking him must have lain elsewhere in the house, or its environs. She was as certain as she could be about anything that there was a girl involved – a snub – out there beyond the reach of the candles in the yard. He had his hand out for her to take, which she did almost without thinking. He pulled her to her feet. 'Come on, we're going.'

She was carried by the tug several stumbled feet towards the staircase before she could gather herself to resist with a jerk in the opposite direction. 'I don't want to go yet.'

He stared at her long enough and hard enough that she saw herself mirrored in his pupils, and only then did he look over her shoulder at St John and Craig. 'It's nothing to do with anyone else,' she said, stroking Max's chin, turning his eyes to meet hers again. 'I'm just starting to have a nice time.'

'Yeah, well don't forget who it was got you here,' he said. He didn't mean just the party. He meant that but for him she could have been sitting there yet in Corn Market with her can of Fanta and hideous blouse. They each turned their back on the other at the same moment. Maxine walked back to the chest. She didn't know how much

Craig and St John had heard, although from the over compensation of their chatter she guessed pretty much everything. She drank the remainder of her Tuborg allocation in two gulps. St John asked Craig if he fancied coming with him on a hunt for more.

'It doesn't take two of us, does it?' The way Craig said it, it might, just, have been a genuine concern about wasting resources, to which St John could think of no effective reply.

For a few moments after he left neither Craig nor Maxine spoke.

'This is so weird,' they said then in unison.

'Jinx, padlock!' said Maxine alone.

'*What?*'

She covered her face with her hands. 'Did I really just say that? We used to say it at school when I was about twelve.'

And now she felt properly embarrassed at the memory of their encounters back then. Craig was lighting a (tactical?) cigarette, hands busy in front of his face, eyes intent on the lighter flame.

'Anyway,' she said, 'you're supposed to wait until the other person says your name three times before you can start speaking again.'

'Maxine, Maxine, Maxine.'

'No: I padlocked you.'

He pinched his lips. She laughed. His eyes widened: *help me out here!*

'Craig,' she said at length and wondered if she had ever called him by his name before, like this, to his face, 'Craig . . .'

Her heart suddenly was beating into her throat. She wasn't playing any more: she couldn't say it.

He breathed out. 'You win,' he said, 'but it's still weird.'

'It is.'

'In a nice way.'

St John showed up with three dumpy bottles of Black Label and a plastic bottle of cider, which his sister, Bea, had been sitting on, or as good as, in the meter box out in the porch. 'You can go next time,' he told Craig. 'I'm not moving from this blanket box.'

It was about ten minutes after that that the motorbike was driven through the downstairs.

'I'm not moving,' St John said.

Half an hour after that that the first of the neighbours phoned to complain.

'I'm not moving,' St John said.

Half an hour after that again that the police arrived.

'I'm not moving,' St John said.

Only the appearance on the landing of the kid brother (*baby*, the Billy Girl had called him), a tow-headed cherub gone leggy, broke his resolve.

'Oh, fuck it.' He got up.

Max returned contrite and smelling like air freshener. He had got no further than the rhododendron at the end of the driveway where he had sat waiting for Maxine to come and find him. And sat, and sat.

'I'm sorry,' he said, and looked it. Max would have been the first to tell you that he was not designed for outdoor use. 'Will you come back with me to Ben and Audrey's?'

'Of course I will,' Maxine said.

In the brief interval between St John's leaving for the second time and Max's reappearance, Craig had asked her for her phone number. 'Just . . . you know.'

'I know,' she said.

He had suggested she write it on the inside of his cigarette-box lid. It was awkward, but as he said there was less chance of him losing it than if he tore the lid off.

'You have a lot of experience taking girls' numbers like this?'

She passed St John on the stairs and banished his look of disappointment with a squeeze. 'That was a brilliant night,' she said and Max, one step behind her, had the good sense this time not to pass comment.

Out on the driveway they met Cathy K, standing a few awkward feet from Stevo and Paula, who had clearly in the hours since Maxine had seen them last become Stevo-and-Paula. 'Am I glad to see you,' said Cathy. 'This pair here make the two of you look like Trappist monks.'

'I was getting desperate,' said Paula. 'If I hadn't leapt him tonight, they'd have had to peel me off one of those candles out in the yard.'

Even Stevo said yuck.

There were more of them than could fit into a single cab, and rather than run to the expense of two (Maxine wondered how she could ever have contemplated it earlier) they decided to walk together as far as the city centre. There was safety in numbers, of course, but there were nights too – this was one – when no matter how dangerous the times you felt as though no harm could befall you.

They didn't see a sinner.

By the time they got to Ben and Audrey's it was nearly half past two.

Max was so tired, so chilled still from his vigil in the rhododendron, that he fell asleep almost instantly, his coat and shoes on, his trousers only half undone.

That was just fine and dandy by Maxine. She had a feeling that there would not be too many more peach-and-cream, lace-trimmed nights like this.

She lay watching the dawn light draw a line around the window blind then she closed her eyes and was gone.

*

St John got rid of the last of the guests at nine, a guy (he didn't look much older than Paddy) who he found asleep in the pantry. He had no shirt on under his jacket and couldn't remember taking it off. Actually he couldn't remember too clearly arriving at the house at all. St John gave him directions back to town and – reckoning he could pass for a half – lent him fifteen pence for the bus out to wherever he had to get to after that.

The house was a shambles, impossible to know where to start with it. He walked out the open back door through the yard – another complete tip – and into the garden. Ethelred was shuffling around behind one of the more opaque sheets of perspex, which was a well-fed-rabbit weight lifted. Fifty yards away Dr Lennox was inspecting the boundary, bending now and then to extract a bottle or a can. St John turned and tiptoed back inside. Bea was up. She was sitting staring at something on the kitchen table. St John walked over for a closer look then took a step back.

'What the fuck?' A used Durex knotted an inch from

the neck.

'I was rolling over in bed and felt it against my leg. I must have lain there all night with it and not known.'

'You don't think . . .' He hardly dared articulate it.

'Don't be stupid. Even if I had been drunk, which I wasn't, I would have woken if anyone had laid so much as a finger on me, never mind . . .'

They looked at the thing, its improbable length.

'Could you . . . ?' He gestured with his fingers.

Bea folded her arms. 'I'm not touching it again.'

It sat there until Paddy came down (Bea had fallen asleep again in her chair) at which point St John, who had been conducting a random and so far fairly ineffectual clear-up, grabbed hold of it, fighting down the urge to retch, and stuffed it in a plastic bag of empties.

'Is there anything to eat?' Paddy wanted to know.

'There's a load of crisps that were never opened.'

Paddy had survived on pretty much nothing else since the previous afternoon. 'Apart from crisps.'

The front door closed. Bea woke as Sibyl came in from the hallway wearing a collarless white shirt that had come home in a job lot on what now appeared to have been Mo's last day working at the WoW shop.

'Who was that?' Bea asked her.

'Mr Nobody.'

She opened the fridge door and straight away closed it.

'Let's go out,' she said.

'It's Sunday,' said St John.

'It's Belfast,' said Bea.

'We'll walk to the filling station.' The filling station had opened a fortnight before, despite a petition by residents opposed to the encroachment of retail on to their solidly residential stretch of south Belfast. 'We'll get bread and bacon . . .'

'Brown sauce,' said Paddy.

'. . . and brown sauce and come back here and make sandwiches.'

'What about all this stuff?' St John asked.

'Maybe the fairies will come while we're out.'

'With a flamethrower,' Bea added, and Paddy liked the idea so much that he flitted ahead of them as they walked down the hallway, dispensing a jet of cleansing fire into this room and then that, this room and then that.

St John could not have told you when they had last stepped out like this, Sibyl, Bea, Paddy and he, which might account for the feeling he had that he should fix this moment in his memory. Sibyl a fortnight off nineteen, a star just waiting for everyone else to realise it, Bea at sixteen, the answer to the question of what would happen if you threw the elements of one sister in the air and they landed the other way, and Paddy who was no baby any more (he must have been pushing five foot), hard though it was for the others to stop treating him as if he was and for Paddy to stop letting them.

He glanced back to make sure they had remembered to pull the door behind them. The curtains had come down – been pulled down more likely – in one of the front bedrooms. It struck him that the dramas within, great and small, had been played out time and again on the windows. The eyes of the house. An arm snaked through his. He turned expecting Bea, but found Sibyl.

'I've decided,' she said, 'I'm never going to get married, never going to live with anyone. I'm going to stay here and turn into a mad old doll surrounded by rabbits and cats.'

'Your head you are.'

'No, I'm serious. You've to promise to come and see me, but, wherever you are in the world.'

'What makes you think I want to go away?'

'Oh, I don't think you *want* to, but I bet you you will.'

'OK then, I'll bring you back a mad old doll hat from wherever I was last.'

'The crocheted ones?'

'What other kind is there?'

At the end of the driveway they wheeled left. St John glanced back again, but all he saw this time was chimneypots.

He felt in his pocket for cigarettes.

*

Craig was still out for the count three hours later. His dreams were the usual midday, drink-addled mishmash, mostly trouble-free. Just before he woke, though, they took a darker turn with chases and blind alleys and all kinds of crazy stuff, which even though he was close enough to the surface to recognise them as anxiety symptoms freaked him out no end. He searched the clothes dumped by his bed for his cigarettes. Of course they would have to be in the last pocket he tried. He flipped open the lid then fell back again on the pillow, hands to his face.

'Bollocks, bollocks, bollocks.'

There was no number.

Growing

I

It took him an hour to get straight in his head what he ought to say. It took him another hour to get through on the phone. Bea answered. I think he's been trying to ring you, she said. I'll bet he has, thought Craig. He heard Bea shout, shout again from further away – on the stairs, perhaps, leaning on the banister – heard at length the tumble of feet, the up-close sound of a hand on the mouthpiece.

'Have you been listening to the news?' St John asked and didn't wait for a reply. 'Hammy's been shot.'

'*Who?*'

'Hammy. Mr Harrison. It's on all the radio stations.'

Craig could hardly ask it. 'Is he . . . dead?'

'They shot him in the head.'

And that was the last of the conversation that Craig remembered, the last, pretty much, of that entire day.

The teacher had been lying in his bed, three in the morning (this from the report in Monday's *Belfast Telegraph*, which Craig was finally in a fit state to read on the Wednesday). His 'common-law wife' – she was Rosalind, Rosalind Proctor – said there was a thump, a series of thumps (that was them battering down the front door) and then before she could gather her thoughts the men were standing over the bed: gloves, hoods, boiler suits. She couldn't be sure if she had rolled over herself or if one of the men had turned her out, but the next thing she was on the floor and the room was filled with the sound of the shots, she felt the force of them too, through the bed, like coffin nails – one, two, three, four, five, six . . . they just kept coming . . . thirteen, fourteen, fifteen – and she hadn't even looked to see, she was ashamed to say, she had curled herself into a tight ball and when the car had roared away she had crawled out of there on her hands and knees, because there was nothing, nothing at all coming from the top of the bed, crawled past the phone in the hall, ripped from the wall, and out into the street, howling.

The IRA said in a statement that he had links with loyalist paramilitaries, a claim denied by his family and the loyalist paramilitaries themselves. Police said it was possible that the murder was connected to an article he had recently published – 'Making the Most of Suffering' – about the republican leadership's manipulation of the prisons dispute.

The funeral was vast. In a spontaneous act of solidarity almost the entire student body arrived in school uniform, although for many this had necessitated an earlier-than-expected dash to one of the three approved suppliers, and hours, as a result, spent waiting in the unseasonably long queues. Craig, despite his initial resolve to mourn in his own time in his own way, couldn't in the end stay away. Yet he did not want either to fall in with the rest of the pupils. He was convinced that he had been more to Harrison than just another schoolboy – more too than a 'project'. He opted for his Sunday sports jacket and a borrowed black tie, slipping in at the back of the church, the last seat in the last pew, as the minister denounced the perpetrators as the enemies not just of democracy and free speech but of ordinary human decency.

Every now and then there came from the front of the church a dreadful sob and Craig felt at once both chilled and cowed, because nothing in his own life had ever come close to the intimacy whose loss those sobs betokened.

The pallbearers were teachers all, Scottie Campbell at the front right, passing unseeing within a foot of Craig as they shouldered the coffin out the door. Ros came after, folded into the chest of her father, her body in the grip of its spasms a haphazard assemblage of bird bones.

Out front – Craig was ideally placed to see them – the Boys' First XI provided a guard of honour, their raised sticks trembling. The camera shutters fluttered apologetically taking only what they needed for the front pages, what the ordinary decent newspaper-reading public needed, before withdrawing.

Craig, in the aftermath, took himself off to a pub near the Albert Clock – Harrison had mentioned it to him once, one of the city's oldest, and surely now its dingiest, and currently emptiest. It suited Craig's purposes perfectly. He installed himself in a corner facing the black-and-white TV, back to the wall, elbow on the counter. He was there when they showed the funeral on the early-evening news, still there when they showed it at nine o'clock. He wanted to say something to the barman, but you could never be a hundred per cent certain in the city centre what way it would be taken. About ten o'clock he fell off his seat. The barman got him out on to High Street and leaned him against a security grille until he was able to flag down a taxi whose driver made Craig give him the fare in advance then ride with his head out the window, so that he arrived back at the house as sober as he had left it at eleven o'clock that morning, but with an ache in his ear that by the following day had developed into a full-blown fever. He wasn't out of bed again for a week.

*

Maxine had heard about the murder, of course. She had even watched the news reports of the funeral on the off-chance that she might see Craig. She was ashamed to say that the sight of the raised hockey sticks had reawakened in her some of the old feelings of disenfranchisement, while at the same time – for deep inside she must be a bad person – making her want to laugh. Emus, that's what they looked like, two rows of nosy emus.

When Craig had still not phoned her at the end of a week, however, she prepared to write the party off as one of those nearly things. So it was a double surprise when a few nights later the phone rang down in the hall and her mother called up that there was someone wanting to talk to her.

'All right,' he said. ('I couldn't make his name out,' her mother had said as she handed her the receiver.) It was St John.

'Yeah,' she said. 'You?'

'Yeah, all right.' Silence. 'Here, you know that was Craig's history teacher got shot last weekend.'

'No, I didn't, I mean I knew he was from your school, but, no, I didn't, God.'

'Yeah.'

She waited for him to say that Craig had asked him to phone her, apologise for the silence – he would be upset, of course, who wouldn't be – but instead he said, 'Have you seen him?'

'Craig? Me? No.' She somehow contrived to make it sound like the furthest thing from her mind.

'I looked for him at the funeral,' St John said, then: 'He's strange sometimes.'

Maxine thought of that enormous house with its turrets and its few bits of furniture. One person's strange . . .

'I don't suppose you would like to go out?' St John asked suddenly and Maxine was caught so off guard that she said, yes, OK, she would.

Friday?

Maybe not Friday. (She had recovered enough to prevaricate.)

Saturday?

This Saturday?

Or next.

Next, maybe.

Maybe?

No, next Saturday, definitely. Then she thought, fuck: Max.

*

St John put the phone down. His hand was sweating. The backs of his knees were sweating. He had thought for a moment when she first came on the line that there had been a huge mistake. He had barely had time to process finding her number written in his cigarette box the day after the party before he heard the news about Hammy. He had carried the box around with him for the next several days waiting for the appropriate moment, for the courage. He would have liked to say something to Craig first – he was the one who introduced them, after all – but Craig seemed to have withdrawn completely and St John, who had not, that he could recall, in all the time they had known each other once heard Craig mention his parents, or anything else about his home life, felt he ought to respect his friend's privacy.

He didn't know about respecting Maxine's boyfriend, or even if he was properly a boyfriend. There was on the one hand the kiss that he had witnessed at the top of his stairs, in the course of which Maxine had got turned around until she was pressed against the landing wall, and there was, on the other hand, the number in the lid of his B&H box. Which was the hand in the end he went for.

2

Craig reached out a hand towards the gate; stopped short. This was his third time trying in the last two weeks. On the previous occasions he had turned about at precisely this point and walked away. The blinds then as now were closed downstairs, but not up. Tilted to repel. He pressed down on the gate latch then let go. He had no call being here. What could his turning up like this do, except reopen wounds that had barely begun to heal? And yet there had been that moment, the last time the three of them met, when they might have altered the course of events, when she and he might have altered them, by agreeing to Harrison's suggestion to get together again on the night that – because they did *not* go along with it? – he died.

He pressed down on the latch again, nudging the gate as he did so with his thigh. It seemed to pull him with it on to the front path. Now when he pressed the latch it was to close the gate behind him. He had not the first idea what he was going to say. *Take a moment, compose yourself*, but his foot had barely touched the front step when the door opened.

'I've been watching you for the last five minutes,' Ros said. She was wearing a gold-and-black tracksuit top that he thought might have been Harrison's, mismatched leg-warmers pulled down at the bottom almost to her toes, which curled away from contact with the slate tiles. *She had crawled out here on her hands and knees to get help.*

'I wasn't sure you would want visitors.'

'I don't really.' She opened the door another six inches. 'But I couldn't bear having to watch you go through that whole pantomime again next week.'

'Ah.'

The hallway was like an icebox. He had never felt cold to equal it within four walls, not an absence of heat, a presence, of what, he didn't care to think. He shivered. Ros slipped round him heading for the kitchen at the end and indicating as she passed it the second of two doorways opening on the left. 'There's a fire on in there.'

The fire was a three-bar affair set into the grate. A newspaper had been abandoned, open, within inches of the bottom bar. Loose pages were strewn across the floor, the single armchair, and the two-seater sofa. Craig stood, hardly even daring to move the paper closest to the fire (he managed to trail it back half an inch with the toe of his shoe) until Ros returned with a tray and told him just to shove everything out of the way.

'Alec never threw a paper out,' she said. 'I'm that used to them I hardly even see them now.'

'If you wanted, I don't know, a hand some day, putting them in order, or . . .' He couldn't think of an or.

'Are you sure you know what you'd be letting yourself in for? I mean, like, never *ever* threw a paper out, or a journal.' She kicked aside the paper that had flirted with the electric fire, set the tray on the square of carpet she uncovered. 'I'll maybe leave it a while yet, though, before I start.'

'Of course.'

She handed him a cup. 'Tea?'

For a few moments she said nothing more. He brought his cup to his mouth. Way too hot. He set it back on the saucer. She was looking at him.

'Do you want to know the worst thing?' she said. 'I already had the candles bought for his birthday cake. He would have been twenty-seven, next month. You know about twenty-seven, don't you?'

Craig had to confess that he didn't.

'It's a cubed, you only ever get four of them in your life.' She made a face. 'If you're that lucky.'

She had been out shopping on her own one day, way last year, and found three large 3s and two Xs – for the Latinists, she could only guess . . . or for kisses – in red and orange wax. When she got home she wrapped them in brown paper and hid them at the back of the cupboard under the sink. He liked to think of himself as a modern man, Alec, but he rarely looked in there for anything other than the washing-up liquid, which she made sure was the first thing he would lay his hand on.

In the weeks after the assassination – Craig was startled to hear her use that particular word – she had got a bit careless. Very careless. Plates with uneaten food left lying around, boxes of cake and what-have-you that people had turned up with sitting on the countertop with the string still around them. So of course, just as her mother had always warned her would happen when she was young, and sneaking packets of crisps up to her bedroom for midnight feasts, mice had gathered. The man who the Council sent out eventually to deal with them said that in a house of that age it was probable that they had been there all along, they had just never had so much encouragement before. They had invited their friends, their entire family circle. It was the council man who drew her attention to what had been going on at the back of the cupboard under the sink.

'They're little fuckers,' he said. 'Pardon my French.'

(Craig felt the heat in his cheeks at that 'fuckers', embarrassed on her behalf not his own, as though she too belonged to that class of people – teachers, parents – in whose mouths such language would always sound like ingratiation.)

The mice had made a hole in the bag of candles and had eaten almost all of one 3 and a sizeable chunk of another. Of the Xs there was no sign at all. No sign, that is, except for the trail of droppings, running from the hole around the overflow pipe (the man from the Council lit the way with his torch) the entire length of the kitchen units.

'Hundreds of them,' Ros said. 'And every one of them orange or red or some marbled combination of the two. I couldn't help myself, I flung myself into the poor guy's arms and cried my heart out.'

She offered Craig a Bourbon biscuit. He must have hesitated.

'Oh, the mice are all gone,' she said.

'I know, I'm just . . .'

'They're not my favourites either.' She picked one up and sniffed it and set it back on the plate, summoned up a smile. 'So, what else can we talk about?'

They managed to put in the best part of an hour without further mention of what had occurred in the room directly above their heads. The last subject they touched on was free gifts in cereal boxes. When did that all stop? Everything was tokens now.

'I'll, ah, call again some time soon,' said Craig as he closed the gate.

She tilted her head to one side then the other, weighing it up. 'That would be nice,' she said.

In fact he called again twice before the end of the following week. On the second occasion, after the ritual with the tea and the Bourbon biscuits, they made love in front of the three-bar fire, on the two-seater sofa, in the space between the armchair and the living-room door. It was frightening the way they went at one another, scratching and biting (in one moment of painful lucidity Craig thought he was about to lose an earlobe) and for a long time after they had rolled apart neither of them could bring themselves to speak.

'It had to happen some time,' she said eventually. She began to gather her clothes. 'I'm glad it happened with you.'

He might have said the same to her.

She was only five years older than him, but common-law widowhood had conferred on her a greater seniority. Students five and ten years older again were girls in comparison. She couldn't be doing with them. For this and other reasons – his still being at school, her former lover being only a few months dead (though what, she wanted to know, would anyone who hadn't experienced it know about that?) – they rarely met outside of the house, but sat in and read or worked on assignments or just watched TV. She was big into her American soaps – 'pure brain porridge' as she cheerfully admitted – and would sit with her feet tucked beneath her for the fifty minutes they were on, hugging a cushion to her chest and tossing comments at the little colour portable on which their too-vivid lives were played out. Afterwards she would be positively coquettish. Just say you had that kind of money . . . Where would you take me? What sort of things would you buy me?

He imagined on those nights the house, seen from afar, vibrating like the box itself when JR's dander was up or when the decanter that Sue Ellen had launched at his head missed and hit the wall.

Some nights, if she was especially sleepy, she put him in a taxi, but more often she drove him home in the car that Harrison had given him lifts in. The first thing that Craig did was lower the window a quarter inch: to let a bit of air in, he said, but really to make sure that all of the air – more concentrated here – that his teacher had breathed was out.

Once, without warning, she turned off the main road on to a street of derelict houses, and off that again up the side of a warehouse where she cut the engine. 'What are you doing?' he asked and was so astonished when she reached for his zip that he practically slapped her hand away.

'Oh, for God sake, nobody can see us.' The warehouse's windows were solid brick. He didn't move his hand. She turned the key in the ignition, put the car in gear.

'How did you even know about this place?' he asked. She moved the gearstick from first back to neutral, looked him straight in the eye. 'Lucky guess.'

Another time she confided in him that she did not always go straight home after dropping him off.

'Where do you go?'

She shook her head. 'Dublin once.'

'*Dublin?*'

'I was looking for Parnell Square, the Sinn Féin headquarters. I got there just as the rush hour was starting and got myself completely lost, so as soon as I saw a sign for the N1 north again I followed it. I had to book into a hotel near Drogheda. My head was nearly touching the steering wheel.'

'That's nuts.'

She didn't disagree. 'I tried for a while counting tricolours to stay awake. I couldn't believe there were so many of them.'

'Look around you,' said Craig.

'Oh, but you know why they have them here, it's a competition with the red hands and the Union Jacks. But there?'

'They fly them in some places to say that they have more right to fly them than the State.' It was a line straight out of Harrison's A-level history class on the legacy of the Irish Civil War. 'Their green is greener, their white is whiter, their gold is . . .'

'Orange, apparently.'

'Tell me you'll go home tonight.'

'I don't know. I hear Kerry is lovely at this time of year.'

He watched her to the end of the street where she indicated left and a moment later right in the direction of home.

A flag flapped above his head. Lashed to the lamp-post, Union Jack. Redder, whiter, bluer.

On the first anniversary of the murder the police renewed their appeal for information. 'There have been no shortage of tragedies in the twelve months since Alec Harrison died,' said the detective leading the enquiry, 'but his killers have to know that we will not let up in our quest to bring them to justice.'

Ros gave an interview on a morning radio programme. 'You think at first you won't be able to get through an hour without him, let alone a day, and then suddenly it's three hundred and sixty-five days and you have done it, you have survived.'

When Craig called round at the house in the afternoon she asked him to go away.

'For now? For good?'

'I don't know. Just, please, go.'

He had a call that night from St John. 'Doesn't seem like a year, does it?'

What could he say? It felt like a decade, a decade in which he had never got around to asking if between them he and Ros could have prevented Harrison dying. As though he didn't already know the answer. 'No, you're right,' he said. 'It doesn't.'

3

St John had only lasted one day in school after the summer holidays before transferring to the Tech. Bea alone had tried to talk him out of it. 'It's because she's there, isn't it?' she said.

'No.'

'Of course it is. Are you just going to follow her around everywhere she goes?'

'I told you, it's nothing to do with Maxine.'

And it wasn't, not directly. It was to do with money. He had never had enough of the stuff, had accepted it as a fact of their lives in that house whose window frames and floorboards, even without Mo's fads, ate every spare penny. Sibyl subbed him the odd time (Sibyl and Mo had come to an arrangement the year before that Sibyl would manage the Family Allowance from now on), but there was a limit to how often he could go to her. There was no limit suddenly to his need: three, four, five, sometimes six nights a week now he was out. He had managed to get a few hours in the filling station down the road, which quickly turned into all day Saturday and Sunday – a fast learner, Eamonn, the manager, said, as though looking out into the forecourt for the pump number before ringing the total into the till called for anything other than good eyesight. What *did* require ingenuity was slipping the odd ten-deck of cigarettes into his overall pocket, letting coins drop on to the floor while giving change

– a 5p here, a 10p there – to be picked up later and not re-placed in the till, activities that he justified by telling himself he was not – surely – the only one at it. After only a couple of weeks Eamonn had offered him hours during the working day, Monday to Friday, which was when St John told him he was still at school, was due back, in fact, the very next day.

'Ah, no,' Eamonn said. He was from some place down south. Years ago, it must have been. It only slipped out in his speech the odd time. 'We couldn't have that now.'

'What if I was at the Tech or somewhere?'

'Oh, Tech would be fine. But you wouldn't want to be doing all that for the sake of a few shifts in here now, would you? I'll get you all the nights you want, six till ten.'

'You don't understand,' St John said. 'I need my nights.'

*

They went to the pictures a lot. After ten years of nothing but closures and conversions to furniture warehouses and car showrooms, picture houses had begun opening again: the New Vic, the ABC . . . They had found the odd little 'film theatre' stuck up an alleyway at the back of the university, with its diet of spaghetti westerns and what until now she had thought of as 'subtitles and sex' (the term 'art house' was another find). In part it was the simple novelty of choice after so long without – Maxine could barely remember the days, before the car bombs of the Seventies, of Regals and Majestics, a picture house in every suburb. In another sense too, though, the pictures just seemed like the safest place to go. She would hold tight to his hand in the darkness. Now and then, and seats permitting, she would let him slip his other arm around her, the heel of his hand coming to rest on her ribs, fingertips stroking the side of her breast. One particular night coming out of the film theatre and finding the alleyway deserted she had let herself get a bit carried away, pressed against a corrugated iron fence, which gave way suddenly under their combined weight and almost pitched them into someone's backyard.

'Sorry, sorry, sorry,' St John said, trying to fix the fence while holding on to the waistband of the trousers that she dimly remembered unbuttoning.

'Don't keep apologising. It maybe just wasn't the best place.'

All the same, when they got out on to the main road and St John hesitantly suggested that there might be a better place, just up the road, she made her excuses and ran for the bus that would take her into town and home.

She turned at the stop. He had kept up with her.

'Soon,' she said and kissed him.

'Sorry,' he said again.

She was pretty sure he had her down as a virgin, which was a pleasant change from most of the fellas she knew, who seemed to want you to be more experienced than you were and dread it in equal measure. And the break from sex wasn't anything like as difficult as she had imagined.

Max had made things easier by getting himself caught after hours with one of the juniors – Maxine could just see him tossing the towels on the salon floor – although needless to say it was the fact that he had had his own key cut, rather than the uses he had put it to, that got him the sack. He was working now – had his own chair, he claimed, not that anyone in Berlin believed him – in a place with very large windows right on Royal Avenue: a hair supermarket, as Pete disparagingly put it. The junior, Kim, was let stay on. She had only been working in the place a matter of weeks, after all. She wasn't to know that Max had no right going in there when everyone else had gone home, although she might have been expected to know that he had no right to be laying anyone back on the floor beneath him but Maxine.

Kim came up to her the Saturday after it all happened while Maxine was in the back room waiting for the kettle to boil. 'I'm dead, dead sorry,' she said.

'We weren't married or anything,' Maxine said.

'I know, but . . .'

Maxine hugged her. Skinny wee thing. 'We'll both live.'

Maxine had run into Max only once since, in the hairdresser suppliers that all the salons used in an emergency. He was standing apparently lost in thought in front of a bay of red hair dyes.

'Penny for them,' Maxine said when she had judged he might otherwise have spotted her trying to slip by without speaking.

'What? Oh.' (She might have miscalculated. She might in fact have got clean away.) 'I was just listening to that song.'

Maxine had to strain to hear it, coming from the other side of a door marked 'Staff' at the back of the shop. Motown-y. She didn't recognise it, but she recognised now the faraway look in his eyes.

He had a neckerchief on that drew attention to rather than concealed the love-bite on the right-hand side just below the hinge of his jaw.

'How's it all going round there?' she asked.

'Yeah, good.' He lifted down a carton of pillar-box red.

'I'm surprised to see you getting your own supplies.'

'Well, you know, sometimes . . .' he didn't finish but turned and looked straight into her eyes. 'And what about you, are you seeing anybody?'

'No,' the word was out before she even knew she was going to say it. 'Not really.'

He snorted, jealousy released, not derision.

'I needn't ask about you.' She reached out and pulled down the neckerchief. Ouch. 'Make sure she's had her dinner before you see her next time.'

He lifted her hand away, smiled, properly sheepish. 'I don't think there'll be a next time with that one.'

He was still holding her hand. They both looked at it.

A woman came out of the staffroom. 'Yous OK there?'

'We're fine,' Maxine said and took her hand back, though at odd moments in the hours that followed she would catch herself bending and straightening her fingers, stroking the palm with the fingers of the other hand.

That was the afternoon of the night that the corrugated iron gave way beneath her and St John in the alleyway outside the film theatre.

'Soon,' she said again as the bus carried her through Bradbury Place and into Shaftesbury Square. 'Soon.'

But the weeks went by as chastely as before.

Their timetables at the Tech, such as they were, barely overlapped and even where they did St John was rushing off to get to the filling station in time for his next shift.

Thursdays, though, they went for lunch in a restaurant in the Fountain Centre. (The Centre was not long opened. It looked as though it had been beamed down from a distant planet where white-painted walls and hanging baskets were unremarkable.) The same thing every week: two house burgers with all the trimmings, one Coke, one 7-Up, a slice of apple pie with cream and two spoons. And every week the same thing from St John: 'My treat.'

'Oh, come on, you have to let me pay some time.'

'You can get the pictures tonight.'

'If I get there before you.' She didn't often, no matter how early she set out.

She couldn't even beat him to the tip. 'Wait, I have it here,' he would say and count it out on the table, a tower of 5ps.

'How much are they paying you in that place?' she asked him more than once.

'I work hard for it, don't worry.'

She was squeezing through the turnstile at the King Street end of Fountain Lane one Thursday, just across the street from the Tech, when she saw Craig in his sixth-form blazer, looking at her from the passenger seat of a car stopped at the traffic lights. Before she could raise her hand to wave, or call out to St John, who, ever the gentleman, had let her go ahead of him, and was still battling the cursed gate, Craig had turned his head. The lights in that same instant changed and the car pulled away. Of the woman driving Maxine caught only the eyes, reflected in the mirror, intent on the cars behind. Not old. She was fucking him, no question.

St John emerged at last, rubbing his heel. 'Bastard things.'

He tore the cellophane wrap off ten John Player Special.

'Can I have one of those?' she said.

'I never know when you're off them and when you're on.'

'Neither do I.'

She waited a full week before mentioning Craig's name. The apple pie had just been brought. They didn't even have to ask for the second spoon.

'Don't,' St John said and pressed down hard with his fingers on his eyes. 'I keep on meaning to try to get in touch, and then . . .' Eyes uncovered again, bloodshot. 'I don't know.'

'He's hardly been beating a path to your door, has he?' Hadn't been beating a path to hers either. He knew where she lived. He could have found her if he had wanted: a bad penny always comes back, as her mother said, wistfully these days (it had been four years since Tommy left and not a word of him in all that time). Maybe Craig had gained a little false lustre by taking himself out of circulation. Or – there was no way on earth that woman in the car wasn't fucking him – allowing himself to be taken out.

'You're right.' St John seemed somewhat heartened, and heartened still more when Maxine fed him a piece of pie off her spoon. She accepted a piece off his in return – a little more than she had been expecting – swallowed at length.

'Have you spoken to him at all,' she asked, 'since the two of us . . . ?'

'Started going out? Oh, yeah, I must have done.' He thought for a moment. 'No, I'm pretty sure I have.'

So of course she knew then that he hadn't at all. It was shortly after that she decided she would have to finish with St John 'before there was any real harm done' (she actually saw the inverted commas), shortly after that again – there had been a May Ball, more ball-like than she had expected, more fun – that she went home with him for the first time.

She woke to his mother at the foot of the bed.

'So you're Maxine?' St John was still out cold. Maxine could see her knickers lying where she had kicked them, just inside the bedroom door. At another time she would have been impressed by the distance she had managed, the enthusiasm implied. 'I was wondering when we were going to get to meet you.' She handed Maxine a plate. 'I brought you some toast.'

Maxine was trying to tug the bed covers from under St John so that she could sit up without being completely scundered.

'Give him a shove,' his mother said. 'He can sleep through anything.'

She stood up then on some pretext, turning her back, and Maxine was able to reach a shirt lying close to the side of the bed. (There was a torch sitting on top of it, which seemed to have been hewn from stone.) St John's mother sat down again as she got the last button in.

'Sibyl tells me you work in the hairdresser's.'

'Only on Saturdays, helping out, I'm at Tech the rest of the time.'

'Doesn't matter where you work, as long as you're happy.'

Maxine took a bite of the toast. Margarine. Her own mother prided herself on only ever buying butter. Her own mother for the same reason turned her nose up at tinned tuna as a pale imitation of salmon. 'Thanks,' she said, hoping it covered toast and endorsement of Saturday job both.

'I used to worry about him a bit.' St John's mother touched her son's back. He made a sound down his nose. 'His father left, you know.'

'I didn't, no.'

'Boys seem to want a man about the place.'

Maxine nodded. She was trying to piece together the precise sequence of events from leaving the ball to sitting in this bed in a borrowed shirt, eating toast and chatting about the effects of marital break-up. There had been a lovely moment in a field – no, not a field: the front lawn of the university – spinning round and round and looking up at the stars, and something to do with the ridiculously heavy torch when they got back here. She thought she might have done a striptease.

'What about your own parents?' St John's mother said suddenly.

'Mine?' Holy God, what was there to say? 'They live in the north of the city. I mean, we all do.'

'North?' St John's mother smiled as though it was the Bahamas. 'That's nice.'

Maxine took another bite of toast. Her mother was right about margarine.

'Well,' St John's mother patted her on the thigh – *she patted her on the thigh!* 'I'll leave you to it.'

The second she was gone Maxine flung the toast down on the plate and dived back under the covers, which roused St John belatedly.

'I can't believe you slept through all of that,' she said.

'All of that about your mum and dad, you mean?'

And Maxine in one movement had pushed herself up and grabbed hold of his wrists, pinning him to the bed. He was

125

laughing too much to put up a struggle.

'It's not fucking funny,' she said, fully astride him now. The laughter died in his chest. She was looking deep into his eyes, saw uncertainty pass across them, then anxiety. Still she stared. He didn't see the string of spit until it had stretched an inch from her bottom lip. The girls at school had used to do it to one another, their particular take on the age-old game of chicken, less deadly than the version with cars, but ten times scarier. His stomach bucked against her. She tried to suck the spit back up, but it was too far gone. She shot out a hand and caught some of it. Only for him straining to tilt his chin the rest would have landed smack in the middle of his face.

'That's disgusting!'

She wiped the run-off from his ear. 'Here,' she said, then bending applied her lips to his neck, sucking, 'and here . . .' his chest now, 'and here . . .'

That, rather than the night before, was the true beginning for her. Over the next – what was it, even? Ten minutes? Half an hour? – she felt herself let go of something and for a time then – weeks beginning to stretch into months – there really was no one but him.

It came as a complete surprise to her in the end when St John dropped into the conversation that he had phoned Craig.

'What made you do that?'

'It's been a year.'

'I know, but . . .'

'A whole year.'

4

He nearly wasn't going to bother his head turning up. How could he even begin to explain everything that had happened? How would he get through a whole night without saying anything at all? It had been ten days now and Ros still wasn't answering his calls. It was eating him up.

Yet here he was, early Tuesday evening, sitting in the back bar of Lavery's, a third of a pint in already, feeling real anticipation. For such a long time, his best friend, his only friend practically.

St John stepped in the door from the front bar and tipped his chin in greeting. His hair was shorter – choppier – and in defiance of the time of year he had on a grey tweed overcoat, turned back at the cuffs to show the striped satin lining.

'You ready for another one of them?' he said, as though it followed on naturally from the last sentence they had spoken.

Craig contemplated his pint, drank another third. 'Sure.'

St John glanced over his shoulder at him as he waited at the bar. Craig returned his smile then leaned forward and polished off the pint. He has something he wants to tell me.

'Here you go.' St John set a glass in front of Craig and clicked the rim of it with the base of his own. 'Cheers.'

He sat and at once looked over his shoulder in the other direction.

'Are you OK?'

'Just ages since I was in.'

'Where do you go these days?'

'Here and there.'

'You look like you've been hanging around the Harp.'

The Harp was where the punks all went.

'This?' St John ran his hand through his hair. Maxine had talked him into it. 'I just felt like a change.'

'Fair enough,' said Craig and with those words went the remainder of his hopes for the evening. It had been too long. He should never have come here.

St John was trying to centre the base of his glass on the circular beer mat.

'We're still mates, aren't we?' he said suddenly.

'Unless you know something I don't.'

St John tried once more with the glass and the beer mat. 'You're not to breathe a word of this to anyone.'

'Out with it.' Craig sat back against the wall, arms spread along the top of the banquette – the bad-news brace position – obliging St John to lean forward to prevent the word-that-must-not-be-breathed getting out despite him.

'Remember the filling station down the road from our house?' Craig did. 'Well you know I got a job in there?' Craig said he had been given to understand that was the whole reason for his leaving school for the Tech. 'Well, I've been . . . lifting wee bits and pieces.'

'Lifting, like . . . ?' Craig had come forward again to meet him across the tabletop. He couldn't say what exactly he had been expecting, only that it was not this.

'You know . . .' St John held his coat open, made a motion

with his other hand towards the inside pocket. (*Certified by the Harris Tweed Authority*.)

'Right.'

'Like, nothing outrageous, cigarettes, lighters, maybe a packet of chewing gum now and again, some change. A lot of change.' The extent of it seemed to dawn on him afresh as he got to the end of the list. 'And one day I stuck a torch down my trousers,' he added unhappily. 'You know, those big American cop ones? Don't ask me what I was thinking. Got it home and realised it had no batteries so I went in the next day and picked up a packet of them. I was going to pay for them, but then I thought what if someone asks me what I want them for – they were the size of rubber bullets – so they went down the bags as well.'

'And you got caught? Craig said, as much to put the fella out of his misery as anything. He was suffering here.

'No, I didn't, but . . .'

'Wait, will we have another drink?'

Barely an inch left each.

'We'd better.'

Craig went up this time.

'So,' he said when he had returned. 'What happened?'

What happened was the manager, Eamonn, had called St John into the storeroom in the middle of last Wednesday morning. He had put in a little desk down at the back: somewhere he could do his paperwork, although the only paper St John had ever seen on it was the *Sun*, open, as it was now, to the football pools. Eamonn closed the paper, put it in a drawer.

'Sit down,' he said. St John looked around. The only seat

was the one beneath Eamonn. He perched on a pallet of anti-freeze. When he looked back Eamonn had a pink page in his right hand, in his left, a pen, the blunt end of which he tapped down the page at two-inch intervals. He narrowed his eyes.

'I think we have a thief,' he said.

St John felt the blood drain from his face. He could do nothing more than shake his head. Eamonn regarded him a few moments more. 'I know,' he said then set the page on the desk. 'Shocking, isn't it?'

'I'm speechless,' St John said. 'How long do you think, I mean . . . Who . . . ?' He shook his head again. 'Speechless.'

Eamonn picked up the page again before St John, who had, almost without realising, been leaning forward, could see what was written there.

'I can't be everywhere in here, not with all the paper-work,' he said. 'I need another pair of eyes and ears, an ally.'

'An ally?' Craig nearly choked on his pint.

St John had the good grace to look embarrassed.

'Well that's OK then, isn't it? You're in the clear.'

'I don't know, he's talking about getting an auditor in. If anyone was to start checking shift patterns . . . I'm going to give him my notice.'

'And as good as tell him it was you all along? Are you *wise*?'

'My exams and all are over. I told him when I started there was a chance I would be heading off. He won't be that surprised I'm quitting.'

'He will if he sees you walking up and down the street every day.'

'That's the other thing I've been thinking, but: I *am* going to go away for a bit.'

'These all dead?' An elderly barman stopped by the table and pointed at the clustered glasses. Those that weren't dead they killed off then and there and added them to the empties arcing over his right shoulder. St John went for another two, acting the lig at the bar, waggling his arse for Craig's benefit while above the counter he was ramrod-straight talking to the bar's owner. You could only stay serious for so long when you were out like this, having a few drinks. Craig's head was already starting to feel bubble-wrapped. Ros really wasn't into bars, or at least wasn't into the juveniles who frequented them, which, now that he thought of it, was fine for her, but had she never stopped to ask herself what he wanted to do – needed to – once in a while?

'Here.' St John handed him the pint in his left hand, held up the pint in his right. They clinked glasses messily.

'I still think you're mad,' Craig said. 'The stuff people get away with in this place and there's you clearing out over a fucking torch and a couple of batteries.'

Somehow he had in his mind come back around to Harrison. It would be worse than stupid, St John leaving, it would be an affront to all the dead whose killers had never seen the inside of a prison cell.

'I maybe underestimated the number of five and ten pees.' St John cleared his throat. 'Fifties too. Sort of like my own private fuel tax.'

Craig batted this away: the point stood. 'Anyway, where would you go?'

'See, that's the lucky thing, Mo . . . my mum . . . has a

friend in Cornwall, keeps goats.' He was perking up again. 'The day before all that business with Eamonn she was on the phone going on about the terrible time she was having trying to find someone to go down and take care of the place while she was in Australia seeing her daughter.'

'You're making this up.'

'I'm not, I swear. Six weeks she's away. My mum was thinking of doing it herself.'

'A goat-herd?'

'Why not? She says there's not a whole lot to it.'

'Fucking mental.'

They tumbled out of there about three pints later and were amazed – momentarily pained – to find there was still light in the sky.

'Promise me, not a word to anyone, ever-ever.'

'Come on, what do you take me for?'

'Drunk like me.'

A bus drew up at the stop before the bar's front door and as the next shift got out the two friends – because that's what they were, friends – parted, St John to the left, Craig to the right. Craig had gone about twenty feet, to the road crossing, when he remembered what it was he had wanted to ask.

'St John!' he shouted and seven or eight heads besides St John's turned, as seven or eight heads always would when his name was called. 'Did you ever see any more of thingy . . .' Fucking bubble-wrap . . . 'Maxine?'

St John's hands were cupped around his ears. He placed them now either side of his mouth, but the bus pulled away again just then and fucked if Craig could make out what it was he shouted.

The following Friday Craig arrived home to find a note on the pad by the telephone in the hall. 'Sinjin (?) rang – going away party 2morrow – ring him.' Below that, 'Aunt Queenie took sick. At hospital with Dad, ravioli in cupboard.'

Queenie was strictly speaking Craig's father's aunt. She had come to the house every Boxing Day and Easter Monday for as long as Craig could remember, sometimes with other more distant, and to child-Craig's way of thinking more suspicious, relatives, more often with another great-aunt, Jean, who had died the year before, since when Queenie had come one Sunday a month besides. Queenie's husband had fallen from the stern of the ship he was fitting out the year after she married him. Her mantelpiece, with its photos from dancehalls and daytrips and church steps, was a shrine no living man could hope to come near, and none had attempted. There was a son, two months old at the time of the accident, but he had gone to sea when he was sixteen and year by year had come home less and less until after one trip he just didn't come home at all. She had got an envelope once in a while with ten Australian dollars in it then eventually not even that. 'You're all I have now,' she had told Craig's parents on each of her solo visits.

'Poor old soul,' his mother said when she and Craig's father arrived home from the hospital at gone eleven-thirty. 'She'll not last past lunchtime.'

But the old soul lasted past lunchtime and dinnertime and on into the evening, each breath a mighty effort to pull herself up out of the hole into which she at once began again to sink. Craig, who had arrived at the hospital a little before midday, could not in all conscience excuse himself to go to

St John's party, nor wanted to now he was here and privy to her efforts, although he did several times join the queue for the payphone on the landing below (twice as long as it would usually be, the payphone on the landing below that being out of order), deciding on each occasion that what remained of his aunt's life was much too short and going up again to her room to ask did his mother or father want to stretch their legs or get a cup of tea.

The end came a few minutes shy of twenty-four hours after his mother had made her prediction in the hallway at home. One more enormous heave . . . then down, down, down she sank. Stayed there.

They had not seen a television or heard a radio all day, so knew nothing of the rioting that had been going on, on the western edge of the city centre, until they were leaving the hospital an hour later, formalities all completed, and saw the injured being wheeled and carried into Casualty, faces bloodied, arms and legs in improvised splints, a smell entering with them of petrol wrongly used. It was as though the three of them had been given twenty-four hours' compassionate leave from history, or its local variant.

A few months before she died – Craig was at the table in the dinette revising for his A levels – Aunt Queenie had made an unscheduled visit in a taxi to tell Craig's parents she was planning on buying her house off her landlord who was getting on in years himself and keen to cash in on the craze created by the government's scheme for tenants buying their council houses. Craig's father had tried to talk her out of it. Sure she had probably paid for it twice over in rent these last fifty years, why go paying for it all over again? She should treat herself instead: go on a nice cruise. Oh, very good, Queenie had said, can you just see me at the captain's table? I can see you dancing on it, Craig chipped in, which had her in stitches. All the same she went ahead and bought the house – nine hundred pounds, paid in cash: fives and ones – then took off on a three-day coach tour of the Scottish Highlands.

What it was, she said when she got back, she wanted there to be something solid for her to leave. And of course the house being the only thing she had she left it to the only people she had.

'Would you believe that?' said Craig's mother when the solicitor told them. 'We only did what anyone would do in the same position.'

The house, two-bedroom, terrace, door opening directly on to the street, between Tates Avenue and the Donegall Road – 'the Village' – was a ten- or fifteen-minute walk from the university, although there weren't too many then who took it: those who were born there, having little in the way of encouragement or example, tended not to go to university at all; those who were not tended to be put off by the area's reputation, the nature of which was graphically illustrated in the murals that adorned every available gable end. It was Craig who suggested, when his results came in and his place was confirmed, only days after Queenie died, that he move in there.

'I don't know,' his mother said. 'It can be a bit rough round there.'

'Around *there*? What about around here?'

'Yes, but we know everyone here, they know us.'

'Why do you have to move out at all?' his father asked.

'It would mean two buses otherwise, every day, there and back,' Craig said and his father who had no experience of student life or of what constituted a 'full' timetable said, right enough, twenty bus fares a week would soon stack up.

The three of them went round together that Saturday morning to clear the house. They sorted through the food in the cupboards (*seven* tins of carrots in sugared water), the stuff under the sink (Craig couldn't help but think of Ros and the mice) and in the glory hole beneath the stairs. (*More* tins of carrots . . . Dementia? Thrift?) They bundled up all the underwear in a bed sheet and put it straight into the bin. Other clothes, and sheets, they put into bags to take to the Salvation Army.

The bathroom had been built on to the side of the kitchen – the working kitchen as Aunt Queenie had always insisted on calling it – covering what had formerly been the yard, and bringing inside the toilet that had once been out. The roof was thick, yellow perspex. The mats, the toilet-roll holder and toilet-seat cover were candyfloss pink, where they hadn't discoloured. Do not ask, do not think. They went into the bin with the underwear. Stripped of them, the room looked every inch the mouldy lean-to.

'You'll need to take bleach to all those surfaces,' his mother said.

'Paint it,' said his father.

'Knock it down and start again,' Craig thought.

The last thing they tackled was the mantelpiece. Craig's mother, who had never even met the man, couldn't bear to touch the shrine: one photograph in particular – taken on a Dublin street, Forties, must have been, his smile revealing a mouthful of decay only true love could see past – almost broke her heart. It was as though something of his soul and Queenie's was indeed caught there.

When the photos were all packed away, however, she insisted on taking responsibility for the box. 'I'll put it under our bed until we can think what to do with them' – under their bed being where all things relating to the family's life, its finances, its dealings with officialdom, usually found their way.

Craig went back on his own a couple of days later and dismantled Aunt Queenie's bed, about which he felt much as his mother felt about the photographs on the mantelpiece. He flipped the mattress over on the floor. The reverse side did not look as though it had ever been slept on. He put on a clean sheet that he had bought from British Home Stores on his way across town (him buying bedsheets!) and lay down on it, hands behind his head looking at the ceiling, its alien topography of cracks and sags and Polyfilla repairs. So this was home now.

He sent out postcards with the new address. He had spotted them in the window of the tourist office, yellowing at the edges. The pictures of Belfast on the front looked to have been taken around the same time that Queenie was stepping out in Dublin with her soon-to-be-dead husband-to-be: City Hall, Castle Junction, Botanic Gardens, hilariously outdated now, like propaganda from a Soviet satellite state with the tanks carefully airbrushed out.

He sent a City Hall to Ros, to St John a view of the

Floral Hall at Bellevue with 'Please Forward' at the top, double-underlined. He heard back from her eventually – 'It's maybe time we both moved on.' (Simple cliché? A play on words? He couldn't decide which was worse.) From him he heard nothing at all.

*

Maxine had a phone call every night for the first couple of weeks then every other night then every Friday without fail then every now and again then just the odd time then one night he called her and said he was staying on to look for proper work, because really what was there back there for people their age? She was surprised at how hurt she was, how *stupid* she felt, because, guess what, his goat-Good-Samaritan act had filled her with the closest thing she had so far known to love. And yet as the weeks went by she was almost grateful to him. He had freed them both, even if all she had done with her freedom up to now was sit in at night and watch TV with her parents, like she was thirteen again.

She hadn't bothered this time going to get her exam results. The grades weren't important. She had reached the end of the road that she had set out on at the age of four. (*A joy to teach* . . .) That was another liberation, if truth be told. From here on in she would get by on what she knew of the world rather than of the inside of a classroom. She had decided (admittedly while sitting on the sofa, hugging a cushion) that she preferred people who *did* to people who talked about doing.

On her way to and from the Tech she had grown to

recognise many of the weekday army who kept the city ticking over and who abandoned the streets to the shoppers on a Saturday, which was really till then the only day she had regularly spent in town: the deliverymen, the storemen, the road-sweeps, the typists, the clerks.

She took a particular shine to one man, a bank messenger, she thought, well in his sixties, as impeccably dressed as a bank *manager* on perhaps a tenth of the salary, whose passage through the city centre she occasionally tried to shadow, not as easy a task as it sounds: he could not go more than fifty yards without meeting someone he knew – frequently another messenger (who knew Belfast had so many of them?) – leaving Maxine staring into shop windows (who knew Belfast had so many gentlemen's outfitters?) or patting her pockets for what she hadn't had to begin with before giving up and carrying on her way.

There was much she could profitably learn from the messenger and his ilk, and not just the best place to buy Argyle socks.

Pete – a definite doer, not an academic qualification to his name – tried to talk her into training as a stylist.

'You've been around the salon that long you're probably half trained already.'

'That's really kind of you,' she said, 'but I'm happy just helping out on Saturdays if you can still use me.'

'We'd need our heads examined if we couldn't.'

She signed up with a temping agency, London-based, which had just opened an office in the city, testing the waters, calmer than at any time in the last more-than-decade. Her first placement was in the typing pool of a car dealership behind Ormeau Avenue, where her facility with numbers was quickly recognised, leading to a move as assistant to the wages clerk. Hardly had she got her feet under that particular desk, however, than a bomb went off a couple of streets away blowing out the display windows and writing off two-thirds of the showroom stock. (One city's calmer was another city's holy fuck.) There had been a warning, and two full hours between the bomb-disposal crew showing up and their attempt at disposing loudly failing. Most of Maxine's colleagues were in a pub on Great Victoria Street by then. The cars weren't the only things written off that afternoon.

After that she was with an accountancy firm for a month, then a construction company. The day she started in that place the company got the contract for the car showroom where she had worked previously. It was a peculiarly Belfast coincidence, a vicious circle become virtuous. 'All I need now,' she said to the girl sitting at the next desk, 'is to meet the bombers.'

'Chances are,' the girl said, 'you already have.'

5

For the first couple of weeks in the house of goats St John slept. Anne, the owner, had timed her trip to coincide with the goats' drying-off period between litters. (Confusingly the smallest goat, Nut, was herself the mother of the other three: Hefnut, Nepthys and Seshat.) All that was required of St John was that he feed them and sweep down their sleeping platform and clean out the pen every week or ten days. 'You'll know,' Anne told him. 'Believe me, you'll know.'

Exposed on a hill though it was, and built entirely of stone that from the outside appeared to be perpetually wet, the house was a sauna compared to home. (It was called regularly serviced central heating. He was going to recommend it.) The next nearest house was a quarter of a mile down the lane, just short of where it joined what Anne called the 'little road'. The big road was another half mile away. The 'local' shop a mile out along it. There was a bike, an old black Raleigh, although St John rarely used it. The shop had a delivery van; the house had a phone. He didn't even have to get dressed.

When he was coming to the end of his third week a researcher rang from Westward Television looking for Anne. St John explained that she would not be back for another three weeks yet.

'Oh.' The researcher took the news like a death. It was just that she had been talking to Anne several times about a feature for the Westward farming programme . . . She didn't leave a note by the phone or anything? St John looked. She didn't, no. 'Oh.'

'If you have already talked to her, though . . . What did you say your name was?' Trudy; the researcher hadn't said it, but her name was Trudy. '*Trudy*, I don't suppose there would be any harm, I mean if she rings I can always mention it.'

'Would you? Would you do that?' Her voice was tremulous with hope resurrected.

Anne, as it happened, rang two nights later to check on Hefnut who St John had told her last time they spoke had seemed to be off her food. 'Shit,' she said now when he mentioned Westward. 'It went right out of my head. Tell them . . . Tell them . . .'

The line went dead.

St John improvised. He called Trudy. Why didn't the camera crew come over tomorrow or the next day or whenever they were free and film the goats in their pen then interview Anne at the big kitchen table when she got back from Australia?

'Brilliant idea,' Trudy said.

She arrived two mornings later in the passenger seat of a transit van in the back of which rode the camera crew with their equipment, or half the crew and equipment. The rest came a minute later in a pair of Volvo estates, the first so full of cigarette smoke that it looked to St John, watching from the doorway, as if it was actually on fire.

Trudy was not at all as he had imagined her from talking on the phone: an inch or so taller than him, a stone or so heavier. He remembered, and at once tried to banish, Mo's description of a woman she had worked for as someone who didn't so much catch the eye as block the view.

She took his hand in both of hers. 'Thank you *so* much for sorting this out.'

She explained over tea in the kitchen – because by the time everything was unloaded from the transit and the Volvos it was tea break – that the piece was for a package called 'Is Small Beautiful?' They were hoping it would fill ten minutes of their half-hour programme.

St John ran through again the roles of the people seated around the table: cameraman, soundman, assistant soundman, focus puller, gaffer, grip, spark . . . Throw in Trudy and they outnumbered the goats by two to one.

He set down his mug. 'Will I take you out and show you where they are?'

The cameraman checked his watch. 'Five more minutes,' he answered on everyone's behalf.

'Did you grow up on a farm yourself?' St John asked Trudy as they crossed the yard a quarter of an hour later.

'God, no: city girl, me. Bristol.'

'So how did you get into this?'

'I just marched up to the front desk of the station and told them I wanted a job. Anything, making tea, cleaning toilets, as long as it was television.'

'You're kidding?'

She made an awning of her fingers over her eyes, peeked out from beneath it. 'I know, it's a bit embarrassing.'

'It's not at all. I'd just never have imagined it could be so easy.'

The awning was gone in an instant. 'Oh, listen, you could walk in there yourself and do the same thing.'

'I doubt it.'

'Bet you a tenner.'

They had reached the goat pen. The occupants stood in an uncertain huddle. St John in their limited experience of him meant food, clean straw, but it was any goat's guess what the other, larger human was for.

'Well, here we are,' he said. 'What do you think?'

'Honestly?' Behind her hand: 'They freak me out.'

He felt oddly protective of them. 'It's the eyes.'

She shuddered. 'It's the whole goaty package.' And almost despite himself he laughed. He liked Trudy.

The filming took four hours, allowing for lunch, during which the crew drove to an inn five miles away, and another tea break. Trudy spent most of the time on the phone in the kitchen – they would add the cost of the calls to the facility fee – setting up the next day's filming, at Britain's smallest perry maker: two hundred bottles a year from half a dozen White Longdon trees.

'You've never heard of White Longdon?' she asked St John. 'Red Huffcap? Stinking Bishop? Neither had I until about a week and a half ago.'

Between calls she asked him about home and his route from there to here. 'It's kind of a long story,' he said.

She drove back by herself the following night – risking the lane in the pitch black – with one of the two hundred White Longdon bottles next to her on the passenger seat of her 126, and a couple of Red Huffcaps besides. She felt sorry for him, out there on his own with only those freaky goats for company. 'By the way, this is 8.5 ABV,' she said, bottle opener (she had stopped at the shop a mile out the big road to buy one, just in case) poised to flip the Longdon's cap.

'What does that mean?'

'It means I'm not driving back down that lane again tonight.'

He told her he had a girlfriend in Belfast. That was OK – she flipped the cap – she had a boyfriend in Bristol.

She also had the next day off. She didn't drive back down the lane again that night either.

He stayed in the house for a fortnight after Anne came back from Australia: it took her all that time to get over the flight; it took Trudy, returning to do the interview at the big kitchen table, to point out that Anne was treating St John like a waiter . . . 'St John, a glass of water please, and St John, put a couple of ice cubes in it . . . St John, my cigarettes! Look beside the Aga . . .' So then he took a room in Torpoint, on the opposite side of the Hamoaze from Plymouth, in the house that Trudy shared with another couple of researchers from Westward, which was when he phoned Maxine to say he wouldn't be coming back at all.

He felt bad, of course he felt bad, but he hadn't realised until he was away from it how circumscribed his life had been by Belfast, by that particular quarter acre of it on which his own house stood.

If Trudy felt bad about the boyfriend in Bristol she certainly didn't let it show. She went back up most Fridays as soon as she had finished work and came down again after dinner on Sunday, nearly taking the door off the hinges sometimes in her eagerness. (The doors it has to be said, like most of the rest of the house, were not in the best of repair.)

Her boyfriend was – get this – training to be a vicar. He had his final-year exams coming up and she didn't want to do anything to upset him, or at least let him find out about anything that would.

She and St John reassured one another that they could stop at any time. Just not this Sunday evening. Just not right this minute . . .

St John never did pay her the tenner, but Trudy was right about getting into Westward. He presented himself one day, exactly as she had suggested – exactly as she had done herself, although with the added advantage of her recommendation – at the reception desk of the studios at Derry's Cross and a week later was taken on in the mailroom from where early the following spring – on nodding terms now with just about every single person in the building and having witnessed at first hand the morphing of Westward into Television Southwest – he graduated to runner on a programme for deaf people. It was not much of a graduation, to be honest, he was still a messenger boy, but running, walking, standing still, it was all one to him: he had both feet, where he would never have imagined they would be when he left home to goat-sit the year before, in the television door.

Trips home were few, far between – farther as time went on – and of necessity flying. Mo practically insisted he stay where he was rather than give the money to the airlines, a bunch of crooks who could get you to Bombay or Buenos Aires for what they daily charged to carry people to Belfast.

He had just started as a production assistant for the gardening programme at TVS in Southampton, covering another part of the regional-television compass, and leaving Trudy to decide once and for all between him and the vicar in Bristol, when, sixty-five miles up the A27, the Brighton bomb went off. Arriving early for work in those first confused hours after the explosion he was grabbed by the deputy head of news and current affairs who ordered him into a studio to explain to the bemused and horrified locals what exactly the IRA hoped it would achieve by this.

As if the panicked decision to throw a PA with no front-of-camera experience into a studio wasn't explanation enough.

He borrowed a tie from the commissionaire. Under the cover of the desk at which he was made to sit he still had on a pair of Air Force 1 trainers. He could barely remember the moment the cameras were off him what he had said when they were on beyond the phrase 'they did it to show that they could do it' (and where had *that* come from?), but the deputy head of news and current affairs sent him a memo the following day. 'If you could work on your accent you could have a career at this.'

That minute and a half in the studio, though, had already made up his mind for him: he was not cut out for news. Give him a garden any day, and, please, point the camera at someone else.

*

Craig awoke to the sound of whistles. Hundreds of them. His bedside clock read ten past three. A helicopter clattered over the rooftops, coming from the east, then took up a holding position a mile or so farther west, its searchlight, even from that distance skimming every now and then across his window, bringing the peonies on the curtains that he had never got round to changing briefly into bloom. It was like the worst days – and nights – of the hunger strikes rolled into one, except that now – he couldn't say how exactly – the whistles sounded celebratory. The radio in his bedroom was medium wave and FM only. He made his way downstairs to the sitting room, trusting to the helicopter for light until he was off the stairwell, and switched the tuner on the music centre to shortwave. After a couple of minutes' fiddling he managed to pick up the police: a squall of static punctuated by clicks and chirps and confused bursts of conversation until the signal was lost again; nothing in short that made sense of the uproar abroad – the euphoria as it sounded.

He heard it on the news at four on an English-language transmission from a territory where it was already noon. His first emotion was not horror, but fear: what further enormities would this provoke? His second, every bit as unbidden, was anxiety for his masters degree. He had taken as his starting point the article that was supposed to have got Harrison shot, developing its thesis and to an extent taking issue with it, arguing that the prison protest had in fact been the first step in a new political strategy. He turned off the radio and, while the helicopter searchlight flicked once more across the window, while rescue workers in Brighton tore apart the rubble searching for survivors, cradled his head in his hands. He might have to rethink.

*

Maxine didn't hear a thing about it until she got on to the bus to go into work. She had recently started full-time in the accounts department of the car showroom where she had used to temp, although – thanks in no small part to the compensation for the bomb that had ended its previous in-carnation – it had grown well beyond 'showroom' now, into the city's largest sales and rental firm.

'Isn't it desperate?' said the woman in the seat across the aisle from her then, settling her bag on her lap, added, 'At least now they know what we've had to put up with.'

At work they stayed on in the staffroom after lunch, crowding round a portable television – wire coat hanger for an aerial – to listen to the Prime Minister's speech to the Conservative Party Conference. 'The bomb attack on the Grand Hotel early this morning was first and foremost an inhuman, undiscriminating attempt to massacre inno-cent unsuspecting men and women staying in Brighton for our Conservative conference . . .' but soon enough it was time for 'business as usual', unemployment and the miners' strike, and long before her parting promise that democracy would prevail all but one of Maxine's colleagues had drifted off to their own usual mid-afternoon occupations.

'Do you think maybe she didn't look traumatised enough for them?' the last man sitting said. He worked in personnel was as much as Maxine knew. 'I can't have the woman myself, don't get me wrong, but I mean her bathroom was blown to pieces twelve hours ago, there are friends of hers lying in the mortuary. It's a pretty gutsy per-formance by any standard.'

Maxine had not yet decided what she thought, though

she tried to suggest from her expression that she would rather not be drawn.

'Alan, by the way,' he said.

'Maxine.'

'Oh, I know. There are no strangers to us in personnel, only files you have yet to meet.' He stopped his mouth with both hands and only slowly uncovered it. 'Sorry, did that sound a bit scary?'

She laughed. 'Just a bit.'

He clapped his cheeks. She registered the wedding ring. 'I keep saying to them all in there we need to get out more, mix with real human beings.'

She switched off the TV, made sure there was nothing left smouldering in any of the ashtrays. He held the staff-room door for her.

'Your hair's changed from your photograph.'

'Stop, now, that really is scary.'

'It's not every day you get a file with someone with hair like that on the front.'

'I helped out in a hairdressers when I left school.'

'You probably don't want me to say that that's in the file too.'

'You're dead right I don't.'

'OK then, I won't.'

'One to be wary of at the Christmas do,' she said under her breath after they had parted, but she stole a glance back anyway as she turned the corner to her office. He was already away.

She spent a long time that night, after her parents had gone to bed, in front of the bathroom mirror, putting her face through its paces, testing her neck and jaw for signs of slackness. She shrugged off her dressing gown. The mirror was portrait only so she had to rely on the gloss of the wall tiles for what even tiptoes could not stretch to. She pinched, she patted. She thought for several wet minutes of Alan from personnel walking in and finding her like this . . . she caught herself on, retrieved the dressing gown from the floor and switched out the light.

She ran into him several times after that, at least once too often for it to feel like an accident, on her part any more than his. Always the chat: nice dress . . . you look like you've been away . . . She dropped his name into conversation with one of the other girls, who rolled her eyes. Alan! Mr *Personal*.

She did, after a great deal of deliberation, go to the Christmas do, in the fortified compound that fear of bombers had made of the Wellington Park Hotel, but she refused one refill in every two that was offered and took the added precaution of leaving before the dancing started. Alan, knocking over chairs in his haste, tried to head her off at the door. 'You're not going already are you?'

A single strand of red lametta had attached itself to the shoulder of his sports jacket. Or maybe *he* had attached *it*: an invitation to her to brush it off. She held tight to the strap of her bag.

'I have an old friend over from Glasgow.' She didn't care if it wasn't convincing. 'Haven't seen her in years.'

He showed her the inside of his bottom lip. Man-boy. Someone must have told him once it was appealing. 'But this is when it starts to get fun.'

She shrugged. 'I could kick myself, but tonight was the

only night she could make.'

Alan fumbled with the flap of his right-hand jacket pocket – wait, not that one – fumbled with the flap of the left, and finally pulled out a plastic sprig of mistletoe, which he dangled in the air between them. 'Before you go . . .'

'Oh, look . . .' Maxine drew her head back a couple of inches and took hold of his wrist. 'Your wedding ring must have fallen off in your pocket.'

He looked, dumbly, at the naked digit for a crucial second then shook it, shook himself awake – 'No, wait . . .' – but by then she was on the other side of the door waving back through the safety glass.

It was a close shave, because actually he wasn't that bad looking and who was to say but that with another drink or two he wouldn't have looked a whole lot better, and let's face it this past couple of years she had slept with worse and had not always been too fussy about what they wore on their ring fingers.

There were queues in two directions at the gates of the Wellington Park when she passed through the security hut at the far end of the hotel forecourt, the queue on the right merging with the queue for the Botanic Inn next door and all of them in communion – shouts, whistles, sudden mad dashes through traffic – with the queue across the road at the Eglantine. Somebody in the queue to the left asked her for a light – don't smoke – somebody asked her where she got her coat – Petal – somebody asked her would she make him the happiest man in the world – depends how easy pleased you are . . . She walked past them all, past the university into town – more queues along the way shading into impromptu parties – swinging her bag, fighting down the impulse to laugh or cry, she didn't know which, only that she was happy. In ten days' time it would be 1985, the decade's midpoint. Everything seemed to open up on that walk. She would be all right. She felt certain of it.

*

St John left the Eglantine about an hour later with Sibyl and Bea and the still underage Paddy. 'It's the Eglantine,' Sibyl had said. 'He'll be old for there,' and indeed he had spent most of his time chatting to boys he recognised from the year below him at school. Sibyl was wearing the hat that St John had brought her and had insisted on her opening before Christmas.

'I couldn't resist it.'

'A mad old doll hat.'

'Hardly.' It was burgundy velvet with an embroidered band, black and gold. He had passed a woman on the street in Portswood wearing one and had chased after her to ask where she had bought it. He didn't even blink when he saw the price tag, although it was twice as much as all the other presents put together.

Sibyl looked at herself in the mirror a long while. She kissed him. 'I love it.'

They crossed the road now to the Botanic Off-sales for a bottle of wine and more cigarettes. They were going back to the house where Mo was waiting for them to dress the tree. The tree arrived on the same day every year on the back of a lorry from a forest outside Newry, another of the things about the economy of their lives in that house that they accepted without question. Almost the only innovation in the last decade and a half was decorating the rabbit hutch. (St John was amazed to find the rabbit still alive, though as squat and heavy now, in its sixth year, as a curling stone.) When they were very small the tree had arrived on Christmas Eve – an almost unbearable wait – but that tradition had been relaxed the Christmas after their father left. He had done his doctorate in the United States and had adopted some of their Yuletide ways: their sadistic ways, Mo had decided. Now it was always the Friday before.

About fifty yards up the road from the bar Sibyl realised she should have peed. She pulled open the door of a telephone box. 'I always wanted to try this.' Paddy hauled her back by the sleeve and they hurried on together, Paddy urging her to think of dry things. 'The Sahara! The Gobi! Belfast on an Easter Sunday!'

St John fell into step beside Bea.

'You're very quiet,' he said.

'You and Sibyl give me plenty of opportunity.'

'Don't be like that.'

She squeezed his upper arm. 'Sorry: sickness.'

It was the word that she and Sibyl had always used for period, from the Old Testament (trust Sibyl to have ferreted it out), the book of Deuteronomy, threatening with damnation any man lying with a woman having hers.

As Sibyl used to say any man lying with a woman having her sickness needed his head examined.

'I'm pleased it's all going well for you over there,' she said. 'Even if I never see you any more.'

He was pleased she had mentioned it. Sibyl and Mo had so far affected – or perhaps it was entirely genuine – indifference. And all Paddy ever wanted to know was if he had met anybody famous yet.

'Is Andrea Arnold famous?'

'Who?'

'No.'

'It's the first time in my life I've felt like I've known what I'm doing,' he told Bea.

'Mo was wondering why you never bring Trudy back with you.'

'Yeah, well she has her own family to go and see.'

Bea let that sit for a moment or two, then: 'Another man?' she asked.

He tried not to and then he laughed. 'Is it that obvious?'

'Sibyl said it all along. I told her it was none of our business.'

'Which is why you are quizzing me.'

'We're the middle ones, we're supposed to have our secrets from the others.' The others were already out of sight. 'I just hope you don't go getting yourself into some awful mess.'

'Part of the reason I'm back for so long is to get myself out of one.' He had told Trudy the last time he had seen her that enough was enough. He had waited for her boyfriend to finish his degree, his curacy, and had agreed not to disrupt his first – he didn't even know what the noun was – vicarship? Vicarage? Anyway: enough. This had been going on for *three years*. He pressed Bea's arm to his side. 'Now, tell me about university.'

'Not much to tell yet. First term is always like a mad mating season. Maybe when I go back I'll get to have a sensible conversation with somebody.'

They were passing the filling station. Behind the bags of coal and peat briquettes the windows were reduced to the size of television screens, the customers the cast of some bleak drama. A large inflatable snowman was tethered to a concrete block at the exit from the forecourt, large enough for someone to have spray-painted across his chest in red, *FTP*. Fuck the Pope. Someone else had obviously tried to scrub it off and succeeded only in toning it down to a less aggressive pink.

'You should call in and say hello,' said Bea. 'They always ask after you.'

'Mm.'

They walked the remainder of the way in silence.

Past the rhododendron and up the drive, the front door was wide open, laying a path of yellow light on the steps. Pine needles and pieces of broken branch littered the hall. A picture leaned against the skirting board below the hook that had used to hold it. The glass, replaced after a similar mishap a few years ago, was cracked, again. St John remembered Christmases gone by, sitting on the stairs in ascending order of age, watching the men wrestle the tree in, like men trying to land a whale. He remembered too the tumblers of whiskey that Mo had handed out to fortify them for the drive back to Newry. They were always handed back empty.

The leviathan was braced in a corner of the sitting room, still breathing: the smell when St John walked in there was pure forest. Whoever had been tasked with selecting the tree this year, he had surpassed himself.

Sibyl was carolling joyfully over the flush of the cloakroom toilet.

Paddy had brought the stepladder in and was trying to set it up to the left of the tree, hard enough when you hadn't drunk four pints in two hours. The twine that had once replaced one of the rope stays had itself been replaced with what appeared to be a wire coat hanger. St John thought about lending a hand then thought he would only make it four pints harder again.

Mo had brought the boxes of decorations down from the attic, Lipton's Tea in yellow, red and white on the side of one, Fyffe's all over the other. Bea at once dropped to her knees and began lifting out baubles wrapped in tissue paper.

Mo came in from the hallway carrying a bowl of satsumas and another of hazelnuts and walnuts. She had on a cardigan that reached almost to the floor, the left-hand pocket dragged down lower than the right by the nutcrackers. She was seventy-five per cent grey now and never went anywhere without her glasses, hooked on to the V of her blouse. She looked better, St John thought, than she did ten years ago. Sibyl followed a few moments later with the wine and the wine glasses. Mo frowned when she handed a glass to Paddy who had wisely left the ladder aside for the moment. Sibyl, reading her face, said, 'Oh, Mo, one won't do him any harm.'

'He looks as though he's had one or two already.'

'We kept him on shandy.'

They all touched glasses, Mo only a little reluctantly.

'Happy Christmas us.'

St John sipped his wine – it was as bad as its £1.99 price tag had suggested – taking in the scene: chaotic and somehow comforting. How could he have stayed away for so long?

'What would you all say if I told you I had had an enquiry about the house?' Mo asked then.

The siblings roared in unison, 'No!'

Mo set her glass down on the hearth. 'All right, then, I haven't had an enquiry about the house.'

'Was it an estate agent?' asked St John.

'Forget it, it never happened.'

'How dare they,' said Sibyl.

'It never happened.'

A moment or two followed of complete silence. Bea peeled back the last of the tissue paper from the decoration sitting in her lap. 'Oh, look, it's the trumpet!'

The trumpet – like the wonky stepladder – pre-dated all of them, part of a set of twelve decorations bought in the States during that doctoral sojourn. The first Christmas of their parents' marriage. Mo took the trumpet in the palm of her hand, looking at it as though at a bone fragment from which the whole creature of the past might be reconstructed.

Paddy slid across the floor on his knees to Bea. 'See if you can find the lantern.'

It was close to midnight by the time they finished: so many memories to be unwrapped (curious how completely they faded when the box was back in the attic, the tree collected and taken to the sawmill), so many personal favourites to be hung, taken down, hung again where they could be seen to best advantage.

The wine had not lasted long. Mo, despite Sibyl's scepticism, claimed that there was no drink anywhere in the house. There was no hot chocolate either. They fell back on a punch of satsuma and lemon and Robinson's barley water.

As they were going up the stairs St John found himself walking with Bea again.

'Do you think she would sell the house?' he asked.

'Ever?'

'Any time soon.'

'I would love to say no, but I mean look at it. Would you like to be here on your own?'

'Sure, isn't Sibyl going to stay?'

'Maybe it was Sibyl I was thinking of. Maybe it was Sibyl Mo was thinking of.'

On the landing now. The pine needles had been tramped up here too.

'Do you know who I keep seeing around the university?' Bea said and St John knew the answer before the words were out. 'That guy Craig who you used to knock about with.'

He affected surprise. 'Gosh, Craig. I thought he would have been finished by now.'

'Postgraduate.'

He wished he didn't have to think about Craig, his own dereliction in regard to him, not now, but he knew the conversation had to run its course. 'Do you ever get talking to him?'

'Just hello. I don't think he can quite place me.'

'How does he look?'

She shrugged. 'I don't know, really. The same.'

'Next time you see him will you get an address or a number off him?' Why had he said that? He had them both, somewhere, or assumed he still did. They had arrived on a postcard at Anne's house a couple of days after Trudy appeared on the scene.

Bea shrugged again. 'Sure.'

*

Craig went home to his parents that year on Christmas morning and left again after *The Two Ronnies*. To begin with he had gone back for a week at Christmas and Easter, taking his cue from the other students, but all he did at home now was eat and watch TV. His MA tutor had told him that the students who excelled were those who realised that the winter break was a month and a half without classes, not a month and a half on the lash.

His father insisted on driving him back to Aunt Queenie's (for that was how they still referred to it), insisted when they got there on helping him in with the new books, which were all Craig had asked for, all he ever asked for these days, and the other bits and pieces that his mother, looking at the uniform rectangular parcels, felt compelled to add if only for variety – gloves, three pairs of underpants, a Chocolate Orange and a six-pack of blank C-90 cassettes – plus a Tupperware full of leftover turkey and an entire Christmas pudding, neither she or his father being much fussed on pudding or cake or mince pies, anything really with raisins. Craig told her every year not to go getting a pudding on his account, he could take it or leave it himself. 'Take it,' his mother said, this year, every year. 'Take it.'

'I feel bad leaving you here on your own on Christmas night.' His father cast an eye around the sitting room. It didn't take long to arrive back at Craig.

'I've got a pile of work to do tomorrow.'

'On Boxing Day?'

Craig bent to flick a plug switch and the electric fire came on in the grate. He flicked another and a small Christmas-tree-shaped lamp lit up on the windowsill. That had been Aunt Queenie's too. He had found it at the back of a closet when they were doing the clear-out – had thrown it straight into the bin bag then as an afterthought taken it out again. For the comedy value, he told himself. But this year as in previous years he had got a real kick out of bringing it down in the second week of December and plugging it in.

He and his father looked at it.

'Well, if you're sure you're all right.'

'I'm sure.'

When the door was shut he stood for a few moments with his eyes closed then drew from his trouser pocket a fol-ded sheet of newspaper, rescued from the pile his parents kept for making spills for the fire. Square by square as he opened it out the most noteworthy, or photogenic, of the University of Ulster's winter graduates were revealed. The largest photograph was captioned 'Well tried' and showed Ros holding her doctorate scroll alongside 'Ulster rugby star Barry Kerr'. Her husband.

He had his face tilted to one side, cheek almost resting on top of her head, the same pose (albeit with more in the way of neck and shoulders) that Craig had adopted in the only photograph he and Ros ever had taken together. It had used to sit, unframed, on the bedside table. Waiting for her in bed one February afternoon he had noticed that the photograph was gone. He tugged open the drawer and there, below some receipts and a repeat prescription, it was. Ros, coming in the door at that moment, had been furious, practically turfed him out on to the floor. How *dare* he? What else did he touch in there? When eventually she calmed down she told him that her mother had been round that morning to help with the cleaning. Craig tried to sustain his sense of affront, but he couldn't say in truth that he blamed her.

He imagined Ulster rugby star Barry Kerr coming across the picture, asking the obvious question. Imagined Ros taking it out of his hand and . . . what? Laughing it off? Ripping the thing to pieces?

But, no, Ros was too careful, and Barry Kerr had the look of a man who knew when he was well off. (To think Craig had once considered her unremarkable.) He had her now, what else mattered?

Some kids passed in front of his window preceded by the beat of their boombox (so what did *you* get for Christmas?). He saw their midriffs only in the gap – one Christmas-tree lamp high – between the bottom of the blinds and the sill. Half a dozen of them at least. He had had a bit of bother when he first moved in, kids playing thunder and lightning, milk stolen from the doorstep, that sort of thing. Then one evening early in the first spring he was there he answered a knock at the door to find a guy, a year or two older than him, shaved head, neck tattoo, shaking a collecting tin in his face. 'Uniforms for the band.' Demand, not request.

There were tattoos too – letters – on the middle three fingers of the hand that shook the tin: N, E, D.

'Sorry?'

'Pride of the Road Flute. We're collecting for new uniforms.'

Other band members, Craig now noticed, were shaking their tins in doorways further down the street, turning away again all smiles. He patted his pockets, stalling. Ned was trying to see past him into the house.

'The wee woman who lives here always gives.'

'She died,' Craig said.

Ned pulled the tin away as though it had just that moment happened. 'I'm sorry, I'm a few streets away . . .'

'No, it's OK.'

'She let me use the toilet one time. Sound as they come.'

'I know, she was my—' he went to say 'great-aunt' but what came out was 'granny'.

Ned patted him on the arm. 'Listen, don't worry. I'll tell the other lads to give you a by-ball this year. I remember when my own granny died. Takes you a right while getting over it.'

Craig wanted to get in the door before any of the neighbours heard.

'Well, I can't say it's been easy.'

Ned nodded. 'See you around,' he said.

'Yeah, see you around.'

Craig had indeed seen him around several times after that, coming out of the local newsagent's as Craig was going in, standing chatting to his flute-band mates at the door of the Royal Bar, further down the Donegall Road into town. Always had a little wink for Craig, like good to see you're coping OK.

And when the bunting was going up in the middle of June, zigzagging across the street, Craig had another knock on his door, a kid standing there, clearly under instruction, asking if Craig minded them anchoring a zig (or maybe it was a zag) to his fascia board.

'Go on ahead,' Craig said, for of all the trappings of the Twelfth of July he minded bunting and its Christmas-streamer echoes least. Besides, he was starting to feel a little uncomfortable with the deference, not least because he feared what would happen if – or more likely when – it came to light that it was based on an initial untruth. He even wrestled himself into a decision to put some money in the tin – in Queenie's name – when the band came collecting again in the spring. But spring came and the Pride of the Road did not. He saw Ned just once more after that – a few months back in fact – hair all grown out, and a sleeveless jean jacket on him with patch badges: Def Leppard, Marillion, Iron Maiden.

He was in West Germany now working, he said. Building sites. Good money if you weren't afraid of hard graft. The flute band? He thought that had died a death. It happened sometimes, a whole crowd of you got into it together and then, I don't know, you grew out of it.

Just like that.

The boombox carried on up the street. Craig folded the newspaper and sat on the settee. He lifted a book from the bag at his feet – R. F. Foster's *Lord Randolph Churchill: A*

Political Life – then squeezed his hand down the side of his seat until he had located the tobacco packet. (Him? Paranoid? Much?) He took out the Rizlas, laid three of them on the back of *Churchill*, and dislodged the nub of resin from the corner of the packet. In a couple of minutes he had his joint. A deep stoned sleep and he would wake tomorrow, Christmas behind him, ready for work. He set the book aside, sparked up, and pulled his legs up under him on the settee.

Ros was married. To a rugby player. Harrison would be spinning.

A couple of days into the new term he was running up the steps towards the door of the Students' Union building when he brushed against a girl coming in the other direction in deep conversation with a friend. 'Sorry,' he said. The girl – he had seen her from time to time; always smiled – put a hand on his sleeve. 'Craig? I'm Bea, St John's sister.'

'Of course,' he said: *that's* who she was. 'I know.'

'Have you a minute?' she asked. The friend had continued down the steps. She looked back over her shoulder. Bea waved her on. 'I'll catch you up!'

They stepped out of the flow, leaning against one of the large windows that flanked the Union's doors.

'I said to St John that I saw you around but was never quite sure if you remembered me.'

She was looking at him too closely for him to lie. 'I *thought* it was you.'

Actually, he had fondly imagined on those previous occasions that she had been smiling because she liked him. Some errors, it seemed, age could not cure you of.

'We only really met properly that once, at the party,' she said.

'If you can call that meeting. I have this horrible feeling I was really drunk.'

'You weren't the drunkest, not by a long chalk.'

She looked up to see how far her friend had gone. He looked down at his watch. She caught him at it.

'I'm keeping you back.'

'No, you're not, I'm just thinking about you, next lecture.'

'I've nothing now till after lunch. We were heading across to the library.'

'Will your friend keep you a seat, do you think?'

She looked up again. The friend was passing under the arch of the Lanyon Building. 'I'd say she would.'

'Quick coffee?'

'Quick one.'

The Snack Bar was bunged so they headed back down the stairs to the Speakeasy. By the time they arrived, Bea had already sketched for him St John's journey from goats to the gardening programme on TVS, his cameo in the reporting of the Brighton bomb.

'St John?' Craig stopped in the Speakeasy doorway. *'Television?'*

'I know. We hardly ever even saw it when we were growing up,' Bea said, either not hearing or choosing to ignore any slight, however unintended, against her brother's abilities in the questions, or their tone. 'He made it sound like the simplest thing in the world to get into.'

The clock behind the bar read ten past eleven and already

there were people sitting with pints in front of them. They both ordered orange juice and both stared at the disappointing two inches that the Britvic bottles yielded in the bottom of their glasses. Warm too. There had been a run on ice the night before, nothing in the buckets this morning but a slick of grimy water.

They sat. Craig said it again. 'Television? St John?'

Again no offence was taken. 'It's mad, isn't it?' She reached for the ring binder sticking out from her shoulder bag, for the red biro clipped by the lid to the spine. 'I promised him I would get your address, and your number if you've got one.'

He didn't bother telling her about the postcard he had sent, but took the pen and the notebook she passed to him, folded open to the back page, and wrote.

She read them back for verification.

'Yep, that's me.'

They picked up their orange juices at the same moment; set them down again at the same moment after a solitary sip.

'It's too early isn't it to be having a *drink* drink?' he said.

'Probably, but let's have one anyway.'

It was late afternoon, already dark, when they got up to leave, having seen off the lunchtime crowd and held their own for a time against the evening vanguard and having talked in between about everything under the sun, his course, her course (English: one missed lecture wasn't going to make a difference), the state of this place at nights, the state of the economy, the latest Woody Allen movie (she had seen it, he had not), Kampuchea, crisps and how to shrink the packets . . . It occurred to Craig that the last time he had lost track of time in a bar like this had been with St John.

For the last while the students coming in off the street had snowflakes in their hair.

Outside, on the steps where they had met, they watched the snow come down with the force of rain. As often happened in Belfast they had both made the mistake of dressing for the day – the season – they had awoken in. It was spring come early when their alarm clocks rang. Instinctively they huddled together as they made a dash for the next available shelter, then the next and the next till they found themselves in the doorway of the Club Bar where they kissed for the first time.

'How did this happen?' Bea asked when they broke apart, her eyes still closed. 'You of all people?'

They kissed again, for longer, till a bouncer moved them on. 'Are yous in or are yous out? You can't stand there blocking the road on other people.'

'Take me home with you,' Bea whispered.

'We're out,' Craig told the bouncer and with her arm around his waist danced between the cars negotiating the slope of the road into and out of town.

They went by Sandy Row and Donegall Road, walking backwards much of the way to keep the snow from blowing into their faces. At one point she asked him to wait while she nipped into a chemist's shop and when she came out smiled apologetically, causing his heart to sink a little, until she swiped an armful of snow off the roof of a parked car, all down one side of his canvas jacket. He ran, roaring, after her.

The snow was three or four inches deep around his front

doorsill. His hands were so cold and the lock was so stiff he had a hard job getting the key to turn in the lock, even without the distraction of Bea, behind him, putting her own hands in his trouser pockets, 'for my sake more than yours'. A door across the street opened a fraction and an over-weight dog came out, with a bit of coaxing from a slippered foot. The dog battled to the nearest upright – a green Tele-com junction box – and cocked its leg. The stream was almost fluorescent against the snow. The dog sniffed, was satisfied, battled back to the door, which opened again a fraction. A hand came out and dragged the animal in. They must have been watching at the window. Craig blew on his fingers then put the key in the lock once more and gave it a twist.

He fell into the tiny vestibule, kicking snow before him and dragging Bea behind. The inner door was never locked, he managed the handle with his shoulder. For a moment they seemed to have brought the cold in with them too. 'Wait.' He stretched to hit the switch on the electric fire. The fan started up noisily beneath the moulded coals.

'I'm all twisted,' said Bea. Her hands were still in his pockets.

'No, I think it's me.' He tried to adjust the lining, which was when they both felt him, caught in that instant between one hand and the other, stiff as a door lock. 'Oh dear,' she said and her right eyebrow crept up.

'Maybe it would be easier if I took them off.' He undid the first button then the catch. With his other hand he had pushed her coat back off her shoulders – it was soaked through – and was tugging her shirt out from the waistband of her jeans. He leaned in towards her mouth.

She worked a hand free at last, put it to his chest. 'I'm sorry. Where's your bathroom?'

He stopped tugging, 'Through that door into the working kitchen and turn right.'

She hitched up her coat and her shoulder bag with it.

'The light's on the wall outside!' he called after her.

He sank down on the settee. What kind of a thing was that to say? 'Maybe it would be easier if I took them off'? And just there now, 'working kitchen'? He never said working kitchen, it was Queenie's term. He only hoped that he had left the bathroom in a half-decent state. (It had neither been knocked down nor painted, although thanks to regular assaults with bleach the mould had at least been kept at bay.) There was a wet spot where his Y-fronts protruded from the opening of his trousers. He pushed them – *it* – down with his thumb and, with less difficulty than he might have had half a minute before, did up the button again. He did not quite register the tapping at first, what with the noise of the fan, the buzz of his own tormented thoughts. Only when those thoughts turned to the possibility of her being too afraid to come back out did it finally penetrate. He turned in the settee. Bea was standing in the doorway, knuckles arrested just short of the frame, holding in her other hand a toothbrush he didn't recognise.

'I couldn't find your toothpaste.'

'There should be some there.' He got up, relieved to have something practical to focus on. 'No, do you know what it is?' He saw himself in his mind's eye put his foot on the pedal of the little plastic bin. 'I finished the tube this morning.'

She stood aside to let him into the bathroom. (It maybe smelled a little too strongly of bleach; she would be thinking he had some sort of problem.) 'I looked in the cabinet, I hope you don't mind.'

The cabinet barely had room for his shaving foam and razor. 'I don't mind at all.' He knelt by the bath and opened a small door in the panelling.

'I'd never have found that in a million years.'

'I must have been here six months before I discovered it myself.' A lie, a week or two at most. Still. He stood. 'Signal do you?'

The packaging for the unfamiliar toothbrush was next to the cold tap.

'Is that what you went into the chemist's for?'

She nodded. 'I just hated the thought of getting into bed without cleaning my teeth.'

She held out the brush. He scrolled toothpaste the length of it then got his own brush from the cup by the other tap and squeezed toothpaste on to that. They stood face to face each mirroring the other's brushstrokes, snow piling up on the perspex sheets above their heads. After a few moments they circled one another's waists with their free arms, drawing close. He felt her heart beating an inch or two below his, picking up speed. They were brushing their teeth now over one another's shoulders, trying not to laugh, at the same time moving their hips slowly together. They drew back their heads to look at one another. He brought his brush towards her mouth. She didn't hesitate, but opened wide, showing him her teeth. Not a single filling. He brushed each tooth in turn: molars, premolars, canines, lateral and central incisors. Her own brush was in his mouth (fillings all over the place, not that she seemed to be looking), gently, gently, but even gently working up a froth at last. Then – whatever had happened to his brush and hers – it was her tongue in there. She was turning him around, pushing him back against the wall, turning him again, pulling him on to her, almost tipping them both over into the bath, finding a place finally, a way. Now it was her hand at the button of his trousers, her hand pulling at her own shirt, pushing it up. The water continued to run into the sink. He could hear it throughout tumbling out the end of the drainpipe and into the drain on the other side of the alleyway gate. It was nearly too distracting, but only nearly.

Afterwards they curled up under an eiderdown on the settee listening to the silence that was the snow still falling beyond the window. Not even the kids with the boombox were out.

'Can I use your phone?' she asked.

He trailed it over by the lead from its station by the hearth. There was a small brown mole on the handset where a coal from the end of the joint he had been smoking lodged itself one night while he searched all around the carpet for the source of the burning smell.

She leaned out of the eiderdown to dial. He was holding on to her legs as she spoke, kissing the small of her back. 'Paddy? It's me, Bea. I'll not be home . . . Isn't she . . . ? Right, but Sibyl's there? How long did she say? That's OK . . . Tomorrow some time. Bye.'

Twenty-five words start to finish. She shoved the phone away.

'Everything all right?'

'Have you met my mother?'

'No.'

'Then it's too hard to explain.'

He didn't want to ask it, but couldn't see either how he could avoid it. 'What do you think St John would make of this?'

'Bizarrely we don't talk an awful lot about my sex life.' After a moment though she added, 'I don't think you should say anything to him, not yet.'

'He and I don't talk an awful lot about anything at all any more.'

'But he's going to have your number now, remember?'

'Stupid of me to forget.'

＊

St John nearly had a fucking fit.

Bea had waited, she told him, until she was certain she had news of something more than a snowy night's fling to impart. Two weeks to be precise, in the course of which she had not spent more than four nights at home.

'What does he think he's playing at? What do you think you're playing at?'

'For God sake, St John, calm yourself or I'm not giving you this number.'

Do you know what? St John didn't fucking want it, not now.

Do you know what? St John could have it his own way. 'I think I'm old enough to make up my own mind.'

It didn't matter what age she was, though, St John said to Trudy when he had put down the phone (Bea infuriatingly had beaten him to it by a couple of seconds), it just wasn't right, for fuck sake, your friend's younger sister.

'One of the lesser-known taboos,' said Trudy with the authority of one who had violated a few herself: the vicar, last she heard, was in therapy.

'Thanks for your support.'

'Any time.'

6

Victor, Maxine's brother, phoned her at work one day. 'Get over to the Royal straight away. Dad's had a heart attack.'

All the way across town she was telling herself hospital was a good sign. Hospital trumped heart attack. Hospital said recovery.

The boss had insisted on her taking a hire car – quicker than waiting for a taxi – but the traffic was horrendous, the standard of driving she had to deal with even worse. She shouted out her window at a stupid man who was sitting in the middle of a box junction on Great Victoria Street. He shouted back, leaned across to throw her the fingers as the cars in front of him at last started to move. Then she stalled with her own nose in the cross-hatching as the lights changed again and the car horns behind her blared. Fuck fuck fuck.

And the car park, of course, when she finally got there was full. She abandoned the car in the end at the back of a building without windows or discernible function, in another time zone practically from A&E.

She wiped her eyes with a Kleenex as she walked, getting rid of the mascara that had run during the drive. She finger-combed her hair. Don't let him see how scared you were.

Victor was waiting for her in the lobby. 'Ah, Maxine,' was as far as he got before she started to cry unchecked.

'I stalled the car,' she said through the tears. 'The stupid man was in the middle of the junction then I stalled the car.'

Victor caught her by the shoulders. 'It's all right, it's all right. There was nothing you could have done, he was already dead when I got here.'

'But I thought when you said the Royal . . .'

No, she told herself, you let yourself think. You knew from the moment you heard his voice.

'Mum wanted some time on her own with him,' he said when she had composed herself sufficiently to get in the lift. People around them carried flowers and magazines and bottles of Lucozade. One little girl clutched a blue satin ribbon at the far end of which, almost touching the ceiling, was a foil balloon: 'Bouncing Baby Boy!'

'She won't know what to do with herself,' said Maxine.

The lift stopped and the doors opened and then there was the two of them for the last three floors. They watched in silence the numbers rise. Maxine contemplated the question of soul. The lift stopped.

A nurse was coming out of a room as they turned into the corridor.

'I brought her in a cup of tea,' she said to Victor, 'plenty of sugar,' and to Maxine, 'You must be the daughter, I can see the likeness. I'm terribly sorry.'

She carried on down the corridor. Victor took his sister's hand – 'You all right?' – and they opened the door.

'The good thing is he didn't suffer,' were the first words her mother uttered. She appeared quite calm, even content that this potentially messy event had gone over so well too. 'He just got up from the chair and said he felt light-headed and then the next thing he was stretched out on the floor at my feet, not even a murmur. They worked on him and worked on him, of course, in the ambulance and after they got him here, but they couldn't bring him back . . . Not a murmur.'

Maxine caught sight past her shoulder of her father's face. In truth he didn't look as though dying had taken a lot out of him. She thought of the poem she had learned in school, 'Rage, rage against the dying of the light . . .' 'Remember,' the teacher had said above the uproar that was habitual in English and most other classes, 'it's "gentle", not "gently": "Do not go *gentle* into that good night."' Her father had gone gentle. She wanted to touch his forehead, but checked herself in case she should disturb him.

'Only we had taken the morning to go and look at washing machines I wouldn't have been with him.' Her mother was still talking. 'I told you about the washing machine, didn't I?'

'The hose,' said Victor.

'It hadn't been right for weeks.'

'Drink your tea, Mum.'

'It's too sweet.'

'It'll do you good.'

For a time then there was only in the room the sound of cup meeting saucer, of three people breathing. Three. Then her mother said with a firmness that was new to Maxine's ears, 'He would have wanted Tommy back for the funeral.'

'But you don't even know where he is to get in touch with him,' Maxine said.

'Somebody knows.'

'I wouldn't get my hopes up,' said Victor. 'It's been nearly ten years. We only have a couple of days.'

'It's what his daddy would have wanted,' she said, as firmly as before.

'I'm not even sure that I would know the right people to talk to any more,' Victor said later as he and Maxine rode the lift back down to the lobby. He had been home off the rigs these half-dozen years and was living in the house he had bought – in cash – with his earnings, a little way out in the country, mending farm machinery, bothering nobody.

'But it's not the ones who chased him we need to talk to, it's the ones they accused him of working for.'

'Maxine, he was a wee lad. Maybe he told the police the odd thing, but he never knew enough to be working for them. A couple of the UDA fellas themselves told me, he was a pain in the you-know-what, he annoyed people, they were chasing him away to save him from worse.'

All the same, to satisfy their mother, the funeral date was set for three days hence to give them time to make enquiries, which Maxine, glad to be spared from the house, from the same lines endlessly repeated by well-meaning neighbours, offered to undertake.

The main police station in that part of town was surrounded by a twenty-foot-high fence of corrugated steel with a fortified pillbox jutting out from it into the road itself, its sides bearing the scars of dozens of paint bombs, any number of bricks and lumps of concrete and even, close to the roof, three high-velocity bullets. Maxine knew better than to attempt to drive in. ('Keep the car for a couple of days,' her boss had said. 'Till you've the funeral and all over you.')

She parked a couple of streets farther on and walked back past terraces of mill houses that had long ago lost their mill, sidestepping to the very edge of the kerb at one point to avoid the arc of a scrubbing brush wielded by an elderly woman kneeling on a folded towel before her front door. 'Well, you've got to keep up your standards,' the woman said, as though in response to a question Maxine hadn't asked.

The constable manning the pillbox gave her the twice-over and a click sounded behind a turnstile, which she had to put her full weight to before it finally yielded and trans-lated her on to the other side of the wardrobe. Guns is what she saw, whichever way she turned her head: guns leaning against walls, guns cradled in arms, guns sagging with their holsters from uniformed hips. A patrol was getting ready to go out, an RUC Land Rover and its two-Land-Rover mil-itary escort. A soldier, barely out of his teens, seated in the rear of one of the army vehicles was looking at pages torn from a girlie mag: a bottle-blonde, tongue out as though to lick her breasts, cupped to the camera, was as much as Max-ine saw before she registered what it was she was looking at and averted her eyes at the same moment as the soldier no-ticed her and stuffed the pages under his seat.

'Take a reddener, you,' said one of the policemen.

'Apologise,' said another.

The soldier did the first all right – almost made Maxine blush for him – and mumbled a few heavily accented words (Birmingham was that?) by way of the second.

The station itself was, in stark contrast to the façade, a simple redbrick building, two storeys, whose roof only

Maxine had been able to see from the bus since the fences and pillboxes had gone up while she was still in primary school. Baskets of pansies, violet, lavender and white, hung from brackets on either side of a door whose letterbox and doorknob were polished to an almost liquid sheen.

Inside was a further throwback, a middle-aged sergeant sitting at a counter with a hatch to one side in the up position. He might have been in here all these years and known nothing of the changes outside.

He smiled at Maxine. 'Help you?'

'I was hoping I might be able to speak to someone about my brother. He hasn't been seen for a while. A good while, actually.'

'How good a while are we talking?'

'Nineteen-seventy-seven.'

The sergeant blew out his cheeks. He should have been in black and white.

'He was arrested once and brought here and then taken to Castlereagh for questioning,' Maxine said.

'Bad boy?' said the sergeant and Maxine shrugged: 'You let him go without charging him.'

The sergeant picked up a biro. When he looked down to write the lower half of his face lost all definition. 'What was the name?'

'Neill. Tommy Neill.'

'Means nothing to me.'

He let the hatch down – in case she got any ideas? – and put his head around the door behind him to start a conversation. The rest of his body followed bit by bit until finally only the left hand remained on the reception side of the door, its fingers drumming on the frosted glass.

While she waited Maxine kept her eyes on a small screen set at an angle above the counter. A cat crossed an empty street at a low run and jumped on top of a dustbin. The bin lid slipped, the cat leapt away, then another figure Maxine had not noticed before moved – straightened up – in the corner of the screen. The old woman with the scrubbing brush.

'There are cameras all round the place,' said the sergeant, reunited at last with his drumming fingers. 'Have to be. The year before last the Provos took over a house and shot one of our guys as he jumped out of a Land Rover at the front gates.'

Maxine remembered seeing it on the news. She thought of the young soldier with the dirty pictures. If that was the last thing you were ever to see, a woman letting on to lick her own breasts.

Her eyes flicked back to the screen. The old woman had the bin lid in her hand. She looked about her then dipped her hand in the bin and pulled God alone knows what out.

'Doting,' said the sergeant. 'Poor oul' doll. Out there all hours and all weathers.' He lifted the hatch again and stood aside to let Maxine pass. 'There's a wee room down there on the right. Somebody will be in in a few minutes to see you.'

The posters stuck haphazardly about the walls of the room were of a kind that, she would have thought, anyone getting this far would have no need of: phone the confidential telephone line, your finger on the dial can take the finger off the trigger, never, ever drink and drive . . . There was a table and two chairs. The table's formica top was chipped round the edges – you would nearly have said nibbled – and the centre furrowed by a deep, brown burn mark. She went to sit on the chair nearest the door, but when she pulled it out from the table she saw the seat was ripped, so she pushed it back and walked round to the other side, facing the door, which was opened at length by a balding man in rolled shirtsleeves. She wasn't sure whether she should stand.

'Don't get up,' he said, settling the matter. 'Detective Inspector Rogers.'

His hand was in front of her. She shook it. He took the chair with the rip in it and swung it round one-handed until it was at right angles to hers and pulled himself up close against the table. Sharp smell of deodorant beginning to lose the underarm war.

'Sergeant Wilkinson tells me you're Tommy Neill's sister.' He was looking into her face, half smiling, like this was some sort of light relief from whatever it was he had been doing in that other room.

She pressed her thumb against one of the chips in the table edge. 'We thought you might know how to get in touch with him.'

'I haven't seen Wee Tommy this donkey's years.'

He does know something.

'His dad's dead.'

Rogers sat back in his seat. 'I'm sorry to hear that,' he said and looked it. 'I lost my own father last year. Bowel cancer. The final few weeks . . . ?' He screwed up his eyes. 'You wouldn't wish it on your worst enemy.'

'It must have been terrible.'

'Yours?'

'Heart attack.'

'You were lucky.'

He was right. It was not just some foible of her mother's: they had all been spared. Stretched out gentle on the living-room floor. Not a murmur.

Rogers looked at his hands, clasped on the formica, then unhitched his thumbs: 'What harm can there be in it?' they seemed to say.

'There was a car accident, about a year and a half ago,' he began.

'Wait,' said Maxine, panic rising, 'is this Tommy we're talking about?'

'A man in his eighties' – proper procedure; he was not going to be hurried – 'hit another vehicle and bounced off it into a lamp-post. Killed him outright. The eyewitnesses said it was his fault entirely. Turned out he was on tablets, shouldn't have been driving at all. The police all the same had to make enquiries. They did a check on the driver of the other vehicle . . .'

'Tommy?'

Now he consented to a nod. 'I was surprised myself when the request landed on my desk.'

'And was he . . . ?'

'Hurt? Not a scratch on him.'

'No, I mean, was he, you know, easy to identify? I was wondering if maybe he had changed his name.'

The smile had returned to Rogers' face. 'You're thinking of the supergrasses. Tommy was more what we used to call a ten-bob tout.' She couldn't help herself, she quailed inwardly at the term, graffiti-lurid. 'Enough for a couple of tins of beer, a packet or two of fags. We had scores of them running about the place, wee lads with big mouths . . . Sorry.'

She shook her head. She had already heard the worst word; she couldn't argue with this description.

'The mistake we made with Tommy was pulling him in that time. A bad case of the left hand not knowing what the right was doing. There was nothing on him. All it did was draw attention. We put him on the Heysham ferry, gave him enough to pay his first month's rent on the other side then left him to make his own way. Looks like he did OK.'

He took a Polaroid from the breast pocket of his shirt and set it on the table in front of her. She was conscious of the other car, the lamp-post almost bisecting the bonnet, and of the horror that must lie beneath the sheet covering the windscreen on the driver's side, but her attention was fixed on the small white van sitting at a slight angle to the right of the frame. On its side, next to a cartoon plumber shouldering a plunger, was her brother's name and phone number.

'That's a Blackpool code, in case you're wondering. He didn't move far from where he landed.'

Hiding in plain view. She covered her mouth and nose with her hands. The first sound that escaped was a laugh, quickly followed by a sob.

'You can hang on to the photograph,' Rogers said.

She looked again at the scene's other components. 'Actually if you just had a pen I could write the number down.'

'Of course.' He patted his trousers – 'Ah!' – raised a buttock (air escaping from the ripped cushion that they both ignored) and drew a pen with a chewed lid from the back pocket. 'Paper?'

'I'm all right.' She had taken out the address book she had had from she was at school. She had long since ceased to observe the alphabet. It was strictly chronological. Every entry necessitated an encounter with some at least of her past as she flicked through looking for a page. The experience, not infrequently, was salutary. *This person too will pass out of your life* . . .

Her hand as she copied the details from the photo was shaking. Tommy would have been somewhere nearby when this was taken, clutching the mug of tea, maybe, that someone had brought him from the café, whose daily-special sign (*Hotpot £1.50!! £1.00 OAPs!!!*) she could just see over the van's roof, or, more likely, going over for the tenth time with a police constable yet to be convinced the moments leading up to the crash: 'He just shot out in front of me, ask this lady here on the footpath, she saw the whole thing. Didn't you, missis? Just shot out.'

'I hope he has the good sense to come home,' Rogers said when she gave him back the pen. 'It will haunt him otherwise . . . his dad's funeral . . .'

He leaned in across the table again. 'And I hope you don't think badly of us over this.' He tapped the photo, but she knew his 'this' referred to more than just that. 'It's a difficult balance to strike, protecting the greater number.'

He was still sitting at the table looking down at the photo when Maxine left.

'You all sorted?' the desk sergeant asked. No cat on the monitor on the wall now, no old woman. Just the bin and the empty street. The less anything happened the more it seemed something would.

'All sorted,' said Maxine, and told herself she would take another route back to the car.

Victor insisted as the eldest child and the person who had shared a room with Tommy all those years that he should be the one to make the phone call. He took the number with him back to his own house. Maxine was half expecting him when he rang her later to say that it was a wrong number after all, that Tommy had changed it after the exposure of the accident. But no. 'He's coming back,' he said. 'He wants to arrive and leave again on the same day, and we're not to say to anybody that he's coming.'

'Apart from Mum, obviously.'

Victor breathed out heavily. 'I get the sense he'd rather we didn't even tell her until the morning of the funeral.'

'How did he sound?'

Victor considered a moment. 'Embarrassed.'

'Is he married or anything?'

'I never thought to ask.'

'But you spoke to him, that's the main thing.'

'Yes.'

'And he's definitely coming home.'

'That's what he said.'

She told her mother anyway, the minute Victor was off the phone. She couldn't not.

'I'd better get his bed made up,' her mother said and shaped to get out of her seat.

'I said already, he can't stay.'

'I know, but in case he changes his mind.'

And having told her Maxine couldn't not go along with the fantasy that Tommy just might. 'I'll check there are clean sheets.'

The following night Victor picked the two of them up and drove to the funeral home, in an otherwise residential street behind a parade of shops. The chapel of rest was a converted double garage, its lighting pitched a few dozen lux below museum special collection, but even that was sufficient for Maxine to recognise as soon as she approached the coffin that her father was gone, slipped out by the back door since last she had seen him in the hours immediately after he was pronounced dead.

'His suit looks well,' she said to cover the shock.

'I think I was with him when he bought that one,' said Victor: 'John Collier.'

'It was the one thing I refused to do with him, shop for his clothes,' said their mother. 'He was worse than you boys, fretting about lapels and turn-ups and what he should and shouldn't wear.'

Maxine glanced sidelong at her.

'You didn't know?'

She couldn't quite believe that she didn't, given the regularity with which the same few stories were told, the same few observations made, in her parents' conversations, but, 'I don't think I did, no.'

'Oh, he was mustard,' her mother said; after a moment she said it again: 'Mustard.'

They sat by the coffin in that induced twilight and recited the Lord's Prayer together, their voices coming back to them from rafters that had once stored deckchairs and windbreakers out of season, garden hoses, lawn rakes. When the last echoed Amen had disappeared into silence her mother made a small adjustment to her father's tie, which, for what it was worth, he should not have worn or been made to wear with that suit, then bent and whispered something in his ear. Her face when she turned was set.

'I think we should leave him be now. Ask the undertaker, Victor, to cover the casket.'

'Maybe we should leave it open until tomorrow, just so, you know, anyone coming who wanted to . . . you know.'

'I already told her,' Maxine said.

'Anyway,' said her mother, 'Tommy hasn't seen him since he was a man in his prime. Better his memories are of him as he was, not of this . . . effigy.'

Of course she had seen it too. She had been married to him thirty-five years.

The morning of the day of the funeral was wet and ferociously windy. A plane was blown across the runway at Aldergrove Airport. At the docks all the ferries were delayed. Victor drove down to the Liverpool terminal twice (the Heysham route was long gone) and was told the second time it would not be long now. The funeral service was due to start at a quarter past two. When there was still no sign of the boat at half past one he drove back to the house.

'We may go on,' he said. 'Imagine how it would look if we were all late.'

Tommy arrived during the second hymn, 'O God Our Help in Ages Past'. Maxine had closed her eyes against the tears brought on by the line, 'Time like an ever rolling stream/Bears all its sons away', and when she opened them again he was standing there, changed, but undeniably himself, holding the hymnal for his mother while she underlined with her forefinger the words they were to sing: 'They fly, forgotten, as a dream / Dies at the break of day.'

When the hymn was over his mother held tight to his hand, held it until it was time for Tommy and Victor to step out to the front and help lift the coffin.

Outside the church the wind had dropped, but the rain was still coming down in sheets. Mourners had to tilt their umbrellas back to converse, those who talked at all. Most stood in silent huddles, waiting their turn to offer their condolences.

They had already decided to forgo the walk with the coffin. Tommy lit a cigarette the instant it was in the hearse, before Maxine even had a chance to say hello properly. His fingertips were orange. He pulled his bottom lip under the top and blew smoke down his chin, as Maxine had seen him do countless times, standing on the street corner, one foot planted on the ground, one foot resting on the wall behind him.

'Rough journey?' she asked.

'Rough enough.' He was watching the umbrellas closely, alert to every twitch, every glimpse of face afforded. He threw down the cigarette. 'Should we get Mum into the car out of this rain?'

Just before Maxine herself got in, one particular huddle broke cover to speak: Pete and Dermot and two of the Berlin girls. It took Maxine a moment to recognise the smaller of them as Kim, who had fucked Max on the floor of the salon back when Maxine was two-timing him with St John.

'It's awful for you,' she said now and rubbed Maxine's back.

'We saw it in the paper,' said Dermot. He had put together the closest thing to a mourning outfit that his wardrobe could supply. His shirt was black satin.

'It was really, really good of you to come.' She meant it sincerely, although she couldn't stop herself as soon as she had said it glancing past them to the car, where Tommy was gnawing on the pad of his thumb.

'Call in some time and see us,' Pete said and gave her hand a squeeze, releasing her. 'We've missed you.'

Tommy relaxed on the journey to the cemetery. There was just the four of them now, a couple of cars carrying relatives following in their wake. (Most of the sweet and chip shops round about had shut, out of necessity as much as respect.) With so much to say they ended up saying little of consequence at all. Odd things about places they passed – Was that not the cinema they used to use for the Saturday Morning Club? What did you call the old boy who ran the wee hardware shop on that corner? – now and again their associations with the man they were taking to bury: there was where he used to stop to get his paper on the way to work, here was where the dentist was that he swore he would never go back to. (And never did.)

They hardly even noticed that they were passing through the cemetery gates.

As soon as they were out of the car, however, linking arms to walk to the graveside, Tommy started to cry. 'I'm so, so sorry,' he said, over and over. He only stopped when his mother told him to pull himself together. His father wouldn't have wanted any of them making a spectacle of themselves.

He did his father proud after that. They all did.

Afterwards they had high tea at a hotel on the Antrim Road. Victor bought them all a Bushmills. 'I don't drink it,' Tommy said. 'No more do I,' said Victor, 'but we'll drink this one anyway. To family.'

'To family,' they repeated.

Tommy went and got another.

'So you're out on your own?' Victor asked him when he had sat down again.

'That's right.'

'Plumbing?'

'It was the one good thing I took away from that school of ours. Your man who took us for metalwork . . . '

'Stewart,' Victor said. 'Nasty piece of work.'

'He was, but he always said a plumber will never go hungry.'

And from there it was an easy step to asking about his 'home set-up'. (An easy step, but even with their mother's new-found resoluteness they still were not the best at saying a thing directly.)

Did they mean was he married? Tommy asked. No, he wasn't married, but he was living with a woman, Barbara, a couple of kids, not his, although as good as now, which makes you, turning to his mother, as good as a granny.

'Like I need to feel my age any more on the day I buried my husband.'

As afternoon turned to evening and the whiskeys mounted up, Tommy's anxiety returned. He kept asking the time, wondering was the wall clock right. He went to the toilet at one point and came out looking spooked. (Maxine had to nod to him to do up his flies.) He was standing at the urinal and a guy came in and just stood at the sink, watching him in the mirror.

'Maybe you just got lucky,' Maxine said and he scowled at her, another of those looks she remembered, though with a good deal less affection. They had spent close on fifteen years living on top of one another, he had had plenty of opportunity to exercise it.

At last it was time for him to leave. He was giving himself an extra hour in case the traffic was bad. He could probably have walked it in half the time.

He disappeared into a little side room with his mother for five minutes while Victor, who had drunk more than he intended, went to order him a taxi.

'I've told her not to come out with me,' Tommy said when he emerged. 'Maybe you'd go in and sit with her.'

Maxine, though, followed him into the lobby.

'I don't blame you, you know, for not wanting to come back before.'

'I did want to, every day.'

'All right, I don't blame you for not coming back even though you really wanted to.'

'What about you?'

'Me?'

'From you were no age at all you were telling us the things you were going to do.'

'That's the way all kids talk.'

'Tell you the truth, it used to get on my wick.'

Ah, yes, Tommy the slagger. *Who do you think you are, wee girl?* She batted his arm. 'There was plenty *you* did that annoyed me, you know.'

'I can believe that.'

Victor stepped in from the front steps. 'That's your taxi now.'

'Right,' said Tommy over his shoulder then he – who had never before he arrived in the church today so much as brushed a hair from his sister's shoulder – grabbed Maxine in both arms and hugged her. 'Don't make yourself the same as everybody else here,' he whispered and before she could say please don't let it be another ten years was out the door and away.

Six and a half hours his visit had lasted.

A couple of weeks after the funeral, Maxine was daydreaming at the bus stop into town.

She had a suitcase with her of her father's clothes for the Seaman's Mission. Imagine they were her clothes in there . . . Imagine she walked right past the Mission to the ferry terminal . . . Imagine being herself somewhere else . . .

A man, Victor's age or a little older, dandered up and looked at the empty frame where the timetable ought to have been. (It was very simple, there was a bus every half hour, unless there wasn't.) He glanced left and right.

'Maxine, isn't it?' he said. 'Maxine Neill?' He had the look – apt given her thoughts a moment before – of a travel rep, the slacks, the pastel sweater, the gold chain on the burgundy loafers, the unseasonal tan. The smile, which never wavered. 'I'm not sure you would know me, but I know you. I know your whole family. And you can tell your brother Tommy from me if he ever sets foot in this town again I'll kill him myself.'

He showed her his open right hand as proof of capability and intent – it did indeed look like a weapon – then in one movement he fetched the newspaper out from under his left arm and unfolded it to the inside back page, and off up the street he went, working out today's bet.

He had gone about fifty yards by the time Maxine had recovered enough to trust her voice.

'Bastard!' she yelled. The man stopped, turned slowly, as though unable to believe his ears. He pointed at his chest – *Me?* – mutely appealing to passers-by, who, to a man, woman and child put their heads down and hurried on. He looked almost wounded. 'Yes, you!' Maxine yelled again. 'Cowardly, cowardly bastard!'

The bus had pulled up and opened its doors in time for the passengers to be treated to these last three words. Maxine hauled the case on.

'Whoa, whoa, whoa!' the driver said. 'I'm not having language like that on my bus.'

'I was just . . .'

'You were just nothing. I heard you.' He nodded to a notice above the ticket machine. 'I have the right to refuse carriage, you know.'

The travel rep had started back down the street. Not running – he would have thought that beneath him – but folding the newspaper again into a baton and walking as though he expected the world to slow to the beat of his cold fury.

'That man there attacked me,' Maxine said and pointed.

The driver looked from him to her and back again. He

didn't hesitate. If you had been driving buses around the city for any length of time at all you would have seen enough walks like that to know – almost to the precise combination of initials – where the owner of that walk was coming from. He shut the door and with a sweep of his right hand swung the bus away from the kerb, throwing passengers out into the aisle.

'Sorry, folks,' he shouted into the mirror.

Maxine lurched towards the back, suitcase banging off her legs, deaf to the grumbles on either side of her, watching through the rear window as the slacks, the pastel sweater, the loafers, the tan and – no trace of a smile now – the jabbing finger receded.

She hoped before she became a dot to him that he got a good look at her face too. She hoped he could see that the fear had gone.

No more car-ferry daydreams. She would stay here. She would outlast him and his kind. Whatever it took, she would outlast them.

Making it

I

Eighteen months more on gardening, a six-month stint on sports (sick-leave cover: he was nearly ready for sick leave himself by the end of it), consumer affairs, health, a brief spell in farming where it had all in a roundabout way started: St John earned his production-assistant chops.

Sometimes still in the middle of the day he would nod off sitting at his desk. Now, though, rather than mock, people around him sympathised, praised him for it even: I mean, the *hours* he must be putting in . . .

Trudy meantime had made the step that he had baulked at to news and current affairs, front of camera too, despite the opinion of one senior executive – loudly expressed to a colleague in a packed lift – that television did the 'girl' no favours. Justice was what it did not do her, and actually it was not television itself, it was the unattended-studio, locked-camera format. Trudy was bigger than that.

Her break came in the aftermath of the Great Storm, which temporarily knocked out the TV-am studios, leaving the producers in London casting about the still-functioning regions for material. As luck would have it – although it hadn't felt like luck the night before – Trudy had been on the Isle of Wight when the storm hit. (A story about a prisoner breeding goldfinches in Camp Hill Prison.) The crew she was with filmed the wreckage of Cowes pier and filmed her reporting from the helicopter that was suddenly, and only a little melodramatically, their only hope of getting back to the mainland. A short time later she got a call from someone in Camden Lock who mentioned, in passing, a reporter's post that was about to be advertised. It meant them living apart again for part of the week, but they told each other that it was worth it. Besides, remember those nights when she had used to come back to Plymouth from Bristol . . . ?

Paddy was in England now too, the south-east, doing a degree in something called Development Studies, which Sibyl described as an advanced Scouting badge. Mo was on the phone constantly to St John. 'I don't think he's very happy. Can you *please* go up and see him?'

'It would be easier if he came down to see me,' St John said, but after several invitations had been declined and several more phone calls from home fielded, he gave in and took the coach up after lunch one late November Friday afternoon. It was dark by the time he arrived. Paddy was waiting for him at the bus stop across from the porters' lodge. He was supposed to have checked about a room, but he hadn't been able to find the room-booking service. 'It will be in the administration building.' Paddy didn't know where that was. St John showed him on a map of the university screwed on to the porters' lodge wall. 'Look, it's marked.'

'Oh.'

Of course, when they got there, it was closed for the weekend.

'Have you got a spare duvet?'

'There are some blankets in the cupboard.'

'I'll sleep on those . . . Do you remember nests?'

Paddy shrugged, stole a glance over his shoulder. No one there.

'You're not embarrassed, are you?'

Paddy shrugged again and St John saw him exactly as he was in his nesting days, standing by his big brother's bedside. The warm feeling that this memory produced was dispelled by one glimpse of the halls of residence. The halls might have been designed and bankrolled by Lebanese cannabis farmers with the express intention of driving students to use their product. The apotheosis of featureless concrete.

'Have you made many friends?'

'Not really, people tend just to sit in their rooms and smoke,' Paddy said, confirming St John's impression. 'Then those who can clear off home at the weekends.'

They stopped at the room only to drop off St John's bag then walked together along empty corridors and draughty walkways to the refectory and from there, one forgettable plate of macaroni cheese later, along more walkways and corridors to the Union bar, about which the most that could be said was that the lights were low enough to disguise the full extent of its ghastliness. No wonder Mo was worried.

St John tried to convince his brother of the virtues of English ales – it had taken him several years to be convinced himself – but Paddy preferred to stick with what he knew, Guinness with a dash of cider to take the bitter edge off it.

'Let's see if we can find a table . . . Oh, look, here are five right here.'

They picked the middle one in order to subdivide the emptiness.

'Would you not think about going into the town the odd time?'

'It's supposed to be full of soldiers.'

'You should be used to that.'

'Off-duty soldiers. Twice as bad. They hate the students. They threw a fella off a bridge the other week.'

'A *bridge*?'

'That's the story.'

'So you haven't met anybody who saw it happen?'

'What, are you thinking of getting your girlfriend to do a report? Do you want to get me killed or something?'

'No, I'm only asking because, you know, stories . . . they grow legs.'

'You know what? I think I would rather not risk finding out how long its legs were to begin with.'

They took refuge from the momentary tension in the topic that had kept them going over dinner and on the trek through the concrete wastelands, the unholy trinity, Mo, Sibyl and Bea, although not in that order nor in the same proportion.

'So, what's all this about Sibyl and the nightclub?'

'Club night.'

'Right.'

'Well you know the fella who was bringing in the Levi's?'

'Wait, is this the Ray-Bans man?'

'No, no, no, the Ray-Bans man has been off the scene for ages. This fella had a contact who could get vintage 501s straight from the States.'

All the fellas Sibyl knew had contacts who could get something that everyone wanted, often before everyone knew they wanted it, and always twice the quality that you would find it elsewhere. What Sibyl's role was in their enterprises was not exactly clear. She wore the stuff around the town. She made phone calls, lots and lots of phone calls. Now some fella she knew, or some contact of his, was starting a nightclub. Club night.

'He wants to call it after her.'

'Sibyl's?'

'Sibyllism.'

'My God, she's like a cult.'

'Funny, that's what Bea said, nearly.'

'How are they getting on?'

'Same as ever.'

'I thought Bea would have moved out by now,' St John said.

'I'm not sure it's that serious, her and Craig.'

'How can it not be? It's been going on long enough.'

'I'm only going by what Bea's said to me,' Paddy said.

'And what has she said?'

'Just that it suits them both to keep things exactly as they are for now.'

'Is he still in that school?'

'The borstal, Sibyl calls it. I think that's one thing Bea wouldn't mind him changing.'

They were a couple of pints further on in this vein when two girls who had been propped up at the corner of the bar for the past half hour came over and stood in front of their table.

'We were having an argument,' the taller of them said. 'Are you two brothers?'

St John and Paddy answered as one.

'See?' said the other girl, but her friend went on undaunted.

'I told her you were gay, and you' – pointing at St John – 'were a tutor picking him up.'

The brothers leapt apart.

'Sorry, she's drunk,' the other girl said.

'I'm *Mags*, and I'm drunk.'

'I'm Shaz, and I'm not.'

'Oh, but you fucking are,' said Mags.

'This is St John,' said Paddy, 'and I'm Paddy.'

Here it was his brother's name not St John's that excited comment. 'What?' said Shaz, 'like Paddy the Irishman?'

'Only I'm actually funny,' said Paddy, but with such a disarming smile that the slap down landed like a caress. Mags dropped into the seat beside him.

'Do either of you smoke?'

St John pushed his cigarettes across the table towards her.

'No: *smoke*.'

'Mags has some fantastic grass.'

'My sister goes out with this guy, right, from Brixton . . .'

'We were smoking some last night and . . .'

'Hold on,' said Mags, pointing again at St John. 'He's not a cop or anything, is he?'

'I work in television.'

'What, like acting?'

'Not exactly.'

'The thing is,' said Paddy, 'my brother's only here for one night and we have a whole lot of stuff we need to catch up on . . .'

St John cut across him. 'Don't mind me.' He started drinking up. 'I was going to say it was time I was getting back. I've an early coach to catch in the morning.'

Shaz, though, took hold of his arm. 'Come on, the night's hardly started yet.'

His glass empty, St John allowed himself to be dragged out the door, down a corridor and out on to one of the concrete walkways. Shaz glanced back over her shoulder.

'Wow.'

'What?' He stopped and turned. Paddy and Mags were a tangle of arms and heads moving together.

'She's not usually this bad. *We're* not.'

Shaz was staring up at him. That unmistakable look, all normal rules of attraction temporarily suspended: tomorrow's tomorrow, you'll do for now.

St John was aghast. Going on the pull with his baby brother? Going back to Shaz's rooms or Mags's and . . . ?

'Do you know what?' he said. 'I really do have to be up dead, dead early.'

The look went out of Shaz's eyes. 'Didn't I make a grab for the wrong one?'

Paddy and Mags were coming along the walkway, trying for decency's sake to keep one another at arm's length. St John met them halfway. 'I should head on here.'

'Wait, well, you'll need this.' Paddy shoved his hand down the front of his shirt.

'You're not serious,' St John said.

'What?'

'You don't still keep your key down there?'

Paddy pulled out the string; evidently he still did. 'It

makes more sense than a key ring.'

Mags let out an *aw*. 'Do you see this, Shaz? Shaz?'

St John clapped Paddy's shoulders, pulled him to him. 'I am bound as your big brother,' he whispered in his ear, 'to mention the letters HIV to you.'

'We were only messing about,' said Paddy, unconvincingly. Shaz had taken hold of his other arm.

'And I'm only saying,' St John called after him.

The laughs of them as they rounded the corner out of sight . . . You did make the right decision, St John told himself. You did. No, really, you did.

The cupboard in Paddy's room yielded two grey blankets and a pancake of a pillow, marbled with mould, by way of nesting materials. The pillow went straight back in again. Instead, St John laid his head on jeans folded inside his jumper. He woke in the middle of the night, cold and aching. He raised himself on one elbow. The bed above him was empty. He climbed in. It was colder again. He was never going to get back to sleep now.

When his travel alarm went off at seven he nearly cracked his head off the headboard. He was still on his own. He washed as best he could in the tiny sink in the alcove next to the cupboard then set the key, wound round with its string, on the desk where Paddy would see it.

It was Saturday morning. What were the chances of anyone even being awake to try the door?

What was there to take if anyone was, and did?

Like all of his family, Paddy was *stuff*-poor. The door of his cassette player, which had used to be Bea's and before that St John's, was held shut by blue tape. There were two pairs of trousers on his clothes-rail, a pair of desert boots beneath them gone shiny at the toes. No coat: he had that on him when he went out last night.

St John wrote a note and slipped it under the cassette player. 'Come down and see me soon: weekend all on Trudy and me.'

The coach station was full of off-duty soldiers with hangovers and carry-outs. Partly on the assumption that it was the last place any of them would think to go, St John passed his time until his bus left in the book section of the newsagent, although bar a shelf of Mills & Boons, the stock consisted almost entirely of books about the Second World War and the SAS. He bought a postcard showing an aerial view of the open-air market, the coach station itself in the top of the frame, and addressed it to Mo. 'I think,' he wrote, and heard again the laughter echoing down the concrete walkways, 'Paddy is going to be all right.'

A couple of weeks later he received a long letter in reply explaining why Paddy had decided to quit his course and go back to Belfast, although in truth he did little more than skim it. There was another letter in the same post bearing the TV-am logo. Trudy it was who had spotted the vacancy for a PA for a new segment on home improvement.

'Didn't you tell me your mum used to be an interior designer?'

'Well, not qualified or anything, and, like, years and years ago.'

'Still, family tradition, it would be worth putting on the form.'

'If I apply.'

'Of course you'll apply.'

There was no of course about it, although finally he did, and now here was the envelope, catching his eye despite his best attempts to ignore it while he read the letter from Mo.

Fuck it. He snatched up the envelope, tore it open.

'Trudy,' he called down the hall. 'I've got an interview.'

'So, you've had two years' experience in – let's try and cast it in the best possible light – a *modest* state school. What makes you think you are suited to a position in a school with our history and reputation?'

'Well, I was fortunate enough to go to a school with a similar history and reputation,' said Craig. The expression on the face of his interrogator – the vice-principal, potential future employer, or that for now was the fiction – said that was open to question. 'What I learned was that opportunity alone is no guarantee of academic success. An inspirational teacher is as important there, or here, as in schools of more limited means. I like to think that I have already demonstrated my ability in my short time in my current post – if you look at the exam averages in every class I taught over those two years – where, to accept for the moment your characterisation of that school, it might be thought it was harder to make an impression.'

The vice-principal pursed his lips. His school, in whose boardroom they were sitting, was out along the A2 to Bangor, set in an acre and a half of woodland running down to the shore of Belfast Lough and the school's very own boathouse. Craig had arrived – by train – as instructed two hours before the interviews began. It was a Monday, half term, so he had not yet had to tell his own headmaster that he was thinking of leaving. There were five candidates in all. One – the only other man – had flown in from Hong Kong where he had been teaching in private schools for nearly thirty years. The women were all closer in age to Craig. They had tea together, stiffly, in the vice-principal's sitting room (he had a sitting room!) before being taken by him on a tour of the school. The facilities were like nothing Craig had seen at his current school, at any school he had ever been in. A full-size recording studio, a whole suite of golf-ball typewriters, three computers, four rugby pitches, on the largest of which the All Blacks had played a practice match, a fitness suite with resident physiotherapist, a swimming pool and diving pool, and the boathouse, of course ('the pupils call it the Shack,' said the vice-principal with a wry smile), for a school of only five hundred including prep. Just under a quarter of this number boarded full-time, although the school also operated a casual boarding arrangement for parents whose work took them away from home for short periods. 'Parents tell us their children are forever pestering them to be allowed to stay weekends.'

You could hardly blame them.

The candidates met the head boy and head girl – giving up a part of the holiday – in the social area of the sixth-form centre, built the year before last thanks to the generosity of a past pupil, who preferred to remain anonymous. (It said much for the achievements of alumni that there were at least a dozen names put forward in the press as possible donors.) That meeting was almost an interview in itself. 'You can tell pretty quickly if someone is going to "get" the school,' the head girl said, to which the boy added, 'Teachers as well as pupils.'

Craig had been so well prepared he had even managed a full night's sleep, but with every minute that passed in the company of these two impossibly poised teens his confidence leached. He was second last into the boardroom.

Besides the vice-principal the panel was made up of two members of the board of governors, one a retired judge, his name if not his face familiar to Craig from high-profile terrorist trials in the early Seventies, as well as the head of the history department, whose contribution so far had been limited to tuts, sighs and a single but eloquent 'Ha!'

'You're not married?' the judge asked now.

'I didn't think it was one of the requirements.'

'I have found in the past that marriage grounds a young man. Of course that is just my opinion.'

'It's an interesting one, certainly.'

(A sigh from the head of history.)

'And how,' chipped in the other governor, 'would you feel about being, by some distance, the youngest member of the department?'

'It would be a very poor teacher indeed who was unable to learn from a more senior colleague.' Craig had realised after about two weeks in his current school that he was going to learn nothing. The vast majority of the teachers were putting in the terms until they could get the fuck out and work on their gardens. 'And a very poor teacher who wasn't open to new ideas from a more junior one.'

'That's a smart answer.'

'I didn't say it to be smart.'

'Which is an even smarter one.'

Stuff him. This had been going on for a quarter of an

hour already. Craig had given up on the job after the first five minutes, couldn't think why they had ever called him for interview, unless as a rebuke for getting ahead of himself. Seriously, stuff the whole lot of them.

The vice-principal was loosening his lips in readiness for re-entry. 'We encourage all our teachers to take an active part in sports. Your CV is a bit thin in that regard.'

'I play darts.'

He didn't.

'I don't believe we have ever had a darts team.'

'Calls for mental as well as physical agility. How many of you could calculate the checkout from one hundred and three in a matter of seconds?'

The judge made a note of that! He should have tried them with shove-halfpenny.

The vice-principal looked to his right and left. 'Any more questions anyone would like to ask?' To the right and the left heads were shaken. 'Very well, unless you have any questions you would like to ask us . . . No? I think that will be all, then, thank you for your time today.'

The final candidate, a woman who had almost made a point of not talking to him or anyone else on the tour of the school (was she afraid they were going to steal her ideas?), looked up as he came out into the waiting area. She had the school prospectus open on her lap, file cards arranged on top with lines highlighted in yellow, pink and electric blue. The strain of the moment was etched around her eyes and mouth . . . to speak or not speak?

'How did it go?' she managed finally, brittly.

'Oh, it's in the bag,' Craig said and her face fell. 'Joke.'

Her face recovered, a little.

He got off the train in Central Station and went straight to the cinema on the Dublin Road in hopes of wiping the whole experience from his mind. (Would that there was something that could have erased Meryl Streep's black wig and strangled Australian accent from his mind.) It was near nine before he got home. Two messages on the answer machine: first Bea wanting to know how he had got on, then – he had wandered into the kitchen and was filling the kettle so could not for a minute place the voice – the retired judge from the interview panel. He switched off the tap just as the message was ending. He went back into the front room and pressed play again. Bea asked him a second time how he had got on. Then the retired judge spoke. Excellent interview, good all-round attitude, head boy and girl as one that he – and only he of the five candidates – 'got' the school, trusting he would be as glad to accept as the panel was to offer him the post . . .

The first thing he did was look up restaurant '44' in the Yellow Pages and book a table, the second was phone Bea. 'Dinner, eight o'clock tomorrow night,' he said as soon as she came on the line. 'Oh, and wear your glad rags . . . Did I get it? I don't know how, but yes, I did. I got it.'

He rang his parents to give them the good news and arrange to take them out for lunch the following Sunday then he sat down with his own copy of the prospectus and allowed his imagination to infiltrate him into its scenes of academic and sporting endeavour.

He sat up in bed at three in the morning, wide awake on the instant. 'This isn't what I want at all,' he said into the darkness.

The vice-principal, needless to say, could not believe, when Craig phoned at nine o'clock sharp, that he was turning it down. The chance of a lifetime . . . Highly unlikely that any future application . . .

'Believe me,' Craig said, 'there won't be any future applications.'

Bea too was baffled.

He had decided not to cancel the restaurant booking, nor countermand the glad-rags directive (nobody did glad rags like the Nimmo women), only modify the toast with which they began the evening seated at the '44' bar.

'Here's to knowing when you're well off.'

'I don't understand.'

'I'm not accepting. It would have been a betrayal.'

'Of what?'

Harrison, he wanted to say. 'The fees for that school are higher than the average industrial wage. It would have been completely out of reach of my parents, of everybody's parents that I knew growing up.'

'You went to a school that was out of reach to most of the people you grew up with because of the qualifying exam.'

'At least the qualifying exam leaves the door slightly ajar . . . Anyway, I'm not talking about where I went to, I'm talking about where I am, where I'm staying.'

He liked Bea well enough – loved her – but he wondered at moments what they were doing together. No matter what position he adopted she seemed almost compelled to adopt its opposite, even if that was the opposite of something else he remembered her having said, a month, a week, ten minutes ago.

She had concluded midway through her degree that English was a dead-end, from which point on her sole goal had been to get the highest grade possible to take with her to a law conversion course, which would enable her one day to argue to her heart's content. She got a first: the conversion to professional arguer was continuing apace.

She took a drink belatedly – 'To knowing when you're well off' – swallowing with it whatever it was that she had been on the point of saying to perpetuate this particular argument, although the ghost of the disagreement hovered around them as they were shown to their table by the curtained front windows.

'I've got some news too,' she said after several sullen mouthfuls of her first course. Craig braced himself. 'St John's going to be a dad.'

'But that's . . . Wow . . . With Trudy?'

'Of course with Trudy, who else?'

'When?'

'Start of the year.'

'And is he, were they, I mean, planning it, or was it . . . ?'

'I'm so glad it wasn't me telling you I was pregnant.' She pushed back her chair and tossed the napkin on the table. 'Excuse me.'

Craig was sitting with his back to the room so he couldn't tell for sure when she got up that she had gone to the toilets and not walked out altogether. A minute passed, two minutes . . . five in total. She sat down again in front of him.

'I was nearly getting my coat there.'

'I was worried that you might be.'

'But not so worried that you would come after me, or stop

215

eating.' She flicked a fingernail off his plate, emptied of its starter in the time that she had been away.

'I was building up my energy in case I had to run to catch you.'

'Funny man.'

He lifted the bottle from the ice bucket, tilted the neck towards her glass. She nodded: *oh, all right then, go ahead.* They let the rims of their glasses touch again, preferring to look at them now rather than into one another's eyes. Seven years' bad sex . . . ? They'd take the chance.

It occurred to Craig that they had arrived almost without their realising or expecting it at the moment when they had to go one way or the other. The next thing either of them said could be decisive so of course for a minute or two neither wanted to take responsibility, or perhaps it was just that neither was entirely sure which way they did want to go. Each made a performance of swirling and smelling and finally swallowing the wine.

The waiter came and stood by the table. 'All finished?'

Bea made a gesture of surrender towards her half-eaten starter. 'Thank you.'

At least it was speech. Craig held his tongue until the waiter had gone.

'What would you think of it?' he asked then. Bea did her best I-don't-follow face, but he could tell she knew fine well what he was talking about. 'A baby.'

She shook her head, smiling: *so that's what you meant.* He topped up both their glasses.

'I'm not saying right away, some day. Because, if it was something you wanted, I would' – the conviction was growing as the sentence formed – 'love it, actually.'

He felt a little light-headed but at the same time absolutely grounded. He *would* love it. She had stopped smiling, stopped play-acting altogether. Don't rush her. Even saying the words is an enormous commitment. The waiter returned with their main courses.

'The salmon for Madam . . . and for Sir the duck. Your vegetables are coming. Will there be anything else?'

'I don't think so,' Bea said and the waiter left, but it was Craig she was looking at. He nodded. Fair enough.

They finished their meal and went back to his house. They made love her preferred way and fell asleep in one another's arms, but from that dinner on they were teetering on the brink.

*

Maxine had not told a living soul about the threat at the bus stop, reasoning that by going to the police she would only be bringing more trouble on her family and giving that scumbag – who would walk away from any charge, guaranteed: her word against his – the satisfaction of thinking he had got to her.

All the same when, a few months later, her mother announced (for widowhood had turned her into a woman who announced) that she was moving to Bangor, where she had grown up, Maxine was secretly relieved. Maxine had only a fortnight before agreed a house-share with two of the girls from work, but at the last minute one of them got cold feet and the whole thing fell through. She accepted the invitation to move in with her mother for the first couple of months in Bangor: help her adjust, she told Victor. She told *herself* she was not running away, for there would be no hiding, even if she had sought it, in Bangor. The town had changed beyond all recognition from when her grandparents were alive and she had visited every second Sunday. Then every one of the eleven miles between Belfast and there had had the weight of ten. You felt when you reached the end of them as though you had arrived somewhere truly other. Her grandparents were working people, living in a two-up two-down with a toilet in the yard, but walk half a minute from their front door and you were standing on the seafront, with its ornamental gardens, its putting green and curious clocktower, around whose base teenage boys and girls, dressed for the effect and never the weather, sat eating chips, giving one another the eye.

Now there were acres of retail park to pass through, housing estates like her own with their familiar flags and murals, their *Touts will be shot*, before you caught so much as a glimpse of that old Bangor. The house her mother found was halfway along a sloping street that began at one of the sequence of roundabouts whose only purpose seemed to be to deter the casual visitor and ended several twists and turns later at the sea wall.

It was a better arrangement than either she or her mother had a right to hope. They went for walks a couple of evenings a week along the seafront, past the chippies and amusement arcades that Maxine remembered so well, to the quieter beaches of Ballyholme, stopping on the way home for ice cream or occasionally a drink in the lounge of the

Marine Court Hotel. Sometimes Maxine would wake in the early hours and go out again by herself. (Her mother took a sleeping pill most nights and once her head was down rarely roused.) She couldn't say why – the local newspaper reports reinforced the impression given by the murals and flags on the approach to the town that there was no shortage of trouble to be found at chucking-out time and long into the night – but she had the feeling that nothing bad could happen to her here, while the ropes tinged against the masts of the boats in the old harbour, keeping time with a rhythm dictated from hundreds of thousands of miles away.

On one such night, it was a Friday, about a year after the move (because, really, the arrangement had turned out very, very well), she was passing a small car park close to the clock, its hands joined at ten past two, when a sporty-looking white car lurched towards the exit then stalled, started up, lurched, stalled again. Anywhere but Bangor seafront she would have kept walking, fast, instead she turned, waited to see what would happen next. The driver's window came down jerkily. A woman's head appeared. Blonde, late thirties at a guess.

'Do you think you could give me a push?'

'You've flooded the engine.'

A look at the grille told her it was a Mazda. They were notorious for it.

'That's impossible,' the woman said.

'No, it just means there's too much petrol in it.'

'What do I do?'

Maxine was already walking towards her. 'Don't rev it.' She revved it. Maxine shouted, 'That only makes it worse!'

She smelt the drink off her before she arrived at the open window. A half-empty Bacardi bottle lay in the passenger-side footwell.

'Here,' Maxine said. 'Why don't you let me try?'

She reached in through the window and turned off the ignition. The woman stared at her, holding on to the steering wheel a few moments longer then, facing forward, let go – of the wheel, of everything – her hands in springing back making a sound like a sigh. 'Fucker,' she said, of whom Maxine could only guess, though for reasons that were all too easy to imagine.

Maxine waited until the woman had dragged herself over the handbrake and into the passenger seat before opening the door. She settled herself behind the wheel, moving the seat back a couple of inches, hoping that some of the too-rich fuel would in the meantime evaporate. She let out the clutch and pressed down gently on the accelerator. Did it again. At the third attempt she got the thing going. She let the engine run a while in neutral to make sure that it had definitely caught.

'Now, where are we going?' she asked.

The woman was looking out the other window. 'Culloden Hotel.'

'Are you a resident?'

'Not yet.'

'It's after two.'

'So?'

'They'll never let you check in at this time. Is there nowhere else you can go?'

The woman turned to her finally. 'Get out of my car.'

'You're in no state to drive.'

'Who are you to tell me what I can do?'

'It isn't safe.'

She's going to hit me, Maxine thought, a split second before the woman's hand made a grab for her face. Maxine ducked and the knuckles of the flailing hand caught the rear-view mirror. The woman fell across her lap, sobbing.

'Fucker,' she said again.

Maxine helped her to sit straight. 'Look, I'll get out of the car,' she said, 'but promise me you won't try to drive it until the morning.'

'All right.' The woman was nursing her hand. Maxine opened the door. 'Wait,' said the woman, soberer. 'Don't leave me here.'

Maxine closed the door again. *How in all conscience could I?* 'If you wanted, you could come back with me to my mum's house. It's only round the corner and up the hill a bit.'

The woman sucked her knuckle then, 'OK,' she said.

'It's Maxine, by the way.'

'Right. Gerry.'

A bunch of clubbers appeared out of a side street as they drove along the front, weird day-glo get-ups that seemed to pulse in the middle of the road until Maxine turned the car left and began to climb the two hundred yards to her mother's front gate.

'Here we are.'

Gerry looked at the house, its twin hanging baskets. 'Nice.'

'She's widowed,' Maxine said by way of explanation or apology, she wasn't sure which.

The light was on in the covered porch. Gerry stumbled a couple of times on the gravel path that led to it. Maxine settled her against the meter box (the 'Milk Today' sign on top was set to one pint) while she patted her pockets for the key.

'I'm not an alco, you know.'

Maxine did not reply.

'Did you hear me?'

'Yes' – there it was, back left – 'I was just looking for this.'

'As long as you know.'

In the hallway, for the first time, Maxine wondered where she would put her. She couldn't risk the lounge – imagine her being sick on the sofa! – and the box room was still full of (what else?) boxes. Her room, it would have to be. She would talk to her mother in the morning, explain everything.

'Would you mind taking your shoes off?'

'Shoes.' Gerry toed each heel in turn and handed the shoes over like contraband. Bally, cork wedges. Without them she stood a good three inches shorter.

For some reason, she chose that moment to smile. When Maxine turned to lead the way upstairs, Gerry hooked two fingers in her back belt loops leaning her head between Maxine's shoulders to stifle her giggles.

'Please,' Maxine said as loudly as she dared. There were limits she was sure to what even a sleeping pill could blot out. 'No messing.'

'No messing,' came the echo from behind.

Her bedroom fortunately was at the very top of the stairs, to the right of the bathroom.

'Do you need the toilet?'

'It's OK, I went back there.'

The car park? Wherever she had driven from to get to the car park?

Maxine walked round to the far side of the bed and switched on the lamp.

'Aw,' said Gerry. 'Sweet room.'

'I worry it's a bit sickly sweet,' she said even though she had helped her mother shop for the Laura Ashley curtains and bedspread. Why was she talking like this?

She crossed to the wardrobe where the spare bedding was kept, took from it a tartan blanket, a pillow, a crocheted throw. When she turned back Gerry was already in the bed. Her eyes were shut, or seemed to be. Maxine walked round to the far side of the bed again to switch out the light. In the space between the bed and the wall, Gerry's clothes were a dark puddle with a pair of pink briefs floating on top. She reached for the switch.

'Get in,' Gerry said. Her eyes didn't flicker.

'I'm OK.'

'Don't be daft.'

She remembered, as she began to unbutton her jeans, many years ago in another bedroom, Heather Nixon watching her dress, making it Maxine's problem, not hers . . . She normally wore pyjamas here, but in the circumstances that would have felt like a rebuke. She cast off her bra and knickers, got under the covers and turned her back. After a few minutes Gerry's hand flopped across her hip. Maxine shifted. The hand shifted with her. She was on the very edge of the bed now, nowhere left to go, so that was how they slept, the two of them, the first night of their acquaintance, that was how Maxine woke in the morning, ejected so violently from the dream she had been having that not a single detail of it survived.

The clock was behind her, obscured by the mountain range of her unexpected guest. Who was lightly snoring. She lay for a while trying to work out the time from the sounds inside the house and out: kettle being filled at the kitchen tap, shutter going up on the car-repair shop further along the street. After eight anyway. Gently, fingertip by fingertip, she uncoupled herself. The spot where the heel of Gerry's hand had lain burned like a brand. The warmth between her legs she dismissed as a morning thing, a memento of the world from which in waking she had been banished.

Her mother was coming in from the porch when she arrived at the foot of the stairs. She had her coat on, her handbag over her arm, ready for town (well after eight then), and in her other arm three bottles of milk.

'That stupid man left us three pints.'

'That might have been me. I brushed against the basket on the fuse box. I might have knocked the wee arrow.'

'Even so, over eleven months I've been here. When did I ever take three pints?'

Maxine followed her into the kitchen.

'Mum . . .'

Her mother closed the fridge. 'Do you know there's a car parked right across our gate?'

'That's what I was going to say . . .' What? What was she going to say? Another minute and her mother would be gone up the town. 'A friend called, after you went to bed, asked me could she leave it.'

'That's strange.'

There was a creak above their heads.

'I think she'd maybe had a drink,' said Maxine, covering.

Her mother nodded at this: sensible girl. She tore a page from the pad attached to the fridge by a pair of magnetised teddy bears. 'It's nice you making friends. You never know, you might decide to stay permanently.'

'You never know.'

Maxine watched her down the path and up the hill towards the roundabout then went – actually, ran – back inside and boiled the kettle.

As Maxine came into the bedroom Gerry's eyes finally opened.

'Oh, dear God,' she said, a face on her like she had been kidnapped.

Maxine set the mugs on the chest of drawers and sat at the foot of the bed, all feelings of pleasant confusion dispelled on the instant.

'You were in your car, down by the front. You couldn't get it started. Do you remember?' Gerry nodded slowly: she didn't remember at all. She had retreated into a corner of the bed, knees up defensively, covers pulled tight around her. 'You're still in Bangor. I drove you here – it was way after two. You took off your own clothes.'

She scooped up the puddle from the floor and tipped it on the bedspread. She grabbed a few bits of her own from the drawers. Gerry's nose and mouth appeared above her knees.

'And what were you doing out there at way after two?'

Maxine stopped short of the door. 'Going for a walk.'

'By yourself?'

She started to explain and then thought, wait a minute: my fucking house, why am I the one making excuses?

'I have to go out in a few minutes,' she said. 'I'll see you downstairs.'

She dressed on the landing and had barely sat down at the little table in the kitchen when Gerry appeared still doing up the buttons of her blouse. She had wiped off most of last night's make-up. She looked better without it, younger.

'I'm sorry,' she said. 'It's all come back to me. Or most of it . . . Maxine, isn't it?'

'Very good.'

Gerry gave herself a silent cheer, knocking another couple of years off Maxine's initial estimate.

'I hope I haven't kept you back.'

'Sorry?'

'Going out.'

The silent cheer had knocked a bit of the flintiness off Maxine's resolve too. 'Oh, no, I was only . . .'

'Not work then?'

'A rare Saturday morning off.'

'Poor you, having to work Saturday mornings,' Gerry said, without a trace of sympathy, and like that Maxine's flintiness was back.

'What about you? Where are you going to go now.'

Gerry thought, or pretended to. 'Home, I suppose.'

'That would be to the "fucker"?'

She might not have remembered saying it aloud, but the sudden flush said she remembered thinking it all right. 'It's

226

all a bit complicated.'

Maxine didn't want her to imagine she could get away with it that easy. 'Life's like that.'

'They don't teach you that at school,' Gerry said.

'No, but you learn it there all the same.'

'Isn't that the truth?' Gerry leaned out to this side then to that putting on her shoes and bringing her back, almost, to Maxine's level.

'Well . . .'

Maxine for some reason offered her hand. Gerry looked at it a moment then slipped hers inside it, the hand that had rested all night on Maxine's hip.

They both laughed, made great play of pumping one another's arms, old-codger style, because what else had they sounded like just now?

'You know where I live,' Maxine said. 'For the time being anyway.'

'Here's hoping I remember where I do.'

The car started first time, glided from the kerb.

Maxine's mother came back half an hour later, carrier bags full of the fresh vegetables that between now and next Saturday, in the tradition of Belfast mothers of her generation brought up to distrust food, she would boil to mushes distinguishable only by colour.

'Your friend came for her car, I see. Did you not think of asking her in?'

'She was in a bit of a rush.'

'She's not the only one. You want to see that town up there, it's as bad as Belfast getting.'

'Will I make you tea?' Maxine asked.

'Do you know, I'd love a cup.'

They sat at the table for two with their tea and the *Radio* and *TV Times*. The sun came out, finding the gap between the houses one street over that gave it access to their garden, with its bird table and bird bath and plastic drinks bottles upturned in the flowerbeds to deter next-door's cat.

Little by little, over a period of minutes it seemed to Maxine, for whom it eventually became a distraction, a smile spread from the corners of her mother's mouth into every last crevasse of her face. She felt the need in the end to ask if everything was all right. Her mother brought the smile to heel, set her magazine on the table.

'It's the strangest thing. There are days when I can feel your daddy about the place, even though I know he never actually *was* about this place. It's as if we brought him with us, or he followed us here. Like this morning, when I got up ... I couldn't shake it. There was a definite sense of someone here with us, just on the other side of the door from me.'

'Do you want a warmer in that?'

A letter arrived, first post, middle of the following week, addressed to Maxine 'Walker'.

'That's funny,' her mother said, more worried than amused.

'An in-joke,' said Maxine, who had already opened the letter and started to read it now as she walked up the stairs to her room. *Dear Maxine, about the other night* . . .

It was as light an expression of contrition as was ever committed to paper. (Fountain pen, Maxine noted, as she had noted the weight of the paper itself, the quality of the envelope it came in.) These things happened was the gist.

Still and all she was grateful that, of all the people who might have been, it was Maxine who was passing – not at all weirdly (underlined) – by herself (double-underlined) – when this particular thing had happened to her. Maybe the next time Maxine had one of those rare Saturday mornings off – when would that be, next year, the year after? – the two of them could meet for a natter.

It was little more than seventy-two hours later when Maxine walked in the door of the Skandia Restaurant on Main Street. Correction, it was seventy-seven and three-quarters: one forty-five. She had come straight from the train. Free mornings were a rarity, but as she explained when she wrote back to accept, the showroom and all its offices closed their doors at one o'clock sharp every Saturday afternoon.

Gerry stood up as Maxine approached the table. 'I still wasn't sure you would come.'

'I think you fancy you're a lot scarier than you are.'

Gerry's smile was constrained, although that might have been to do with the amount of lipstick it had to contend with. She had the full make-up on again. Maxine tried to hold on to the image of her without it.

A swish of a polyester tunic and a click of a ballpoint pen announced the arrival of a waitress at Maxine's shoulder.

'They do a very good open sandwich.' Gerry slid a menu to Maxine, who slid it straight back. 'Actually, I'm fine with just coffee.'

'Two coffees,' Gerry said, sounding disappointed.

'Please, don't let me stop you.'

'Oh, go ahead then, a prawn open sandwich too.'

The waitress held the pad close to her face as she wrote, clicked the ballpoint pen again, and swished off towards the orders hatch. They both watched her go.

'Did you ever waitress?' Gerry asked.

'No. You?'

'When I was at school. Hated every minute of it.' She kept her head turned towards the hatch, away from Maxine. 'Do you like where you are at the minute?'

'You mean work? It has its moments, I suppose, good and bad.'

'A lot of responsibility?'

'You'd always like a bit more, wouldn't you?'

'You might be surprised to hear it, but not everyone would, no.' She had faced round again. 'I have been thinking a lot of things through since last Saturday. I'm going to be on the lookout soon for someone to come and work with me, someone I can trust.'

'You're kidding me, right?'

'I'm not kidding you at all. I'll start you on a thousand more than you're getting now.'

A woman stopped in the street directly outside the window to skelp the back of her daughter's bare legs. She swiped more air than flesh, though that didn't stop the wee girl shrieking, arching to get out of the way. Gerry shuddered. The child wiped her nose with the back of her hand. The coffees came.

'Your sandwich will not be a minute,' the waitress said.

'Do you know, I've changed my mind again.'

'But it's ordered.' The girl showed her the pad: *there*.

'Well cancel it.'

'The cook has the prawns and all put on it . . .'

'I'll pay you for it, here' – a ten-pound note on the table – 'take for the coffees too.'

'Oh, but . . .' Maxine reached for her purse. Gerry stopped her. The girl put the tenner in the front pocket of her apron, shaking her head.

'I know what you're thinking,' said Gerry when she had gone. 'Why would I want to work for that flake?'

'I'm not.'

'So you will?'

'Well . . .'

'Give it some thought at least.'

Maxine sipped her coffee. 'All right.'

They said goodbye at Gerry's car, parked facing oncoming traffic about fifty yards from the restaurant. Maxine had gone about fifty yards farther when she turned and ran back. Gerry was still waiting for a gap to pull out into.

Maxine rapped the passenger window. 'I've given it some thought,' she said. 'I will.'

'Oh, good.'

'What is it you do?'

*

St John was travelling back from a recce in Solihull when Shelly arrived, three weeks premature. So when, barely thirteen months later, Trudy went into labour again he made damned sure he was with her every managed contraction of the way. A little boy. St John held him, mesmerised. 'Can you believe it?' Trudy was too busy weeping to speak.

She had talked about Oscar, but St John, who knew all too well the unwanted attention that a name could attract, favoured James. He said it now, looking down at the baby's worried face, while behind him the nurses stitched and swabbed, and it being the first name ever spoken in his presence James his son was ever after.

He took a week's annual leave and on the third day of it drove out to Heathrow, Shelly asleep in the back most of the way, to collect Mo.

They would need the extra pair of hands, she had said. 'One's a pet, but two's a zoo.'

It was like that with mothers, only with teeth, said Trudy, who insisted on packing her own mother back off home to Bristol before St John's arrived.

His heart, when he saw her walk through the door into Arrivals, shrank. His first thought was that she had done something to her hair — backcombed it possibly — in a hideous attempt to appear youthful. But, no, it wasn't that at all. 'Those *pinheads* in the Special Branch, kept us queued out on the tarmac in the driving wind like a bunch of refugees while they went through everyone's papers, children and everything. Because of course we're *all* bombers to them.' This delivered in a near shout as she strode through the terminal pushing the stroller that she had taken from St John in exchange for her cases. They were almost out the doors when she stopped and crouched down in front of her granddaughter.

'She's the image of Sibyl when she was that age.'

'Everyone here thinks she's got very like Trudy this last while.'

Mo undid the straps. The child put out her arms, not at all strange. It was the hair she went for first, trying to touch it, or tame it. 'No,' said Mo, 'her mouth and everything: definitely Sibyl.'

Which St John thought could be a mixed blessing.

Bea had been filling him in on recent goings-on. (Things were a lot less frosty on that front since the break-up with Craig.) The club night had turned into what St John had always mistaken it for, an actual nightclub, with premises down at the bottom of Corporation Street, if he knew where that was. St John remembered it principally from its frequent occurrences in news bulletins throughout his teens.

'But I mean she's – what? – twenty-nine coming?' St John said. 'I thought that was just kids.'

He and Trudy had knocked all that on the head during her first pregnancy, but even before then he had started to feel ancient whenever they were out up the town. Besides, it wasn't called TV-*am* for nothing.

'No, there's all sorts involved,' said Bea. 'That's what's worrying me. It's not just a music thing. And now she has Paddy doing stuff for her too.'

'What sort of stuff?'

'Designing flyers.'

'I didn't know he could.'

'I don't think Paddy did.'

'I think Paddy might be gay,' Mo said as they slipped into the traffic headed eastward on the M4.

'*What?*'

'I have always thought it, to be honest.'

She had Shelly out of the car seat and sitting on her lap

with the lift-the-flap book she had brought her. Trudy would have a fit if she could see them, although St John remembered a trip once to Dublin Zoo – three, maybe four summers before his father left – most of which Paddy had spent on Mo's knee, when he wasn't trying to clamber over the handbrake to get in the back with his big brother and sisters.

He remembered the night he visited Paddy at his university halls.

'I don't know how to tell you this . . .'

'You're going to say girls,' Mo interrupted. 'They're all over him. That doesn't count for anything.'

'Doesn't it?'

'You forget, back in the Fifties, even the Sixties, it was very hard for people to come out, especially in Belfast. Nearly all the men I knew who were gay went with girls. Some of them, I don't think, ever went with a man at all.'

'Which makes them straight.'

Mo's eyes and his met in the rear-view mirror.

'You don't really believe that, do you?'

They drove on in a silence broken only by baas and moos from Shelly as she turned the hardboard pages.

He opened the door of the apartment rather than ring the bell and risk disturbing Trudy and the baby. They, though, were coming from the main bedroom into the hall, bringing with them the warm milky smell that bound them from the day's beginning to its end.

'Just awake!' Trudy said and, not without hesitation, surrendered her son to his grandmother's outstretched arms.

'Little scrap,' Mo said, and from her tone you would

have thought this was a baby that had been lucky to hang on until she got here, rather than one who had weighed in at close to ten pounds and had wasted no time in adding to them.

'She outed my brother in the car,' St John whispered as he passed Trudy with the bags and Trudy almost bounded into the sitting room before Mo could make any thirteenth-fairy pronouncements on James.

In fact, she was great with him and managed too to include Shelly in the fuss she made: wasn't she a clever girl, finding herself such a beautiful baby brother?

Again, watching her, St John was assailed by a memory, long submerged. Another trip to Dublin, before Paddy was born, Bea not out of nappies, stopping by the side of the road for tea and sandwiches, Mo beating down the tall grass to clear a place for him to pee, his father's voice carrying as it rhymed off for Sibyl the towns they still had to pass through: Laytown, Balbriggan, Skerries, Rush, Swords . . . Mo's hand in his hair (she was doing it now with Shelly) as he squeezed out the last of the piddle, *good boy*, *good boy*. Back in the car then, sitting forward, arms around the back of her seat, drowsing while she kept up a constant flow of chat and song, through Laytown, Balbriggan, Skerries, Rush, Swords . . . inexhaustible.

'You would nearly think she had done this before,' he said to Trudy as she sat with him in an armchair a couple of nights later, content now to listen to the sounds of splashing from the bathroom.

Later still, lying in bed, neither of them able to sleep for wondering at the basket in the corner, their baby's near miraculous self-containment, Trudy asked him why he thought his mother had never found anyone else.

'It wasn't for want of looking,' St John was about to say, but 'There were boyfriends, all right,' he said instead, 'more than a few, the first lot of years especially. She was still young, I suppose. You don't recognise it when it's your parents, when you're the age I was then, but she couldn't have been more than six or seven years older than Sibyl is. Some of them were OK, you know, the boyfriends, could talk to you like human beings. Some of the others would take one look at the four of us kids and you'd see the panic in their eyes. One or two of them mind you, would look at Sibyl and you could see the panic in Mo's.'

Trudy gave a grunt: miraculous self-containment or not, she was gone.

St John though, despite his exhaustion, was still awake long afterwards. Not much over thirty-five, beautiful beyond even a child's partial reckoning . . . Why hadn't she found someone after all?

'You never divorced him, did you?'

The following morning, breakfast cleared away, a second pot of coffee just coming to the boil on the stove.

Trudy had James out for his first taste of city air. Mo was on the floor, where she had been helping Shelly fit together the two parts of a duck jigsaw – 'The other way, see, like this . . .' St John was sitting with one elbow on the table, one on the back of the chair.

Mo looked up at him, an additional tilt to her head such as he had seen her affect in the presence of teachers or functionaries of any stripe unwise enough to turn up on the doorstep. Almost at once, though, she relented.

'No, I never did.'

'He couldn't have contested it. It was desertion, clear-cut.'
Shelly clapped her hands: the duck was done. 'And it would
have made it easier for you, if ever you had, you know . . .'

'Met a man I wanted to marry? There was a woman used
to come into the War on Want shop had a great saying: "If
they cheat with you they'll cheat on you," which ruled out
more or less every man that came after your father.'

'Like Dr Lennox.' Another memory resurfaced: bobbed
up and out before he had the gumption to button his lip.

'Dr Lennox?' Mo tilted her head again. Kept it that way.
The lid of the coffee pot rattled. Hallelujah.

'I'm sorry, it's not my business,' St John said and went to
the stove. 'Milk in this?'

He could feel her eyes on him as he stirred. Please just let
it drop. Please, please, please . . . She didn't.

'I don't know what you're talking about.'

He put down the spoon and turned around. 'I shouldn't
have said it, but, look, I know what I saw. He came out of
the house one day. You were in there in your dressing gown.
I'd talked to you on the landing, there was someone in the
bedroom. I'm not stupid.'

Which was probably the stupidest thing he ever said to
her. Mo looked at him a moment or two longer. 'He helped
me out with something once,' she said. 'Now' – to Shelly –
'what does the duck say?'

'Quack,' said Shelly. 'Quack, quack, quack.'

*

The half-term interview date notwithstanding Craig's head-master – the 'Chief' – had got to hear of Craig's planned defection and his decision ultimately to reject it.

'Many would say you were a fool to refuse, though thank God you did,' he said.

The next year, after Mrs Fielding crocked her knee coming down the assembly-hall stairs, he made Craig acting head of the department of five history teachers. When Mrs Fielding returned three months later – slower, older, somehow, by a good ten years – the Chief let it be known that he wanted the current, temporary arrangement to continue for another term, then another. By the following September Mrs Fielding was gone altogether.

One of the first things Craig did, in consultation with the Chief himself, was strongly discourage (he would have preferred 'ban', but the Chief strongly discouraged him from styling it as such) the practice of a teacher standing with his back to the class for an entire period, writing screeds and screeds on the roller board for pupils to copy, or just as frequently fail to finish copying before the board was pushed up and screeds more were written: whole eras flashing un-interrogated – unintelligible – in front of their eyes.

Teachers, he said at the meeting in his room to discuss the changes, ought to engage the pupils.

'We do engage them,' Wilson was first to protest, as it might have been predicted from his nickname – 'Chalkie' – that he would be.

'We engage their arms, not their imaginations.'

'Oh for God sake,' Wilson said. 'They don't want us anywhere near their imaginations. That's the deal. You'll have the mas and das down on you if you go mucking around in there.'

'Well, actually, I've told the Chief I want to hold an open night for the parents, let them know what we're planning on doing.'

'A fiver says you don't get more than ten of them.'

There were nearly four hundred pupils doing history across the school's five years, so eight hundred parents give or take.

He got eleven. He had deliberately not set out chairs, but left them folded against the wall to be opened as required so that no matter how many, or how few, did weigh in there wouldn't be an empty seat to be seen.

He talked in the main about Robert Shipboy McAdam. Did any among them know the name? The shrugs, the glances at the ground between their feet told him no. Not to worry, not many people did know him, but once upon a not so very long ago he had been a big name in the city, had a foundry on Townsend Street, a Presbyterian and an Irish speaker, if they could imagine that, commissioned a floral tribute on the occasion of Queen Victoria's visit to Belfast – *Erin go Bragh* spelt out in dahlias, or misspelt as it turned out. Still it's the thought that counts, isn't that what they say? (And, no, don't ask him what *that* was in Irish.) They weren't looking at the ground now, his eleven parents, they were looking straight at him. History, he told them, taught us that we were a more interesting and varied bunch than the newspaper headlines might lead people to believe. With their permission, and without neglecting the curriculum, he would like to take their children on a journey to help them discover how they had become who they were and to take pride in where they were from.

What do you say?

Yes, they said in concert, with our permission, please, do it.

'The caretaker says he only counted nine,' Wilson said at break the next day and Knowles ('Know Less'), who taught science, said, well, the Chief needn't be expecting them all to offer nights like that now unless he could afford the over-time.

'Overtime?' said Wilson. 'What's overtime?'

Craig left them at it. He had a field trip for his fifth years to arrange, into town for lunch in the coffee shop of Anderson & McAuley's. The pupils themselves laughed in his face when he told them. 'We're going to a department store? No harm to you, Sir, but are you right in the head?'

'Perfectly. It wasn't always a department store. Started life as the family home of Sir Stephen May, Collector of Customs for the town of Belfast and the third May in only twenty-five years to be elected Lord Mayor. He would have pulled back his curtains on his first morning there – sorry, his curtain-puller would have pulled them back – on to a view of the old castle walls. The present building was com-pleted in 1899 by a Mr Young and a Mr McKenzie, the same architects who had just finished Robinson & Cleaver's at the far end of the street . . . Now, you have a week to come up with as many interesting facts of your own as you can muster. But, remember, don't just look in books. Ask your mum and dads, your grannies and granddads, listen to what they have to say.'

They brought with them to the coffee shop stories of

Christmas Clubs and tick books ('You wouldn't have got tick off of Robinson & Cleaver's'), of two yards of lace bought in the haberdashery the year before the war began to turn a hand-me-down into a wedding dress that everyone who was there agreed looked as though it had cost thirty or forty guineas, of the fella who had put the windows in one night when times were really, really hard so the police would arrest him and at least give him his dinner.

And over chips and Coke he gave them more on the Collector of Customs and how his family, the Mays, had come to hold such sway in the town. A familiar Georgian tale of debtors' prisons and bastardy, and, yes that was the correct word.

'Can we go to the Co next time, sir?'

'No, no, the Chalet d'Or.'

'We'll toss a coin for it and whichever one loses we'll go to the time after that again.'

There had been about half a dozen such outings, the last two with the active participation of Wilson and the other history teachers, by the time – one pig of a late winter's evening – he slipped out of the little side gate he always used at home time and noticed a man leaning forward over the wheel of a blue Ford Ghia peering at him through the rain running down the windscreen. Craig had an instant, eerie sense of familiarity, as though the same car with the same man in it had sat in the exact same spot once (many times?) before. As Craig drew level the man opened the driver's door and levered himself up, burly in his tweed car-coat.

'Excuse me,' he said, and Craig's instinct despite the unthreatening tone was to quicken his step. 'Craig, isn't it? I think you know my wife. Ros?'

Craig stopped, turned, blinking rain off his eyelashes. Well that accounted for the eerie familiarity.

'Barry Kerr,' the man said, a split second after Craig had worked it out. 'Sorry, I know it looks a bit odd, hanging around the school gates. That's me trying to be discreet. Do you want to get in? I can run you home.'

'It's no distance, really.'

'Do you want to get in anyway? I'd appreciate a couple of minutes of your time,' Barry Kerr said and ducked back into the driver's seat, a man confident of getting his way in the end. Craig did nothing now to shake that confidence. As he pulled the passenger door shut behind him, Barry Kerr offered him his hand. A huge thing. The bulk Craig had observed was not all car-coat. 'I'm on a double-yellow here, do you mind if we talk and drive?'

Even as he spoke he was applying his hand to the wheel again, turning the car in the opposite direction to the one Craig had been heading in.

'Ros has told me a lot about you. She says you were very supportive when Alec died.'

So that was how she characterised their year together.

'Well, Alec had been very good to me.'

'People tell me he had a real charisma.'

He glanced sidelong at Craig. Was that what this was about? Help me know the man she loved before she met me? He had waited a long time for it if it was.

'He inspired me,' was as much as Craig could say. Barry Kerr nodded. They had turned off the main road into a rat run that brought them out at length opposite one of those small Belfast hotels that had long been strangers to overnight guests. Barry waited for a gap in the traffic and swung the car across the road before chopping down on the indicator with a meaty pinky.

He turned in his seat. 'Have you time for a drink?'

This was getting stranger by the minute. 'It would have to be quick.'

Barry popped his seatbelt.

'You OK leaving the car here?'

'It's all right, they know me.'

And indeed from the doormen on through they seemed to. The main lounge was almost full – commuters glad of the haven from the rain, or the excuse to slip in a swift one before the bus or train. Barry led the way down the corridor into a smaller, emptier bar whose walls were a shrine to Ulster rugby. Barry affected not to see his own photograph as he took his seat, although anyone unfamiliar with the game or the society pages of the *Belfast Telegraph* might never have made the connection between him and the figure framed above his head, face contorted in the moment of victory, gum shield spinning from his wide-open mouth.

'I'm buying,' he said to Craig, and to the barman who had tailed them to the table: 'Lime juice and soda water for me, and a . . . ?'

'Coke.'

'Nothing stronger?'

'No: marking later. Coke's fine.'

Nilsson was singing distantly. Not 'Without You', the film theme . . . no, it was gone.

'I'll tell you what it is,' Barry began then straightaway

stopped. 'I take it you follow the news?'

'It has a way of ensuring that you do whether you want to or not.'

'I hear what you're saying,' Barry said, and paused again as the barman returned, set down the drinks and left. 'A few of us have been watching developments lately . . .'

'A few of you?'

'Just friends, a couple of rugby guys, some people I've met through work.'

'Which is?'

'PR.' He dug in his pocket and coaxed out a stainless-steel case the size of a Zippo but a fraction of the depth. He pressed an indentation in the base and the short end of a card appeared. 'Go ahead.'

Craig, with difficulty, removed it. Kerr Communications: Tailored to Meet Your Needs.

'Just had these ones done.'

'They look the part.'

'That's what I thought.'

Each went for his pocket then his drink.

'You were saying about these friends . . .'

'Yes. We all get together, once a month, have dinner – in here the odd time – and talk about what's going on.'

'I wouldn't mind knowing myself.'

'Oh, I think you are doing yourself a disservice. You've been on our radar for a while. Ros says you have it in you to be one of the best.' Craig thought he remembered Ros getting carried away one time in her hallway and saying something very like that. (Remembered – even though he knew she was getting carried away in word as well as deed

– getting carried away with her.) Barry moved a fraction closer, dropped his voice a fraction lower. 'I don't know about you, Craig, but we – my friends and I – we have detected a change in the mood music from the other side of the house.'

How easily he assumed which side Craig was on.

'We get the feeling that they are preparing something – they would probably offer it as an initiative, but a strategy is what it will be, something aimed over our heads at the government in London. We are going to have to be a bit quicker on our feet than we have been in the past.'

'This is all very interesting,' Craig said, 'and I don't disagree with you, but I have to tell you, I don't think of myself as a Unionist. There's a difference between a background and an allegiance.'

'So much the better. We're not entirely comfortable with the label ourselves. We want to start conversations that challenge and extend us. Besides, I'm not asking you to join anything, just come along some time, talk to us.'

'I would have thought Ros would be better placed than me to provide that service.'

It came out more bitter than he had intended.

'Ros doesn't want to get too involved, for obvious reasons – you know, give each other a bit of room – and then . . . well, I'm sure you can guess.'

The barman had ghosted over again. Their glasses were empty. 'Anything else for you?'

'No, I think that's us,' said Barry.

Outside again he tried to insist that Craig get back into the car. 'I've probably taken you miles out of your way.'

'It's Belfast,' Craig said. 'Nowhere's miles. Anyway the walk will help me think.'

He tucked his chin into the collar of his coat and pressed on into the rain, but before he had got around the first corner his head was up again and he was laughing – real, shoulder-shaking laughter – at the absurdity of what had just occurred.

For the past four or five months he had been going out with Yolanda, one of the Spanish assistants. On their first night in bed she told him she was probably going to get married when she returned home and she wanted before she did to have a couple of flings. Craig was her second – her 'blond', a designation that said more about where she came from – the southernmost tip of Andalusia – than it did about his colouring, which at its lightest, in his pre-teens, was only ever dirty fair.

She was in the kitchen when he got back to the house, a fork clenched between her teeth. She took it out, wiped it on the back of her hand.

'I didn't know what time to expect you,' she said.

There was hissing and spitting coming from under the grill. Craig pulled out the pan: fish fingers. Yolanda practically lived on them. ('Why do people here think that all Spanish women can cook?')

She elbowed him aside, flipped the fish fingers soft side up with the fork.

'I think someone just tried to recruit me,' he said.

'I'm sorry, "recruit"?'

'Get someone to join.'

'Like a club?'

'Maybe, or a party. He says he wasn't, but I'm telling you he did a pretty good impression of it.'

She pushed the pan back under the grill. 'I had to send one of the fourth-year boys to the Chief this afternoon.'

(He wondered if she had understood what he had said.)

'He made a gesture at me, with his hand and his tongue in his cheek, like this . . .' She demonstrated, reversing the angle of her fist after a few strokes and switching her tongue, convincingly, to the other cheek.

(Perhaps it had been the word 'impression' . . .)

'Who was it?' he asked.

'It doesn't matter. The Chief has dealt with it.'

'Tell me. I'll find out soon enough anyway.'

She sighed. 'Brown.'

'Duncan Brown?'

She took two rounds of sliced pan from the bag in the breadbin. 'I shouldn't have said anything.'

'He's a little shit, so he is.'

'He is not so bad most of the time, he stepped over the line . . . is that what you say?'

'Overstepped.'

'Right.'

'He mimed you sucking his cock.'

'It's ugly when you say it like that.'

'That's why they do it, to make it ugly.'

She had laid three fish fingers on one of the rounds of bread and was pressing another round down on top. 'Ach! Look what you made me do.' She tossed the top layer of bread on the plate, spread it with salad cream and replaced it. There were fish fingers left over. 'Will I make you one too?'

They ate with their books in front of them. He didn't trust himself to start marking yet. After a while he became aware that she was watching him.

'What?' He touched his cheeks, his nose, for anything that might have stuck to him, or, worse, fallen out of him.

'Nothing,' she said, then, 'I don't understand you. On the one side you are like Mr Chips with your trips into town.' She had seen Peter O'Toole, dubbed, in the musical remake when she was growing up. (¡Adiós, Señor Chips! Adiós!) It was one of the things that made her want to come here and be gesticulated at by the likes of Duncan Brown. 'On the other side you are so *hard*. And then, living here . . .'

'Hold on a minute,' he said. 'What has where I live got to do with fourth-years doing blowjob signs to you?'

'You don't even fix the roof of the bathroom. It's plastic. I don't know. I ask myself sometimes what it is you are waiting for.'

'To fix the roof?'

'OK, play games.' She massed her brows into a formidable frown, but her toes, which had crept up on to the edge of his chair, were dancing inside her socks. 'What do I care? I am going home in ten weeks' time. So long, have a happy life!'

He made a grab for her feet, but she pulled them out of the way. 'See you,' he said, and went after them under the chair and that was the last he thought about Duncan Brown and Barry Kerr and his dinner-club friends that night. The last he thought about marking.

3

Turned out that what Gerry did was textile rentals (no, neither had Maxine until then), everything from dust-control floor mats to individually tailored personnel uniforms.

She had the contract for two of Northern Ireland's four main banks and one of its biggest councils. Or she and her husband had. *Had* had. The fucker. The week after Maxine agreed to work for her, Gerry walked out on him, on all the trappings of the contracts for two of the four main banks and one the country's biggest councils, and set up on her own. The first thing she did was go round all the companies she and he had worked for together and offer to undercut their current contract by ten per cent. Only one of them took her up on it, which was one more, if she was being honest, than she had expected. Five thousand pounds a year in roller towels. No: four thousand five hundred. It was a start.

Her husband's name was Andrews. Her own, which she had reverted to, was Young. To get ahead of him in the Yellow Pages she named the new company Aardvark. 'Repairs, rewashes, and renewals,' ran the entry. '*No stone left unturned* to bring you the COMPLETE SERVICE.'

'Do aardvarks turn stones?' Maxine had asked when she saw the copy, with its logo of a cartoon aardvark (a pretty cute-looking aardvark it had to be said) leaning against a rock it had just upended.

'They do while they work for me,' said Gerry.

Maxine's training was all on the job. No better way to learn than by doing, as Gerry said. She accompanied Gerry on visits to factories whose processes, with their chemical cocktails and asbestos-clad ovens, seemed better suited to producing explosives than overalls. She toured laundries with her, met bank managers and even trailed around car auctions in search of a van until she was able to persuade Gerry that she, Maxine, could find her something newer and cheaper and less likely to have had its clock tampered with. And when there were no meetings or tours or auctions to attend, no paperwork on her desk to be dealt with, she read and read and read.

(Just anyone try her on the subject of table napkins. Go on, try her, anyone.)

Gerry would still come in some mornings a little the worse for wear. Her husband had not taken the separation, or the competition, lying down. His lawyers were all over his and Gerry's memorandum of association (had she forgotten that she had signed that? He hadn't) looking for the words that would pull the rug from under his ex-wife's feet. She would get calls from them three or four times a day. She would get calls, from whom, she could only guess, in the middle of the night, silence on the other end of the line. 'You don't scare me,' she would say, would even on occasion sit on the floor with the phone to her ear until whoever it was could hold his breath no longer and hung up. She changed her number more than once and each time was obliged to make it known to her husband's lawyers, and each time, after a gap of a couple of days, the calls would start again.

And some nights the mood just came on her and she drank.

Maxine would make a pot of tea on those mornings after – Darjeeling appeared to do the job best – and leave it, without a word, on Gerry's desk, the one facing the window, the post beside it already sorted: for your eyes only; for discussion; and (by far the largest number) don't worry, all in hand.

Her Christmas card at the end of the first year – wherever Gerry had found it – was some piece of generic American Fifties tat featuring a boss with a Colgate smile, side-parting and pipe, a speech bubble coming from his mouth: 'Thanks for being a swell PA'.

In her own hand Gerry had added a capital L.

Maxine knew from doing the books that, even before the cost of her own lawyers was taken into account, Gerry was barely making enough that first year to pay her. She was barely making enough to cover the pencils, the paper and the batteries for the calculator with which Maxine worked it out. Gerry, on the one occasion when Maxine tried to broach the subject with her, shrugged.

'That's the way it works,' she said. 'And when we do really start to earn I'll be making four times as much as you.'

To which what could Maxine do but laugh, although she was never again so tempted, standing a little later in the al-cove that served them as a kitchen, giving the tea leaves a stir before serving, to let go of the string of spit that she dangled experimentally above the open pot.

Nah: she slurped it up again. Keep that one in the armoury.

The second year was better. The second year in fact was a bit of a blur, so many were the stones that Aardvark was turning. Maxine had forgotten to take a summer holiday. She looked down and it was June, up again and it was the end of September and she and Gerry were running – literally – a few minutes late for a meeting, on the northern edge of the security zone, in one of those concrete and steel bunkers, on the site of a linen warehouse, mid-nineteenth century, bombed early in the eighth decade of the twentieth, that constituted the Belfast Troubles vernacular.

They arrived windswept at the door, which was of course locked. The lobby was presided over by a security man (another essential of the vernacular), ex-services by the looks of him, in a uniform that Gerry herself had provided, with the assistance of Maxine and a chain of suppliers stretching as far as north-west China. They watched for the best part of a minute while he, fifteen feet away on the other side of the door, studied their images on closed-circuit TV. When at long last he deigned to admit them he asked them both for ID then checked the names against the list of the day's expected visitors. He checked the exact spelling, tapping Gerry's driving licence with his pen. 'See what it is, I get Gerry for short,' she said. She was craning to see the name on the badge pinned above his breast pocket. 'What do you get yourself . . . Richard? No, let me guess.'

His face!

They are less intimidating, she said to Maxine on the stairs up, when you can picture them standing in nothing but their socks. She had just introduced a new line of double-knit polyester sock specially designed for door staff and other personnel whose duties exposed them to the elements. It was still a growth area in Northern Ireland.

Maxine's period had started a couple of days before: started, then, in what was becoming in its own way a pattern (not entirely unconnected perhaps to the overlooked summer holiday), almost as quickly stopped again. The days immediately after *that* were less predictable. Sometimes the period would switch on again the following day. Other times – forty-eight, seventy-two hours later – it would come back in a sudden burst.

Forty minutes into the meeting she realised with a lurch this was one of the other times.

The tea and coffee had just arrived on a trolley pushed by a woman wearing a turquoise tabard overall manufactured in Mauritius. (Even in the grip of her terror Maxine couldn't stop working.) If she could only hold out until they broke for refreshments . . . But, no, the man sitting next to Gerry signalled to the woman in the tabard that they would carry on for a minute or two more and she stopped in the act of taking the clingfilm from the biscuits and left them to shift for themselves. Bugger. A minute passed. Two minutes. The man next to Gerry kept talking. Maxine grabbed her bag, stood up. If they could excuse her for a few moments . . .

Gerry flicked her eyes towards her then away.

'Is it the toilet you're looking for?' one of the other men asked. 'Only it's a bit complicated.'

Maxine told him she was sure she would be all right.

'No,' he said, up out of his seat now, walking with her to the door, 'believe me,' and he launched into directions that included a left turn then a right turn and a couple more doors. She was nodding like mad before he had got through the second of these. Something cataclysmic was about to descend on her, from her, she could feel it. She started walking, fast.

'Hold on, there's more,' he called down the corridor after her. She walked faster. 'If you get lost just ask someone.'

She turned left, she turned right, she went through one door then another then saw coming towards her the woman who had brought the tea trolley, who steered her the final leg: another door, a right turn . . .

She made it to the cubicle with seconds to spare.

And, oh, God, the mess . . . She must have used half a toilet roll in there.

The sweats had passed, but she still felt faint. She leaned forward resting her elbows on the edge of the basin a few moments then washed her face with cold water.

Outside again she tried to remember which way she had come. Left, she thought, then after a fruitless few seconds walking, decided it must have been right. She doubled back, turned a corner, and there was a door with a push-bar handle. There had been a door like that earlier – hadn't there? She pushed and the door swung shut behind her. She found herself on a back landing. Not where she needed to be at all. She tried the door. It wouldn't open. She walked the length of the landing looking for another one, and found it, finally, bottom right. She opened it and was outside standing at the top of a blue metal staircase. Not knowing what else to do, she started down, hardly daring to glance in any of the windows she passed lest she should find herself face to face with the people she was supposed to be meeting.

A train appeared briefly travelling towards its own reflection in the mirrored walls of the Royal Mail sorting office, then like the snake that ate itself disappeared from both sides at once.

She had arrived in an alleyway full of industrial bins and rat-bait boxes, tossed rather than laid on the ground, as though even the pest controllers had been unnerved. She picked her way with care, and as much speed as she dared, round to the front of the building again and presented herself at the door. The security man's voice came out at her from the vent in the wall: 'Yes?'

She told him her name, who she was here to see. There was a long pause. 'Sorry,' he said, 'somebody of that name is already in.'

She laughed. 'I *was* in, with my boss, Gerry. Remember, you checked the spelling of her name? See?' She waved, but he wasn't looking at her or even at her image on the monitor. He was looking at the visitors' book.

'She hasn't signed out.'

'I know, that's because I came out the back way. I got a bit lost.'

'If she hasn't signed out,' the man said, refusing even to meet her in the second person, 'I can hardly sign her back in again.'

'But she is me.' Maxine was shouting into the vent now. Passers-by glanced over their shoulders at her. 'Will you please just let me in?'

The pause this time was twice as long.

'Sorry, no can do.'

She stomped back round to the alley, forgetting in her anger (who even said that, 'no can do'?) the implication of the scattered bait boxes. Another security man had come out and was standing at the top of the metal staircase, hands on his belt. 'You're not supposed to be round here. It's a security risk.'

Maxine was trying to imagine him in his double-knit polyester socks. It wasn't working.

'Did your man at the door put you up to this?' She plunged her hand into her bag, pulled out a handful of Lillets. 'Do these *look* like suspect devices to you?'

The man smirked and went back inside.

In the end she had to go into a newsagent's in the next street over and ask to use the phone. 'Go ahead, it's not my shop,' the girl at the counter said. 'I'm only standing here minding it.'

'Here,' Maxine gave her twenty pee. 'Give it to them or stick it in your pocket.'

The phone was on a shelf behind a curtain. Maxine hunched over the receiver for still greater privacy. Directory Enquiries, switchboard ... *finally*.

'You're not going to believe this,' she began.

The man who had given her directions to the toilet came down to the front door to vouch for her. The security man behind his desk was unrepentant. He asked Maxine to initial the note he had written in red biro beside her name: 'Temporary unauthorised absence 10:10–10:23.'

It was barely twenty minutes since she had got up from the conference table. But, still, twenty minutes ...

Gerry ignored her as she came back into the room, as

though an absence of that duration was nothing remarkable.

As soon as the meeting was over and they were clear of the place, though, she launched in.

'What were you playing at?'

'I wasn't playing at anything, I was . . .' It was nearly too surreal for words. She felt the laughter rising. 'I just wasn't myself for a while, apparently.'

Gerry snorted. 'Silly wagon.' A nod then in the direction of Maxine's groin: 'And you need to get that seen to, by the way.'

There was only the two of them in the office. Not much passed beneath notice.

'I will.'

'Do. Soon.'

*

The feeling among the small team St John had working for him on the home-improvement segment was that they were ahead of the curve. That feature on the house in Solihull? Generated more phone calls when it was broadcast than the rest of that week's stories put together. And then just when they were really hitting their stride, TV-am lost out in a blind franchise bid to Sunrise. With the clock ticking the channel began to cut its losses, and its staff. Trudy had seen it coming and had already hopped it to the BBC: 'moving in with Auntie', as St John liked to say until she told him to stop, seriously, he was making her feel like some tweedy old lesbian's plaything – and don't even think about going there. So St John didn't. When the time came for *him* to make a move he swung the other way entirely. Mike Warren, another who had bailed out of Camden Lock early, called him one day. He had got involved with the Local Channel in Swindon. 'All this guff about satellite?' he said. 'Forget it: cable is where it's going to be at in a few years.' So far in Swindon it was news and sport. 'Makes your average regional programme look like a Hollywood blockbuster, but leave that to one side.' The trick was to minimise the content cost without cheapening the look of the product. 'Do you remember you did that feature last Christmas – the best of the seasonal DIY books? What I'm thinking, each week, a different book, a different household task, follow the instructions, step by step, and – does it work? Does it not? – there you have it. We call it *Home Test*.'

'And you seriously think people are that interested?'

'In doing it themselves? Of course not, but they'll be interested in watching somebody else struggle with the instructions for half an hour.'

'And who had you in mind for the talent?'

'Well, you know and I know it's the talent that really costs.'

'So . . . ?'

'We're talking about a whole new way of making programmes.'

'So . . . ?'

So Mike persuaded him to give it a go.

Just as the camera was about to turn over for the beginning of the first programme, he had an idea. When the lights came up he had his head down on the book he was supposed to be reviewing.

'Sorry,' he said and gave himself a shake.

Which was the birth of *Home Test*'s Dozy DIY Man.

*

It was several months before Craig heard again from Barry Kerr, a letter inviting him to dinner, not in the hotel where they had previously had a drink together, but in the members' room at Barry's rugby club.

Craig had been there once before, in his teens, for a New Year's Eve disco, and had been copiously sick in the shrubs at the side of the wooden security hut, replaced now by a striped barrier operated remotely from inside the clubhouse. The clubhouse itself had undergone a transformation, an extra storey having been added with, in the centre, above the door, a clock face incorporating the club crest, the hands, as Craig's taxi deposited him on the front step, reading five minutes to eight.

Inside, the curtains were drawn on the windows overlooking the pitch – sounds from that quarter of training in progress – and a concertina partition had been pulled across the room, or most of the way across, about a third the way down, no doubt to create a sense of intimacy, but actually, to Craig's mind, making the gathering seem a little forlorn. The shuttered bar didn't help. Club stewards stood in a rectangle of lit doorway to one side of it, with drinks on a trolley.

Barry greeted him with that huge handshake of his, steering him meanwhile with the other hand towards this trolley. 'Have whatever you want. It's all on us tonight.'

Craig, as ever in such situations, asked for a gin and tonic, which he otherwise never touched, and one of the stewards entered it in a ledger while the other poured.

He had wondered in advance – had been awake in fact since five this morning wondering – whether, despite what Barry had said about her reluctance to be involved, Ros might be there, but, no, turning with his drink (God, it was strong) to the table he saw that the gathering, like the rest of the club, was an all-male affair.

Barry aside, Craig knew no one. There was a pair of solicitors, identifiable before they were even introduced by their chalk-stripe suits, a man who was the And Son of one of Northern Ireland's largest haulage firms, another man like Barry with a background in PR.

The four remaining were in finance.

The talk over soup was all rugby, on which subject, of course, everyone deferred to Barry Kerr. The mid-Eighties had been a false dawn: it would be at least ten years before Ireland produced another side capable of a tilt at the Triple Crown . . . No matter how much money the broadcasters were prepared to throw at it the game would never go professional, and so on.

Already, though, by the time the soup plates were being cleared, Barry had begun to take a back seat. Craig, who had been scouring the table for water with which to counteract the effects of the gin, missed the precise moment when the conversation segued into politics, though it was possibly around the question of anthems at Lansdowne Road. One of the bankers said that he had always found 'The Queen' to be singularly uninspiring.

'Land of Hope and Glory', And Son offered by way of alternative and conducted himself in a bar or two with a swinging dessertspoon: 'God who made thee mighty make thee mightier yet . . .'

The 'might' said a solicitor *might* just be the problem . . . Barry Kerr intervened briefly to ask if anyone objected to him smoking, which no one did . . . His PR colleague said that nobody in the South seemed too bothered about the 'soldiers' in the 'Soldier's Song'. (They were bothered enough to disguise it in Irish these days, quipped another banker.) It was the anthem's job to rouse and deceive: a sixty-second ad campaign for a product only its producers, the anthem singers, ever bought.

The main courses started to arrive: Viennese pork. 'A signature dish here,' Barry said, presumably for Craig's benefit.

A head, recently showered, appeared round the imperfectly drawn partition, eyes dancing about the table before alighting on Barry, widening then in surprise. 'Oh, I beg your pardon.' A friend must have been waiting somewhere in the shadows at his back. 'What's that all in aid of, do you think?' the showered one asked him as they withdrew.

Barry laughed. 'A good question,' he said, although for a time after it was posed no one at the table seemed able to find his voice to answer. Conversation fragmented, became localised. The man to Craig's right – his name was Mervyn – confessed to him that he had been a dunce at history when he was a boy. Nowadays, he knew, it was fashionable to say there were no bad pupils, just badly taught ones, but he didn't even have that excuse – couldn't fault a one of the teachers unfortunate enough to have had charge of him – it was all down to him: a dunce, pure and simple.

'Oh . . .' Craig stretched out the prefatory vowel.

Mervyn stopped him with a raised palm. 'No, I tell that to everyone who comes to work for me: own up to your weaknesses, before someone else discovers them.' Down came the hand, firmly, on the tablecloth. 'Or if you won't own up, bone up.'

'How many people do you have working for you?' Craig asked.

'We took on our eightieth at the end of the summer.'

'And what are his weaknesses?'

'Hers. Chief among them would be that she doesn't recognise yet that she has any. Early days, though, early days.'

'Potatoes?' a steward came between them offering a dish with mashed on one side, roasted on the other.

'A bit of both,' Mervyn said; waited, watched. 'Perhaps a bit more.' And Craig, looking sidelong at the food heaped on his plate was a little surprised not to have to sit through a second confession.

Barry waited until pudding – apple pie – had been served and the cups set out for tea and coffee before addressing the table again. He hoped that by now everyone had had an opportunity to exchange a few words at least with this evening's guest, whom he would now like to call on to suggest a few headings for discussion.

That was it – a few headings for discussion? Craig had spent most of the previous week's evenings writing and rewriting a formal presentation, which he could not now bring himself to take from his pocket.

'Well . . .' he picked up the spoon from his saucer and

squinted at the hallmark. 'I suppose, in very bald terms, what I would want to begin by asking is why does it matter?'

The man facing him – another banker – leaned forward. 'By "it" you mean . . . ?'

'The Union.' Spoon on saucer again, hands folded. 'Only a zealot would claim that it had anything to do with defending the Faith any more, and you of all people can't imagine either that culturally much would change if it was to go, that you wouldn't be able to carry on with pleasant evenings like this. I mean, let's be honest, we could be sitting in Dublin, at Old Belvedere, or in Cork Constitution . . . Garryowen.'

The banker jabbed the air with his index finger. 'I'll tell you why it matters in one word,' he said and proceeded to make of it four: 'e-con-om-y.'

'Would be addressed to our advantage,' said Craig. 'Northern Ireland would be granted special status for maybe forty or fifty years. The EU would get involved, the US: just think of the kudos you would get if you happened to be sitting in the White House when peace finally broke out. The Union is intact not because its supporters have been so good at making the argument for it, but because those against it were too busy disagreeing about how it should be dismantled. Except now it looks as though they might at last be getting their act together.'

'So what do you suggest?' This from And Son.

'Me? Oh, I would probably say do something radical, the Danzig option, make Belfast a free city within a reconstituted federation of the islands . . .' Their mouths, some of them, hanging open at this, 'but short of that, the best bet would be to get your compromise in first. Make nice, as the American mommies say.'

And Son again: 'Make nice?'

'Well, how many friends has making ugly won you?'

'Another good question,' Barry said, though the banker sat back shaking his head and was noticeably half-hearted in the tapping of the tabletop that was the signal called for to show their appreciation at the evening's end. Barry made a presentation of a commemorative fountain pen, which Craig, a strict Bic man, put into a bedside drawer when he got home and did not give another thought to until the phone rang, six months and a day after the date inscribed on the fountain pen's barrel, and Barry asked him what he thought of repeating his rugby-club performance at a week-end brainstorming session.

'I thought maybe I had got a few people's backs up the last time,' Craig said.

'No, not at all. Your contribution has often come up at our dinners. We even have a little "Danzig" grouping.'

'You know that I wasn't being entirely serious when I suggested that? You know Danzig didn't end too well?'

'I'm only saying it as an example of how open we are to exploring new ideas, and not just us, but people further up the food-chain, which is what this weekend away is about, pulling together the results of all these informal debates, seeing what there is there of value.'

This was all beginning to sound a bit too official for Craig's liking.

'Honestly,' Barry said, 'no strings attached. Treat it as a break, nice hotel, you and a guest.'

That was very kind, but Craig didn't think there would be a guest. Yolanda had returned to her southernmost part of Andalusia, from where she sent him the occasional very funny letter: the places to which her hunt for genuinely *bad* Irish-style fish fingers had taken her! The furtive shame of cooking and consuming them – when a girl might be other-wise occupied – in an apartment shared with her husband-to-be!

Guest or no, Barry was saying, he was sure Craig wouldn't turn up his nose at a weekend away. The assumption that he *wouldn't* was almost reason enough for Craig to turn it up as far as it would go. But then, 'bring a guest' . . . Was it likely that Barry would be there on his own?

'Where did you say it was?'

'We're still working on the venue, but it will be some-where nice, somewhere we can all relax, enjoy the food and the architecture – it was Leuven last time. Just keep the third weekend in March free.'

Craig left a moment's silence. 'OK,' he said then. 'The third weekend in March.'

*

Maxine was able to tell Gerry in January that Aardvark was on course to record its first five-figure profit, net, that was, of overheads and wages for the two of them in the office, the warehouse staff of six, and the three drivers, driving the three new vans. They had even had an approach from one of the banks that had been with Andrews all these years. Perhaps it would be to their mutual advantage to arrange a meeting in the coming weeks?

'They kept us waiting long enough. Let them sweat till after Prague,' Gerry said. She meant the trade fair, the weekend, as it happened, of Maxine's thirtieth birthday. 'Speaking of which I thought maybe you should come too. You're not my PA and you're not my pal, although you can still be that. You're my partner. I'd be kidding myself if I thought that any of this could have happened without you. I'll organise a meeting with the lawyers as well when we get back.' She paused. 'Unless of course you would rather spend your birthday at home.'

'I think you know the answer to that.'

The truth was that what Maxine had been dreading most about the birthday was her mother's desire – repeated at ever-shorter intervals since her birthday the previous year – to mark the occasion in 'suitable fashion'. Maxine had a vision of one of those early-Seventies family meals, the table fleshed out with cousins yelling at her to blow out the candles before they set fire to the hotel.

'We could do something the night before,' her mother said when she broke the news about Prague.

'I'll have such an early start, I'd probably spend the whole night with one eye on the clock.' Her mother looked prepared to carry on arguing the point, till Maxine delivered the line to which there was no answer. 'It'd be a terrible waste.'

So instead they passed the last evening of her twenties at Victor's, where in actual fact there was far more food than the three of them on their own could eat: poached salmon, ham off the bone, four different types of salad and an enormous forest-fruits Pavlova.

'You went to an awful lot of trouble,' Maxine said.

'I went to an awful lot of shops, it's not the same thing.'

'That Pavlova didn't come out of a box.'

'No, a friend left it over.'

'What a shame she couldn't stay and help us eat it,' their mother said and Victor turned his head away so that she couldn't see what Maxine saw, the sudden rush of colour to his cheeks.

And, oh, how stupid could she have been all these years never to clock it? How stupid could they all have been? Although maybe the failure was not so much with what their eyes saw as what their words directed them to look for. Fairies, her father had called them, fellas who were a bit light on their feet, her mother preferred. A fella less light on his feet, less fairy-like than Victor it would have been hard to imagine.

They toasted, as they always did these days when they got together and drink was taken, absent family members.

'And friends,' said Maxine and managed to catch her brother's eye. Again the blush. No, she was not wrong.

'And friends, of course,' her mother said.

Gerry insisted on champagne on the flight across to London, working on the steward – 'it's the girl's thirtieth birthday, she's having a breakdown here' – until he smuggled some down from First Class. Four miniature bottles. At seven forty-five in the morning. That set the tone. They wangled another couple of bottles when they switched planes at Heathrow then after touching down in Prague had a cocktail at the hotel bar before heading to the fair where they ordered a bottle of Sekt with their late lunch, during which they were joined by a group of men from a Belgian trade association who Gerry had met the year before at a fair in Ghent. Which called for another drink. The men had uniformly short hair and wore matching suits with the initials of the association stitched into their shirt collars. 'Like fucking Kraftwerk,' Gerry said when she and Maxine were alone again, 'and I speak as someone who spent the whole of 1975 wanting to ride Ralf.'

Every so often Maxine was reminded that Gerry hadn't arrived on this earth the age she was when she flooded the engine of her Mazda in that Bangor car park.

There was an arrangement to meet later at a beer hall near the Kraftwerk men's hotel, but in the course of the afternoon she and Gerry secured a deal with a financial services company with headquarters in, of all places, Ballsbridge (talk about round the world for a shortcut? They could have saved the plane fares and bought themselves a day-return to Dublin), so needless to say they had to go to dinner with the team – four more men – from there. And needless to say Gerry let it slip that it was Maxine's special birthday, so the celebrations were doubled, and then before Maxine knew it it was five to twelve and she had forgotten to phone her mother, but then as everyone kept telling her the night was young, and so was thirty really, when you thought about it. Some fella who would never see forty again, or very soon hair, sidled up to her, wanting to know where the mister was. 'I'll let you know when I find him,' she said, and then it was all 'get away with you' and 'a fine-looking girl like you?', which, in content if not in tone, was exactly the sort of conversation that Maxine had fled home, and the threat of cousins, to avoid. Gerry was on the other side of the table, getting the full Dub treatment from the MD. Maxine signalled to her – 'I'm away' – and was pleasantly surprised when Gerry too stood up and lifted the MD's hand, like an exit barrier, from the table.

'We'll love you and leave you, gentlemen,' she said and, shoulder to shoulder, she and Maxine stepped outside and flagged down a cab. Before they could get in, though, Gerry turned and cocked her head. 'I can't believe us letting them spoil our night like that. *Your* night.'

'I don't know, I was starting to think I might be hitting my limit.'

'*Starting to think* you *might* be? That sounds like one more to me.'

'At least one.'

Gerry slapped the roof of the taxi and the driver with a few no-doubt choice Czech words over his left shoulder sped off.

Instinct rather than familiarity with the city led them down side streets until they found a neon sign at the top of a staircase into a basement where beautiful young women raised their arms to the ceiling, in order, as it seemed, to make room for the beautiful young men who slinked around them making complicated patterns with their hands before their faces.

'Look at them all,' Gerry said, or shouted, above 'Oh, L'Amour'. 'So at ease in themselves.'

'Hairdressers,' Maxine shouted back.

'What?'

'Two-thirds of them: hairdressers. Any money. Spot

them the world over.'

They bumped hips for a time on the edge of the dance-floor then – 'what's a boy in love supposed to do?' – plunged right in, one hand held high, one hand clutching their Pilsner Urquell to their chests.

It was four when they got back to the hotel. Even the night porter had given up on them. He appeared eventually, in response to their knocking, from behind the door marked 'left luggage' and let them in. Over his shoulder a red-headed woman slipped out of the left-luggage room and tiptoed down the corridor in the direction of the breakfast lounge, as inconspicuous as a fluorescent bat.

They bottled up the laughter until they were in the lift, Gerry sliding, helpless, down the wall, Maxine dancing on the spot to keep from peeing. They barely knew the lift had started until it stopped on the third floor. A moment, then the doors opened. The laughter shut off like a tap.

'This is me,' Maxine said.

'Pity,' said Gerry.

'It is, isn't it?'

Neither of them had moved and yet it seemed suddenly as though the space between them had shrunk. Maxine still had her thumb on the door-open button. She let it go now. The lift went up another floor, stopped, and repeated its offer of a way out. They ignored it. With a sigh the doors closed again.

They kissed messily, suspended there in a box in a shaft in Prague Old Town.

'Don't do this unless you mean it,' Gerry murmured, getting in close, fitting herself somehow between Maxine's shoulders, hands flat again against Maxine's breasts, and leaning forward Maxine kissed her again, but whether it was the words did it, or whether it was the thought of Victor and his hidden friends (for it wasn't the hands, no longer flat, on her breasts, the tongue exploring her mouth) something inside her shrivelled. She lowered her head.

Gerry let go a breath that took with it all the desire that had been building in her, blind, since she boarded the plane twenty-one hours ago in Belfast, gathering force from the British Midland steward, the Belgians, the leery Dubs, the jostling of the bodies on the dance-floor, the heat of them, but not finding focus finally until the doors of this lift had opened then closed again opened then closed again.

'Never mind,' she said, with the last of that breath into Maxine's hair.

But Maxine did mind. That she had led Gerry on like that, or had let herself be led, one minute she thought it had been one way the next that it had been the other. She was too embarrassed to sleep, to do anything when she got to her room but pace up and down between the bed and the table with the little cube of a TV. After half an hour of this – leader then led, leader then led – she put on her coat and went out again – by the stairs – into the early-morning streets. She sat for a time before the Astronomical Clock, perhaps, like the other waifs she found there, unconsciously in need of a little of the faith of the Apostles who made their jerky circuit once an hour, although before they had put in an appearance the street-cleaners arrived on their motorbikes to hoover up yesterday's dog shit. Maxine moved on, crossed the river by one bridge, crossed back a short time later by another.

Around seven she walked up to a café whose owner was setting out tables beneath the awning.

'Too cold still,' he said when she went to sit down and held the door for her. 'In, in.'

He showed her to a window seat then brought her coffee in a porcelain pot and a pastry, still warm, sagging under the weight of the jam in its centre. She began to think that she might not want to crawl off somewhere and die after all.

She watched a man cross the square at a diagonal and go into a newsagent's and thought how peculiar it was that after only a couple of days in any city you began to see faces you 'recognised' from home. A sort of survival instinct, perhaps, a way of helping you take root, should the winds of fate carry you far from your own people.

The man came out of the newsagent's again carrying a copy of *The Times*. He was headed straight for the café, turning the pages as he walked, becoming with every step more definitely familiar. She stood up, abandoning coffee and pastry and, feeling as though this was all happening in slow motion, that she was re-enacting a near miss, pulled open the door at the same moment as the man veered off towards an alley out of which a party of early-bird Japanese tourists was emerging and the café owner at her back called out, 'Madame!'

'Craig!' she shouted and the man jerked back, not, she thought, in recognition of the name, but of the accent, the unmistakable imprint of native English – Belfast English – she gave its single syllable.

It wasn't him. Not even close.

'Sorry,' she said.

'Madame!' The café owner had come right out on to the street, almost tripping over his own tables in his haste.

The man with *The Times* frowned.

'Jesus Christ,' he said and changed again before her eyes from not even close to him and only him. 'Maxine. What are you doing here?'

A glance around to see whether, whatever it was, she was doing it on her own.

'I was thirty yesterday,' she said.

'Happy birthday.'

She began to laugh then suddenly, stupidly, she was crying.

And then the newspaper was on the ground and his arms were around her, hands grasping her arms, while by some miracle of physiology, she thought, until she saw the café owner's shoes in amongst theirs, simultaneously patting her on the head.

'So, so, so,' the café owner soothed, 'so, so, so,' and *The Times* blew sheet by sheet across the square.

*

Craig's own route to the square that early morning had been a little less eventful. The Chief had allowed him a day's leave the day before, but even so it was after six before he got off the plane, alone, in Prague. There was a note at reception from Barry Kerr: 'In closed session. Meet in lobby 7?'

He barely had time to wash his face and change his shirt.

The first person he saw when he came down again into the lobby was the Party leader, bumptiously requesting that the piped pop music was turned off. 'It's Prague,' he said, as much for the benefit of those in his entourage as those behind the reception desk, 'some Dvořák, perhaps, some *Emmy Destinn*, if that name means anything at all, but, please, not this drivel.'

Craig's heart sank. A couple of the Party's other MPs were installed at tables around the lobby, pointedly not hearing, and just as pointedly not looking at each other: factions in the making.

'You got here!'

He looked round: Barry, coming in off the street, and there beside him – 'You two know each other of old, of course' – both less and more the woman he remembered, Ros.

Their year together passed before Craig's eyes, a capsule.

'Of course,' they repeated in sync.

Their hands went out towards each other's, but no sooner had their fingers touched than she drew hers away. 'Sorry,' she said and blew on it. 'My hand must be freezing.'

Barry laughed. 'So much for Prague spring.'

'That was poor, even for you.' Ros turned towards him, glad, Craig thought, of the shift in focus, although there was nothing feigned about the stroke of the arm that softened the rebuke. Barry accepted it gratefully.

'Dinner's at eight-thirty,' he said. 'You're welcome to join us for a drink beforehand.'

'Craig probably wants to get out and see a few of the sights before the light goes altogether,' said Ros.

'No, a drink would be nice,' he said and then wondered, seeing her smile appear and disappear in a heartbeat, if it had been the wrong thing.

She squeezed her husband's forearm. 'I'm just going up to the room to change.'

Barry, watching her go, was smiling. 'She's been looking forward to seeing you,' he said and Craig wondered how she would have reacted if she hadn't been.

The pre-dinner drink, though, was entirely without awkwardness, or at least awkwardness of his and Ros's making. If their past was a capsule, he quickly realised, it was floating somewhere far off in space, incapable of communicating, destined never to return. The three of them were joined by another couple, Willie and Fay, late middle age, country accents, and a woman, Harriet, who had something of the stage Sunday-school teacher about her (expect a scene later in which first impressions were proved to be well wide of the mark) and with whom Craig, finding himself seated next to her, thought he might be being paired. He wondered how to signal to her that he found it as amusing as he was sure she did that couples were always trying to get their single friends together.

The Party leader came through the lobby again – 'Do you hear that?' he said, his face lit up in triumph: 'No music!' – and stopped at their table to talk, telling everyone not to get up, at which point everyone did and remained standing for the forty-five seconds before he moved on to the next table, his parting shot to Craig being that he looked forward to what he had to say, it would make a nice change from the learned stuff he was usually subjected to.

When they sat again Craig was somehow beside Ros. 'He means well,' she said. 'He just has trouble putting what he means into sentences that don't instantly get your hackles up.'

'My hackles are just fine. At least I know now I'll never embarrass myself by saying to someone, "Oh, but he's not really like that in real life."'

She smiled, but her eyes at once strayed back to Barry who was talking over his shoulder to the MP for East Antrim.

'Do you think he will ever run himself?'

She faced round, 'Barry?', faced away again. 'No, Barry's your classic prop: better at giving someone else a boost than running with the ball.'

Did they really once tear into one another in that room full of newspapers?

He turned to look for Harriet. She was leaning forward to listen to something Willie was saying. Craig caught 'Enniskillen' a couple of times, caught too a glimpse, at the end of her straining neck, of the curve of Harriet's shoulder, cut across by a coral bra strap. She glanced Craig's way, a quizzical kink in her brow, and he lowered his eyes, though over the next half hour's comings and goings to toilet and bar he gravitated away from Ros and back towards her.

Just as they were about to go in for dinner a tall, prematurely bald man strode across the room. 'So sorry I'm late.' Harriet sprang up and the man leaned forward – down: he was that tall – to plant a kiss on her cheek, hand curling round the small of her back.

'This is Robert, my fiancé,' she said to Craig and to Robert, 'This is Craig's first time at one of these too.'

'You and I should stick together,' Robert said and saw to it that they did, pleading with Harriet to talk to someone to swap a couple of place names. 'There we are,' he said as they sat and all through the dinner regaled Craig with stories of his job with a construction firm in Faro and the apartment he and Harriet had there to which they tried to escape at every available opportunity.

'I love Belfast as much as the next man,' he said. 'Just don't ask me to live there the year round.'

He paused just long enough to ask Craig what it was he did – 'Harriet hasn't briefed me.'

'I teach history.'

A nod – 'Good for you' – and on he went again about a school his company had worked on and then about the English-language bookshops in Faro, the newspapers, the redundancy of the weather reports in a place where it hardly ever rained and finally the sea temperature at this time of year along the Algarve coast.

The best that could be said was that he left Craig no time in which to be nervous. His moment came, once again, with the arrival of the coffee. He was the last of three people who had been invited to contribute, following on from a journalist 'from the People's Republic of Cork', and an ex-priest whose views the Party leader seemed particularly keen on drawing out and who answered every question with a question of his own. 'Do you want my honest opinion?' or, 'Can I be perfectly frank with you?' and more than once, 'Off the record?'

Craig, reprising as requested his Danzig routine (with a detour through Monaco and a cheeky nod to Vatican City), acquitted himself well enough for the Party leader's press secretary to seek him out afterwards to convey the leader's sincere thanks, the leader himself having bowed out directly Craig had finished speaking to make a few calls before bed. The other senior Party people retired soon after – a handshake for Craig from each of them: early starts all. Harriet and Robert went too.

'I haven't seen him all week,' Craig overheard her say to Ros, her voice so low as to be almost a growl.

Ros, when she had gone, looked at her watch. 'Gosh, is that the time?' It was only just eleven. She stifled a yawn. 'I'm still on kiddies' clock.'

'You have children?' Craig asked.

'Two boys and a girl: six, eight and ten . . . like stairs.'

'As the old woman said, it's not like you didn't know what caused it,' said Willie, the Fermanagh man, who had stopped by at that moment to say his own goodnights.

'Did Barry never mention them to you? What's he like?' Again the rebuke softened by a stroke of the arm. It was obviously a routine with them.

'Craig never asked.'

Ros was searching in her bag for something – found it: a mini-album of photos. Two little hims and a pocket version of her.

'Lovely looking kids.' Craig gave them back. 'So who has them this weekend?'

'Oh, we're very lucky. Their school has a casual-boarding arrangement, so they're all there.'

'Having a ball, I'm sure, down at that Shack,' said Barry, and Craig didn't have to bother asking what school it was they were at.

He and Barry parted a little after midnight, a couple of

fifteen-year-old single-malt Scotches under their belts. (It was typical of the Party that it would book into a hotel with no Irish whiskey, not even a Bushmills.) As he let himself into the room he felt suddenly, profoundly weary, not the day catching up with him, but the days, the weeks, the months, the accumulated years of Craigness. Undressing, he caught sight of his behind in the big bathroom mirror. He backed towards it, looking over his shoulder – surely not – backed a bit more – Oh, Lord, it was . . . a fucking fold . . . *sag*.

He sat – flopped it felt like – on the edge of the bathtub. If he wasn't careful his entire life would have passed him by.

He woke at six on top of the bed wrapped in his hotel dressing gown. He phoned reception to check that the gym was open. By the time he stepped out to buy a paper at a couple of minutes before seven he had already run two and a half miles, which was two and a half more than he had run in the whole of the previous decade, two and a half more, as it was to turn out, than he would run in the decade that followed.

'I'm thirty,' she said, and started to cry.

'So, so, so,' the café owner said.

4

To the traditional disappointment of both mothers, the wedding took place in the registry office of Belfast City Hall. Maxine walked up the carpet between the banks of chairs (you could not have confused it with an aisle) on Victor's arm. She could barely turn to look at him, so much had he begun to resemble her father at the age when he first took root in her consciousness, so unlikely was he ever to be able to experience a moment like this himself, a public declaration, this is the man who forsaking all others I love.

Tommy sent a telegram. 'Hope to see you and make Craig's acquaintance soon.'

Maxine had not yet told him that he had made Craig's acquaintance once before. There was a lot about those days indeed that was still difficult to come at. A month after that life-altering meeting in Prague they had gone for dinner – 'call it our first anniversary, why not?' – in a restaurant on Shaftesbury Square whose lights, suspended above the tables and reacting to sound waves, it can only have been, brightened and dimmed as the conversation beneath them rose and fell. Maxine waited until the end of the second course, when Craig went out to the toilet, before taking the package from her bag and propping it against her plate.

'What's this?' He stopped short of his chair, stricken, as though something had been expected of him in return.

'Open it and see.'

He sat, slowly. 'You didn't have to . . .'

'Open it.'

He picked at the Sellotape – 'It's OK, it isn't going to go off' – then ripped into the paper with his thumb.

He looked down, looked up at her. She thought for a moment that he might be about to cry, that he had in that instant recast everything that happened since he walked out of the Prague newsagent's with his *Times* – everything since he last clapped eyes on *this* – as an elaborate practical joke. 'I don't understand.'

'It's yours, from years ago.'

'I know it is, that's what I don't understand.'

'I picked it up,' she said, as she picked it up now. 'In the old Spar, remember? You'd dropped it.'

'I got chased every day.'

He touched the key ring hanging from the pencil case's zip with the very tip of his finger. *He's afraid to believe in it.*

'The pens and all are still in it.' She held it towards him. He took it finally, drew back the zip. There were his initials, CR, in faded purple felt-tip.

'And you kept it?'

'I wanted to give it back. Tried to, one time.'

She wondered how different things might have been if she had succeeded then as they sat in her back garden, before Heather Nixon came back and threw herself on to his lap. (She had not found the moment yet to ask him if he had fucked her.) Would they have lasted this distance, or have been over and done with before the dark nights kicked in?

How strange to imagine him consigned to her past

instead of Heather Nixon's. (He *hadn't*, she was almost certain. Heather would have said. She did plenty of times later: kept a tally of their names, for heaven sake, on the girls' toilet walls.)

He had taken out the protractor, its semicircle quartered by fissures. 'I think I might have done this myself,' he said. 'I think I was going to see if I could separate it into a hundred and eighty individual degrees . . . a bit like a fan.' He demonstrated.

And he wondered why other boys used to chase him.

He covered her hand with his. 'Thank you,' he said, but for the remainder of the meal the lights above their table were subdued. By the time they left the restaurant he was practically silent.

'What are you thinking?' she asked.

'You don't want to know.'

She honestly thought that might be it, finished. 'Try me.'

Another silent step or two, then: 'I think we ought to get married.'

It was so not what she had been expecting that she laughed. 'Oh, you do, do you?'

He stopped – they were outside the oddly named Scruples Chicken Ranch – turned to her. 'Yes. What about you?'

The two words were on the tip of her tongue, but they were much too potent for a footpath in Shaftesbury Square. She wanted to say them once and for ever. But she did want to say them, of that she was in no doubt.

She put her arms around his waist. 'As quickly as possible.'

The business in the City Hall lasted about two minutes. Just because it was required by law to facilitate civil marriages it didn't follow that Belfast was going to *celebrate* them.

The facilitator, a council employee, had the kindly but no-nonsense air of a school nurse: 'Say "ah".'

'Ah.'

'Say "do".'

'Do.'

'Now you.'

'Ah . . . do.'

So much for potency.

'Right, off you go.'

'That seemed to go over all right,' Victor said as they traipsed down the stairs to the back door and Maxine, who had turned to share a laugh with him, caught his expression, and caught herself just in time.

'Yes,' she said, 'it did, didn't it?' She kissed his cheek. 'Thank you.'

Out in the courtyard, the photographer arranged the principals in the various combinations that tradition dictated then marched the entire party round to the front gates and lined them up with the 'Belfast Says No' banner slung below the dome in the background. (Maxine had always thought there ought to have been a second part: 'Now what was the question?')

'On a count of three,' he said. 'One, two, three . . .'

'Yes!' they shouted, guaranteeing him grins.

Some traditions are newer, and more local, than others.

*

St John heard the news in passing from Bea, several months after the event, sitting on a bench in Hyde Park. He couldn't say why he felt quite so affronted, or even if it was on his sister's behalf or his own.

'I don't see that lasting,' he said.

'Oh, I don't know,' said Bea.

She had told him she was coming to London to do a bit of shopping, which ought to have alerted him that something was afoot (St John's sisters had never done 'shopping': they came by things, turned them up) and if that hadn't then the suggestion that they meet in the park certainly should have. 'I thought it best if no one could overhear us,' she said when they had installed themselves, and allowed an elderly couple to pass, slowly, slowly. 'I mean, you being in the public eye and all.' Bea rather overestimated the size of the cable audience and *Home Test*'s share of it. There was as much chance of their meeting a survivor of the *Titanic*, roller-skating.

'Don't tell me,' he said: 'Sibyl?'

'Paddy tells me there's a lot of drugs around the club.'

'Stop press: drugs in nightclub shock!'

'No, this is scary stuff, pills being imported to order from Amsterdam.'

'Sibyl's doing this?'

'Sibyl's not able to stop it. There's a crowd has moved in to that whole scene' – lowering her voice still further – 'Paddy's pretty sure they're connected to the IPLO.'

St John turned and looked at her.

'Hang on, wasn't the IPLO put out of business?'

'They stopped using the name, if that's what you mean.'

St John couldn't even begin to frame the next question.

The IPLO was a breakaway of a breakaway of one half of the Old IRA. The IPLO was supposedly where you arrived if you faced away from the Provos and kept going left for two decades, murdering backsliders as you went. It seemed extraordinary that his sister, following the route that she had devised for herself at the age of about ten or eleven, should have ended up at the same destination.

'Paddy's petrified,' Bea said.

'Not a bit of wonder. Could you not have a word with her, tell her to go to the police?' But even as he asked it, St John knew the reply.

'The last place that tried to get rid of them got firebombed.'

St John leaned forward, elbows on his knees, holding his temples with both hands, tight. 'I can't believe Sibyl letting herself get mixed up with those headbangers.'

'If it was anyone else I would say we try and think of a way to get her to leave Belfast for a while, but you know what Sibyl's like.'

He did, but still. 'There has to be something we can do, somebody we can talk to,' he said.

The news about Maxine and Craig was the sour cherry on this bitter little cake.

'On the bright side,' said Bea, when they had sat for a minute and more unable to muster a word between them, 'I have only another month to go of my articles.'

It would have been churlish to suggest that the first thing she might have to do was defend her sister. 'That's fantastic.'

'Do you know what? I think it is too.'

She took his arm as they rose finally and walked back towards the street. It was February but felt as warm as a

Belfast June. A jogger in a singlet, sweat-soaked, overtook them. A group of teenagers passed in the opposite direction, boys and girls alike long-legged and flaxen-haired, scintillating in their simultaneous conversations.

'I always get this feeling when I'm in London,' Bea said, 'that there's a tour-bus parked just round the corner: THE MOST BEAUTIFUL PEOPLE IN THE WORLD ANNUAL OUTING.'

'If you're quick enough you can still get on it.'

'You're sweet, but you know what Sibyl would say, "I'll go by cab in case I show them up."'

And it was a relief to have a pleasant Sibyl-thought at the very last to take away. The only shame was that the relief was not longer lived.

Trudy switched on her bedside light at four. 'Are you going to tell me now what's eating you?'

'It doesn't matter,' he said.

'It matters if you're tossing and turning and I can't sleep.'

'There has to be *somebody*.'

'What?'

'Nothing.'

She turned on the light again at five. 'What is it now?'

'Irps.'

'*What?*'

'Sorry. A thought.'

'I'm very happy for you, but the kids are going to be up in an hour's time.' She pushed him with the sole of her foot. 'Please, St John, go and think somewhere else.'

He got out of bed and rang Directory Enquiries, standing with the cordless phone between the curtain and the kitchen window to keep the noise down. Directory Enquiries told him he would need the exact name of the college, and the town. 'Maybe,' the operator said helpfully, 'if you were to leave it till it was light, and you were a little less tired . . .'

It took him two days to get the names of every college within commuting distance of Derry, another two to pluck up the courage to start ringing round them, sitting in the little room he had use of at the Local Channel. He found him in the third college he tried . . . just.

'I'm afraid we don't have anyone of that name,' the receptionist said, then hesitated, the penny dropping: she was talking to an idiot. 'We have a Dr *Ó Nimm* . . .'

'Sorry, that's what I meant to say, Ó Nimm.'

'Right, so' – brighter, brisker – 'I'll fire you on up then.' And she did, like that, fired him on up, and there was his father's voice, in Irish, then, when that got no response, English.

'*Dia duit* . . . Hello?'

'This is St John.'

A pause. St John saw his face as clear as clear. The way his brows would knit. The way increasingly his own did when he played for time. 'I'm sorry? I didn't quite catch . . .'

'I think you heard me well enough. It's St John.'

A longer pause, then: 'Is she dead?'

St John was eleven again, Paddy's head sticking up from the nest at the foot of his bed. *Is he dead?*

'You mean Mo?'

'You still call her that?'

'Yes, and she's keeping the best, thanks. We all are.' Nothing. *Don't let yourself get annoyed.* 'I was wondering if I could ask you something.'

287

'I have a class soon.'

'I'll be quick about it.'

And he launched in and told him the story of Sibyllism and the Amsterdam pills and the remnants of the IPLO. His father listened so quietly that St John stopped a couple of times to ask was he still there.

'Still here,' he said. 'Still here,' then, finally, 'And what was it you wanted to ask me exactly?'

'I remembered Mo telling us that when you were arrested that time you were on a wing with the IRSP.'

The IRSP – as St John understood it – lay several stages back along the evolutionary road that terminated in the blind alley of the IPLO.

'They took me in, yes, for the fortnight I was there . . . nearly twenty years ago.'

Twenty years and at least two splits. St John pressed on feeling more hopeless with every word. 'If there was any-one you knew from back then who might have any sort of sway . . .'

'I wasn't a member of any organisation. I am a republican by virtue of being a socialist, I am not a republican socialist, still less a violent one. The RUC had trouble understanding that, so had your mother.'

St John couldn't let that one pass. 'I don't think it was the politics she minded so much as who you were practising them with.'

The voice at the other end turned steely. Steelier. 'Don't let her convince you that it was all my doing. Now, I am sorry about your sister, but I do have to go.'

St John still hadn't moved – hadn't detached his hand

from the receiver in its cradle – when, a minute or two later, the phone rang. 'I got the number off our receptionist,' his father said. 'You're in England?'

'Swindon, as we speak.'

'I was there once a long time ago, when I was at Oxford.' He paused. 'I'm sorry about the way I spoke earlier. And I am sorry, really, about Sibyl. I am sorry about a whole lot of things. I don't expect you to understand, I'm not sure I understand it now myself, but a clean break seemed like the best solution. Those were more extreme times.'

They talked for a quarter of an hour (St John didn't ask about the class he was supposed to be teaching), in the course of which St John told his father that he was now a grandfather twice over.

'Actually it's three times,' his father said. 'My youngest lad and his girlfriend . . . they were much, much too young, but what do you do?'

At the end his father gave St John – half-uncle St John? – his home phone number. 'Maybe we could talk again some time.'

They spoke briefly on the final day of that summer when the IRA declared a cessation of its campaign. It was one of those days, everyone was phoning everyone. *Do you think this is it? Do you think will it last?*

St John had more reason than most to wear out the dial. Mike Warren had called him first thing that morning. Sky had been in touch. They wanted *Home Test*, they wanted him: the Dozy DIY Man.

'That's satellite, but, right? Not cable.'

'It's *Sky*,' Mike said. 'Fucking Sky.'

*

Gerry had turned down the invitation to the wedding – Maxine, she hoped, would forgive her: she was a bit allergic to marriage ceremonies having had such a bad reaction to her own. Delayed, like, but bad all the same. She did, though, give them the most beautiful present of an antique love-seat, which went into the big bay window of the bedroom in the new house, Craig having at last been persuaded to give over the keys of the Aunt Queenie house to tenants, a pair of junior doctors at the City Hospital. And, too, Gerry made good on her promise to have Maxine formally recognised as a partner in the business. (*Junior*, like the doctors, but partner was partner.) Not that a big lot changed day to day. Though outside the office the company continued to expand, within its doors there were still just the two of them and there were still times when it seemed all they did was talk, still other times when they could go from morning to evening without exchanging more than half a dozen words. Prague obviously had to be dealt with. It was Gerry who came up with the formula, or fell back on an old familiar one. 'God I was pie-eyed. I don't remember a single thing after we left that nightclub.'

As for the other consequence of the trade fair – the Dublin contract – that, within a twelvemonth, was accounting for over a third of their turnover, to say nothing of the other doors it had opened in the South. Gerry was up and down a couple of times a month on the train, although not always up on the same day she went down. Maxine, needless to say, had her suspicions, but said nothing.

On one of those mornings after, while the first train from Dublin was still somewhere between Lurgan and Lisburn, a woman phoned the office, Maud, a friend of Gerry's friend Abbie. They had been introduced at dinner a few weeks ago and Gerry had expressed an interest in a meeting the woman and some other friends were holding to urge all political parties to increase the number of women candidates at the next election. 'I just wanted to give her a wee reminder, eight o'clock tonight . . .'

Gerry, when she did get in, could not have been less interested. 'I didn't say I'd go, I said I'd think about it, and I only said that to shut the bloody woman up. She had me cornered. Horsey bake.'

She scrunched up the Post-it Maxine had handed her and tossed it towards the bin. It landed two feet short ('Did you move that bin?') and despite several nudges in passing with the outside of their feet throughout the day ('I don't see why I should be the one to pick it up' . . . 'It wasn't me moved the bin') was still on the floor when Maxine was getting ready to go home, a little later than usual.

Craig was across in Fermanagh for a couple of days with Barry Kerr – providing yet more 'analysis'. At least now he was being paid for it, although he might need to be paid a whole lot more if he carried on stretching the patience of his headmaster. (Maxine – I'm sorry – baulked at 'Chief'.)

It was only to save her from having to stand and look at it tomorrow that she bent and picked the Post-it up.

The venue was a hotel she and Gerry had been trying for a while to woo. It would do no harm to be seen patronising the place – she assumed there would be a drink in the hotel bar afterwards. That was how all those things ended, wasn't it?

Anyway, she had no other plans. She could just go and sit at the back of the room and, if it was the load of rubbish Gerry was predicting, sneak back out and say hello to the duty manager.

She ought to have realised how badly she had miscalculated before she opened the function-room door.

She was only a couple of minutes late: was it likely that everyone else had arrived on time? Even if she had put her ear to the door before her hand she would have *heard* the emptiness. But hand it was that led, not ear, and in she walked on a vision of the utmost bleakness.

Besides the three women behind the table at the front of the room there were five people in attendance, all of whom looked over their shoulders as Maxine entered. There could be no hiding or escaping.

'Come in,' said the middle woman of the front three. It did have to be said, there was something ever so slightly equine about her show of teeth: Maud, so. 'We had just got through with the introductions, it being such an intimate gathering.'

'It's Maxine,' she said. 'Maxine Neill.'

'Actually,' said the woman, sitting to Maud's left, 'I don't want to criticise those who have come along for the failings of those didn't make the effort, but this turnout just proves what we've all secretly been thinking: no one's going to get very excited by a call for more women candidates. I mean, do we honestly imagine hearts will soar if we get an increase of fifteen per cent across the board at the next election? Not that we have a snowball's chance of getting anywhere near that of course. We need something gutsier to rally around. We need a party.'

'Our research shows that "party" has negative connotations for a lot of women,' said Maud.

'We can argue later about what we call it. We need to make sure that whatever emerges from this stage of political uncertainty takes account of the concerns of women of all religions and classes, whether it's equality in the workplace or maternity care or sex education, and whether the discrimination emanates from the State or those individuals and organisations who have taken it upon themselves to usurp the role of the State . . . I think you all know the kind of people I'm referring to.'

'Yes,' Maxine said, and that was the moment when she ceased to berate herself for her stupidity in picking the Post-it up off the office floor and began really to listen.

She left the room, two hours later, Treasurer.

Craig told her she was a soft touch. Like he was one to talk, haring around after Barry Kerr for a party he claimed not to support or even to like. Gerry told her she was a mug. 'They can talk all they like about changing the face of politics here, but when it comes to the crunch people will vote the way they have always voted: creed first' – a tap on her crotch – 'gee last.'

'I'm going to pretend you didn't just say that.'

An election had been announced to a forum for political dialogue, which, even Maxine had to admit, was the equivalent of an invitation to the opening of a porch into an anteroom. All the same her group and other like-minded groups, operating now as 'Women in it Together', decided they would field candidates: one in every constituency if they could manage it.

To make sure that all the right people made it into the porch – all the people, that is, who might otherwise be tempted to take potshots from the outside, and had the wherewithal to do it – the government had put in place a system of top-ups. Maud had calculated that six thousand votes across the whole of the country would be enough to get WIT – because WIT inevitably and almost instantly they became – in there too.

Maxine allowed herself to be persuaded to stand as number five on the list for Lagan Valley and with a team of three volunteers – two of them still at school – set out in search of converts. They were pitching their message to the voters of the big parties, but really they were scrapping for first preferences with the very few, like the Greens, whose voters were, as Gerry would have it, traditionally gee-friendly.

Some of the places they canvassed they got absolute dog's abuse. One man answered the door to them in his boxer shorts, or mostly in. Others simply shouted at them from their armchairs, 'Fuck away off.' (Craig, after the first night, offered to accompany her, but (a) – she said – you're tainted goods and (b) – his face in her hands – I love you and all, but seriously what could you do?) Women who opened the door to them were half the time looking over their shoulders. To be honest, the evenings couldn't have ended soon enough. Maxine, though, loved the number-crunching that followed: if two-thirds of the nine women in the hundred and fifty houses they had between them covered who said they would *at least consider* voting WIT did, and if *that* was repeated across the whole constituency then . . .

They were reckoning on four hundred first preferences, they got five hundred and twenty – Maxine herself thirty-six of them, twice as many as the Natural Law candidate, twelve times as many as the combined votes of the two candidates running as independents (the No-Friends as everyone else, WIT included, referred to them) – and though their overall vote was barely above one per cent, they broke the magic six thousand: they got their top-ups, their two tickets to the Forum.

Maxine took a day's leave the second Friday in June, the first day that the Forum sat (Gerry to her credit had tried to persuade her to chalk it up as work), and met up at Stormont with all the other candidates whose thirty-six votes here and there across the country had carried them over the line and into the talks.

Standing at the foot of the steps up to the parliament building – conscious for the first time of the size of the place, the spread – she instinctively linked arms with the women on either side of her, who had each, acting on the same instinct, linked arms with the women to their left and right respectively, and so on down the line, so that when one moved all moved, a wave washing right up to the revolving door, irresistible.

Craig left the house half an hour after Maxine and arrived at the parliament building with Barry Kerr, who had managed to get accreditation for them both. (One of the 'Danzig Group', cured of his folly, in public at least, had made it on to the Party's talks team.) He too hesitated at the foot of the steps, stumbled almost, his feet seeming to refuse the command to walk.

'You all right?' asked Barry.

Craig nodded, trying to regain his composure. 'I never told anybody this,' he said, 'but when I was a kid I had this bizarre feeling, everything that happened was being scrutinised and controlled . . . I think I imagined it was all coming from here.'

'What year were you born, '63? It all was.'

'No I mean the smallest, smallest detail, who sat down beside me on the bus, how many fillings I needed when I went to the dentist, whether or not it rained on my birthday, where I came in the sack race at the school sports . . .'

'I believe the term you're looking for there is delusions of grandeur.'

'You obviously don't know where I came in the sack race.'

He met Maxine in one of the intervals between sessions in the melee at the foot of the grand staircase. As successive party leaders appeared at the top and the press closed in he and she found themselves by degrees pushed to the very edge until they were right up against one of the enormous rectangular pillars separating the hall from the arcade on either side. 'I feel like dragging you behind this thing,' she whispered close to his ear.

'How quickly power goes to the head.'

'Believe me, it's not the head.'

A bell rang: ten minutes to the start of the next round.

'Let's get away from here as soon as we can,' he said.

'OK.'

But the remaining sessions took a little of the heat out of

them both – the story of their lives just now, as they had, several bedtimes of late, ruefully and wearily acknowledged to one another. Instead of going straight home – and resisting all too easily the opportunities afforded by the bushes and the trees bordering the mile-long driveway to the front gate – they followed the herd across the road to the Stormont Hotel for a drink.

The bar was a babel of correspondents and their crews, American, French, German, Italian, Spanish, Norwegian, Russian, Israeli, Danish, Portuguese, Northern Ireland once again demonstrating a pulling power out of all proportion to its size and the scale of its conflict. Unless of course the news teams just wanted to make sure that this really was the beginning of the end and that they would never again have to bother themselves or their viewers with the self-regarding place and the minutiae of its hatreds.

Among the Forum teams, their supporters and observers, meantime, there were many hugs and tears, because whatever the scale of it they had lived with this thing nearly all their adult lives, since childhood, some of them.

Hugs and tears and rounds called in quick succession.

Craig and Maxine found a couple of seats eventually next to a crowd from the SDLP, intent it appeared on obscuring every last inch of tabletop with empties. They were on their third drink themselves when Maxine happened to turn her head as out of the ruck at the bar, a few feet to their left, a hand emerged clutching the unspilled portion of a pint of lager, and behind it, bit by bit, the somewhat buffeted but unmistakable figure of St John Nimmo. She touched Craig's arm, which was the movement that alerted St John to her presence and to Craig's.

It was the first time they had all been in a room together since the party in St John's house back when they were seventeen, before Maxine and St John, before Craig and Bea. Actually it may have been the first time since that party that they had been in the presence of so many people drinking so much so fast.

For a moment none of them spoke; for a moment it looked as though St John would take back the steps he had taken towards them.

'My partner's supposed to be here,' he said, 'BBC.' He glanced back over his shoulder, glanced here, there and nowhere in particular about the bar. 'Looks like I missed her.'

After which there was nothing from any of them for several moments more. Craig and St John went for their pockets at the same moment, produced from them identical packets of cigarettes. Marlboro Lights. Maxine spluttered into her glass.

'What?' they both asked. 'What?'

She pulled over a stool from the no man's land between their table and the SDLP's. 'Come on,' she said and patted the cushion, 'sit.'

Four hours later, St John having discovered in the meantime that Trudy had headed into town to voice-over some pictures at Broadcasting House, and was already back at Mo's, there was just the three of them in the bar. All around them bar staff stacked chairs on tables, tipped ashtrays into buckets, and made gravity-defying parabolas of empties. Time's call had gone unheard so often there remained only these practical demonstrations of the fact that it was well and truly up.

The lights went on, the vacuum started up. From the restaurant came the sound of tables being set for breakfast.

'I think we're going to have to go somewhere else,' St John said and Craig and Maxine nodded: good idea.

The bar manager was only too glad to phone them a taxi – minutes was all it took to arrive ('Hello, 999 Cabs . . .'). As they drove down the Newtownards Road towards the city centre – clouds, blacker than the night sky, piled on the hills beyond – they did their best sober-in-a-taxi routine, asking the driver had the town been busy and was he staying on long and what time was he back in tomorrow. The driver was having none of it.

'Were yous up there at the talks today?'

They all answered at once. Yes . . . No . . . Kind of . . .

He shook his head. 'No harm to yous, but it's a waste of fucking time.'

He gestured towards the glove compartment. 'Open that there,' he said to St John, who trapped as he was in the passenger seat could only comply.

'What do you see?'

'Books.'

'Books is right. Do you know what's in them?'

'Um . . .'

The driver leaned across him – driving for the moment with his eyes not much above the dashboard – and pulled a book out. 'Freemasons,' he said. 'And, here – stick your hand in the map pocket.'

St John did. More books, more Masons. The car was a mini mobile library of esoterica.

'Some of the things in there, let me tell you, would turn your blood cold. That's who's really running the show. See compared to that? See what's going on up there . . . ?' A nod backwards, aimed up the Newtownards Road, up the mile-long driveway and the flight of steps to Stormont's front door: 'Mickey Mouse stuff.'

They tumbled out of his car in front of the Europa Hotel, where St John had the security guard phone reception to page a colleague of Trudy's who was staying there and who sent word back, via reception to the guard, that they were good people and true – his exact phrase – on the strength of which they were able to carry on for another hour and a half in the first-floor bar in the company of men and women whose own record of falling into bed with one another was a Masonic conspiracy compared to their own cartoonish efforts.

There was an element of not wanting to blink, or bail, first: too much still, in their various combinations to fear being said. Craig it was, in the end, ran up the white flag. 'That's me.' He pushed his glass into the centre of the table. (What was even in it?) 'No more.'

Maxine, with only a slight time-delay between brain and mouth said, God, yes, they should really think about getting another taxi.

St John got up with them, a little stumble, steadying himself with a hand splayed on the tabletop. 'OK, OK, but there's still something we have to do.'

'That sounds worrying,' said Craig.

St John wagged a finger; it was easier than speech. The same finger led the way to the lifts, pressed the button to go up.

'St John,' Maxine slurred, 'We can't do *that*.'

The lift doors opened. St John's finger lit the topmost light. They concentrated on their stomachs as the lift ascended, lest they should overtake the rest of them, and when the doors opened again – oh, fuck, Maxine whispered – it was on to a vast window looking west to east across the city. They tripped forward like communicants to the altar.

The black clouds had cleared and in their wake the new day was mustering in pinks and mauves.

St John draped an arm around each of them. 'It's really bad of me not to have said it before now, but I'm dead pleased for the two of you. Dead, dead, dead, *dead* pleased.'

'Like we're ones to complain,' said Craig, 'you with your babies . . .'

'School any day now, for fuck sake,' St John said, more in wonder than anything.

'. . . and not even a card or a call from us.'

'Mnah.' St John dismissed the omission. Maxine took up the refrain.

'Let's not be too hard on ourselves here. I mean, OK, there's a whole lot we could have done differently – done better – but you think of all the things that might have happened . . .'

'I suppose when you look at it like,' said Craig. There were lines in his head, a Heaney poem, from back around the time of the ceasefire, which had troubled him oddly then, but which came into its own now, something about being alive and sinning, 'Ourselves again,' something else again, *'not bad.'* Yes. His arms up around the others' shoulders now too, pulling them in until their three foreheads touched.

'We haven't done too bad, have we?'

Fucking

I

Late one April evening, a matter of hours before the final text of the Belfast Agreement was arrived at, Maxine came out of the room in the east wing of the parliament buildings where the WIT team was in conference and found herself face to face with the man who had once promised her he would kill her brother. The man was with two others in ill-fitting suits whom she recognised from all the to-ing and fro-ing and room-hopping of recent days. He, though, was dressed as Maxine remembered last having seen him at the bus stop in the aftermath of her father's funeral, like a travel rep, his jumper today knotted loosely about his neck.

He smiled. 'Well, well, well. Maxine, isn't it?'

He thrust out a hand, which Maxine, caught off guard, was unable to get out of the way of. He gave her wrist a squeeze for good measure.

'You moved away. Bangor wasn't it? Oh, but then of course you got married.'

Her mouth – she was powerless to stop it – fell open. The men in suits were looking at her closely, critically.

'I used to run around with Maxine's brother, Tommy,' he said, by way of explanation. 'Long, long time ago.'

She managed to get her hand back.

'I didn't expect to see you here,' she said.

His smile broadened. 'Did you not know? I have to be

here. These fellas here – they won't mind me saying it – are only the lieutenants. There can't be an agreement until the brigadiers have approved it.'

At the far end of the corridor at that moment the Prime Minister appeared in his shirtsleeves, accompanied by the Secretary of State. The Secretary of State peered then her hand went up in salute.

'I think they might be looking for us,' said one of the men in suits.

The travel-rep brigadier gave Maxine a pat on the back, winked. 'Looks like your Tommy backed the wrong side,' he said.

Maxine in her agitation was halfway down the corridor in the opposite direction before she remembered what it was she had come out to do. By the time she had faced about the corridor was empty, but in all the euphoria of the days that followed she could not shake the memory of that encounter, nor yet when she went out to cast her vote in favour of the agreement that the brigadiers had given their assent to. It was a new Northern Ireland, and one that her brother did not feel safe coming home to.

The travel rep was killed a couple of years later, as he sat in a car outside a bookmaker's to which he had been lured by a call from – police later confirmed – a stolen mobile phone. A motorbike skidded to a halt in front of him and the pillion passenger emptied a full magazine through the windscreen before shouting to the driver of the bike: 'Go, go, go!'

One of the lieutenants who had stood with him in the corridor at Stormont went on TV (his suit was a better fit for him now, or he was a better fit for it) and said that while he deeply regretted the incident it was well known that the deceased had been estranged from his party for some time and was widely believed to have been involved in extortion from his own community, which, God knows, was having it hard enough without gangsters leeching off it.

The Prime Minister's office issued a statement, the Prime Minister himself being on holiday, saying that this dreadful murder should not be allowed to derail the peace process, which the people of Northern Ireland had voted for in such overwhelming numbers. It was almost word for word the statement put out when an organisation styling itself Direct Action Against Drugs, but with all the weaponry and the logistical capabilities of the IRA, killed a number of dealers the summer before, including one who was alleged to have been 'preying on' the Belfast club scene for many years.

No one was arrested then. No one was arrested now. Now as then Women in it Together made no official response.

Craig was at a conference in Sarajevo when news of the shooting broke. He had at long last written up his free-city spiel into a monograph and even though, as far as it pertained to his home town, it had been overtaken by the Agreement, it had struck a chord. Invitations followed to conferences on conflict resolution, as well as to other cities with a bit of 'Belfast' form – starting with the Bs, of course: Berlin, Beirut, Bogotá – allowing (the governors might have said 'obliging') him to take the plunge and resign from his school.

The fifth-year pupils had made a presentation at the final assembly of the year, a framed 'Plan of the Town of Belfast' dated 1757, its key marking only seven buildings of note: Custom-house, English Church, Market-place, Shambles, Presbyterian Meeting-house, Barracks, 'a new built dinner hall'.

'That's *Linnen*,' Craig said, puncturing Maxine's delight at the discovery. 'Two *n*s, curly capital *l*.'

Maxine went to some of the overseas conferences too – spoke at them, drawing on her experience of the talks – although not as a representative of WIT, with which in truth she had felt herself increasingly at odds, not least because of its silence on the drug-dealer murders. She never failed at those conferences to mention the meeting in the corridor at Stormont with the man who had threatened her brother. And now that man was dead too.

Maxine phoned Craig twice, even though she knew that he was more than likely in session with his mobile switched off.

'I am trying very hard to remember not to take pleasure in anyone's death,' she told the answer service the second time, conscious that she had once vowed to outlast him and his kind; this was not at all the way she had meant it. 'Oh, and guess what just started?'

She had asked him the same rhetorical question every month, or five weeks, or very occasionally three, since they had decided to stop trying not to have a baby. It had been a bit of a joke between them to begin with, the near impossibility of predicting her fertile period. 'Do you think your body is trying to tell me something?'

'Tell you? Tell me, more like.' That she had maybe left it too late already. That Gerry was right, there was something going on there that she should have had checked out long, long ago.

She did eventually go to talk to her GP, who had suggested she go on the Pill for six months, which – whatever she told her about getting things back on an even keel – still sounded like an admission of defeat to Maxine. She and Craig had talked it over and agreed to give it another Pill-free go or eight in the weeks before the Sarajevo conference.

And here, for their troubles, she was again, nearing the end of her thirty-eighth year, being rhetorical and as stoical as she could muster.

Craig phoned her later that night – the early hours almost in Sarajevo – said, what she expected him to say, that he already had, in her, everything that he had ever wanted, or needed, although saying it with a vehemence that nevertheless disarmed her. Of the murder he said, 'I have a horrible feeling it's what we voted for and a horrible feeling that if we were offered it a second time we'd vote for it again.'

Because chains that would never before have dreamed of it were opening now in Belfast, because glass was replacing blind brick as the façade of choice, because the security gates and turnstiles around the city had been dismantled and even the concrete barriers that replaced them were disappearing, because along with everything else house prices had been processed up. In the last eighteen months alone Craig's great-aunt's house had nearly tripled in value. The last estate agent he had gone to see told him to do nothing for the moment, except, if he could, buy more property: they were still on the lower reaches of the upward curve.

Better off with each day that passed, they did what

everyone around them was doing and shopped, reinvesting their little portion of the peace dividend. Habitat, on a Saturday morning, appeared to them the creation of neo-Marshall-planners, intent on boosting morale as well as growth, their presence there not so much a lifestyle choice as a civic duty.

Maxine's mother, ignorant still of his threat to her own family, went to the travel rep's funeral. 'For his mummy, God help her,' she told Maxine. 'She is as good a wee woman as ever drew breath. Knit me bootees and a matinee jacket when Victor was just born, and I tell you at the time we were glad of them. Anyway, nobody asks for the children they get.'

*

Slowly, slowly, *Home Test* built its Sky audience, coming in from the fringes of the lunchtime schedule to early evening. The format remained pretty much unchanged for the first couple of series. Each week St John would tackle a piece of basic home improvement, guided – or occasionally flummoxed – by a manual: sanding a floor, rehanging a door, wiring a dimmer-switch, with a precautionary fire-extinguisher standing by, or (a high point of series two) fitting an electronic cat flap. With the move to evenings, however, came a number of innovations. There were studio guests, usually people who had made their names on other parts of the Sky schedule, given a task to complete, with St John as mate and interviewer combined; there were 'how we used to' shows, making use of tools and tips from bygone eras. (Conclusion?

A person in possession of a sharp knife and a tin of baking soda could get by in most situations.)

Back in Belfast one pre-Christmas with Trudy and the children, he presented Mo with a brand-new aluminium stepladder, with an extra-wide (and therefore ultra-safe) crosspiece and adjustable tension strap. She did not know until well into the New Year when Bea phoned to tell her she had caught that night's programme (Mo did not have access to Sky, which was not a sentence she could have imagined ever saying when she was nineteen, or even forty-nine) did not know until then that he had taken the old ladder back with him as a prop for a 'how not to' special: finally the star of its own public-information film.

Mike Warren had cashed in his interest in the production company after the fourth Sky series – he hadn't got into this line of work to sit in meetings with fucking bank managers and accountants – and had returned to making actual programmes with a company called Verbal.

St John switched on his phone one day coming out of a production meeting and Mike's name popped up at the head of his missed calls. They played phone tag for a couple of hours before finally managing to speak.

'Mike?'

'St John?'

'Hey.'

'Hey. Thanks for getting back to me.'

'What's new with you?'

'Funny you should ask.'

'Oh?'

'Mm.'

So.

What it was.

Verbal had pitched this idea to 4 – who were going with it, Mike was pretty sure – taking personalities back to the place where they had spent their childhood, seeing what it revealed about them.

'We're calling it *Where I'm Coming From* and I thought, you know, satellite is still a bit of a closed world, it would be a good next step for you.'

'To be one of the . . . people' – St John shied away from Mike's *p* word – 'sent back to where they came from, you mean?'

'Yeah, "This is the room I slept in when I was a kid," sort of thing, "This is where I got my end away."'

'I don't know.'

'Oh, come on, I'm joking about that, I mean unless you want to talk about getting your end away. No, we'll talk to any brothers and sisters, your parents . . .'

'Well that's what I don't know, things were a bit, what would you say, *complicated* when I was growing up.'

'Perfect! Viewers *want* complication, they don't want to see family trees that come embroidered in little gilt-edged frames any more. Simple went out with Sooty and Sweep.'

St John, as it happened, had been thinking for some time about what came next. Shelly and James were hurtling to-wards their teens. In a very – scary – few years they would be away, or on the point of going. Trudy, he sometimes felt, was already limbering up in front of the starting blocks, her mind set on the overseas post that her CV lacked.

And it would be good to be able to spend more time

in Belfast, where – it was pleasing to remember – he had friends. Good too to make contact again with his father.

'Sixty minutes, twelve-day shoot,' Mike was saying, 'two months' prep with a full-time researcher and PA.'

'You're not exactly leaving me much room to say no.'

'Oh, and the fee's not bad either.' He named it.

St John laughed. '*Any* room.'

But still he didn't say yes until he had talked it over with Trudy – one of their shorter conversations. 'What are you, insane? Of course you are going to do it' – and at least run it by family in Belfast.

Sibyl wanted to know if this was really what it had come to, meaning – he supposed – television, the world that it channelled. (Or was that projected?)

Mo said, with what amounted to a shrug, that she didn't have access to Sky.

'It's not Sky, it's 4.'

'I don't know, do we even have that?'

'Everybody has that.'

Bea, the only one to whom he had mentioned talking to his father, was the only one who was openly discouraging, 'It'll not end well,' she said.

Bea was in the middle of divorce proceedings, victim of a two-and-a-half-year itch; she was not disposed to see anything ending well.

Paddy had one only question: *Why you?*

It was the researcher, Tom, a skateboarder without the wheels (the cap never left his head), who let slip the answer, several weeks later, that one of 4's stipulations in commissioning the series had been a good regional spread.

They had been racking their brains in the production office for someone from 'over there' – preferably *not* a sports personality with a drink problem: like they needed that on their shooting schedule – when Mike came up with St John's name.

'I mean,' Tom had the gumption to realise he had said rather more than he ought to have, 'we were all, *of course: St John Nimmo . . .* We should have thought of you straight away.'

St John looked at his stricken expression and tried hard not to smile. *I think I'm going to be able to depend on you from now on, Skater Tom.*

*

For a while the conference invitations continued to come in from all parts for Craig and Maxine both. As time passed, however, and politics shrank into its old WIT-less party shape, they came increasingly for him alone. He sensed in any case that Maxine had been steadily losing her appetite for the apparently endless reiteration involved, even the reiteration of doubts – 'I mean, I had plenty of reason to dislike the man, but to see the process just absorb his murder like that . . .'

Sooner or later you were bound to run out of steam.

He had said several times that he would cut down himself, but then an offer would come in to speak, with an honorarium attached equal to his monthly standing orders, and that would be him, off again.

Inevitably the same faces tended to recur: Iurie, the Mad

Moldovan (it was how he introduced himself), with his theory of the *stabilising* effect of unrecognised states; Liesl, the Afrikaner ex-ANC cadre, now in flight from two identities.

The new faces, by the same token, tended to stand out. Devon's appeared for the first time in Sarajevo, on the fringes of a reception hosted by the European Union Delegation in Bosnia and Herzegovina. Not young, exactly, but carrying youthfulness into the next age. She was from Wyoming – 'Carbon County, if you've heard of it,' delivered with a wry smile.

'No, but I've a faint impression I know its twin.'

The smile subtly changed. 'You're quick.'

'That's one of the kinder things that's been said about me.'

She was currently on a post-doctoral fellowship at a centre for international understanding in Massachusetts. Didn't drink. At all. She had done enough of that, and other stuff, before she went back into college in her early twenties. The grimace said she would prefer not to talk about it, so Craig didn't ask.

'I played guitar in a band,' she volunteered a moment later.

'Right, I see.'

'I don't know if you do. One of my band mates died after a gig: freebasing. We had been in kindergarten together.'

'Christ.'

'Yeah, well.'

They carried on talking when they got back to the residences sitting in the little café-cum-TV-room-cum-bar, long after everyone else had turned in, fuelled by nothing stronger than filtered water, sliding down in their seats until they were both resting their heels on the seats opposite. They turned to one another in laughing at a certain point and then didn't turn away again. There was no saying how long they held that look . . . The laughter dried up. They shook their heads. This was hopeless, wasn't it? Their individual circumstances, the vast distances between them.

Still, they exchanged email addresses.

They wrote as soon as they got home to make sure the addresses were working. They wrote after that twice weekly, then daily, then once or twice an hour.

It got so that she was waiting for him getting up before going to bed. Some mornings they exchanged ten or twelve emails before he started to work and she called it a night. The *x*s with which they signed off multiplied.

When she began describing for him what she was wearing sitting at the computer Craig set up another address.

He passed up two invitations to conferences that he knew she would be attending – 'a paranoid person would think you were avoiding her,' she wrote. The third he accepted: Rome; which of all of them he ought to have known to avoid.

Maxine was waiting for him when he got home in the airport car park. He threw his bag in the boot.

'How was it?' she asked.

'You could pretty much write the script.'

'Oh, dear.' She leaned forward to check in her wing mirror for cars coming up on the right as she nosed out of the parking bay. She was beautiful. How could he have let himself forget for a moment, never mind a dark Roman hour or two, the miracle of their having found one another? Her hand slipped from the gearstick on to his. 'At least you're home.'

It crossed his mind that she knew, or suspected something, that this was her way of saying that whatever it was that had happened it didn't mean anything to her, so long as it went no further.

'Oh, and I should warn you, St John is looking for you.'

'You were talking to him?'

'He phoned.'

'He timed that well.'

'I don't get you.' She was still trying to concentrate on the traffic.

'He phoned last time I was away too.'

'Did he?'

'Well you told me.'

'Really? Maybe he did then. I don't remember.'

She either does not recognise what you are at or she is shaming you by not rising to it. Stop. Now. Breathe.

'Did he say what it was he wanted?'

'You know St John, a bit vague on it sometimes. Some new thing he's working on, I think.'

'I don't see how I'd be able to help him.'

'He mentioned that teacher of yours that was shot. Harrison.'

2

They met in a café looking across Donegall Square and the Garden of Remembrance to the western flank of the City Hall. St John had grown a moustache and goatee since last they had met. The beard was flecked with grey. They gripped one another by the upper arm as they shook hands, but from the moment they were seated there was a tension between them, concentrated on – emanating from – the A4 envelope that St John had set on the low table separating their seats.

A man in fluorescent waterproofs had come out of the City Hall to pick up litter from around the Cenotaph: a conveniently distracting midpoint to which they addressed the majority of their comments. Which were to begin with confined to the health of those they each held dear, a little more circumspect, even now, in the case of some – Bea had come down with some glandular-fever type thing: dizziness, stiff neck, nausea – than others.

Eventually, however, the envelope could not be ignored. St John several times moved it with his splayed fingertips, lining up the shorter edge with the edge of the tabletop.

'So Maxine tells me you're branching out?' Craig prompted.

'I don't know about that. It's more a one-off thing.'

The council worker had gone back into the City Hall. St

John turned the envelope through one hundred and eighty degrees.

'Is that anything to do with it?' Craig asked.

St John pulled his hand away as though burned, replaced it slowly.

'Listen, this might all come as a bit of a surprise to you,' he said. 'It did to me, but just bear with me for a couple of minutes, will you?'

*

Skater Tom had phoned him at home one night the week before he was due to travel to Belfast. 'Sorry, I know it's late, but I'm sitting here looking at something . . . funny.'

'Funny how?'

'Like peculiar, like . . . I don't know. Was there a teacher when you were at school . . .'

'I know what you're going to ask. Harrison, his name was.'

'Right, and he was mixed up in some kind of shit?'

*

'What do you mean shit?'

'That's what I asked. I mean part of it, you know, is the way Tom speaks. It's shit this and shit that, good shit, bad shit, crazy shit.'

'OK then, but "mixed up", that's pretty unambiguous.'

St John took a deep breath. 'He came across a document, a list of names the IRA had of people who were being used

319

to undermine the hunger strikers' cause.'

'Used by who?'

'Well, the document seemed to suggest elements within the security services and some loyalists they were running.' He laughed entirely without volition, glanced around at customers addressing themselves to lattes and overblown muffins, or thumbing messages into phones. 'Sorry, it seems mad to be sitting here now saying it.'

'But you believe it all the same or else why would you have called me? Why would you have brought your envelope?'

St John nodded: you're right. 'I think some of it could be true, yes. Don't get me wrong, I'm not saying it's a reason to kill anybody, but as an illustration of how fucked up things were, it's worth sitting down with an open mind and looking over.'

He slid the envelope across the table. Craig stared at it. He stood up. 'No.'

'No?'

'I won't let you do it.'

St John let out something else in the territory of a laugh, of bemusement this time, mixed with a degree of genuine sympathy. 'Craig, mate, I hate to say it, but you can't stop me.'

*

He came home that night like a bear. No point even asking him how it had gone. Silent through dinner, he got up as soon as he had finished eating and went to his study. They had rooms enough in the house for one apiece, although she preferred 'office' for hers: easier to shut the door on and walk away. They had a mini-gym whose doorstep she was fairly sure he had never darkened. It was to there that she went when she had made her evening call to Gerry in Dublin to reconcile their diaries for the morning.

(Gerry was more and more inclined to open an actual Dublin office, seeing as how more and more of their income was being generated from there, as indeed was more and more of everything else on the island. Besides, eight years' commuting to get a ride, she said . . . it would wear you out.)

At regular intervals as she worked out she heard from the far end of the landing the ping of mail being sent and received.

She heard it again as she dried herself after her shower.

Downstairs, moisturised, dressed only in a bathrobe, she took a large glass of red wine into the odd little Art Deco sunroom that more than anything else had sold them on the house and that was, in all types of weather at all times of day, the room to which they most often repaired. She eked out the wine, hoping he would join her before bed. It wasn't good for anyone's morale all this time alone under the one roof.

She tapped on his door on her way up to bed. He looked at her over the top of the computer. 'Are you going to be much longer?'

'Not much.'

The last thing she heard, half an hour later, was a ping.

*

Craig replayed the afternoon's conversation dozens more times as he lay in bed. He would have said he didn't sleep at all were it not for the moments when Harrison himself was in the room, on the chair where the clothes got dumped, an empty coffee cup dangling from the forefinger of his right hand; for the trail of orange and red pellets, glowing like the lights in the floor of a plane, leading from the chair out the door to the landing.

'It's up to you,' he said to Craig, more than once.

*

St John's phone rang almost as soon as he was out of bed.

'I'm sorry about yesterday,' Craig said. 'It was all a bit of a surprise.'

'Maybe I could have brought it up better.'

'What was it you wanted me to do exactly?'

'I was thinking an interview, walk and talk, maybe along the front of the school, putting things in context. The idea isn't to condemn, but to understand – why people made the choices they did in those days.'

(The idea in structural terms was to put into perspective his own father's sudden departure, leading up to a reunion, possibly on Derry's Walls.)

Craig whistled. 'How far were you imagining we were going to walk?'

'I'm talking very generally here,' St John said. 'It's a one-hour programme, this will be a two-and-a-half-minute segment, at most.'

'Two and a half minutes?'

'Edited. Take us maybe a morning to do, an afternoon, we'll work around you.'

'All right.'

'That's brilliant. See you at the school gates, then?'

'Yeah, see you at the school gates.'

*

They settled on Monday morning at eleven-twenty: directly after break. The school had expanded, upwards rather than outwards, since their day, two-storey classroom blocks become three or four, a new tower block rising up in the centre where, from memory, the anachronistic junior girls' playground had used to be. It had the air now of an island city, rather than the overgrown market town where between them they had spent thirteen years of their lives. Still, at twenty past eleven, that familiar quiet reigned, of classes in session.

'I feel like we're mitching off,' St John said, his hand on Craig's shoulder. 'Come here till I introduce you to the crew.'

They were standing at the raised boot of a nearby Volvo estate, all two of them: Andy on camera, Conor on sound. St John drew his head back looking at Craig. 'Sorry if you were expecting a whole crowd.'

'No, no . . . Actually, I don't know what I was expecting.'

'Time was you would have needed a bus, nearly, for all the focus pullers and second assistants. The only thing that hasn't changed is the Volvos. Isn't that right, Andy?' Andy's smile was enigmatic, but before he could respond or St John elaborate, a woman arrived in a quilted anorak that polar explorers of old could only have dreamed of, four coffees held at arm's length (the anorak was ice-white) in a cardboard carrier. 'Oh, and this is my producer,' St John said. 'Hazel.'

Craig smiled, held out his hand. 'Craig.'

'*You're* Craig,' she said. 'Hi.'

The 'I' bloomed like an exotic flower. 'Fantastic to meet you finally. I'm really looking forward to this.'

'Me too, actually, now that I'm here,' said Craig.

While St John and Andy paced out together the route of the walk and talk and Conor looked displeased with something in the atmosphere – squinting into the middle distance, alternately covering and uncovering his right ear with the headphones as he tried to pinpoint the source of his irritation – Hazel took Craig through the release form.

'It looks scarier than it is. Basically it just says that you consent to us making use of the interview material in whatever form we decide. It's pretty standard.' She made a cross as she said this at the foot of page one and another where the text ended a third of the way down page two. Craig without hesitation signed his name beside them both.

'I better watch I don't say anything I regret.'

'I'm sure you won't.'

Conor gave him a radio-mic pack to put in his back pocket – 'Phone off?' Craig nodded – then fed the wire up under his wool polo shirt and clipped it in just above the second buttonhole.

'Everybody happy then?' St John called.

'I'm still picking up a bit of buzz from somewhere,' Conor said. They all stood and listened. Heard nothing. Conor shook his head. 'I suppose it'll have to do.'

St John walked Craig back to the starting point he had

agreed with Andy, about thirty yards from the school gate, next to a car with a Jesus fish in the window.

'Just try to ignore the camera,' St John said. 'When we get right up to the gate I'll lean against the pillar and we'll carry on talking till we're done.'

Craig's face broke into a smile. 'I've never seen you in action before. I'm impressed.'

'It's like anything, isn't it? You do it often enough you eventually cease to be a complete incompetent.'

'As the actress said to the bishop,' Craig said out the corner of his mouth as they waited for the signal to walk.

St John stifled a laugh. 'Now don't you start me going.'

'Turning over,' Andy called, but Conor held up a hand – not yet; a bus passed, dieselly; the hand yielded to a raised thumb.

'Three, two, one,' St John whispered, and Craig took his hand from his jacket pocket.

Visuals
EXT *School, wide shot:* ST JOHN *and friend* CRAIG *walk*

Sound
Continuous street ambience

Narration
ST JOHN
This is a bit strange, Craig, being back here.

CRAIG
Well, of course, you've been living away a right while, which makes it even stranger.

ST JOHN
So, what is it now, thirty-something years since the two of us met?

CRAIG
Thirty-two. You sat beside me on our very first day.

ST JOHN
Did I?

CRAIG
You did: first day, first class.

ST JOHN
That's the historian's memory, you see.

CRAIG *(laughs)*
You made an impression.

ST JOHN
Seriously, though, history was your subject, wasn't it, from pretty early on?

CRAIG
I suppose it was.

Visuals
ST JOHN *and* CRAIG *arrive at School Gate.*

'Hold on a second,' Andy said. 'I just want to change the shot. If I could cheat you round this way a touch, Craig.'

His hand reached out, like some extension of the camera that he kept to his eye, and tried to manoeuvre Craig into position.

'Like this?' Craig asked. He was faced more towards the camera than St John.

'A touch more . . .' Craig's back was practically flat against the gate. 'That's it.'

'It's going brilliantly,' said Hazel. 'Really natural and re-laxed. You would never think you hadn't done this before.'

'Conor?' said Andy.

'I can live with it.'

'All right, turning over.'

Visuals
ST JOHN *and* CRAIG *chat at the School Gate.* ST JOHN *frowns.*

Narration
ST JOHN
And there was one teacher in particular who you looked up to?

CRAIG
Mr Harrison, yeah.

ST JOHN
What was it we used to call him?

CRAIG
Hammy.

ST JOHN
Hammy. That's right.

CRAIG
Every teacher had to have a nickname. He hated it.

ST JOHN *(after a moment's reflection)*
And could you tell us what happened . . . ?

CRAIG
He was murdered.

Hazel, to Andy's immediate left, raised her hand. Craig stopped. Andy shouldered the camera.

'Is everything all right?' St John asked.

'I was just wondering if we were happy with Craig using that word.'

'Murdered?' said St John.

'Yes, are we sure that's what it was, because this is such a lovely chat and I would hate us to have to lose the whole thing because Compliance . . . ?'

'Our legal eagles . . .' St John turned to Craig to supply the gloss.

'Sorry,' said Hazel. 'Because the Legal and Compliance Department objected.'

'No, I think we can definitely say murdered,' said St John.

'Well,' Craig's tone was even, 'three men broke down his door in the middle of the night and shot him fifteen times in his own bed, so, yes, I think we're justified in calling that murder.'

'Oh, God, no, don't get me wrong, it sounds *aw*-ful.' Hazel's eyes creased awfully at the corners. 'It's just we've not had to deal with anything like this on *Where I'm Coming From* in the past and with this peace process and everything . . . ' Finally she waved away her own objection. 'Listen, I'm probably just fussing over nothing.'

Neither Andy nor Conor offered an opinion, any more than they would have if they had been standing at the side of the pitch while the referee and linesman discussed a tight penalty call, but waited for the signal of Hazel's silence to turn over again.

'Do you need me to pick up from before the last question?' St John asked her without taking his eyes off Craig, to whom he gave a little grimace of apology.

A passing lorry driver tooted his horn, as passing lorry drivers the world over were programmed to do. Conor, as soundmen were programmed to, looked daggers.

'If you wouldn't mind,' Hazel said.

St John took another second to think himself back to where he had been emotionally.

Visuals
ST JOHN *and* CRAIG *at School Gate as before.*

Sound
Continuous street ambience as before

Narration
ST JOHN
I'm sure a lot of people watching can relate to that, giving your teachers nicknames: a normal part of school life. But there was nothing too normal about *any* aspect of life in Belfast in those days, was there?

CRAIG
No, well, that's the whole rationale of terrorism *[NB flick of the eyes off-camera: cover with reverse-shot noddy or GV]*, it renders all arenas suspect: home, work, school . . .

ST JOHN
So, Hammy – Mr Harrison . . .

CRAIG
. . . was murdered. I was – you and I were – seventeen. The Provisionals – the IRA – broke down the door of his house one Saturday night and three of them ran up the stairs and shot him while he slept.

ST JOHN *(shakes head)*
And he had a girlfriend, if I remember, who lived with him, a partner.

CRAIG
That's right.
(Silence)

ST JOHN
And, um, was there any indication at the time why this would have happened. I mean, a schoolteacher . . . ?

CRAIG
The hunger strikes were just getting going then.

ST JOHN
This was when Bobby Sands died?

CRAIG
That was a bit later, but, yeah, Bobby Sands and nine others, and Harrison – his name was Alec, Alec Harrison – Alec had written an article about the use of the hunger strike as a tactic . . . and, well, they've always had a very tight editorial line, the IRA.

Visuals
Close-up ST JOHN, *smiles faintly, acknowledging this attempt at Blitz humour. Glances off into School, biting his lip: this is not going to be an easy question to ask.*

Narration
ST JOHN
Were you aware that certain allegations have been made . . .

CRAIG
Mm.

ST JOHN
. . . suggesting Alec Harrison might have had connections to . . . I mean, while I've been making this programme I've been shown papers that seem to indicate a connection to some pretty shadowy people, not that that's a reason to kill anyone, but I'm wondering, does it affect at all your memory of him, because you were more than just pupil and teacher, you two, you were . . . ?

CRAIG *(nods)*
Friends. First of all I think you have to say that even though we have put the guns away, or most of them, we haven't stopped fighting here altogether: the past is the new front line and reputation is its cannon fodder. We're all vulnerable.

ST JOHN
Well, I don't know if I've said this, but part of what I'm trying to do here is understand what went on in my own family, with my father in particular . . .

CRAIG
Yes, but, you see, the problem, revisiting the past, is that you can't really control it once you start. Let's say for instance someone was to get hold of something else about you from when you were growing up.

ST JOHN (*a backwards nod*)
I'm sure the teachers in there would have a few things to say, those who still remember me . . . the Crafty Fag Club . . .

CRAIG
Something worse than that, something less glamorous, like stealing money from the filling station where you used to work . . . Remember you did that? Just up the road there at the back of the school.

ST JOHN (*to camera*)
Can we stop there, please?

CRAIG
It wasn't just a little either, was it? Like, it was starting to show up in the books. You were really sweating it you were going to get caught. Remember? That was why you went away to England. That was how all of this came about, if you think about it. That's how we have ended up standing here talking today.

ST JOHN
Andy, please . . .

Visuals
ST JOHN'*s hand closes in on the lens.*

Commentary
ANDY (*off-screen*)
Don't touch the fucking camera.

Sound
Scuffling intermingled with further unattributed swear words.
[At this point the interview is terminated.]

They were all talking at once. 'Who the fuck do you think you are?' said Andy to St John.

'The lead! You're stretching the lead,' said Conor to Andy.

'I can't believe you would do something like that,' said St John to Craig.

'I hope you got all that,' said Craig to Conor and Andy, and to St John, 'I told you I wouldn't let you do it.'

'Maybe we should all take a few minutes, collect our thoughts,' said Hazel to everybody, but Craig was already unclipping his mic and trying to trail the lead down his jumper.

'Watch out for the wee windshield,' said Conor, and with that straw, Hazel's diplomat's back was finally broken.

'Oh, fuck the windshield!' she shouted. 'And fuck that fucking word "wee"!'

St John watched all this with the same bewildered expression on his face as when he opened his eyes in first-year geography class to find Uprichard kneeling beside him. 'Welcome back from the Land of Nod.'

*

'I can't believe you would do something like that,' said Maxine: St John verbatim.

She had been in the sunroom, crossword on her lap, half complete, when Craig got home and threw himself into a chair. He felt exhausted.

'Somebody had to,' he said now. 'Alec isn't here to defend himself.'

Even with his eyes closed he could sense her standing over him.

'But you know all they'll do is cut that bit and use the

rest,' she said. 'You signed the release.'

'I don't think they will. St John will be too afraid of it getting out. He knows Hazel and those guys there heard it: he knows they know it's true. Anyway' – he put his hand into his jacket pocket and, without opening his eyes, pulled out the phone – 'your man Conor wasn't the only person recording.'

He pressed a couple of buttons and there was a sound, amplified almost to distortion, of other neighbouring buttons being pressed then a swoosh, consistent with a hand being rapidly withdrawn from a pocket, then the soundtrack settled into polyester-lining static interrupted at regular intervals by a thud – Craig's right foot hitting the pavement – followed by a fainter thud: the left. Thud, fainter thud, thud, fainter thud. Then from very far away, from the beginning of recording history as it might have been, St John said, 'This is a bit strange, Craig, being back here.'

Maxine sank down into the seat beside him. She sat very still listening.

'They know you have this?' she asked when it was over.

'I played it for them before I left.'

She sat a moment more then stood and walked back towards the kitchen.

'So?' he called after her.

She turned in the doorway. 'I don't think I like you very much.'

3

She tried to speak to St John, but every time she rang the phone went straight through to voicemail. 'Call me back,' she said. Days passed, then weeks. He didn't call.

She and Craig meanwhile climbed into bed beside one another at night, sometimes even at the same time. In the morning they climbed back out and got on with their days.

She arrived for work one Monday morning on the back of another silent breakfast to find Gerry already in.

On a Monday. Morning. She stepped out, looked at the door, stepped back in again. 'What are you doing here?'

'I came for the comedy hour, obviously,' said Gerry. 'Anyway, I should be the one asking you. You look like . . . I'm too polite to say shit.'

'Gee.' Maxine paused unbuttoning her coat. 'Thanks.'

'You know I'm kidding. Half. I'm just worried you're a bit run down.'

'Hmm, I wonder why that would be.'

'I'm going to tell myself this is still all repartee. It is repartee, isn't it? I mean, you are not seriously trying to suggest that you are carrying this company?'

'God forbid.'

'Because just for a minute there, from where I'm sitting . . .'

'Ah, see now, that's it isn't it: where you're sitting.'

Gerry did the thing with the head and the eyebrow that

334

she had got off *Friends* or *Will and Grace*. 'Meaning?'

'Oh, come on,' said Maxine. 'I'm sure you can work that out.'

'Whoa, whoa, whoa,' Gerry said. 'Where's all this coming from?'

'Forget it.'

'No, tell me. I'm all ears.'

'Do you know what?' Maxine started doing up the buttons of her coat again, turned around and walked to the door. 'I can't be doing with this today.'

'Well let me know when you can be. I'll be waiting here for an explanation.'

'Nothing would surprise me more.'

'I have a suggestion,' Gerry shouted after her: 'Take it out on the person who got you into this state.'

Craig was out when she got back. She tried St John's number. Voicemail. She didn't speak, yet she needed to get the words out, to find a way to begin to make good the fault, or faults, in whichever direction they were travelling, because otherwise there was just no hope any more.

She sat in the sunroom. Think, think, *think*.

And then . . . the production company! There would have been emails, with perhaps another number tucked away.

*

Craig came home, not at all late, to a house in total darkness.

Maxine's keys were on the countertop. Her coat was in the sunroom. He called her name as he retraced his steps towards the front of the house, going from room to room downstairs, then commenced climbing up, still calling, but going through the motions now, because he knew long before he saw the rim of blued light around his study door where he was bound to find her.

He pushed with his fingertips. Her eyes only were visible, uplit above the back of the screen.

'You forgot to do your thing with the emails today.'

'I don't know what you're talking about.'

'Well that's odd, because it looks to me as though you do it pretty much every day . . . Bundle them up and send them to the secret Hotmail. Except it's only secret if you delete them from the Sent folder too.'

He reached over the top of the screen and took the mouse out of her hand.

'You have no right to look at my mail.'

'So it's my fault for looking, not your fault for fucking her?'

'It's a basic principle.' The former, it was understood, not the latter.

'Craig,' she said, 'please. It'd only hurt if I laughed.'

He was round beside her now. She wouldn't get out of the chair so he rolled her to one side as he knelt before the screen. The blasted cursor was frozen.

'I'd like you to leave now,' he said.

'That's not the way it's going to go, sweetheart,' she said. 'That's not the way it's going to go at all.'

*

He stayed on his knees for an hour, rerouting and deleting, resetting passwords. The rest of the house was still in darkness when he came out. He didn't know if she was in their room and didn't dare (care?) to go in and check. He went for a walk instead round the block trying to decide what to do. He thought about going to his mum and dad's, but they were old now, easily rattled. He sat on a wall and smoked half a dozen cigarettes one after the other. He threw the rest of the box away and went back to the house. *Still* in darkness. He eased his key into the lock and pushed. The door wouldn't budge. She had only gone and put the fucking deadlock on.

He spent that night in a guesthouse off Botanic Avenue. The taxi driver who picked him up had recommended it. 'I'd say it was your best bet. Actually, at this hour I'd say it was your only bet.'

The landlady wore a bright pink trouser suit. She took one look at Craig, standing in the doorway, no bag, not obviously drunk. 'Throw you out, did she?' she said and when he didn't reply at once, shushed herself. 'Don't mind me. I come from a long line of plain speakers. I'm the first of them to live past fifty.'

'Not thrown out,' Craig said, 'locked out, but it comes to much the same thing.'

The landlady handed him a key. 'I hope whatever it was you did was worth it.'

The wall of the stairwell was lined with autographed photographs – Telly Savalas, Kris Kristofferson, Eartha Kitt.

He turned halfway up. 'Did they all stay here too?'

'That's the hobby,' she said. 'Something to keep me out of mischief. And, here, do you know the only person ever refused me? Van Morrison. Presidents and all sorts, I have, but could your wee man see his way to obliging? No he could not.'

She walked down the hall and pulled the blind on the front door: closed. Craig had made it and no more.

'People here lose the run of themselves very easy,' she said.

By happy coincidence – at least he was happy about it now; *happier* – the couple in the Aunt Queenie house, Eric and Bathilde, had decided not to renew their tenancy when it ran out at the end of the month.

Craig had called round to see them, make sure everything was all right, because to be honest the past couple of years he had maybe been too inclined to leave things to the letting agents to sort out. The terrace of houses opposite had been demolished and a small city garden built, which, against the odds it might have been thought, had not only survived but thrived. There was even a bronze plaque: most improved street (medium), Belfast, South.

Eric had answered the door, pulled it almost closed at his back. Bathilde was having a lie-down on the sofa.

'What it is,' he whispered, 'she's pregnant. Completely unplanned, but you know how these things go.'

'Yeah,' Craig said. 'I do, of course. Congratulations.'

It was nearly ten before he woke that first morning in the guesthouse. The landlady (she was in a turquoise trouser suit this morning) wouldn't hear of him going out for breakfast: he had only missed it by half an hour. While she poached him his eggs he rang Maxine – 'There's nothing to talk about,' she said – then the letting agents for the Aunt Queenie house: would they mind taking the listing off their website for the time being?

He moved back in at the start of the following month, having left off until then letting Devon know what exactly was afoot. He emailed her the second he had the computer connected then checked fifteen minutes later to see if she had replied. And checked fifteen minutes after that and fifteen minutes after that and fifteen minutes after that again. He checked every quarter of a waking hour, which is to say all but a small handful of the twenty-four available, for three days until she emailed to say she needed a bit of time to think this all through.

He had just enough sense of humour left to laugh at himself. Himself laughed back, in reverse, from deep inside the screen. What a prick. What a complete and utter prick.

She didn't write again, ever.

Starting . . . again

I

St John's name for a time was frankly toxic.

It had been his decision and his alone not to carry on with *Where I'm Coming From*.

Mike Warren did actually use the words 'never' and 'in this town again'. The fact that he used them on the train between Water Orton and Coleshill Parkway was neither here nor there. The malediction was portable and universally applicable.

Publicly Verbal covered itself with a press release citing an illness in the family. This was not entirely fiction. Bea's 'glandular' symptoms had worsened and were soon accompanied by headaches and bouts of vomiting. Her GP, Dr Park – Sarah: daughter of, and inheritor of the practice from, the late and not unanimously lamented Dr Lennox – referred her to the hospital where a scan revealed a tumour nestling in her brain, 'looking quite at home', as Bea reported it. The whole thing developed with incredible speed. Within five weeks of her going to the doctor – while St John was still trying to manage the fallout from Craig's sabotage – she was having her first course of chemo. It didn't go well. She decided after the second that she would fight the thing on her own. That went even worse. By the beginning of the summer it was clear she was dying: six months at the outside was the oncologist's best guess.

She collapsed midway through the fifth and was rushed into hospital. For a couple of days it was touch and go. Then she rallied. On the morning of the third day she took a little tea and toast.

'I think I'm ready to go home now,' she said.

No one in the family hearing this was in any doubt where she meant by home.

Paddy was living there with his girlfriend and his girlfriend's young son and his own two daughters by the girlfriend before last. And Sibyl, of course.

'So, it's a big house,' Mo said.

Paddy it was who answered the door the day Craig turned up. As with Bea those years before Craig wasn't sure he would have recognised him out of context. He must have been fifteen or sixteen stone. His head was hairless and polished to a high shine.

Paddy would clearly have had no such trouble recognising Craig, who having stumbled on a style – a look – in his late teens had stuck with it, a little more grimly with every passing year. 'Well, fuck me,' he said. 'I believe I ought to box your ears.'

'It was Bea I was hoping to see. I only just heard she was ill. The hospital told me when I rang that she had been discharged to home.'

'You know why, don't you?'

'I guessed.'

Paddy considered a moment longer. 'Let me go and see how she is,' he said and shut the front door.

Which he opened again a couple of minutes later. 'Bizarrely, she wants to see you.'

The smell in the hallway was on the fungal side of damp. Craig glimpsed through a half-open doorway the shoulder of a familiar sofa, positioned, he would have been willing to bet, to the exact inch where it had been when last he saw it.

Up the staircase they went (shrieks of children playing somewhere in the rear of the house), along the landing, blanket box still in situ, left before they arrived at it, through the door into Bea's room.

She was lying on her right side facing the door. He thought she was probably not long awake. She didn't try to move.

'This is unexpected.' The voice weak, the smile, happily, less so.

Paddy, in the doorway, spoke to her past Craig's shoulder. 'If you're sure you're all right, then . . .' He started to pull the door to. 'Five minutes,' he whispered to Craig.

'I'm not deaf yet,' said Bea with surprising force. 'Fifteen!' She waited then until the door was properly closed. 'Was he giving you a hard time?'

'Tell you the truth I thought it would have been harder.'

There was a chair under the window. Old paint or make-up stains on the white-glossed wood. He brought it over beside the bed.

'I'm not sorry St John didn't go through with that thing,' Bea said. 'I told him all along he was asking for it.' She paused to catch her breath, or perhaps to swallow the laugh that was bubbling up. 'Mind you, I never thought that the *it* was going to be you.'

'Maxine and I separated.'

'Over *that*?'

'And a few other things.'

'Oh, dear.' She shifted on her hip. 'I always quite liked her. I thought once upon a time she was The One for St John.'

'What changed your mind?'

'About Maxine? Nothing. I just realised there isn't a One. There are Several – Lots maybe – but most of them we don't get to meet at the right time, if we ever get to meet them at all.'

'Do you think you and I met at the wrong time?'

'Oh, no.' Another pause for breath or laugh. 'There was never going to be a right time for us.'

'That's good to know.'

'I wouldn't want you pining unduly when I'm gone.'

'Bea!'

'What? I am going, but don't worry, I'm coming back.'

He didn't know what to say.

'I've been reading up. The crematorium is built on an Iron Age rath. I'm going to have a tin box put in the ground below my name, hedge my bets. If I miss out on resurrection maybe I'll be scooped up in an exca— . . .' The 'ca' kicked off a cough, which took a hold of her for ten, fifteen seconds. She reached to the wicker cabinet (white, like the chair) standing by the bed and pulled out a Kleenex, which – 'excuse me' – she spat into.

'Ugh! That's the worst about lying here all day, fluid builds up.' She dropped the Kleenex into a bin between the cabinet and the bed. 'My mouth tastes horrible.'

'Can I get you some water or something?'

'I feel as though I've drunk a river since I came home.'

He glanced, wondering if he had remembered it correctly and, yes, there was a sink in the far corner. His eyes lit on the glass by the cold tap with its single toothbrush and well-squeezed tube of toothpaste.

He wandered over and picked the brush up, turned to her with it in his hand. A smile crept across her face.

'Yes, I think that is exactly what I need.'

He filled the cup with water and knelt with it by the bed.

'That reminds me, once when we were kids, watching Errol Flynn doing his Robin Hood thing and at the end King Richard comes home and is going to knight him and says, "Kneel Robin Hood", and here's Sibyl, "Oh, that's nice, they're using his full name."'

All this time she was watching him squeeze toothpaste on to the brush. He slipped his hand behind her head to bring her up straighter. With his other hand he guided the toothbrush into her mouth, back teeth, front teeth, bottom teeth and top. Her tongue was a compliant tortoise, moving its head now to this side now to that in counterpoint to the brush. The toothpaste turned to a pink-flecked foam, filling her mouth finally.

'Spit!' she said, or its foam-filled, open-jawed equivalent.

'Christ,' he said, 'I forgot. Spit.' He scrambled up looking for something.

She was giggling, trying to hold it in. There was a bowl by the head of her bed, which he felt instinctively he should ignore. For one mad instant he contemplated removing his shoe. In the end he grabbed the glass, launched the water down the sink, and returned it to her empty, just in time.

'I thought I was going to choke,' she said.

He rinsed the glass in the sink, filled it again after the third rinse to the very brim. His hand behind her head again, she sipped. Closed her eyes, 'Mmmm. Smell my breath.'

He leaned in close. 'Beautiful.'

He left a kiss on her lips. She didn't open her eyes. Paddy came back. 'Craig's just going,' she said.

He walked with Paddy to the bedroom door. He looked back. She was smiling.

*

Craig thought it might be politic to stay away from the funeral, but he had asked Maxine to call him as soon as it was over, which she did. 'Too good sometimes for your own good,' her mother had told her more than once since the separation and the start of the long, slow rapprochement, which stopped short – would for ever remain short – of a reunion.

The funeral, she told him, had been a desperately sad affair, for which she was, in all honesty, pleased. The last thing she wanted was to be told to celebrate the life and be robbed of the chance to grieve. A bulb had blown in one of the clusters of lights to which she had to keep on raising her smarting eyes, so of course she got that Smiths song in her head, which made her eyes smart more even after she realised it should have been the other way round, all the bulbs blown and a single light that never went out.

Needless to say, it being Bea, she had gone to great lengths to ensure that all the arrangements were made. In one of the lighter moments Sibyl suggested that she had probably checked the availability of slots at the crematorium before deciding to die. (As the result of an aneurysm, mercifully, before the tumour could exact its full terrible price.) Her mother had said, 'I always hoped she would be here to bury me, because God knows the others are clueless.'

'Was the dad there?' Craig asked.

'He was.'

'And?'

'I shook his hand in the line-up, but there was such a crowd coming behind me – I mean *such* a crowd – I didn't get speaking. Not the least like any of the children. Isn't that funny? It's as if they've all followed a different evolutionary path from being with the mum for so many years.'

Sibyl, in fact, had grown into the woman her mother was when Maxine first got to know them all. 'She should have been in films,' Maxine said.

'And St John?'

'Looked stunned, as you can imagine. They were always so close, the two of them.'

Maxine had managed a couple of minutes alone with him coming out of the crematorium. He was holding a tin into which family members had placed mementoes, a parchment scroll with a note, in Bea's own hand, to future generations:

I was here too for a time.

He had got the call at half-ten the night before Bea died and was on the first flight out of London the next morning, praying – don't ask him who to – that he wasn't too late. She was already pretty far gone by the time he arrived at the house – scarcely even a flicker of the eyelids in the previous two and more hours – and it had upset him to think that she might not know that he had made it back, but then he was taking his third or fourth turn by the bed, holding her hand, stroking it, and talking to her, to the room in general, about the day he discovered her rhododendron den, its Gitanes butts and miniaturised crisp packets, and he felt for a moment her fingers close over his . . . A look down at his fingers as he relayed this, to Maxine, as though reminded anew that he would never again feel his sister's touch.

'And before you ask, no, he didn't mention you,' Maxine told Craig.

'Maxine, come on, what do you take me for?'

'It's tempting, but I'm not going to answer that.'

*

A few days later Craig bought the biggest bunch of white tulips Belfast had to offer and caught the bus out the Castlereagh Road to the crematorium at Ballygowan. The road bent and narrowed dangerously a few hundred yards from the crematorium gates. A posy of irises had been tied, heartbreakingly, to a lamp-post just beyond the bend, like a windblown seed of death from within.

He walked among the memorial garden's silver birches, the plaques with their heart-shaped surrounds, their photos and their bedraggled teddy bears, until he found the tree with her name before it. Beatrice Annabelle Nimmo: daughter, sister, dear, dear friend. For a moment he saw her sitting with her back against the trunk, finally getting to finish her joke about the rath and the hope of eventual excavation. He hunkered down fingering the cards on the wreaths and sprays already there, but unable now to read a word of what was written on them.

As he was straightening up he caught the eye of an elderly man who had been leaning his right hand for support on the trunk of a neighbouring tree. 'Someone belonging to you?' the man asked.

'Friend.'

The man wandered over in the way that someone of his generation would.

'Young, was she?'

'Well . . .'

'Your own age, I mean.'

It was a long time since anyone had called that young, but give it another decade he would probably start to think it was too. 'A couple of years younger,' he said.

The man shook his head.

'That's my son over there,' he said, since, in the way of someone of his generation, Craig hadn't asked. 'Fifty-five, never a day's sickness in his life and then, boom, just like that . . .'

'Bomb?' Craig was about to say and was glad he didn't.

'Heart attack, getting out the shower one morning.' The man shook his head again. 'You never know the minute, do you?'

'You do not,' said Craig.

And oddly, given how often he must have heard them down the years, these words spoken so artlessly there among the trees gave him a lift as he rode the bus back to town, gave him a lift whenever he recalled them, long weeks later. 'You never know the minute.' They were like a signal to get going. Keep going.

The question of the house could no longer be dodged. It needed a new damp-proof course, insulation, a complete rewiring. The window frames were so rotten it was a wonder the panes hadn't already fallen out and now they had discovered woodworm under the stairs, an entire cosmos of holes.

'That kitchen could do with being replaced too,' said the builder who came out to give them a quote. 'Even without that you're not going to see much change out of a hundred thousand.'

Sibyl it was who said what the rest of them had begun to think. 'Knock it down, sell the land. I would rather see it gone in one fell swoop than have it fall apart brick by brick. And, let's face it, it's a hundred grand this time, who knows how much it will be the next? I don't know about the rest of you' – though in fact she knew fine rightly – 'but I don't have that kind of money.'

If only they had decided to sell six months ago, the agent handling the sale told her, before Belfast was flooded with all that land – the decommissioned police stations and great lumps of former shipyards – they would have made an absolute killing, but now . . . 'We're still doing pretty well out of it,' Sibyl said.

They had a dinner, those who remained, the night before

they left, gathered round the kitchen table, the dining room having already been stripped and boxed up. St John wasn't able to get back. He left it as long as he could before ringing. One of Paddy's girls – St John had no idea which – picked up, said hello fifteen times, each one louder than the last, before Paddy himself came on the line.

'I thought they would have been in bed,' St John said.

'Yeah, well, you know . . .' Paddy sounded exasperated. 'Special circumstances . . . Wait, here's Sibyl.'

The phone was taken – *whisked* (for it had a sound) – out of his hand. St John had an almost physical sense of being carried along – the hallway, must be, then – a change in the acoustic – into the drawing room.

'What are you doing?'

The acoustic changed again: she had turned around – he could feel as well as hear it: doubled back on herself. 'I am walking from room to room with a video camera.'

She called them out as she went: living room . . . dining room . . . family room . . . maid's pantry . . . kitchen – 'Say hello, everyone'; 'hello,' everyone said; 'hello back,' said St John – laundry room . . .

'I never ever thought you would leave there,' St John said into a lull.

'I never ever thought I would live to be this age.'

He could hear wind all of a sudden.

'Are you out in the yard?'

'Yes . . . Hold on: the garden now.'

'How good a camera have you got that you can film in the dark?'

Thirty seconds passed of continuous suburban garden

ambience, night, then, 'Aw, fuck,' she said. 'Battery's out.'

Back inside she passed the phone over to Mo.

'You did the right thing staying away,' she said.

'I didn't "stay away". I wasn't able to get back. Shelly—'

She cut him short. 'As you wish. Anyway, it's an empty vessel. The soul has already departed.'

Sibyl was shouting something in the background.

'What's she saying?' he asked.

'She thinks she's being funny. She's telling you to ask me about the curtains.'

'What about the curtains?'

'I took them all down. Well, Paddy did. I told him there wouldn't be time tomorrow morning.'

Sibyl's voice sounded again nearer at hand. 'Last weekend, she made him take them down. Last weekend.'

'You never know what hitches there could be,' Mo went on evenly. 'Anyway, I don't see what all the fuss is about, you get lovely light at this time of year.'

Well into the evening and first thing in the morning. He understood now the exasperation in Paddy's 'special circumstances'.

Mo insisted on a four-way split. She wanted to donate her portion to a North Down Hindu meditation centre, which she had started attending with Bea in the weeks after the first, soul-destroying course of chemo. She had the offer of a room there in perpetuity, with a door leading straight on to the garden. Vegetables only, but the leeks when they flowered were very pretty.

Paddy and his ever-growing patchwork family (his girlfriend had just discovered she was pregnant) put their names down for one of the dozen houses that the developer who bought the old house – a Dundalk man – was planning to build on the site. 'I'll let you have a big four-bed detached for the price of the entry-level semi,' the developer said. He could afford to be expansive. His bank in Dundalk was giving him one hundred per cent loans for properties bought in the North.

Sibyl preferred to get very far away. She bought a wreck of a farmhouse in the Glens of Antrim – no electric, no running water, no paved road leading up to it – and spent what was left of her money on the conversion. St John mourned the glorious opportunity lost by her refusal even to *listen* to what the producers of the various makeover programmes he put her in touch with had to say.

'I suppose I should be pleased that you've stopped moping and started working again,' she said, 'but this is strictly family. Anyway, Mo needs a project.'

Mo travelled out from North Down once a week, by taxi, sometimes bringing bolts of material, although she might more usefully in those first couple of years have brought a few sheets of plasterboard, a suitcase full of nuts and screws. It was to Sibyl's that she went eventually when she fell out with the Hindus running the meditation centre – bunch of charlatans – and from there that she conducted her protracted legal battle to recover the money she had already donated.

It was to Sibyl's house too that Paddy and his family repaired when the Dundalk developer went bankrupt, him and his bank, the whole bloody country, leaving the foundations of the big four-bed detacheds and the entry-level semis only half begun and the old house a heap of rubble behind a corrugated iron fence, warning signs all around it:

Notice to Parents. Please warn your children that this site is NOT a playground and can be dangerous. It is important that the risks and consequences of entering are made clear to children.

3

The estate agent, Andrew, with whom Maxine had, over the previous few weeks of general enquiries, enjoyed several bantering phone calls, was something under half her age and clocked it the moment she walked in off the street and introduced herself.

'Ah,' he said (*recalibrate*, went the message that passed across his brain furrowing his brow, *recalibrate*), 'that's right . . .' – glancing at the face of his Blackberry, finding nothing there to save him – 'Maxine . . .'

'You had told me you might be able to show me a couple of rentals in the city centre in my price range?'

Andrew opened a drawer, closed it, went to stand up, sat back down and opened another drawer.

'Maybe this is a bad time?'

Whether it was the tone of her not-question that put manners on him, or the approach from the rear of the office of a more senior colleague – 'Is everything all right?' – he smiled at last.

'No, it's absolutely fine.' One answer for the two of them. He reached across to a peg between his desk and the next and took from it a suit jacket, grey with wine-coloured piping along its narrow lapels. 'Tell you the God's honest,' he added to Maxine in an undertone, 'I could do with getting out of here for a while.'

He led her through the late-morning traffic across the road to the car park of an apartment complex, a bakery in a former life, whose every second window had a 'To Let' sign with his company's name above it.

The car lights blinked on while they were still thirty feet away. Maxine not noticing at first the key in his other hand thought he had activated them with his Blackberry on which he had continued to type one-thumbed while they walked (his pace and the cut of his suit jacket afforded her plenty of opportunity to observe his broad bum: a bum that when he was twice the age he was now would be all too depressingly in proportion), walked and, very occasionally, talked.

He had been in the firm for four years: 'My boss says it must have been me started the downturn, because things were great till I arrived.' He saw her size up the car, a red BMW coupé. 'No family responsibilities yet.'

'No,' said Maxine, 'me neither.'

He stole a glance at her, arrived at who knows what conclusion. 'Right.'

The first place he showed her was a former retail unit (the word shop had disappeared from the lexicon) beneath a YMCA at the foot of the Albertbridge Road. As they entered he pulled down the faded 'Last Few Day's' banner from the door.

Massive place. Get over the smell of abandonment (at least she hoped that was abandonment), take the optimistic view on the future of the peaceline (it was bound to come down: they were all bound to come down), whose final barbed-wire layer she could see above the buildings opposite, and it was actually not bad. Not bad, but not, she said, turning to

Andrew with a smile, strictly speaking city-centre.

Half a mile down the road, over the Albert Bridge, arriving in the city centre proper, he didn't even bother looking for one of the cheaper parking places but drove straight down the ramp into the basement of Victoria Square, where he repeated the trick with the locks and the Blackberry. (Maxine could see the key now, but it still looked to be entirely passive.) Through the lower arcade of shops they walked, up the escalator to the Corn Market side of the square, through Argos on to Arthur Street and up a flight of stairs to a modern and entirely feature-free one hundred and eighty square feet without natural light.

'I'm wondering,' said Maxine, 'would anybody hear me scream?'

'That's a no, then.' He gave the office – the 'space' – the once over before switching out the lights. 'I can't say that I blame you.'

Out again, walking, up Arthur Street across Corn Market, where an enormous steel sculpture, the *Spirit of Belfast*, had replaced the bandstand that had replaced the fountain, him telling her about his parents, and how they had never bought new houses. Three times they moved when he was growing up and each house was a bigger challenge than the one before. But see when they had finished with them . . . ? People didn't believe him when he told them – his boss, he was sure didn't believe him – thought it was all about the money, the nice car, but he wouldn't have got into this game at all if it hadn't been for his love of old buildings.

After all her private sniffiness about him and his Blackberry, she was embarrassed when her own phone rang, full volume, before he could add anything more.

Bank.

'I'm sorry,' she said, 'do you mind if I take this?'

'Go ahead,' he said, Blackberry out, thumb working.

'Max*ine*,' said the bank manager. She always pictured him pushing himself back from his desk, the precise length he got on the last syllable corresponding to the distance travelled.

'To-oh—' There wasn't much you could do with Tom, but as ever she gave it her best shot in return '—om.'

As ever, he laughed, for about half a second. 'I've some good news and bad news for you.'

'It's a lovely morning, let's start with the good news.'

'That draft finally cleared.'

The decision to dissolve the partnership with Gerry had in the end been mutual and painlessly arrived at. Like a couple of Disprin dropped in water, said Gerry, reaching for an analogy familiar from the early months of their working relationship, when Gerry was in what she referred to now as the Bad Place. She was far, far away from it these days. In Wicklow, to be precise. In love, with the MD she had met way back when in Prague. 'Dubs,' she said. 'Masters of the long game.'

Mutual too had been the determination not to let the lawyers crawl all over the dissolution papers, but even with them both pulling in the same direction, or shouting encouragement to one another while pulling in opposite directions, it had still taken the best part of three years to get to this point, this phone call.

'The *bad* news . . .' said Tom, but Andrew meantime had stopped unexpectedly, just short of High Street, and was

360

pushing open a door next to an outdoor-pursuits supplier.

'This place just came up the day before yesterday,' he whispered. 'No lift, I'm afraid, but the stairs aren't too bad.'

The stairs in question rose up out of a tiled hallway whose left-hand wall was largely taken up with a cabinet of brass-handled mailboxes.

'What's that?' said Maxine, distracted, into the phone. 'Sorry? Listen, Tom, I'm going to have to call you back.' Andrew's broad bottom had already reached the first-floor landing. 'I'm, ah, starting to lose the signal.'

She put the phone in her pocket at the second attempt. 'Oh, my God.'

'Some place, isn't it?' Andrew said. 'Apparently there's an application in for listed-building status.' He was poised to point out the words 'shipping broker' on the glass of one of the first-floor doors. Maxine, though, did not wait. Past the thing that looked very like 'furrier', she went, past the door from behind which the sound of sewing machines had used to come, up the next flight of stairs.

The door was locked. She had imagined for a moment that she could simply walk right back in to Max and Magazine, 'Shot by Both Sides'.

Andrew had caught her up, sounding a little out of breath. 'It's this one here.' He took out the key to a door next to the one whose handle she had not yet let go of.

'I think there was a clothes shop or something in there,' he said over his shoulder, teeth gritted.

'Hairdressers,' she said, to the door rather than to him.

He switched keys, tried again, putting his shoulder to it. Not without difficulty, the door finally gave. '*There!*'

He worked it backwards and forwards on its hinges. 'I don't think a preservation order would prevent you planing a bit off this.'

Maxine walked past him to the window – same sash, although cleaner than she remembered the one on the other side of the dividing wall having been. She peered out, but, no, she couldn't get the angle.

'Does this window open, do you think?'

Andrew came across and undid the catch. He needed both hands to push the sash up far enough for her to lean out, on tiptoes, stretching, feeling it in her calves, the backs of her thighs . . .

The sign was gone, but the bracket, tantalisingly, remained. She would see about having it moved over ten or twelve feet. Or perhaps just leave it where it was, fix an arrow to it angled from there to here . . .

She looked back suddenly over her shoulder. Andrew, caught out, dragged his eyes up to meet hers.

'How much did you say the rent was?' she asked.

Andrew hadn't said it at all. He did now, tripping over his words a little. She smiled. 'You're on.'

She leaned out the window again. Below her, to the left, would-be b-boys were six-stepping around the *Spirit of Belfast*'s giant unravelled spring.

She felt in her pocket for her phone, got Tom back on the line.

'Oh, that's much better,' she said. 'Now, do your worst.'